Watchdog

Robert Anderson

Copyright © 2014 Robert Anderson
All rights reserved.

ISBN: 1500750700
ISBN 13: 9781500750701

For H, A & E (But Mostly Me)

Chapter 1

City of London, 15 September 2008

For a moment the closing meeting was almost beautiful- like a ballet in space, like *2001*. That was before it started, of course, while the meeting room was being set up. If there was one truly worldclass department in the firm, it was Client Catering, and *The Blue Danube* seemed to shimmer through the board room as orbiting chrome vessels of coffee intersected flying saucers laden with pastries, then danced through glinting asteroid storms of jelly beans and mint imperials.

By then I hadn't slept for more than 48 hours, and I was starting to lose the plot in a big way. When all those days of accumulated stress and adrenalin gradually start morphing into euphoria, you love it, but at the same time you know the crash is coming hard on its heels. After you've done a few of these deals, you start to fear it way before you get there. My mind felt like one of the firm's 100% recycled pencils- too hardened and desensitised to work without exerting massive pressure on it, too brittle to take much of that kind of punishment. The more I tried to sharpen it now, the more quickly the fractures appeared. The waste paper basket in every meeting room in the office was full of splintered 100%

recycled pencils, presumably smashed to smithereens by exasperated visitors. So far as I could estimate, my brain was about two hours away from joining them there. On the other hand, I was undeniably reaching a significantly higher state of consciousness. Higher- and much, much lower. Pretty much the place occupied by Carl, although he was a permanent resident there.

Carl always had a keen sense for when I really didn't want to speak to him, so he immediately shuffled into the board room and wolfed down a raisin Danish in two ravenous bites. He looked alert and stimulated, which did worry me. He had recently developed a Marxist-Leninist persona, and was only interested in development by paradigm shift, catastrophe and revolution. Hardly the ideal person to run the post room in a law firm.

"Er, Houston- we have a problem, man."

"Cannabis psychosis?"

"Hardware, man. The signing pens, to be precise. Sweet tools, man, super-calligraphic, erm, expialidocious..." He kissed his fingers. "Oh, you beautiful, bourgeois beasts!"

"What about them?"

"Try to keep in mind the, er, fundamental impermanence of all material chattels when you're processing this data, man..."

"Carl!"

"Well, to cut a long story short- we are, er, we're one short. I don't want to make a mountain out of a, er, Mont Blanc, heh heh heh, but someone would appear to have half-inched one of them. I repeat: We got a Blackhawk down, we got a Blackhawk down."

"We got what? What? How could this have happened? What are we going to do? People are flying in from all over the world for those bloody pens! You think they give a damn about anything else in that room? Judging by their comments on the drafts, most of these guys haven't even read the documents they're going to sign with them…"

"What can I say, man? The post room is fatally compromised."

"You think? But I thought you were keeping the signing pens locked up in the real estate title deeds room anyway? That place is like Fort Knox!"

"Yeah, but remember what Citizen Proudhon said: 'Property is theft', man."

I groaned and involuntarily massaged my temples with my fingertips.

"Bugger me! So now we have to tell our most high-maintenance client that someone nicked one of his new five hundred quid pens- inside our office?"

"I think it may be best to manage disclosure of the whole 'inside job' aspect of it, man. The last thing we want to do is start a witch-hunt here. Reactionary hysteria. Kangaroo courts. McCarthyism, man! I mean, did you even see *The Crucible?*"

"No, I don't like snooker. So just find me a replacement pen, will you? And for Christ's sake look after the rest of them, Carl, we can't afford to have any more broken arrows out there, OK?"

Carl nodded again.

"Kula Shaker, man! The title deeds room is in total lock-down. Bikini State Alpha."

He tugged hard at a chain around his neck, making a loud rasping noise to feign asphyxiation. I assumed that the chain held the key to the deeds room and that Carl was indicating that he wouldn't let go of it, whatever inhuman duress he was subjected to. That was certainly the explanation I was most comfortable with.

"Tell me one more thing though, Carl- why are you here at all?"

"Here in the office?"

"Here in the client suite. Where someone might see you."

"I volunteered to help out with the closing, of course, man. Lay out the papers. Just one more step in the Long March."

"From post room to paralegal?"

"Yeah, that's my vision, as you know: '*Paralegals Sans Frontières*'..."

"There are plenty of *frontières* really though, aren't there? Two words for you, Carl: 'Ketamine' and 'Incident'."

Carl looked at me pityingly.

"What's happened to you, man? Were you always so- so uptight?"

"I don't know... I've been to some pretty dark places in the last six months. With all these deals, you know? Well, of course you do know, because now you've been directly responsible for two utter fiascos yourself. So, like I say- no client contact for you while I'm here."

"But how long will that be for, man? When you're sleeping with the fishes, I'll be reaching for the skies."

"Is that Engels? What are you trying to say, Carl? Is this struggle entering a militant phase?"

"Force is the midwife, man."

"Yoda?"

"Marx! Force is the midwife- of every old society pregnant with a, er, new one."

"Is there something you want to tell me, Carl- are you confessing to nobbling the missing Mont Blanc?"

"Like I told you before, man- I'll move any mountain to reach my goals."

The truth was out there, just not as far out there as Carl. Before I could travel deeper into the heart of darkness, the doors of the board room swung open. Xavier was now standing between them, teeth clenched in his habitual expression of bloody-mindedness. They gleamed brilliantly in his perma-tanned face.

"Ah, shit," I said, to no one in particular.

Xavier swept into the meeting room, followed by his genial, Brummie executive assistant Darren, a glut of private equity guys and their investment bankers and lawyers. Carl stared at Xavier suspiciously through red-rimmed eyes for a moment, then shuffled out of the room.

"The euro-trash can of history, man..." he muttered.

Xavier closed the doors theatrically behind him, and then turned confidentially back to us.

"You know, I'm really hot! I came here on the, uh, 'Tuuube'. That's what they call the London Metro here, you know! The Tuuube..."

He looked around the room, nodding sagely as he pushed his long, receding grey hair up from the roots with his fingertips.

"Wasn't it hot, Darren- hot on the Tuuube?"

"Totallay!" said Darren.

Xavier stared intensely at me.

"Oh, yes- they said in the hotel it would be quicker than a, uh, cab, you know. Have you ever done that?"

"Taken the Underground, you mean?"

"The Tuuube, you know! That's what they've called it here- for over one hundred years, you know?"

He nodded his way round the room again. "The Tuuube!"

"Thanks for the Dick Van Dyke guide to London, Xavier! Yes, I've been on the Tube. Twice a day, as a rule. Taxis aren't a hugely practical way to get in, unless you do actually happen to live in a hotel in the West End."

"Hey, loik Omar Sharrrif," said Darren. "Yow know, Dr. Zhivahgow! Played contrrract brrridge. Had no crrrib. Lived at Clarrridge's."

There was an uneasy pause, before Xavier spoke again.

"Well, you know what we really need to make some progress here? Get this, uh, party started on the road, you know?"

He cracked his knuckles, with an air of determination.

"No? No? You don't know?" he said. "Iced latte! Yes. What we really need is some iced latte, you know! Would you like some iced latte, Darren?"

"Oiced lattay would be awesome," Darren said. "If yow've, loik, got some, oi mean," he said to me apologetically. "Do yow actuallay 'ave a Starbucks in the buildinggg? 'Cause oi think they do at Clifford Chaaance."

Xavier nodded brusquely.

"Nothing was too much trouble for them over at 'CC', you know? That's what they call, uh, Clifford Chance LLP, in the City, you know. CC! Or 'Cliffords'. But Cliffords doesn't sound so cool, you know?"

"It's bostin'!" concurred Darren. "Cee-Cee…"

"Yes, anything we wanted, you know, no, uh, no questions asked…"

"Great Tube service over there at Canary Wharf as well, isn't there?" I suggested. "But listen- we've got a lot of documents to sign here. If you all want to sit yourselves down, shall we get cracking?"

We needed Churchill, but we got a Chigwell scout-leader- that's just my public speaking style. Obviously Xavier hadn't been a boy scout though, because he wasn't having any of it.

"No, no, no! First things first, you know! Is there really no way we can manage to get some, you know, coffee in here?" he said.

I gestured towards the huge industrial vats of coffee on the board table. There didn't seem to be any better way to put it, these things were naked monoliths, they were like the Sheffield cooling towers. They still didn't appease Xavier though.

"But is it- iced? I don't think so! Maybe you didn't hear me, but I'm talking about iced coffee, you know!"

This was becoming a serious client management issue. I lunged inelegantly for the phone in the middle of the board-table and dialled reception.

"Ye-es?"

"Do we have any, er, iced coffee?"

There definitely weren't any yuppie sympathisers on reception that day.

"Xavier, they say it's cold outside and we've got plenty of de-iced in here already. The show must go on, I guess!"

Xavier pouted and gestured out of the window, evidently intending to indicate an ultra-chic modern metropolis outside, awash with iced beverage opportunities. Unfortunately this was post-industrial London, not downtown Tokyo. The window he had chosen for this particular demonstration looked out onto a vista of nineteen-seventies tower blocks and grim Victorian warehouses- the latter probably solely populated by decrepit Steptoes, slurping watery grease-tea with four or five sugars in it. None of this fazed Xavier though. He believed in looking at life through the lens of his own ego, not a mere window.

We seemed to be accelerating into impasse, so I was actually quite relieved when Carl re-entered the room. Only on the actual point of his entry, I mean, because immediately after that I realised that he was muttering some repetitive mantra under his breath and trailing a line of trainee solicitors and junior associates behind him.

"Not the tribal shaman persona…" I breathed.

Except for Carl himself, who had his hands clasped before him like a badly dressed undertaker, each of them was holding a black leather pen-case out at arm's length in front of them. Before I could do anything to stop them, they walked around the signing table in Indian file, each reverentially laying a pen-case in front of one of the signatories at the table, before stepping back to stand behind that grandee's chair like a medieval page. It was a truly degrading spectacle, and the bankers loved every minute of it.

For a moment it appeared that Carl's masterstroke was actually succeeding, so I had mixed feelings when he himself stepped forward to lay a black biro in front of Xavier, with the complacent flourish of a *maître d'* placing a rare delicacy before an unusually discerning patron. On the one hand things were now going wrong in a way that would clearly have unspeakably ghastly repercussions for everyone concerned- on the other hand the world had not actually detached itself from its axis and started free-wheeling through the universe. I mean, this thing wasn't even a Bic, it probably wouldn't even make it through the dating of the share purchase agreement. Carl hauled himself out of his customary slouch to his full height, which was actually quite tall. He gave a signal to his accomplices, and they stepped forward as one and flipped open the pen-cases, like waiters removing silver *entrée* covers in unison. Carl himself flicked back his lank, brown forelock, removed the lid of Xavier's biro, spun it round theatrically and wedged it firmly onto the end of the pen.

"Locked and loaded..." he muttered.

He took a step backwards and then, one hand behind his back and the other outstretched towards the ball-point on the table, proclaimed: "Gentlemen, I give you the pen: Still mightier than the sword!"

There was some muted applause from the bankers, but Xavier just sat staring at it, until Carl finally dropped his hand heavily onto his shoulder.

"Hey, I hope you don't suffer from pen envy, man!"

Xavier was now staring at Carl as if he was completely insane, and you'd have to say that he had pushed the boundaries of the business meeting pretty far- further than I would ever have dreamed possible. Xavier reached out into the void for some psychic spar to cling to. Unfortunately what his hand found first was the subscription agreement in the pile of signing documents. He started flicking myopically though it.

"You know, here on page 90, this is, uh, this is really not the way to spell my name…" he said. "It's 'Van der' Tempel, you know. Here just- Tempel. A spelling mistake, you know! And after all the fees we're paying you!"

He hitched his leg up onto his chair.

"You know me, I think you all know how I work by now, I'm a practical man, a businessman. I've made my name- *Van der* Tempel that is, huh huh- by getting straight to the point. Not getting lost in the detail, you know. I cut through it like a…"

Here he mimed a decisive, thrusting motion.

"Knoife through margerrrine?" suggested Darren.

"Sword through stone, you know!"

"Right…" I said.

"Contracts and, you know, lawyers, are a bore to me, you know? I'm in the value-creation business, and you guys are just an over-head!"

He looked around the room for affirmation. That wasn't particularly forthcoming, but to be fair that might just have been because so many of the people in it happened to be lawyers themselves.

"So let's just put this- this regrettable mistake- behind us and move on, huh?" he concluded magnanimously.

Painful, you'll admit, but probably no more than a minor irritant, if that hadn't also been the moment that Kenneth Smythe chose to join the fray.

Ken was the lead client partner for Xavier's fund, and an undisputed silverback at the firm. That made him 'boss' to me and Carl, and he exercised about the same level of moral ascendancy over us that Boss Hogg exerted over the burghers of Hazzard County. He bustled in to the meeting room catastrophically late, erratically shaven and sporting a ridiculously countrified shooting-jacket. This rustic garment had a row of cartridge-pouches like a Mexican bandit's bandoliers above the breast pocket. There may even have been one in there, although I couldn't swear to that. In any case the dark stubble on his top lip served to emphasise the *bandido* look. The resemblance had obviously struck Carl too.

"Whoah! ¡*Viva la revolución*, man!"

Ken looked at him, with a suspicion bordering on panic.

"I beg your pardon, Carl?"

"You've got a bit of a Pancho Villa thing going on there, *jefe*. The 'tache could still use some work though... ¡*Vaya con dios*, man!"

This certainly wasn't what Ken had reluctantly left the bucolic delights of his house in the country for. Still, at least he hadn't bothered to take the early train. That reflection seemed to give him some comfort. He rallied the troops.

"What's the hold-up then, chaps? Someone told old Xav he has to get his wallet out to buy this company? I thought it looked a bit, ah, dusty in here, eh?"

This type of anodyne corporate humour was what had paid for Ken's country pile in Hampshire in the first place. It got an appreciative chuckle from Xavier. Pumped up, Ken started moving his hands together in a characteristically non-committal fashion, somewhere between a clap and a rub.

"Come on, team, let's get this show on the road, alright?"

"Just what I said, you know!" said Xavier. "But there was no iced latte, if you could believe it! Sometimes I wonder if we should use a European firm instead…"

"You know that we are actually English, Xavier?" I said. "Only the firm is American."

"Yow English, Matthew?" said Darren. "Oi actuallay thought yow was Austraylian! Yow've got a sloightly strynge accent, don't yow?"

Ken took me to one side.

"Now, Matthew- a quick sit-rep, if you please. Everything under control?"

"We are cooking with gas, Kenneth!"

"Signing pens make quite the splash, did they, eh? Heh, heh- I thought they would, I thought they would!"

"Ah, now it's funny you should ask that… We were one short. But Carl improvised a bit of a presentation ceremony. And I think we got away with it…"

"He did what?"

"Picture- as you probably can- a Masonic ritual. Vaguely sinister. Carl and the trainees processed in with the pens, then handed them over personally. No hoods though, fortunately."

"And that went down well, did it?"

"They loved it, it brought the house down. Darren says it's the most significant innovation he's ever seen from this firm."

Ken considered this.

"Yeah, I know. You can take that different ways…" I admitted.

"So- what did you make of it yourself?" he asked eventually.

"Have you seen *Jacob's Ladder*? It was a bit like that. In fact, a couple of people did ask me afterwards if we've secretly been testing Agent 15 on our trainees and falsifying the records."

Ken sighed.

"Is it true? Shit!"

"Listen, Matthew, my point is really, why the bloody hell aren't there, ah, pens for all?"

It's a good question, when you come to think about it, and one that- maybe in a wider context than writing implements- we should probably all be asking.

"Carl thinks we have a mole in the post room."

"But he is the post room, isn't he?"

"Er- yeah."

"Hmm. Well the main thing is that Xavier got…" He paused. "What did Xav get?"

There was no easy way to put this.

"Erm- a ball-point," I confessed.

"A Parker?"

"It was, er, own brand…"

"Jesus Christ, Matthew!" He stamped his foot pettishly. "I'm more than a little disappointed at the judgment- or lack thereof- that you've shown in all this, let me tell you. Stationery is bloody important, you know?"

I was still absorbing this insight when Carl seized the moment to sidle over to us. The guy was like the loose nut in a space shuttle- he wasn't going to stop rattling around until he had destroyed the whole fucking thing.

"Hey, er, what does 'mezzanine warrant' mean, guys?"

"Just jargon, Carl," I said. "Listen, I'm having a quick word with Ken here. Keep up the good work out there, and we'll continue the on-the-job training later, alright?"

"Hey, that's great news, man," said Carl. "'Cos one of the banker dudes over there was just saying that we're one short in the signing bundle. They reckon it's lucky that Ken has arrived in the nick of time to sort it out. Kind of like the US cavalry, you might say, heh heh heh!"

He looked apologetically at Ken, then rested his hand lingeringly on the epaulette of his shooting-jacket.

"Only they, of course, were no friends to Pancho Villa," he said. "They hunted him like a, er…"

"Pheasant?" I suggested.

"No, man, like a dog," said Carl.

Ken stared at him in total bemusement. His eyes actually seemed to bulge somewhat from his head. Perhaps he was just shocked by the suggestion that he would be of the slightest assistance to anyone requiring legal documentation. Unfortunately there was no time to bring about an unlikely meeting of minds between Ken and Carl, because by now some of the sprightlier signatories had managed to sign their names where Carl had tagged the signature blocks in the documents, five times in a row. They were beaming around complacently and shaking hands with each other to emphasise this. Ken was onto it in a flash, his finely-tuned dealmaker's antennae twitching.

"I'll take it from here, chaps…" he said. "Ladies and Gentlemen, I am delighted to announce that after months of hard work by, er, everyone around this table, Project Behemoth has completed! Oh, not at all, not at all, you're welcome, you're welcome, you're very welcome… Yes indeed, the 'fat lady' has sung the, er, rather tricky Wagner aria! All bar one small, but crucial, detail…"

Now he performed his own ungainly sprawl towards the telephone in the middle of the board-table, burying a female private equity executive in a moist tweed armpit in the process, and was instantly immersed in a highly involved conversation. Finally, he covered the mouthpiece with his hand. The room held its breath.

"Well, that *settles* it..." Ken said. I had never heard him speak with such authority. "If it's warm Dom Perignon or cold Veuve, I'd go for the, um, 'the Widow' any day- wouldn't you agree, Xav?"

Xavier removed his glasses and squinted earnestly at Ken.

"Oh, I couldn't agree with you more, you know. That's the 'pop' we serve at our own, uh, 'shop', you know!"

He turned to the bankers nearest him.

"Shop! That's what you call your office, in the City, you know! Even though, you don't actually sell anything there. Maybe cans of Pepsi-Cola, Wagon Wheels or, uh, something like that in the cafeteria, but that's strictly for personal consumption, you know? Not for general retail purposes. We keep a few cases of Veuve Clicquot, uh, Ponsardin 'fizz' though, that's 'the Widow', of course, for special occasions. A mega-deal, you know. When we hit the front page of the *FT-* again! Then- pop goes the weasel, you know!"

Xavier mimed a Formula One-style shake-and-spray with an imaginary magnum of champagne. I tried to picture a meeting room at the fund's stark, utilitarian Hanover Square offices with champagne dripping off the ceiling, whilst Xavier, Darren and their crack cohorts of super-serious MBA graduates and eurotrash interns pogoed frenetically to celebrate the headline in the *Financial Times*. It seemed far-fetched, even in 'Hangover Square'. For one thing, there would have to be a tactical pause pre-spray, while everyone wrapped their silk Hermès ties in cling-film.

Ken nodded appreciatively at this hedonistic account.

"The perfect fizz for it, Xav!" he affirmed. "I salute your choice. Love those little notes of pear that creep up on your palate at the end, right? And in actual fact, we do something very, very similar here."

I was still trying to work out what we had ever done at the firm that was remotely similar to that, when Ken turned to me.

"Sort out that missing mezz warrant will you, Matthew?" he hissed. "What the bloody hell are you waiting for?"

"Do you want fries with that?" I said, but it was actually quite a relief, because I knew from past deals that once this fine wine double-act got going, it could take hours. I left the meeting room and staggered back up to my office on the third floor. It was only as I slumped down into my chair that I realised how exhausted I really was. I blinked to clear my eyes, as I brought the warrant document up onto the computer screen. The part where my peripheral vision should have been was just fading to black now. Total sensory collapse could not be far away.

"Hey, man!" said Carl from somewhere behind me, his voice ringing out of the void, making me jump involuntarily. "I'm certainly not chasing you, man- but that Ken dude does want to know what's going on up here? Where's the, er, 'bloody document', is what he's asking, man? His words, not mine…"

"I'm printing it now! Christ! I haven't been to bed since Friday! For two pins I'd just go ahead and have a nervous breakdown right now, and let him see how the closing goes then!"

"Hey, cool your boots, man. But I don't think that printer actually contains any paper anyway, does it? Isn't that what that flashing red light is striving to indicate, man?"

"Oh, for Christ's sake!"

I grabbed a new packet of printer paper and started trying to tear it open. The wrapper seemed to be made of some super-high tensile strength, Kevlar-paper weave, defying my increasingly desperate attempts to get to the paper inside. I poured my last reserves of energy into one final assault, but only succeeded in tearing a narrow strip off the cover, sending the packet flying out of my hand and smashing into the printer, which growled menacingly. My mobile phone started ringing.

"Open that sodding thing, will you?" I said to Carl, as I scrabbled for my phone. "Show no mercy- whatever it takes. Hello- Matthew Verreaux?"

"Matthew? Matthew- who are you talking to? What on earth do you think you're doing?" said Ken at the other end. "Don't you realise that we're all waiting for you to, ah, honour us with your gracious presence down here? And I might tell you that that includes Xavier himself!" He was clearly playing to the crowd around the conference phone in the board room.

"Yes, we are waiting, waiting, waiting, and we don't have all day long here, you know!" said Xavier in the background. "I've been up since six a.m. this morning, you know? And that's after Michael Winner and Lord Jeffrey Archer kept me up all hours at the weekend, after Jeffrey's latest, uh, Sheep Herder's Pie and Krug party! Oh, they're real party boys those two, you know- crazy, crazy guys! Some revolting meat pie with champagne of all things, you know, who ever heard of that? Absolutely mad! So if you lawyers could please just hurry up and do your job, we'd all be very grateful, you know?"

Carl was now rolling around on the floor, tearing at the packet of printer paper with his long, yellow canines as he tried to wrestle it open. Gradually the wrapper was being obliterated, ripped into tatters. Long, thin scraps of it fluttered in the air like confetti before coming to rest on the floor around him, curved and twisted like mocking crimson smiles.

"Do you think this will still fit into the printer, man?" said Carl, handing me a bizarrely contorted, mis-shapen block of A4. "It normally looks a bit, er- flatter..."

"And rectangular. But this'll have to do," I said, cramming it into the printer tray. The printer ground and whirred in protest, but I slammed the tray shut with the flat of my hand, which seemed to subdue it. I gave into my anger and frustration, and gave it a few more juddering blows for good measure. There was not a peep back from it now.

"I don't think you need to keep on hitting it like that, man," said Carl. "It seems more submissive now. You've broken its spirit…"

"Maybe for now. It's making me feel better though, you know?" I said. "I could smash this whole bloody office to pieces right now! Why does nothing work properly around here?"

"Matthew? Matthew!" said Ken's voice over the phone. "For goodness' sake have the common-or-garden decency to answer my perfectly clear question! When the devil is the document going to be ready- by which I mean, down here, in Xavier's hands, in apple-pie order and fit for signature?"

"Just give me five minutes…" I said.

"Mayday, mayday!" shouted Carl.

The printer's gears and motors were howling and crunching now, as it chewed and concertina-ed the document into a crinkle-cut paper fan. The LED display was lit up like a Christmas tree.

"Core reactor meltdown, man! Ladies and Gentlemen, we will shortly be landing on Three Mile Island!" yelled Carl.

"Ten minutes, Ken," I said. "We'll be right down…"

Carl gingerly tried to remove the shredded paper from the printer. It was so tightly wedged in that he was reduced to tearing it scrap by scrap from the gear train, leaving an insolent stub jammed in the works. This remnant of paper was tiny now, but something told me it would unerringly bring the whole process to a halt. Just then, the printer suddenly growled and snarled back into life. Carl yelped and jumped back, clutching his hand.

"It got me! I'm bleeding, man! Bleeding…"

"Fifteen minutes…"

"I really don't know what else to say to you, Matthew- just get down here as soon as you possibly can, is that absolutely clear?" said Ken, and rung off.

Of course we should have got rid of him immediately, because freed from the crippling pressure of trying to coax obsolete office printers into effective action on a live call, between the two of us we did eventually manage to get a fifteen-page document printed off. I sprinted breathlessly back down to the board room. They didn't seem to have made much progress in my absence. Ken was now engaged in a monologue about Billecart-Salmon champagne, which wasn't too encouraging, because he generally favoured the alphabetical system for these wordy rambles through the world of wine. Everyone else had downed tools by now, and stood clustered around Ken and Xavier- presumably because the former was doling out champagne, in volumes directly proportional to his perception of their usefulness to him. I noticed that the other side's lawyers, all the accountants and our trainees were on particularly Spartan rations.

At some stage, Ken had gleaned a sufficient smattering of acceptable behaviour to realise that he couldn't openly boast about the moolah. His response to this did have a certain ingenuity, in that instead he bragged about the wine he drank and the restaurants he ate at, as though those were in some way an indicator of exceptional discernment that other people simply lacked. In Ken's world, the choice of the masses to flock to Ronald McDonald instead of to Heston Blumenthal would have been incomprehensible, were it not for his own connoisseurship. But then perhaps the strange thing wasn't the fact that Ken thought this was a socially acceptable way to flaunt it, but the fact that he was probably right.

What really upset me was that Emily obviously thought so too, because she was not slow to involve herself in a debate about the 'biscuity' qualities of Krug.

"You know, I never really understood what people meant about that until I first tasted it- it almost seems to crumble on the tongue, doesn't it, Xav?" she said.

"That's exactly what dear, dear Jeffrey says, you know!" he said.

Everyone nodded eagerly, anxious to avoid any suggestion that they themselves would balk for a moment at spending the price of a second-hand car on a bottle of champagne.

"So what exactly is a *blanc de blancs* champagne, Xav?" asked Emily.

"Well…" Ken started.

"No, no, no- I've got this, Ken…" said Xavier.

He smirked with indescribable smugness, and hitched his leg up onto a chair. Ken pouted sulkily, and when I approached him with an empty glass, he grudgingly poured me the barest thimbleful of champagne, without even the most formulaic words of congratulation on closing the deal.

I certainly wasn't about to force my company on Ken of all people, so I slumped down in a chair outside the charmed circle to drink my splash of champagne. It tasted minging anyway, because I'd eaten my own body weight in mint imperials that day, in a vain attempt to keep my mouth feeling fresh for 48 hours without the aid of a toothbrush. I knew from experience that all booze was really likely to do at this stage was hasten my inevitable, fatigue-induced descent into a catatonic state. But then that might have seemed preferable to consciousness for some of the people in the board room, because by now Xavier was giving a detailed account of a driving tour of Champagne-Ardenne he had made in 1987. He was one of those cussed raconteurs who don't necessarily have all of the facts at their finger-tips, but can't be persuaded to gloss over the most immaterial scintilla of them either.

"So I wasn't staying in Reims itself, you know- but actually in a teeny, tiny, uh, 17th Century *château* a very good friend of mind keeps up, just south of the city. So I drove up on- now what was the, uh, what was the road again?"

Xavier chuckled. Suddenly he clicked his fingers.

"The A4! It was the A4..." he said. "No, it wasn't the A4- it was the, uh, the A34, you know, huh huh huh..."

I don't know if I actually nodded off in my chair at this point, but it must have been touch and go, because Emily squeezed my arm quite sharply.

"Matt, a few of us are going to grab some lunch to celebrate. Why don't you come along? I'm sure they can manage without you for a couple of hours, now you've got it over the line?"

I hoisted myself out of my chair. We were heading for the door when Ken intercepted us. He assumed the hideous, rictus smile that I recognised as Ken turning on the charm for the ladies.

"Oh, Emily, can we borrow young Matthew for a sec?"

Emily smiled back.

"Of course, we were just popping out for a spot of lunch," she said.

"Oh, that should be fine..." said Ken. "Just check none of the other partners in the office needs a hand with anything first, will you, Matthew?"

"Maybe operating some heavy machinery?" I suggested. "Because I've still got at least 40 per cent. vision..."

Emily and the other bankers set off, and suddenly I noticed that Ken and Xavier were standing shoulder-to-shoulder. Perhaps I wasn't at my sharpest, but I could still recognise an axis of evil when I saw one. Xavier was like a freakish exoskeleton, propping

Ken's invertebrate form up into some semblance of an authority figure.

"We did just want a word- a little, erm, real-time feedback on the deal," said Ken.

Xavier nodded sternly.

"We? You and Xavier?" I said. "Now? Really?"

"Yes, now! You know how important Xav's business is to this firm, Matthew…"

"I basically pay your salary, you know!"

"Oh, thanks- can I have a raise then?"

Ken shook his head. His technique in these circumstances was to give the impression of being more sad than angry at his employees' failings. That may have been true, but at the same time he was infinitely more self-interested than he was sad.

"I don't think you understand the seriousness of the situation, Matthew. I'm sorry to say that Xavier really hasn't been happy with your, your *attitude* on this transaction."

"It's been, uh, markedly unprofessional to our minds, you know. There are plenty of other law firms who would sell their own mothers to work with us, you know!"

"And so would we, so would we, oh yes, we would indeed!" said Ken quickly.

Now Ken was feeling the heat himself, and you certainly didn't need to be a weatherman to know which way the wind was going to blow that.

"To be perfectly honest, I haven't been especially impressed with your attitude either, Matthew. You have to jolly well understand your client, and *their* needs. What makes *them* tick and fires them up, really gets them out of bed in the mornings. Maybe they already have a large Victorian house in town, but do they have a, ah, really *decent* pad in Nice or Antibes yet? Do you know what *their* hot buttons are, and how to push them? At this firm we all have to be prepared to go the extra mile to add value, in a, erm, really *value-added* way."

This type of banal marketing-speak was what had paid for Ken's own third home. He even used the same intonation as the expensive management consultant he had learnt it from. Pad No. 3 was indeed in the south of France, and had almost mythical status in the firm due to the Herculean efforts that Ken and his 'pod' of architects had gone to in shipping heavy building materials in from all around the world to construct it. It made working at the firm feel like putting in a shift as a Giza brickie on a pyramid. You knew that someone was going to end up with a pretty impressive domicile at the end of it, but barring some outrageous quirks of fortune, the chances were that it wouldn't be you.

"And here we all were, waiting for you to get round to printing off a perfectly simple mezz warrant for execution! Not exactly value-added law, was it?"

"Oh, law, you know!" said Xavier. "It's just a product, that we can buy off the shelf from any one of a dozen, two dozens, of US or, uh, English firms, you know? I-banks make you money, lawyers just cost you money! There are fewer decent coffee shops these days, you know!"

"Well- yes. I think I've made my point," muttered Ken. "So do you have anything to say to us, Matthew?"

"Do you, you know? Do you?" said Xavier.

I thought of Ken's inspirational words: Push your client's hot buttons. Maybe it really was time to go the extra mile. I looked Ken in the eye.

"Yes I do- fuck you…"
I turned to Xavier.
"And fuck you!"

Things started happening fairly quickly after that. What I remember most clearly though is how long the smile on my face lasted for. Out of the office, through the first cigarette, down Coleman Street and up onto Moorgate. They call it 'Meltdown Monday' now, of course, but for at least five minutes I was feeling pretty cool- like a character from *Dubliners*, before the whisky flush wears off. I couldn't believe it had all ended like that at the firm, but talent runs this town, right? Only at Moorgate Tube they have this *Evening Standard* billboard. When I was younger, a small boy I mean, not a trainee solicitor, I didn't understand that the *Evening Standard* was actually a newspaper at all. I was under the impression that it was some incredibly low-tech, handwritten news-service, distilling the day into a few, infinitely carefully-selected words for the benefit of passers-by. Even so, I rarely bothered to read them myself. That day though, Monday 15 September 2008, the name of a client on that billboard did catch my eye:

'4,000 CITY JOBS AXED AS LEHMAN FOLDS'.

Now the whisky flush was over for the whole City. For a moment I desperately wondered if there was any way back to the firm. When hope had left on the Northern Line, I was still standing motionless in a busy station, all alone with my fear.

Chapter 2

Bankside, London, 6 October 2008

It's always slightly colder than you expect in the middle of a Thames bridge. I like it, it's as though midstream is another world entirely, a watery no-man's-land between what you left behind on one side and what's about to hit you on the other. Maybe that's particularly true of Southwark Bridge, where otherwise you would plunge straight from the City into Bankside, a confusing, schizophrenic place, with all of the Square Mile's jumble of era and architecture but none of its fixity of purpose. I stopped for a second to admire the view, just as a huge, multi-barge convoy laden with containerised waste chugged through the arches, completely dominating the vista. I was bringing quite a lot of emotional baggage myself, and somehow it seemed an appropriate motif for Bankside- the place hasn't forgotten any of its successive incarnations as hedonistic playground of Elizabethan London, down-at-heel warehouse district, yuppie dormitory or post-industrial art mecca, but the constant shifts in identity have certainly taken their toll. At the time I was fixated by the symbolism of that short walk across the bridge from the City to Ofcable's Bankside HQ, but we'll just have to put that down to boyish enthusiasm- or pre-interview nerves.

Certainly I was exhausted by the time I got there, not by a brisk stroll over the river from Bank Station, so much as the huge reserves of emotional energy I had expended in deciding what to wear that morning. Tie or no tie? Because the fact was that I was starting to really need this job- on the other side of the river, it was another manic Monday, and the FTSE 100 was already down seven per cent. that day.

"Snazzy tie, if I may say so!" said Colin, as he shook my hand gently and led me through Reception and into a meeting room. "Very natty indeed! I'm afraid some of the chaps just don't take the trouble these days."

Colin himself was small and neat, his scanty, brown hair scraped into a sparse parting. You couldn't call him dapper as such, with his cardigan and standard issue lanyard, but he was certainly no slob.

"They think themselves too 'media', if not indeed too 'savvy' for it, I dare say!" he continued. "I mean, just look at all this- 'bling'…"

He gestured expansively round the meeting room. It boasted day-glo plastic chairs in various colours, a large but rather grubby white-board and a forlorn, disconnected spider-phone squatting disconsolately in the middle of a circular desk. The walls were sparingly covered with some phoned-in corporate artwork defiantly, almost aggressively, devoid of any conceivable artistic inspiration. It seemed to fall somewhere between a reasonably well-groomed government department and a very low-rent advertising agency.

"But, media or no media, we are, after all, responsible for upholding 'Standards' here, as I always say! Being the, er, Content *Standards* Supervision Team, I mean…" he explained.

"Right…"

"Just because we are- in many ways- the engine room of Ofcable, is no reason to come to work in a boiler-suit and flat-cap, wouldn't you concur, Matthew?"

"Er, definitely. We actually went 'dress-down' at my old firm for a while. But people soon started wearing suits again. I guess they just found it more conducive to a professional working environment."

"Exactly, oh, exactly!" said Colin. "Don't get me wrong, I'm certainly no enemy to innovation- and I'll provide you with some open-and-shut evidence of that shortly, I think you'll find! But, for me, work life is all about the three 'P's- Professional, Professionalism and…" he paused to take a dainty sip of water, "… doing things Profession*ally*."

I was guessing, then, that it hadn't been Colin who had scrawled either "Fuck Ofcable", or the pithy response "Fuck the Office of Media Supervision of the United Kingdom of Great Britain and Northern Ireland (Ofmedia)" in permanent marker on the white-board behind him.

"Oh yes," he said. "Follow, follow, follow the three 'P's, and you won't go too far wrong! But then I don't need to tell *you* much about professionalism, do I? Being a fully-qualified lawyer, I mean!"

"Er- no…"

"So how exactly did you come to leave your last job, Matthew? I imagine some people would find it rather glamorous, wouldn't they, working in a big Los Angeles law firm! There can't be many jobs in that field around at the moment though- what with Halifax, Northern Rock, Bradford & Bingley and all that malarkey?"

"There's nothing, Colin. The market is dead."

"Oh- right. And your CV says that you're English yourself though, aren't you? Born under the, er, grey skies of Blighty?"

"Yes! I suppose I just found working in a law firm- verbally inhibiting. You know, I studied English Lit at university. I wasn't used to the kind of constraints- on communication and self-expression- you have to put up with in the City."

"So you're interested in communication, then?"

"Yeah, and especially the media of communication. Like- well, like cable, you know?"

"And offices?"

"Yes, offices too, I suppose…"

"A-ha. Which naturally attracted you…"

"To Ofcable!" I concluded triumphantly.

Textbook interview technique, but if it's all about waiting for the interviewer to tell you what to say, Colin was a human autocue. He stood up, seemingly to indicate that he had heard enough, which was great because I was on fire and the only way was down. Unfortunately he then saw the writing on the white board for the first time, blushed crimson and started ineffectually trying to rub it off with a balding board-rubber. Which would have been fine, except it really was permanent marker. His increasingly frantic rubbing was just heightening the farce. It was shaping up to be an embarrassing silence, which I always feel compelled to take desperate measures to break.

"That told them, eh?"

"Who, Matthew? Who?"

"Those, er, Ofmedia… bastards?"

Colin stared at me, aghast, and ushered me hurriedly out of the meeting room.

"They're our brothers in arms, Matthew! I have to tell you that I'm really, I'm extremely upset about that, that treasonous tomfoolery in there!"

"Sorry…"

"Couldn't they at least have used approved, er, Nobo 'Dry Erase' markers?"

"Oh right, you mean the graffiti artists…"

"Who else? Well, listen, it's, er, it's been very interesting talking with you, Matt. I think I have a bit of an idea of what make you, er- tick…"

"Great… I mean, I think that's great. Is that great?"

Colin leaned towards me confidentially.

"I suspect that you, like me, are a firm believer in the three 'P's! So now let me show you what makes *me* tick. This way- this way. We're a, er, couple of floors down."

We stepped into a coffin-like lift. Maybe it was just the disconcerting proximity of the flimsy aluminium walls, but it seemed both an interminable and headlong descent, more like a free-fall mining elevator than a conventional office lift.

"Feeling alright, Matthew?"

"Uh, yes, raring to go!"

He led me down a narrow corridor further into the depths of the building, for what seemed like hundreds of metres.

"Have you seen *Das Boot*, Colin?"

"Oh yes, yes, indeed! Very suspenseful when they're listening out for the sound of the steel hull as it's gradually- gradually- gradually crushed under the overwhelming pressure of the water, isn't it?"

"Er- yeah. Is this, er- is the roof getting lower?" I asked. "Are we under the level of the river now?"

Colin looked thoughtful.

"Do you suffer much from claustrophobia, Matt? Any feelings that the walls are, well, you know, closing inexorably in upon you?"

"Not generally... But then I don't have much subterranean experience. Never worked in a nuclear bunker, super-deep borehole mine or anything like that."

"Any pot-holing? Cave diving?"

"Er- no."

He rubbed his hands together enthusiastically, in an apparent attempt to make light of this gaping void in my CV.

"Well, no matter, no matter. Any other hyper-sensitivities or, er, personal phobias we should be aware of?"

"Like what?"

"Oh, nothing, nothing, nothing in particular. A fear of rodents, for example- especially those associated with, shall we say, the docks and waterside areas of Britain?"

"What! You mean rats? Would that be a problem here?"

"No, no, just making conversation. Nothing so *Wind in the Willows* here! I almost wish there were, don't you? Mr Badger, Mr Mole, Mr Toad and, er, 'Ratty'!"

"Kind of... Good old Ratty..."

He was definitely pondering the musophobia angle though, because we continued our descent in silence for a while.

"I do have a fear of swimming over submerged ships- or any heavy marine equipment," I said.

"Oh?"

"Yeah, I fear that wrecks are going to suck me down under the water with them. You know what I mean?"

"Ah, erm. Sort of, I suppose... It sounds most unpleasant! But, well, that really shouldn't be a problem here. The water and, er, semi-aquatic mammals, if any there so be, are all on the other side of the wall here, if you see what I mean?"

Finally we reached our destination, and Colin swung open the door of what- from the outside- looked incredibly like a broom cupboard. It looked even more like a broom cupboard from the inside, except for a faux-mahogany desk and huge movie billposter monopolising the interior. Two livid red words on the poster dwarfed the rest: 'STALLONE' and 'COBRA'.

We stood for a minute looking at the poster- you really couldn't miss it in there.

"Have you seen it?" Colin eventually asked. "The movie?"

"Yeah, I think so. Not for some years obviously…"

"Well? How did it make you *feel*?"

"It's, er, it's kind of a testament to '80s individualism, isn't it? The name of the actor getting higher billing than the name of the film. The maverick loner outperforming the rest of the LAPD."

Not bad, I thought, but Colin shook his head, smiling ruefully. He drew a laser-pointer from a customised holster that seemed to have been blu-tacked onto the wall. It looked suspiciously like the laser-sight attached to Cobra's 'Super Soaker'-a-like gun in the poster. He flicked it on with a flamboyant gesture and indicated the tag line at the top of the poster.

"Crime is a disease. Meet the cure! That's what… inspires me. You see, Matthew, smut is a disease too. And we're the cure!"

"Smut? I think Cobra would say 'filth'. Smut is more kind of *Carry On*, isn't it? I reckon Cobra would probably just turn a blind eye to smut, wouldn't he?"

"Filth, hmmm… *Filth* is a disease, and we're the cure. Filth is a disease, and *we're* the cure… I think you're going to fit in well round here, Matthew! Do you have any other questions?"

"Er, no, I think we've definitely covered the big issues now. Thanks, Colin."

"Now, let me just ponder whether there's anything else that *we* should be telling *you* at this stage…"

There was another awkward pause, during which Colin grimaced disconcertingly. I hoped that he was simply cudgelling his brains for some elusive, but vastly lucrative, employee benefit.

"Oh yes, how could I forget!" He beamed complacently. "Well, I suppose there's really an unofficial fourth 'P' after all that, er, being Professional, Professionalism and doing things Profession*ally*. And that 'P', my young chum, is for 'Partying'! 'Starter for ten': the annual staff trip to Shakespeare's Globe- that's just a few minutes' walk away along the river, as you might well have noticed. Our very own Bankside neighbours, we like to think! Next: for, er, ten more: there's rather a nice little tradition that somehow seems to have spontaneously evolved here at Ofcable. If someone has a birthday- and people at all levels of the team will tend to do so each year- then they buy an assortment of cakes for the rest of us. Nothing lavish, just something tasteful like- well, like iced yum-yums, say." He moistened his lips sensuously with his tongue. "Even something a little continental, a spot of patisserie like French Fancies, sometimes. What's the French for *ooh la-la*, do I hear you say? Well, don't ask me how it all got started, *mon ami*! But you do the mathematics: nine people in the team equals approximately nine days of the working year when you get a little baked pick-me-up, to jazz up the middle of your afternoon! Because we don't miss out if someone has a birthday at the weekend either, I can assure you- we make sure they roll it over onto the next Monday. Or the next business day, in the case of public holidays, force majeure events or, er, balloted industrial action, of course. Now that's not to be underestimated on a wet Monday in October, is it?"

You can never persuade people who've worked in the same office for their entire careers that every grouping of clerical workers in the civilised world has exactly the same 'birthday cakes' tradition as their office does. But then why disillusion them? God knows there's little enough professional pride to go round as it is.

"Absolutely not! So is it someone's birthday today?"

"No, I'm afraid not, Matthew. Perhaps I shouldn't have used October as an example just then…" He shook his head ruefully. "Because, as ill luck would have it, it really isn't a particularly good month for birthdays in 'Standards'. I can show you the graph some time, if you like? We can even slice and dice it to exclude statistical anomalies- like the so-called post-War 'Baby Boom', for instance…"

Now we were back in the corridor. I had gone far too long without seeing natural light to remember what direction we were moving in. Back to the surface I hoped, because sensory disorientation was setting in fast. Besides, who knew what weirdly mutated protectors of the public morality lay at the building's core. The overall sense of dislocation was heightened by the fact that every five yards or so, we had to stop to negotiate another set of fire doors. I hate the formulaic courtesies of life, but in the circumstances, after each set of doors that Colin held open for me, I felt I had to go through the same diminishing, energy-sapping ritual of thanks.

Finally, Colin jerked open the door of an even more diminutive space than his own office. Inside, a guy of about my own age, but darker, stockier and with decidedly more swagger about him, was lolling back on a lime day-glo chair, speaking on the phone in an unmistakably Essex accent. The walls were covered with Tottenham Hotspur FC memorabilia, including a 12-inch single of *Diamond Lights*, complete with a brooding mood-shot of Glenn Hoddle and Chris Waddle. Chris was wearing a PVC-effect leather jacket that appeared to have the sleeves rolled-up, *Miami Vice*-style. I think Cobra would have found it a little effete for street-work, but you never know- those were different times.

Colin patted me unconvincingly on the shoulder.

"This, Master Verreaux, is your new office! And, er, office-mate. Once you start, you can put your own poster up. Blu-tack only during your probationary period, obviously…"

He pulled out another lime-green chair. Lime obviously hadn't proved a hit in the trendy departments at Ofcable, because it soon turned out that everyone in 'Standards' had a lime-green chair.

"Sit down, sit down- make yourself at home!"

I sat down and leant back in the chair. It cracked ominously, as though an irretrievable hairline fracture was opening up in the fibreglass. It felt as though the whole thing could collapse completely at any time now. I immediately hunched forward nervously, while Colin looked around the office with an appraising eye. He reached out to the wall, making a movable frame with his hands.

"I'm seeing a *Turner & Hooch* poster- right, let me see… Right here!"

"Watchdogs, eh?"

Maybe I should have stuck with the law after all- chat like that could have seen me anointed 'Son of Ken'. Colin slapped me on the back, anyway. My new room-mate looked over at us curiously as he hung the phone up.

"Young Peter, meet Matthew," said Colin. "Our newest recruit!"

Pete thrust his hand out.

"Pete Staines. Made in Essex, raised in Bas Vegas, an' born to trade. Just currently lackin' the necessary academic grades…"

"What grades do you need to trade?"

"Well, some, mate."

Colin was fidgeting impatiently. He obviously didn't consider Pete to be sufficiently on-message for extended pleasantries.

"Well, we mustn't keep you all day, Matthew! Did you have a coat with you?" he asked.

"Actually, I'd really love to see Pete in action," I said.

Colin seemed pleased.

"Up on the wire, eh? Well, alright then!"

Pete was unfazed.

"You're in for a treat, mate! Next up, Chatterbabe TV. Those little minxes will be trash-talkin' before I've entered the friggin' 4-digit PIN!"

There was an incongruously svelte flat-screen TV mounted on the wall. Pete flicked it on with a flourish, then expertly punched in a series of numbers. A scantily clad, highly made-up peroxide blonde was polishing a telephone with exaggerated gusto.

"Now, young Matthew," said Colin. "If you take a moment to look at your timepiece…" he held up his watch. "You'll see that we are considerably before the watershed for broadcasting content of a, ah, explicit sexual nature on television. So just by showing an indecorous acreage of skin like this young lady here," he gestured dismissively towards the screen, "these characters at 'Chatterbabe TV' are walking on egg-shells! They're clever, but sooner or later they will crack. And when they do, we'll be ready to come down on them like…"

"Humpty Dumpty?" I suggested.

"No, no, no. More like all the king's horses and all the king's, er, men!"

Pete picked up the telephone on the desk.

"Everyone ready to roll then? Booooty call!"

He gave the impression of a man who had never lost his relish for his work. He dialled a number, apparently from memory, and then put the phone on speaker.

"If this one doesn't hit the next *Cable Enforcement Bulletin*, then I'm a friggin' Dutchman!"

"We publish the *Cable Enforcement Bulletin* monthly- it's like one long roll-call of all the bad guys we've taken down to, er, Chinatown, that month," Colin whispered to me. "Peter here lives and breathes to get one of his busts into it."

"He never has?" I asked.

Colin shook his head, and patted Pete on the shoulder.

"It's only been five years. Keep the faith, son- keep the faith."

"Have you made any?" I asked Colin.

"Two! And that's two very good reasons why they pay *me* the big bucks…"

A couple of rings later a female voice answered, pleasant, faintly Eastern European-accented.

"Welcome to Chatterbabe TV! You're talking to Jane- what's your name?"

Pete winked at me.

"Clive Allen here, luv."

"Hello! So, Clive, how are you? What have you been up to?"

"I've bin watchin' you in glorious technicolour- an' I can tell you that you are a sight for sore eyes, darlin'!"

"You're sweet… So what would you like to talk about this afternoon, Clive? Things really don't look too good for the bankers, do they? I saw in the paper that the Icelandic banks are all collapsing now. Soon there'll be nowhere safe to put our money. Except maybe under the mattress!"

Pete growled lasciviously.

"Your mattress- that's more like it, luv! 'Cos it certainly isn't the bankers I'm worried about! Why don't you take off that old dressing gown of yours, and slip into somethin' a little less comfortable?"

"I'm sorry, Clive, but this is really not that type of channel. We're here to have a nice chat with you, just like friends. So be a good boy now!"

"Talk to me then, talk to me, it's bin drivin' me crazy seein' you, but not bein' able to touch you! Let's imagine the sweet, sweet music we could make- if other people's rules weren't keepin' us apart…"

"Well, we could talk about something prohibited…"

"Oh, yeah! Now you're talkin', luv…"

Pete winked at us again. Or maybe he just had a nervous tic.

"Something we're not really supposed to talk about with callers…"

"You know I'm not just any caller, baby!"

"Something from the Ofcable broadcasting regulations!"

Pete put his hand over the receiver and grimaced at us.

"Bol-locks!"

The girl chuckled.

"Am I free to go now, officer?"

Pete took a deep breath, and gave it one last throw of the dice.

"Whaddaya' mean, I just want some… relief…"

"Oh, come on, 'Clive', our real callers just want to hear a real woman's voice! Someone who isn't their mother, or the local librarian. A conversation! Surely you must know that after all these fake calls? You know this channel better than I do!"

"So I s'pose a special finish is outta' the question, then?"

"Clive, I'm going to have to hang up if you continue talking like that…"

"Fine, fine, I'm off anyway, I'm gonna' let you off with a caution this time, alright?"

Pete crashed the receiver down with exaggerated venom. Colin patted him on the shoulder.

"You lost this time, son. But that doesn't mean you have to like it."

He turned to me.

"You see what we're up against? The cunning!"

"Every Sherlock Holmes needs his Moriarty…" I said.

Colin nodded- down, but definitely not out.

"True- too true."

He held his hand out again.

"Welcome aboard!"

Pete made a crude gesticulation at me behind Colin's back, and as I gave him the finger on my way out, I think I had already made up my mind to choose Ofcable. Maybe that would have been a more profound decision if the other option hadn't been to choose Jobseeker's Allowance, but it wasn't just the desperation- or at least, not one hundred per cent. the desperation. If I had to start again from scratch, I wanted to do it with people who actually cared about something this time.

Chapter 3

Soho, London, 7 October 2008

Reviewing that celebration dinner dispassionately, if that could ever really be possible, I would have to say that it was a disaster from the moment the *amuse-bouche* arrived. I don't object to an *amuse-bouche* if someone else is paying, although unless you're a Spanish dwarf a tiny glass of cold soup is hardly likely to rock your world. But if you're picking up the tab yourself- well, it doesn't feature on the price-list, but it's just basic economics that you're going to pay through the nose somewhere along the line.

"So my father was asking how the 'State Sector' is treating you," Emily said.

She took a sip of her cocktail, then wrinkled up her own exquisitely angled nose.

"Daddy thinks you're very sensible- he's always said that the Civil Service is the fast-track to a knighthood. Says the City doesn't get a look in. Unless you do a stint at the Financial Services Authority once you've filled your boots financially, that is. That's good for a 'gong', apparently. Especially now, of course."

This was exactly the kind of practical careers advice you could always depend on from Emily's dad. When I was a solicitor, he was always advising me to chuck it in. Not in the way I had, obviously- his idea was more that I should become a barrister, as a shortcut into the House of Lords. I don't know how Emily ended up as an investment banker, maybe there were good opportunities for getting the Order of the Garter or something.

He himself was immersed in incessant jockeying for position in a minor guild or livery company in the City. In fact 'company' was a slight misnomer for the Worshipful Company of Cheesemongers, as it was really a loose gathering of warring cliques, entirely composed of unusually quarrelsome and unpredictable misanthropes. They all had titles, possibly of their own devising, and if you were anything without 'Master' in the title, you might as well have been a woman.

"Yeah, I did try to get the knighthood thrown in with the Tube pass and BUPA membership, but they beat me down to an OBE."

Emily pouted.

"So I take it that you put a good spin on me getting sacked for insubordination and ending up with a 60% pay-cut, then?" I asked.

Emily waved over the waiter. I had a sudden fear that she was going to complain about the cocktail.

"It doesn't hurt to put things in a favourable light," she said. "Accentuate the positives! I mean, would you prefer it if I described you as the guy who managed to get himself fired on the last ever leveraged buy-out in the City? Because that's how someone referred to you at the bank the other day!"

"So what did you say about the job?"

"Working at a quango in the broadcasting sector. Very New Labour, Daddy said. And they certainly look after their own. They're all making out like bandits with final salary pension plans, aren't they?"

She looked at me suspiciously.

"Why, how would you describe it?" she asked. "You have been rather cagey on the subject, I must say."

The waiter arrived at the table before I could answer. Emily held out the cocktail glass.

"What is *in* this? Cooking sherry?"

"The house champagne, madam."

Emily shook her head.

"Can you remix it for me? With real champagne?"

"Real champagne, madam?"

"Yes, yes- you must have something decent on the premises, don't you? Something you don't put on the, ah, 'fish n' chips' as well?"

Emily squinted towards the bar, as though trying to give the impression that she was much older than her years- an aged dowager used to peering through a lorgnette, to be treated with kid gloves at all costs.

"The vintage Laurent Perrier, then."

The waiter hesitated.

"Well- yes, madam. But it will be a little bit more expensive than the list price for the cocktail. We normally just use the house champagne for mixing."

Emily waved her hand airily, to indicate her total disregard for additional expense in any guise. It would have been quite an impressive gesture, if she had been paying herself.

"At least it might be remotely drinkable!"

"Yes, madam."

The waiter hurried off. If there had been any doubt before, it must have been clear by now that he had his hands full with our table. It was a pretty excruciating moment for me, because I certainly wasn't intending to tip him royally to make up for it. On

'Standards' pay, it would be all I could do to cover the tab that month as it was. There was nothing for it but the manly option- disengage from the situation, and try to brazen it out as best I could.

"Really! What is he thinking of?" said Emily.

"He must be thinking you're out of your mind! How can you even taste the champagne in a cocktail? Even some real diva like Mariah Carey or J-Lo would have potted that by now, and be halfway through the next one!"

For the first time, Emily did look a little bit uncertain as to the part she was playing. She was clearly determined to carry it off though, because her mouth was hard when she spoke next.

"Listen, Matthew, I work very hard. If I want to have something nice, then I'll have it. Lots of banking people- colleagues of mine, friends even- are losing their jobs, right, left and centre. Times are really tough, you know. It's a war out there!"

"You don't need to tell me that- I'm an economic refugee! But this is a new one on me- you're upgrading your champagne because of the austerity of the times? If you're so worried about losing your job, wouldn't it be a bit more intuitive to rein in the high life a little bit? Surely you don't actually need to spend so much cash to have a laugh?"

"I'm not worried about losing *my* job, Matthew! You're wilfully misunderstanding me. The point is that other people are getting laid off. We have to respect the sacrifices that they've made, so that the rest of us don't have to take pay-cuts. That makes it more important than ever that those of who still do have jobs enjoy life to the full. You can't just take it for granted anymore, and think the good times will go on forever. We owe it to ourselves, and the people who've been canned, not just to mope around. That's my point. The show must go on, you know?"

I must have looked as unconvinced as I felt by this analysis, because she tossed her Brazilian blow-dried, sunshine blonde hair in irritation. Not for the first time, I was struck by the reflection that with her perfect cheekbones and huge brown eyes, Emily was almost too classically beautiful. But then I do mean, almost.

"What are we talking about here anyway, fifteen, twenty pounds?" she said, shrugging her shoulders. "Big deal. I mean, *big* deal, Matthew! You didn't taste that revolting drink he brought- it was disgusting, real gnat's pee. And besides, we're supposed to be celebrating, remember? It's no time to nickel and dime!"

"Oh, yes- what could be a more fitting way to celebrate getting a low-level clerical job? What would we be doing if I had made partner instead of getting laid off? Buying the vineyard?"

Emily sighed, and changed her angle of attack.

"You didn't answer my question- how would you describe this new job of yours?"

I sought inspiration from Colin.

"I'd say that filth is a disease- meet the cure!"

That had sounded better in Cobra's brooding presence in Colin's office. Outside the precinct, I had to admit that it came across a little feebly.

"What on earth are you talking about? What do you actually do?"

"So there are these chat channels on cable TV, and guys can phone up the girl on the screen and chat to them."

"Sex lines, you mean?"

"No, no, that's the whole point! The girls aren't allowed to talk dirty, they don't have a licence to do that. And they work all day, you see, not just after the TV watershed. That way they can capture the lucrative long-term unemployed market."

Emily raised her eyebrow.

"I know! But when you come to think of it, the long-term unemployed have the fewest readily-available conversational companions of anyone- it's almost a public service. Anyway, the point is that that's exactly what we monitor. We phone up and try to get them to use words of an explicit nature. If they don't, we know they're in compliance, and they don't get another check-up for a few weeks."

"And if they do?"

"I don't know, I've only been doing it for a day," I admitted. "They're not giving it away out there, let me tell you. Life as an *agent provocateur* isn't all it's cracked up to be. Guys have been up on the wire for years without a sniff, and all my girls sound far too polite to get it on... God knows what it would be like trying to get started as a pimp. I just don't know if I'd have the motivational skills."

"It all sounds unspeakably sordid. It's exploiting the perverted!"

"Who cares about the perverted? It's the innocent we should be worrying about, isn't it? But then who knew the taxpayer was devoting so much effort to tempting the non-explicit chat-line industry to cross the line! Ofcable is ploughing a lonely furrow out there. It's like being Batman- sometimes you wonder whether anyone else cares, because they certainly don't lift a damn finger to help you."

Emily shuddered.

"I think I'm going to scream if I hear another one of your stupid analogies tonight, Matthew. I just can't take it, you never stop! I think I preferred it when you were just depressed and droning on and on about your future and how much you hate your job. At least you were engaging with life on some level, you were actually trying to better yourself. This is like speaking to a sixth-former. Christ!"

"Sorry," I said. And I did mean it. But Emily wasn't done.

"And as for this new job of yours... Just imagine the people you must speak to. The dregs of society!"

"Hardly the dregs... I mean, there are rapists and murderers out there. These girls can't even say the 'f' word on the telephone. They're actually more like pen-pals for the illiterate..."

"And you think that's a respectable profession?"

"Call it a victimless crime."

"I call it the thin end of the wedge..."

"Now I can tell you've been speaking to your parents- you've been at your Mum's *Daily Mail* again, haven't you? But just to be clear, we are the regulators. You make it sound like I ice their nipples before they go on air."

"Matt! They do that?"

"I don't know actually, that aspect of it might just be a figment of Pete's imagination. Which is pretty feverish- malarial, really. He's got quite an interesting agenda in all of this- he wants them to cross the line on a philosophical as well as a professional level. He thinks that they should throw off the shackles of Victorian prurience. And then, of course, we do have 'non-binding' quotas to hit, whatever that means- not much in practice, apparently..."

"Can we please change the subject?"

"OK, but I'm definitely going to want your ideas on how I can make my first bust. Colin thinks I'm just not pushing the right buttons out there..."

It appeared that I wasn't necessarily pushing the right buttons inside the restaurant either. Emily was studying the food on the neighbouring tables, not generally a sign of engrossment in the conversation at your own.

"The clams look good- succulent," she commented.

"Hmm, suggestive- but I'm not sure how I can work it into the conversation."

Now she shook her head in annoyance. I reached across the table for her hand.

"Listen, I was joking about getting insights into the girls on the phones from you- sort of…"

"I should think so too!"

"But it is important that we still have a bit of common ground. Work is a big part of life. I don't work in the City any more, and the way things are, I don't see that changing any time soon. There are just no jobs out there- there doesn't seem to be much of anything in the City right now. Except for fear and desperation, and I've got those covered already. So I need to know- is that OK with you, Emily?"

Because I did want to know, I just didn't know what I could actually do with the information when I had it. This is the thing that always seems mysterious when viewing broken relationships with hindsight- one party's failure to accept the loss of the other's commitment to the relationship on an emotional level, even after diagnosing it on an intellectual one. People lazily tell you to look on the bright side, but that's absolutely the worst thing that you can do. You might get some kind of reprieve, but that's partly just because break-ups are never strictly bilateral processes. There are all sorts of factors external to the will of the actual participants in the relationship, which have much more to do with the way you interact with other people around you than with each other. In fact, you should always ask yourself what Morrissey would sing about the situation. Hope would not spring eternal then. You'd understand that reality is always much, much worse than someone with a degree of residual affection for you is immediately willing to tell you. And that sooner or later, you'll have to open your eyes and face up to the advanced progress of this gradual adjustment of emotional expectation. This might be the time when the most crippling damage to self-esteem and to the friendship itself is done, but somehow there doesn't seem to be any way to short-circuit it. There's just a mandatory cooling-off period of decreasing hope and increasing resentment, until you eventually find yourself ready to believe what you've been telling yourself for weeks.

I thought there was a hint of irritation in Emily's voice when she replied, but then maybe I'm over-compensating a bit now- trying to pretend that I saw it all coming, and wasn't just hiding behind the emotional sofa. If so, all I can say in my own defence is that that's probably the only shred of bravado I have left from the episode.

"It was always you I was interested in, Matt- not your job."

I may not have been a lawyer any more, but that didn't mean that I was oblivious to the tense that people spoke in. That was definitely enough facing up to the issue for one dinner.

"Right… Another 'French 75', then?"

"Let's have another look at the wine-list first," said Emily. "Xavier was telling me about this wonderfully flinty white Burgundy he's discovered. Xavier has become very impatient with Bordeaux- he thinks they're resting on their laurels, and have been for a while now. I want to see if they carry it here…"

"Xavier? Work Xavier? Tube Xavier? Frappucino Xavier? Xavier the…"

She pulled her hand away and looked at me sharply, which was a shame because I was just getting going. On the other hand, this was the politer end of the spectrum, so maybe it was a good time to get out.

"Yes, Xavier. He is my client too, you know- still my client. You don't expect me to sabotage my career as well, just because you couldn't take the heat in yours?"

Plenty of interpretations can be put on everything you do in life, and you don't always get to pick your own version of events. Of course I had to accept that a lot of people would see my accelerated career change as an old-fashioned cop-out- it was just that I had hoped that Emily wouldn't be one of them. Maybe it was the correct interpretation though, and I really was just a serial quitter, because one thing was for sure- I badly wanted to get out of that restaurant at that moment. There was only one thing holding me back, and it was no great indication of moral courage in itself: What happens if you leave a restaurant after the *amuse-bouche*, but before the starter? Do they charge you for two thimbles of soup that don't even feature on the menu and, if so, what's the damage? It might sound like a trivial quandary to be defeated by, but I really couldn't afford another serious loss of face at that moment. Emily was just not the type of girl to face implication in a serious breach of restaurant etiquette with equanimity. And even from a legal point of view, I could easily see that there was at least a moral commitment to stick around for starter and main, after pigging out on a *demitasse* of Chef's lovingly crafted radish and watercress gazpacho.

For all the thought that one gives at various stages in life to love, there's no doubt that it can be very easy to get distracted from it at the crucial moments. It's all very well for Andie MacDowell not to notice the apocalyptic rainstorm at the end of *Four Weddings and a Funeral*, but I would have been under the nearest bus-shelter, calculating the distance to Highbury & Islington Station, before that *dénouement* could even have got going. I mean, was it an Arsenal match day? If so, it could take ages just to get into the Tube station.

That's probably why real life is such a tragedy to those who love romantic comedies. There just isn't time to make the most of the poignant moments that creep up on you whilst you're trying to work out how to exit a restaurant before you've had any non-complimentary courses, or boiling water for your morning tea in a saucepan because one of your mates has put your cordless electric kettle on the gas hob and melted it beyond recognition. Because in my experience, the real battlefields of love are mined with distractions- they're Tube platforms and petrol station forecourts, they're supermarket aisles. Other stuff is happening there.

And besides, life's real soundtracks are always, always wrong. Just take that moment in La Corniche- there was some kind of Michael Bublé swing muzack burbling around the restaurant. There just haven't been any moments in my life to which that would be a remotely appropriate accompaniment- or anything but a grotesque, cynical mockery.

I took her hand again, but she just left it hanging limply in mine.

"Emily- do you still love me?"

"Of course I do. But...."

She sighed, and pulled her hand away again. This time it felt a bit more- final.

"But what?"

"Oh, Matt, you know. Things have changed so much, recently. It's just really hard for me to adjust, you know. I thought I knew exactly where everything was heading. You were going to be a partner in a US law firm- I would make MD at the bank. Well, in a couple of years. We were both on the same page, career-wise! And now, I really don't understand what you want anymore. I don't think you do yourself. You don't seem yourself, I feel like anything could happen, that you could suddenly decide to go off travelling or- or anything. Everything is suddenly up in the air. You'll probably go off with some, you know, unconventional girl from Ofmedia..."

"Ofcable."

"Sorry?"

"It's Ofcable- not Ofmedia," I explained irrelevantly. "They do all communications- we're just cable. And according to Pete, they're all mingers at Ofmedia, anyway…"

"Some girl from Ofcable then, who knows all about books and listens to The Smiths, I don't know."

"You listen to The Smiths."

"Not willingly, Matt, that's the point! You bombard me with those dirges."

It was true that she never actually put them on herself. But then she didn't put any music on herself. Except occasionally Dido, and you would think that only someone completely immune to monotony would play Dido records.

"So where does this leave us? You want to split up? How does that work? Do I move out?" I asked.

What was the form with a rented flat? Because I certainly couldn't afford to pay the rent solo. It was in Maida Vale. Public sector employees don't live in Maida Vale- the whole point of the Bakerloo line is to transport people like us past places like that, and on to Kensal Rise and Willesden. And there were tenants in my old flat in Dalston now. I mean, they looked like squatters, but they did generally seem to pay the rent. How would I get them out?

"Well, maybe- for a while, anyway."

"Sorry? Oh, me moving out. For a while? There is no 'while', is there though? We must have been split up for quite a while already, or we wouldn't even be having this conversation. You mean forever, obviously."

She was crying a little bit now. And I mean, a little bit- she wasn't about to start sobbing and beating the floor with her hands in anguish. Somehow I felt that would have been more appropriate. I would have myself, but I felt too numb and sick for sudden movements like that.

"If that's how you want to put it. It isn't easy for me either. Maybe one day we could get back together, you know? If we grew back together again. Started wanting the same things- the same life- again. But right now, I just don't know, I can't predict when that might be. We don't seem to be at the same stages of our lives at all. It's just all so difficult, you know!"

She did look sad, although I could tell that it was more for herself than me. That sounds a little critical of Emily, but I really don't mean it that way- it's perfectly rational to be moved by an emotional experience, without necessarily wishing to undo it. But let's be clear, I was still a long, long way, just at that moment, from being able to appreciate that.

"You know, I'm, uh, I'm just a bit disappointed in you, Emily. You're really not the person I once thought you were."

That's one thing about getting dumped, it takes years off you. I was behaving like a fifteen-year-old already, anxious, vulnerable, rank with spite and self-pity. I could feel it, I could hear it, I just couldn't stop myself.

"What do you mean?"

"I'm sorry- let me take that back. What I really mean is that I'm disappointed that this has happened. I, er, I really do wish it hadn't."

The break-up interlude had removed one potential banana-skin, in that the waiter had now arrived at our table with the starters. There was no question now of leaving without paying. Instead I stared blankly at my food.

"Something wrong with your *foie gras?*" asked Emily.

That was the kind of restaurant it was- *foie gras* was the cheapest thing on the menu. It was like butter in that place, it was *The Killing Fields* for geese in there.

"Kind of cruel, isn't it?"

"You've never had a problem with that before!"

"Yeah, well I've never felt like my own insides had burst before. It hurts."

Because that was how it did feel- almost a physical pain, that made me want to groan or shout out, or just to curl up like an injured animal. Like I'd been poisoned. And if you want to know whether that poison was pure, unadulterated loss of Emily, or how potently laced it was with my own wounded pride and self-esteem, then I'd have to say that anyone who could answer a question like that truly would know a lot about themselves- and probably about love as well. But then Emily showed that she was the one who really knew a lot about me.

"Listen, Matt, I'm not saying this to be cruel, however it might seem to you right now, but all of this- all this emotion, and, you know, a bit of drama with it, really- it's quite strange to me, because you've never taken anything seriously like this before. You know, people, grown-up people in their late twenties, they do get married, and they do talk sensibly about whether they want to have children. They can have conversations without constant wisecracking or stupid analogies, and they can talk about their careers and respect each other for what they do. Without having to make it seem as though everything in the real world is somehow- ridiculous. It's easy to be the boy at the back of the classroom, making fun of everything and, to be honest, that's worked pretty well for you- right up to a few weeks ago. But, you know, that doesn't get much done in the real world, Matthew. You might not want to have a successful career, but I do, I do want to get things done, to achieve something in my life, and I don't see why I should be made to feel ashamed of that. Why should I- what's so wrong with that? What do you plan to do that's so bloody great? Phone sex lines all day? Being, I don't know what- whimsical- all the time doesn't build anything, so at the end of the day, it's just a bit pathetic in an adult if there's nothing else there."

She patted me on the hand.

"You've got so much going for you, Matt- you're smart, you can be funny, you're really quite good-looking, you're, you're pretty tall. So I'm not saying that there is nothing else there- it's just that I don't think you've shown us all what it is yet, have you? So I must admit that it seems a little bit unfair that you get to treat everything with such cynicism, only now it turns out, everything except for your own feelings. I mean, how was I to know? You're always talking about everything in terms of films and books, but what about your life- our life? Things might have been a bit different if you had shown me that you cared like this before- that you really did want to invest a bit of yourself in something. Anything!"

"What if I do now?"

"Well, now- now I'm not sure that there's anything left to invest in, to be honest. Things do change. They- end."

Even at the time, I wasn't all that far from understanding that it was myself I should have been disappointed in. Sometimes you look around, but there's just no one else to blame it on. It seemed as though time was up on the man-child routine, as well as the lawyering. As for the film thing, I think everyone says now that cinema has colonised our consciousness. I was just wondering whether you could even call it colonisation, when the previous occupants of your consciousness somehow seemed to have wandered away at some point, and left it uninhabited.

Chapter 4

Bankside, London, 6 November 2008

"She's a grade 'A' bitch, mate, and that's all there is to it! Of course it wasn't your fault. 'Course not."

That was Pete's take on the subject, and it too was an important part of the healing process. You could also say that he was the real victim in all of this, since I was staying with him in his bachelor pad in Bermondsey whilst the widows and orphans were being evicted from my flat in Dalston. This was more of an imposition than it might sound, because Pete's spare room was actually characterised by him as the 'Darts Room', and by all accounts his game had gone to pot since I had moved in.

It wasn't all beer and skittles for me either, mind you: the Darts Room was a pretty disconcerting place to sleep, in large part because it had a life-size poster of Eric Bristow MBE on each of the three walls not actually dominated by the board itself. Having the Crafty Cockney's decidedly beady eyes on you wherever you were in the room was enough to give anyone the yips. Pete had also painted trophies commemorating each of the Cockney's major victories on the walls. Unfortunately these depictions were so haphazard in execution, no two of them looking remotely identical, that he had had to write the name of each relevant championship underneath them in biro. They all had very long, unwieldy monikers, so the overall effect was to give you the impression that you had inadvertently entered the bedroom of a very naughty five-year-old- or perhaps a dangerous mental patient.

Even to the darts purist, the Darts Room was not entirely fit for purpose. Whilst painfully narrow in dimensions, it was not quite long enough to accommodate the whole of the designated competition exclusion zone around the oche. As Pete was a stickler for all darts regulations, that meant that he had carefully affixed a further line of duct tape outside the Darts Room, in his entrance hall, exactly ninety centimetres behind the rubber darts mat where the throwing player stood. Pete insisted that any visiting player stood out there whilst he was throwing his darts, to ape the professional experience and avoid putting him off. So the social side of it was diminished a bit by the fact that you were essentially playing a game with someone who was in a different room from you at all relevant times. And it was hardly a home comfort to have most of your bedroom floor carpeted in a rubber mat, with a raised throwing line on it. On getting up in the night for any reason, the unpleasant effect of cold rubber on my feet was only mitigated by the exciting realisation that at some point I was likely to stub my toe painfully on the oche. Of course after a few weeks of this, the regulation distances were all etched in my memory so that I could easily pace out the distances in the dark. Which is why I have no sympathy whatsoever with professional darts players overstepping at tournaments- it's just a question of total immersion in the game.

Worst of all though, Pete was not always so punctilious about the precise measures of the game, and after a night out he would stagger into the Darts Room and hurl darts in the general direction of the board from well behind the oche- sometimes even from the doorway. Technically I believe that's perfectly permissible under competition rules, but it could be a little alarming for anyone who happened to be sleeping in the tiny single bed underneath the board at the time.

So all in all, breaking up was even harder to do than I'd expected. And it wasn't really the accommodation I had been hoping for to prove to Emily that I had grown as a person since student days.

"Grade 'A' bitch- with honours!" Pete elaborated, rocking back in his lime-green chair.

"OK, OK, I get it! I should have known what I was getting into, though- she used to wear a fur coat at university."

Pete considered this fresh evidence.

"What's so bad about that?"

"It still had the eyes on it."

"Ah, the 'Cruella de Vil' type- I shoulda' known!"

He hung up the telephone and swivelled round to face me.

"I can't believe the punters wait that long to get on the phone with them. Shockin' at their age, really… Average age of fifty-nine, the KKK Channel's callers."

"You what?"

"The 'Krazy Kids Kall' Channel, to you."

"They actually brand it the 'KKK Channel'? That's pretty punchy. Shouldn't we be cracking down on that, for a start?"

"They're colour-blind in their recruitment policy, from what I can see! No institutional racism at the KKK. Proper rainbow nation down there, mate. They really oughta' reconsider the burnin' cross logo, though…"

"You wonder why they don't play it safe and call it the 'Crazy Cids Call' Channel. 'C Cubed'."

"C to the Power of Four, that would be, mate- even I know that! Crazy 'Cids' with a 'C' though? People would be expectin' to see old Chuck Heston ridin' round the Costa del Sol on a big horse, smitin' the locals with his sword. Probably even worse for race relations than the friggin' KKK Channel."

"Hmm, I don't think there are any 'Moors' around any more though, are there? You don't see it as an option on those 'Ethnic origin' questionnaires. And anyway, El Cid was definitely not 'Crazy'! He was the first Christian Iberian hero."

"Yeah, well Cristiano Ronaldo takes care of all that sort of stuff these days. But listen, mate- how are you goin' to get her back?"

"Who?"

"Cruella! Emily! The girl you've been mopin' about for the past month! An' phonin' on the sly when you think I'm not listenin'... Who d'ya think I'm talkin' about? I mean, you could always throw yourself into your work to try and forget about her. But then you'd actually have to do somethin' in the office..."

"What would you have me do, Pete? You make it sound as though our desks are groaning with vital work!"

"You could get me a cuppa', for a start!"

"Fine. That engrossing task should be more than enough to take my mind off things..."

One advantage of base and shallow people that you rarely hear about is the fact that they're very easy to get to know. I mean, I'm talking about myself as well as Pete. When I was lawyering I never made tea for anyone, which you can easily get away with in professional services provided that you make a point of it, but I had already settled into a strictly observed tea rota with Pete. I was getting pretty good at finding my way to the kitchen by myself by now- the walls creaked differently, depending on how far below water level you were.

The office kettle could definitely have done with its own Standards Supervisor, because it had an element with the shape, colour and noxious aroma of a Scampi 'N' Lemon Nik Nak. The bottom third of the kettle was filled with a swirling mass of flaked lime-scale that, judging from its impact on the toughened stainless steel interior of the kettle, promised severe internal damage to anyone ingesting it. It was a bit like the gyrating plastic bags in the Pacific Ocean trash vortex- a disturbing but ultimately insoluble environmental problem that you just had to put out of your mind if you wanted to get on with your day-to-day life. I poured the dregs of the kettle into Pete's cherished 'Ossie Ardiles Soccer School' mug, and took it back to the broom cupboard. He was liable to look a bit pasty after a hard weekend, so the minerals from the lime-scale would do him good. I could tell that he really appreciated the gesture.

"This better not be any of your posh City tea…" he said.

"You think there is posh Tetley?"

"There's peppermint tea."

"Well that isn't tea then, is it? It's an aromatic herb. I know you can make most things sound pretentious by putting 'City' in front of them. But tea-bags just aren't one of them."

"So is it posh City milk then?"

"Semi. Does that count?"

I would have been interested to hear how semi-skimmed registered on Pete's poshness scale, but just then Colin arrived and mimed knocking on the door. To add an audio element to the gag, he also said "Knock, knock!"

"Anyone home? Now if I can just tear you gentlemen away from your no doubt invaluable, er, hot beverage-related business for a moment, then maybe I can introduce another pair of valuable additions to our, er, little band of brothers?"

The first valuable addition was clearly dressed to impress, with a broken pencil wedged behind one ear and a school exercise book in his hand. This might have looked a bit more professional if it hadn't actually had 'Form 3A' written on it. He was wearing a baggy suit of a shade of grey so pale that in some lights it would have looked white, a white shirt so frequently boiled that in any light it would have looked grey, and a skinny tie that clearly dated from the last time ties were skinny. However, all of these professional accoutrements were trivialised in my eyes by the fact that he was also Carl. He stepped into the office with an extravagantly long step, somewhere between a bow and a fencing lunge.

"Another lawyer, to be precise!" said Colin.

It was clear then that, setting aside the question of his legal qualifications, this was no impostor- fiasco still followed Carl like a shadow. I shook his hand, fairly firmly.

"My learned friend..." said Carl.

Colin looked pleased with this lawyerly shop-talk.

"As a fellow professional, I was hoping you could mentor Carl a little, Matthew. Show him the old, er, ropes. Help him find his feet outside the ivory tower of the legal profession, eh?"

"No problem, Colin. I really would love to speak with him. Right now, actually."

Colin rubbed his hands together.

"Excellent, excellent. I was considering putting Carl in here with you, given your, er, professional affiliations. But Peter has been in this office for five years now, and they do say that 'possession is nine-tenths of the law', don't they?"

"Really?" said Carl. "Because one of my friends actually got cautioned for possession, man."

"I see..." said Colin uncertainly. "But first let me introduce another 'New Kid on the Block'! Thomas Taylor. Come in, Tom!"

A small, cadaverous figure, with short, dark hair cropped austerely back from a pale forehead, stepped into the office noiselessly. He looked disapprovingly around at it and all its occupants.

"Hi, Tom," said Pete breezily. "Pleased to meetcha'!"

"It's actually 'Thomas'," said Thomas. "Perhaps the Chief Executive mentioned that to you, Colin? I asked him specifically to clarify that in advance- to avoid any unfortunate misunderstandings or, ah, unsolicited abbreviations of this nature- when I got here."

"Right, well, er, Thomas is actually on secondment to us- from Ofmedia, of all places!" said Colin quickly. He patted Thomas on the shoulder joshingly, then withdrew his hand as Thomas appeared to recoil from his touch.

"Ofmedia?" hissed Pete.

"Come to see how we do things at Ofcable, haven't you, eh, Thomas?" said Colin. "You'll certainly learn a thing or two about cable regulation here, I would like to think! At the feet of the masters, and all that, eh?"

Thomas allowed himself a glacial smile.

"Scarcely at the feet," he said. "Although it does strike me already that your, er, methods are- markedly different- from Ofmedia best practice, in many material respects. So perhaps we can indeed learn a little from each other. After all, it is important to know what *not* to do, as well as what to do, as the Chief Executive told me himself."

"Really? The Chief Exec said that?" said Colin, with interest.

"The Chief Executive of Ofmedia. When he charged me with the signal responsibility of undertaking this secondment. I felt that I could not refuse it, when he had personally intervened in the matter. He asked me to pass a message to his opposite number, should I encounter such a person here."

"Oh yes? What was that, then?"

"To his opposite number, Colin. Such identity to be verified to my satisfaction. I'm sure that you would not wish me to break that confidence? And you, of course, can have no pretensions to such a status yourself!"

"Quite so, quite so," said Colin uncertainly. "Well, let's continue our little tour then, Young Thomas. We'll pass the CEO's, er, office when we get back to surface level and you can pop in for a nice natter then! Let's, er, regretfully part company with Carl at this point, though. He and Matthew will be wanting to have a good old chin-wag of their own, no doubt!"

Carl looked at me.

"The time has come to talk of many things, man."

"I will see you legal eagles anon, then…" said Colin.

He bowed his way out, in apparent tribute to Carl's lawyerly status. Thomas followed him silently.

Carl slumped down into a lime-green chair.

"Whoah, that went pretty well," he said. "I wasn't sure how you'd play it there, man."

"You actually considered this in advance?"

"It did seem a coincidence, there being another dude with the same name as you already on the books. Moreover, this dude was repeatedly described by Colino as being a fellow lawyer. I feared an embarrassing misunderstanding, man. Especially with that Thomas character twisting my melon. What did Colino call him, Thomas Taylor? More like Tomás de Torquemada, man."

"Well, at least he's well-qualified for the role. You can't really quibble with Inquisitor General of all Spain as relevant work experience. The ideal foil for you, I'd say, what with your legal expertise and all…"

"Like I say, man, a good thing you kept your powder dry in that regard. You could've told Col I wasn't really a lawyer- then if I'd tried to counter with the same damaging accusation about you… Who knows where we would have got to?"

"Yeah, that could have led to a real Mexican stand-off. What with the publicly available online register of solicitors being the only way to resolve it. But no doubt we'd all have looked back and laughed. After you'd done your time for impersonating an officer of the court, anyway. Not to mention any tit-for-tat disclosure of the Ketamine Incident…"

Carl put his hands up in placation.

"Don't get uptight again, man, I had nowhere to go. There was some unpleasantness concerning a missing fountain pen at the last place…"

"Shit! Really? You too?"

Carl chuckled.

"No, not really, man. Actually I got caned at work. Under controlled conditions, as it happens. Perfectly professional. But still, they did not like that."

"You what? In the office? Are you completely insane?"

"Who among us is truly free from insanity, man? But in my own defence- the alleged incident took place squarely within the 'Designated Smoking Area' outside the office. You know, the DSA, man. You had the odd Marlboro Light there yourself, as I recall. Only now, of course, they claim that it was always implied that the 'smoking' part of DSA only refers to 'tobacco'!"

"What sticklers. So what happened?"

Carl's eyes glazed over.

"It was hell in the post room that day, man. There were bogeys like fireflies- all over the sky."

"Meaning?"

"There were a lot of, er, letters to deliver."

"Wasn't that a bit of an occupational hazard in the post room?"

"Listen, it's all about morale in the post room, man. If we feel properly valued, appreciated, we can work wonders- move mountains."

"Like a Mont Blanc?"

"I don't know what you mean, man... But like I say, if treated with, er, kid's gloves, we can generally deliver the overwhelming majority of the regular-sized letters that arrive in the first post- at least by close of business. But that day the, er, yoke of oppression was lying heavy on our shoulders..."

He sighed, and put his feet up on my desk.

"It all started when I- personally- took receipt of a consignment of important letters from a reputable firm of professional translators. Things of beauty, man, elegant epistles on thick, creamy Conqueror note paper. And individually addressed to many of the partners in the firm. Well, all of them as it turned out. Anyway, the courier was especially importunate that these documents be delivered directly to the addressees. Personally. So I gave him, er, certain assurances that I would take full responsibility for safe delivery. He in return promising to buy me a Tia Maria or two in the, er, Alibi Bar later on..."

"But what did translators have to say of any conceivable importance? Surely they were just trying to scrounge some business from the firm?"

"With the benefit of considerable, er, twenty-twenty hindsight- that was how the authorities later interpreted it. Though no one could possibly have foreseen that at the time."

"So these letters were basically advertising flyers?"

He nodded slowly.

"So why was that so stressful? Couldn't you just chuck them in the partners' pigeon-holes with the rest of the obvious junk mail? I always assumed that was what the post room was for. You must have dealt with tons of that crap every day."

Carl winced a little.

"Well, these, er, perfidious polyglots had misleadingly printed 'Urgent' on the front of each envelope, you see…"

"So you barged in on every partner in the firm with some irrelevant spam? Nice one! How did that work out for you?"

"*Urgent*, man. How would you interpret that? I'm not a translator myself- I only speak English. And my first language, Esperanto, obviously. *Urĝa*."

"I would translate it in light of the identity of the addressee."

"Ugh, don't talk to me about translation, man. Those partners were, I don't know, with clients, in completion meetings, holding conference calls at the time. They weren't best pleased to be disturbed. As I said at the time, I was genuinely concerned at the, er, chronic anger management issues that some of these guys appear to have. For their own sake, not mine, man. I mean, do they flip out like that every time they get a takeaway pizza flyer through the letterbox? Don't they care about the potential paper-cut exposure from, er, thrusting crisp envelopes rapidly into employees's faces?"

"But surely you didn't actually get fired for that?"

"Not directly speaking, man. Hasty words were exchanged, without doubt. More by them than, er, by me. Although I was upset too- I don't mind admitting it. Shaken. I had to take some time out to reflect. Consider my position. Well, as it turned out, I did have some gear in my possession, for, er, personal consumption. So, when I entered the DSA, I took that designation quite literally. Designated. Smoking. Area. Which I still think is some kind of basic, er, human right, there are legal cases on it and everything. Although I haven't actually finished all the reading on that yet, man. Anyway, I put some of it in my rollie. Surreptitiously, man, I was aware that there could be uptight characters in the vicinity. I thought it would calm me down a bit."

"And did it?"

"In a manner of speaking, man. Unfortunately I had forgotten that it was actually from a batch I had been retaining for a, er, special occasion. I mean, I knew it was a potent strain. It turned to be the freaking *Andromeda Strain*. To cut a long story short, there was a paranormal, er, photochemical reaction. One that- to this day- I still can't completely explain."

"What happened?"

I don't know what elucidation I was hoping for when I asked that question, because it should have been perfectly obvious that we were a pretty long way from Kansas now. Nonetheless, Carl pondered it for a moment.

"Well, the sunshine kind of freaked me out, man. It felt like that weed was, er, photosynthesising *inside* me. It would probably take a combination of an anthropologist, a botanist, a neuroscientist and a Shaman of Shamen even to scratch the surface of what I experienced that afternoon, man! I became temporarily obsessed with the sun. It was solar shock and awe. It's not really surprising when you consider the, er, ancient tradition of sun worship and solar supreme deities. All over the world, I mean, not just our Aztec and Mayan brothers. But with that gear inside me, there was a supernova going on inside my head. The sun was just swelling, swelling, swelling into a red giant in front of me. I prostrated myself before it, man."

Like I say, I don't know what I was expecting when I asked the question. It definitely wasn't that though.

"OK- so you were kneeling down, worshipping one or more sun gods, in the Designated Smoking Area outside the office? That must have been the most interesting spectacle for the guys in the Property department since- well, ever, I guess... So what happened next?"

Carl considered this.

"In simple terms- layman's terms, I mean- I suppose you could call it speaking in tongues, man," he said. "I began invoking ancestral sun deities, each in their own, er, *lingua franca*."

"What languages were you speaking then?"

"You name it, man, heh heh heh. Old Norse. Quechua. Mesopotamian. Esperanto. Aymara. Sanskrit. Khmer. Forgotten lore, man, lost pagan heritage- these were the, er, ancient languages of the world."

"So who diagnosed this? Surely there weren't speakers of all those on the premises? Is Mesopotamian even a language? Sanskrit I remember- from *Indiana Jones and the Temple of Doom*."

Carl brushed aside this pedantry.

"Some of it I verified, by reference to independent research…"

"You mean you looked it up on Wikipedia?"

"Like I say, I researched it," Carl said sniffily. "For the rest- it's more a matter of what I *know*, than what was 'diagnosed' by so-called experts, man. Believe me, no one would have been happier than me to have had a team of world-class philologists there, to decipher the linguistics and capture that moment. Knowledge was wasted that day, man. There isn't a day that goes by when I don't regret that, believe me."

"And what did the firm say?" I asked.

Carl shook his head sadly.

"Maybe, like Icarus, I had flown too close to the sun to remain long unsinged, man… But the gods chose a pretty strange, er, vessel for their vengeance. The senior partner and managing partner were both travelling on business. So I was interviewed by the most senior remaining partner on the premises. Perhaps unsurprisingly given those, er, selection criteria, he turned out to be one of the most, er, blinkered and reactionary figures within the establishment. You might remember him actually, man- Ken Smythe. Wore a poncho- or some other kind of Mexican garment, I seem to recall. Sort of a rain-maker at the firm. You know the dude I refer to?"

"Pancho Villa. Of course I remember Smythe, Carl! More *Rain Man* than rain-maker, I would say. But yeah, he was the partner on the deal where I cashed my chips in- Project Behemoth. You were involved in that one as well, surely you remember it? The one on which you lost the Mont Blanc and facilitated my professional suicide?"

Carl blinked back at me.

"It was the same guy? He's like my Nemesis, man! That explains everything… 'Cause this Smythe certainly didn't bring much, er, hermetic vision to his inquest. I urged him to get on his knees with me and grope blindly towards the, er, possibilities of the phenomenon I had experienced- to prostrate himself before enlightenment! It scared him, man. A little mind teetering on the brink of its own, er, puny experience was my impression."

"But what- with all the will in the world- could Ken really have gleaned from this experience, Carl?"

"Listen, man, to put it another way: I had inadvertently stumbled upon a gateway to another dimension. One in which solar deities still very much rule the roost. A, er, Stargate, if you will- to the true meaning of religion, quantum physics, time and space. Smythe is a Pandora who left the, er, Box unopened."

"The key to this gateway being the dope that you smoked just before going through it? So to get back there- to make another crossing- all you would need to do would be…"

"To smoke some more of the same batch," said Carl. "Precisely, man. And that's why I offered to do exactly that."

"In front of Ken?"

"Of course. So he could verify it for himself, man. I mean, no one could guarantee that we would be able to align every vibe with the first episode. It's not like, er, crossing the road- unless you live on a pretty cosmic highway! It would basically depend on the gear being absolutely uniform in quality across the whole batch. Although," Carl chuckled, "I think I can vouch for that, heh heh heh! But there was also my state of mind to think of. Whether that could be recreated with sufficient accuracy."

"And no one could vouch for that…"

Carl ignored me.

"To give Smythe the benefit of the doubt, it may ultimately have been quite genuine, er, conscientious doubts- scientific scruples- on that score that led him to veto the experiment, man. But whatever the ethical dilemmas involved, when I over-ruled him and sparked it up, he called security."

"And that brought matters to a head?"

"He couldn't wait to get me off the premises, man… Glibly reasserting the, er, reactionary value system of his 'partnership'. An errand boy, sent by grocery clerks, to collect a bill. Plus, it seemed that I had upset him. In some previous dealings that we had had, I mean."

"That's what I keep trying to tell you, Carl! We were all on Project Behemoth together!"

Carl chuckled.

"Some memory you have, man! Photostatic… So anyway, the next thing I knew was that, instead of the interview requests from *New Scientist* and *National Geographic* I'd been anticipating, I was receiving a P45 in a manila envelope. Low-grade internal stationery, man. A cruel mockery in the circumstances… It was the end of my career at the firm."

He looked quite despondent about it, but it seemed to me that, taking everything into account, things could have turned out a lot worse for him. After all, he had a new job already. Admittedly that was on the basis of a tissue of fairly fundamental lies that could unravel at almost any time, but a job's a job.

"One thing I still don't get, Carl- you took this summary dismissal as a promotion?"

"In what sense, man?"

"In the sense that Colin just introduced you as a lawyer, and you didn't say, 'Colin, I may have deceived you slightly when I unlawfully claimed to have professional qualifications. Actually I worked in the post room until my eventual termination for gross misconduct.'"

"*Touché*, man! Although I did actually, er, sit the A-Level Law exam. But tell me, man, how much of your own back story did you share with Colino?"

"Hmm, fair enough…"

"Listen, man: Please don't feel threatened by my arrival. I know that I've got a bit of a reputation as an innovator- a, er, disruptor, if you will. But don't regard this new role I've taken on as an attempt to challenge the *status quo*. Consider me the Planchet to your D'Artagnan."

"Maybe the Pip to my Dogtanian."

Carl grimaced.

"No way, man. Pip was a filthy rat. I can't have that."

Pete had been listening to this exchange with relative indifference, but like centuries of Essex yeomen before him, he was not one to allow an injustice to go unchallenged.

"Pip was a friggin' mouse! They'd hardly cast a rat as the hero's right-hand man, would they! What was his weapon of choice- the bubonic plague? Who was his boss- the Pied Piper of Hamelin? And besides, d'ya think that I- or any other poor sod who's worked in this office for five years- don't know a friggin' rat when I see one? I could pick a brown rat from a water vole at fifty yards, b'lieve me. It's like the friggin' *Wind in the Willows* round here!"

"I knew it!" I hissed.

But new boy or not, Carl was sticking to his guns.

"Did you see the size of him, man? He had his own sword! And full-length pantaloons, as I recall. Hardly the accoutrements of the diminutive house mouse or, er, *mus musculus*. Besides, *Muskehounds* was produced in Japan. Totally different, er, anthropomorphic perceptions. Anyway, let's not get bogged down in the whole Dumas value system. Not all directly translatable into modern terms, man. At times he seems to show some promising, vestigial sense of social conscience. But then look at his, er, über-reactionary depiction of Milady de Winter. An empowered female class warrior, who most intelligent commentators would now regard as a socialist heroine in the tradition of Charlotte Corday or, er, Ulrike Meinhof. Demonised by Dumas."

"Is this you outwitted?" I asked Pete. "That's got to hurt. This guy got fired from his last job for getting stoned in the office, so I don't know where that leaves you."

"I was distracted," Pete said. "I was thinking about Dogtanian's love interest. A disturbingly attractive spaniel…"

Carl nodded sympathetically.

"One for one and all for one/ Cablehounds are always ready!" sang Pete tunelessly. "One for channel one-four-one/ Surveillin' everybody…"

"Nice one, man!" said Carl sincerely. He turned back to me. "Look, man, my point was simply that, however far my material circumstances may have improved, I still recognise your moral supremacy. OK?"

He held out a decidedly clammy hand. I shook it gingerly.

"OK, cheers. Although if that's true, you must be in a real abyss."

I introduced him to Pete, who certainly was.

"Intrigued to meet you, mate," said Pete. "Tell me some more about this 'Ketamine Incident' of yours, then."

"All will become clear, man. I sense that you will not long remain outwith the Circle of Trust."

He opened his exercise book, pulled the pencil out from behind his ear and licked it. This must have been a purely symbolic act, as it was clearly broken beyond any possible redemption. In fact it was one of the 100% recycled pencils from our old firm- the writing implement of choice for a man sending postcards from the edge.

"Soooo, what exactly do we do here, man?" Carl asked. "Something to do with cable TV, I gather? Just from something Colino let slip earlier… Make cable TV? Not a problem, 'cos I've got a great idea for a show, as it happens. You take a bunch of ordinary people- who don't even know each other, you see- total strangers! And put them all in a room together, with no contact with the outside world, except through us. And we would only communicate through, you know, some type of disembodied voice. To freak them out all the more, I mean. Give them basic food and stuff, obviously, it's not a physical endurance test. Maybe even some booze- the Great British public loves intoxication comedy. Next? Just sit back and see what happens, man. It could be like *Lord of the Flies* in there! Real, er, televisual innovation. I mean, far-fetched, man, but just imagine if we could pull it off!"

"You mean like *Big Brother*?" said Pete. "What planet have you been on for the last 10 years, mate?"

"Has it been done already, man? I don't watch TV myself. Drug of the nation. But, OK, stay with me, man, stay with me, how about if they weren't ordinary people at all- but actually, you know, celebrities? Adds a completely different dynamic, because the celebs are already used to living in a goldfish bowl- but how will they react to the seclusion of the room? It's all about taking people out of their comfort-zone, man."

"So obviously that's complete gibberish- but it would be awesome though, wouldn't it?" I said. "Actually making the shows, I mean. It's what I've always dreamed of!"

"You chose a pretty indirect path to wish fulfilment by goin' to law school then, mate!" said Pete. "Sounds like your careers office dropped the friggin' ball a bit on that one!"

"Yeah, but unfortunately there was no application form you could fill out to do those kinds of jobs. You had to find your own way, and I always went for the route of least resistance…"

"Well, I don't think you'd get much screen-time on the KKK Channel or Chatterbabe anyway, mate," said Pete. "They do tend to favour the lookers, I'm afraid."

"Not all this 'chat' stuff! Real TV. *The Sopranos*. *Panorama*. *Top Gear*. What would you do, Pete? *Bullseye 2.0*?"

Pete rocked back in his chair to ponder this.

"Yeah, definitely darts, gotta' be somethin' to do with darts. But not a straight rip-off of *Bullseye*. A twist on the format- maybe with a datin' angle. A bit of *Blind Date* thrown in. 'Love on the Oche'. Somethin' like that- somethin' romantic, you know?"

"Harnessing the full aphrosidisiac power of the game- got it. Ironic really, since darts people are more notable for their lack of appeal to the fairer sex…"

"Bollocks they are!" said Pete indignantly. "But if so, all the more need for a show like this."

"A depiction of sexually confident and successful darts fans?"

"Exactly. It could be just what's needed, to dispel tired old myths like that. Which were no doubt propagated by the oh-so-glamorous snooker fraternity, in any case. The old sweaty palms brigade… Revitalise the whole scene, that would."

"I hate to interrupt you while you're on a Kool-Aid break, man," said Carl. "But if we're not here to make the shows- then what do we do?"

"Watch and learn, my friend," said Pete. "Watch and learn."

He flicked the TV onto Chatterbabe TV. It was a blonde girl again, the same one I think, although orange people can all look quite similar. Pete picked up the telephone receiver.

"I got tone. Firing!"

Suddenly he passed the receiver onto me.

"What are you doing? What are you doing?"

"Come on, Matt, your turn to hand on the baton to the new boy. Think of it as your initiation! Give 'em hell, mate!"

I put the receiver to my ear.

"Welcome to Chatterbabe TV! You're talking to Jane- what's your name?"

So it was the same girl, with the kind voice. But I was still nervous- insanely nervous. The worst thing was that I couldn't even come up with a *nom de guerre*, which seemed to be such a crucial life-skill at Ofcable.

"You do have a name, don't you?"

"Er, Art Vanderlay."

She laughed.

"Like in *Seinfeld*?"

"You watch *Seinfeld*?"

"Why not?"

"Well, they never really showed it in this country. It was on BBC2 in the middle of the night or something. A real grave-yard slot. So I always thought it was kind of a status symbol for people who'd spent a bit of time in the States."

"I'm sorry to disappoint you! Maybe you could tell people you caught it on Polish TV too? That actually would be quite prestigious for an English guy, because it was all dubbed into Polish."

"How did that work out? Was it funny?"

"Funnier than Polish sitcoms."

"What are Polish sitcoms like?"

"Well, they're very funny if you enjoy jokes about how stupid women are. Half of the population is happy."

"Sounds good. Maybe BBC2 will buy them too. But what about the other half of the Polish population? What are they doing?"

"They're watching *Seinfeld*, of course!"

"Of course. So what else do you like to watch?"

"As you'd imagine, I'm tuning into Chatterbabe TV a lot."

"There must be a lot of pride in having your own TV channel. I expect Ant and Dec watch a lot of ITV."

"It's hardly comparable. We're the heartbeat of this station. If we do our jobs right, it's like performance art, like sculpture. If not- nothing. Ant and Dec don't even operate the phone-lines."

"That's certainly what they claimed- at the time I thought they were just trying to avoid liability for rigging phone competitions. But it sounds like you really like this job- which is something that I didn't totally expect."

"It has potential. Everyone has things they would change about their jobs, right? In our case, there are certain, uh, limitations in what we can do with the format!"

"You are kind of dependent on the conversational skills of your callers. And I guess some of them don't get too much practice…"

"Some of them?"

"Oh, so you force me to accept membership of the ranks of the socially excluded? Live on air?"

"Of course not- I was just interested in your choice of words. As though you're- an outsider. Not really involved."

"That's the story of my life, Jane... But enough about me, tell me how you would change the Chatterbabe TV format? Because it seems like such a winning formula."

"I've got a few ideas..."

"Like what?"

"I can't tell you!"

"You think I'm Rupert Murdoch? And I own a suite of TV channels with no existing content? Actually, I do, and I'm just scouting for new ideas. My colleagues and I were just talking about what we would do- if we had our own cable shows."

"Oh, really? And what did you decide?"

"There were creative differences, to be honest. So our channel would probably end up being a bit like BBC1. No one would really know exactly what it was for, but hopefully we could dumb it down enough to nab a few viewers from Channel 5."

"You're very cynical, Art! You don't know how lucky you are to have the BBC here! We used to pray for BBC shows to come to TVP1- back in Poland. They were so- so beautifully made, so professional... But then we'd be sad, because we never had the money to make anything like them in Polish!"

"Did you work in TV in Poland too, then?"

"Sure, I was a producer. For four years."

"Wow, isn't it a bit of a come-down... Well, you know..."

"Working on the phones, you mean? Maybe so, in some ways... Not financially, though! I get paid more here. And I enjoy speaking to people as well, you know? We're still putting together shows here, in a different way. The caller creates his own content live on air, for others to behold. If that's not art- with a small 'a'- then what is?"

Pete was drawing his finger across his throat. I covered the mouthpiece with my hand.

"What?"

"Time's up, matey. Wrap it up, wrap it up!"

Carl started replicating Pete's gestures. I covered the mouthpiece with my hand again.

"Do piss off, Carl!"

"Are you still there, Art?" asked Jane.

"Er, yeah. You were telling me about your plans to make Chatterbabe a bit more- hard-core…"

"Hmm, that isn't quite the expression I would use, Art! But I would definitely change the format of the channel… You know YouTube? The video-sharing web-site? The users broadcast their own material. Whatever they like, as long as it's decent. I do have an idea for how Chatterbabe could become something like that…"

This time Pete put his hand over the receiver.

"Seriously, mate, you've got to wrap this up p.d.q.- we only get two minutes in and out, or its friggin' entrapment!"

"Entrapment? Really?"

Pete looked at me reproachfully.

"OK, OK. Listen, Jane, we'll have to continue this conversation another time- I, er, left something in the oven…"

"You take care now, Art."

I hung up. Pete did not look impressed.

"What? What's your problem?"

"My problem? What's your problem? You're supposed to get them talkin' about shaggin', it's not the friggin' South Bank Show! There are rules of engagement in this caper, and if you break the two minute rule too often, you're history, you're toast, they come down on you like a ton of bricks."

"But… that girl. She was- nice."

Pete slapped his hand on his forehead in frustration.

"Listen mate, it's their *job* to keep dosy blokes like you chattin' away on the phone. What do you think they're gonna' do- belittle you? Nag you about not takin' the bins out? They're devious- insinuatin'- Delilahs… That's why- when you're up on the wire- you've got to be cold. Stone cold."

Carl nodded sagely.

"And that's why they call him 'Stone Cold' Pete Staines, eh, Peter?" said Colin, walking into the office and perching on Pete's desk.

Pete nodded sternly. He loved that nickname. And why not, since he had quite clearly coined it himself.

"I thought they called you 'Seaman Staines'?" I said.

Pete scowled.

"That's just those twats from Ofmedia…"

"Don't listen to them, 'Stone Cold'- you're the iron fist in the velvet phone manner!" said Colin encouragingly. "But hey, listen, Peter, 'the strong arm of the law'! Who was that? Who did they say that about, eh? Eh?"

Pete sighed.

"Juliet Bravo?"

"No!"

"Judge John Deed?"

"No, come on, Peter, old son- it was Cobra! Oh, yes. Now, young Carl, as Matthew has probably told you already, we do have a little tradition here- you may not have come across it in your previous places of work- of going out for a drink together when we have a new joiner in the office. So see you outside in precisely, um, four and a half minutes. You too, Peter. Strong arm of the law! Strong arm of the law…"

Colin walked out, still muttering the line under his breath.

"One arm is stronger than the other in his case…" said Pete. "But I s'pose we better go for a drink, or he'll only get the hump again. And we do not want that…"

"Does he get really irate, man? Ugly scenes?" asked Carl, with interest. "If you, say, interrupt him with confidential missives from journeyman linguists?"

"Not really, no. But there's a significantly heightened risk of an emergency 'State of the Standards Nation' meetin' bein' convened…" said Pete gloomily. "First Colin plays short bursts of carefully-selected Survivor songs to psyche you up, then- once you're spiritually weakened by that- he kicks off a brainstormin' session to improve morale. There's tumbleweed blowin' through the room before you can say 'Team Hug', and the first person to get chronically demoralised is Colin himself. Before you know it, you're goin' out for a drink just to cheer him up. So the net result in the present case would be spendin' one of the most tedious hours of our collective lives, jus' to get straight back into the situation we were tryin' to avoid in the first place- Team Drinks. It's really quite a dilemma, my legal chums, 'specially since I'm also supposed to be meetin' a sweet young lady from Billericay tonight…"

"Sounds like the start of a limerick…" I said. "But what do you think Cobra would say- confronted with this situation?"

Pete reflected for a moment.

"I think he'd prob'ly say- forget the poontang, and make mine a pint of the lager with my name on it!"

"You think Cobra drinks the family beer?"

"Wouldn't you? If there was a Verreaux beer? Not that it's likely that any self-respectin' beer would ever be marketed under such a ludicrously posh name. It's clearly a wine name, innit? 'More Château Verreaux, Tarquin?' 'Oh, yes please, Minty, dear. It's the last of that vintage, redolent of the fruits of over-privilege and down-trodden peasants.' But you never can tell, maybe it could catch on as a shandy in France."

"Verreaux 1664, yeah, I'd be all over that! But, like the rest of the sentient world, I certainly wouldn't be drinking Cobra. Not unless I happened to be in a curry house at the time. Which I doubt that the good lieutenant ever is. Indian food is weird in America, so Cobra is obviously more of a Tex-Mex man. If he ever ventured away from the Bud or Miller Genuine Draft- say if the pipes were being cleaned in his local…"

"Or if the, er, barrels were being changed and he couldn't be arsed to wait……" added Carl.

"…Then I for one would be highly surprised if he went for anything more exotic than a long-neck Corona."

Pete stood up.

"What utter, utter bollocks! Both of you! Two points, right? Firstly, Cobra is a crackin' pint, an' when I find pubs that have it on tap, I frequent them, I cherish them…"

"On tap? Pah! They don't even have it on tap in India!"

"Well, they do in the Far East."

"What? Where?"

"Far East Essex, Mr Backpacker-Twat! And, secondly, have you even seen the friggin' film? Clearly a hard-case like Cobra ain't gonna' be satisfied with nachos an' avocado dip. Tex-Mex, my arse! He'll wanna' let his hair down, really tie one on. And you know that what that means…"

"You end up in a curry house?"

"Damn right!"

"So your contention is that Cobra drinks Cobra Lager- both inside and outside curry houses?"

"That's exactly what I'm sayin'. It's all I've ever been sayin'!"

"OK, fine. Can we go now?"

"It was you holdin' us up with your bollocks. Tex-Mex!"

"Oh, come on, Stone Cold."

We went to the pub.

Chapter 5

Bankside, London, 7 November 2008

I watched the waiter through a glass darkly- or to be more precise, through the cluster of huge, brown Cobra Lager bottles towering over his flimsy silver tray. They clinked together like the bottles on a seventies milk-float. It was a nerve-jangling, vertiginous soundtrack to what seemed doomed to be a losing battle with gravity for both tray and bottles. The waiter himself looked utterly unconcerned, confident either in his intimate knowledge of the weight distribution of bottled beer, or in the futility of struggling against fate. Either way, I couldn't help but envy his equanimity. There was an alien item on the tray too, a tall, long-stemmed glass filled with some luminous orange gloop, crowned by a burning sparkler. It seemed implausible that this pyrotechnic accessory had been designed for culinary, or even consumer, use. Tiny shards of light fizzed out from a dense cloud of acrid, chemical-infused smoke all around it. The glass also contained a garish paper cocktail umbrella, apparently badly singed by its proximity to the sparkler. The waiter set the tray down on a neighbouring table and reverentially picked up the glass. It was as though it was the only thing he noticed on the tray, a dazzling novelty in a life completely conditioned to the transportation of out-sized lager receptacles. As always though, it was better to travel hopefully than to arrive. Just as he ceremonially proffered the glass towards us, the sparkler finally ignited the cocktail umbrella. The waxy paper flared up into weird, unnatural green flame. Job done, the sparkler itself fizzled out completely. Its wizened black tip broke off and fell into the glass.

"Mango Surprise, Gentlemen?"

It certainly was a surprise. I for one had never seen anyone actually order a pudding in a curry house before. I always assumed that it was just a sop to the professional pride of the proprietors that they listed them on the menu at all, to indicate that it was a real restaurant and not just some form of late-night drop-in centre for booze-hounds. Carl put his hand straight up in the air, no doubt much as he used to do back in Form 3A.

"Hey, thanks man. Got to have a dessert after a curry. Cleanses the palate. After that eclectic barrage of, er, exotic spices, I mean."

"You only had a tomato omelette, mate," said Pete.

"After a meal in a curry house, then," said Carl sulkily. "Anyway, I like the sparkler, man. A timely reminder of the, er, ephemeral nature of this flibbertigibbet capitalist society. Soon, it too will burn itself out."

"Yeah, well just take a look at what happens then, Karl Junior!" said Pete. "You an' your lot always think the collapse of easily-mocked but actually friggin' venerated institutions will make the world a better place, but it's the same old story in practice! All that's actually happened is that your puddin' is buggered, and now there's absolutely no hope of improvin' it. You can't do it yourself, and now no one else can be arsed to either. That's the real lesson here, comrade. That Mango Surprise is a friggin' socialist dystopia- end of!"

"Hem, hem," said Colin, tapping a spoon against a glass for silence. Unfortunately it happened to be the glass containing Carl's Mango Surprise. The charred canopy of the cocktail umbrella crumpled into a black powder and fell into the glass, dusting the Mango Surprise in a grimy film. Carl looked at it glumly. He wasn't totally above material concerns yet, evidently. He winced as Colin gave the glass another tap, putting the disintegrating umbrella out of its misery, and then cleared his throat to speak.

"Thomas here said something to me in the pub earlier," said Colin. "Something that made me sit up and think. About teamwork. About loyalty. And about leadership. What 'Standards' is all about!"

Thomas watched him closely, with an extremely strained smile on his face.

"He said it was a shame that not everyone in the team had taken the trouble to come out tonight- to honour our special tradition here of having welcome drinks…"

"For shame!" shouted Pete.

Colin held his hand out for silence, before continuing.

"He singled out Veronica, of course, although- off the record- I can confirm that she is in fact on special assignment. But do you know what I said to him? Do you know what I told Thomas?"

"Don't be such a dick?" said Pete.

"Er- no. I rallied his spirits, in the great tradition of Good King Harry…"

"Prince Harry, you mean? You gave him a B-52 to drink?" asked Pete.

"King Henry V, Peter… I told Thomas not to worry about those who hadn't bothered to come to the pub with us!"

He pulled out a scrap of paper and surreptitiously referred to it.

"We few, we happy few, we band of brothers... Gentlemen in England now-a-bed, shall think themselves, erm, accurs'd they were not here, and hold their manhoods cheap whiles any speaks, that fought with us upon Saint Christmas Day!"

"Well, I'm certainly not holdin' anyone's manhood, Colin," said Pete. "Cheap or not. And it's Saint friggin' Crispin's Day, anyhow!"

Again Colin extended a regal hand.

"Immortal words- words that the Reverend Tony Blair himself could be proud of," he continued. "And I'd like to, er, download to you a few ruminations of my own, as to how those unforgettable words of King Hal can inspire us in our own work. As Robin Williams so memorably said in *Dead Poets Society*..."

"Don't say it, Colin, don't friggin' say it!" yelled Pete.

"*Carpe diem*- seize the hour! Together we can make the Standards Team- extraordinary!"

"Seize the day, you prat! Its *diem*, not *horam*!" Pete shouted.

"Seize the day! Yes, of course- spotter's badge for you, Peter! The hard-earned motto of 'Team Cobra'. You can see that for yourselves, printed in, er, semi-permanent ink on the Frisbees I had made up for the Summer Ramble. Yes, Peter, they actually said 'Carp Diem'. But I think we all know exactly what it meant! Not 'Fish of the Day', as Stone Cold Pete Staines would have had us believe... But now- to stick with the Latin theme- proposal *numero uno* for seizing that day: We print up some new 'Team Cobra' T-shirts for everyone!"

Now Carl pushed his Mango Surprise aside with purpose, and stood up too. Colin didn't look best pleased to be sharing the lectern.

"Ladies and, er, Jellyspoons..." said Carl. "I think I speak for all of us when I thank Colin for his inspiring quotation from our illustrious Bankside neighbour, Mr Shakespeare! Hearing him speak- Colino, not the Bard of Avon, heh heh heh- it struck me for the first time that we few, we, er, happy few are carrying on a great tradition. A stone's throw from the very spot where the original will.i.am created comedies, tragedies and, er, 'problem plays' to delight and enthral the Elizabethan theatre-going public- we now craft cable TV shows for the delectation of their couch-dwelling descendants!"

"How many times do we have to tell you: we don't actually make the friggin' shows!" shouted Pete.

"Whatever, man. We don't have beards either- we're his *spiritual* successors. But we're, er, we're digressing, man. What I just wanted to tell Colin is: 'I am Spartacus', man!"

He paused expectantly.

"We are Crassus, so get a friggin' move on, mate!"

"Oh- OK, man... So the only question I would drop in the, er, metaphorical suggestion box at this point, is whether the mooted Team Cobra T-shirts really achieve the, er, unequivocal statement of proletarian unity that we crave? Would not some more perennial gesture of our socialist solidarity as, er, workers, be more suitable- more contemporary?"

"What- what did you have in mind, Carl?" asked Colin cautiously.

"Team Cobra tattoos, man!" said Carl. "Regulatory body art."

"Facial tattoos! Tear drops! Let's get matchin' friggin' spiders' webs on our faces!" yelled Pete.

"I mean, all kinds of, er, obsolete bourgeois institutions- banks, choirs, charities and, er, so on- have their own T-shirts and baseball caps. It's become just another smug corporate emblem, man. The trite insignia of a false consciousness. Inking is more personal- more enduring. I would be honoured to accept the charge of drawing up some Cobra designs. I'll come up with a short-list for everyone to look at before we go to get, er, inked. So it only remains to propose a toast- to my, er, mentor, Colin- and Team Cobra!"

He took a loud slurp of Mango Surprise, as though it were a cocktail. It must have tasted like an ashtray-flavoured Opal Fruit. Colin slapped him on the back unconvincingly and raised his own glass.

"*Carpe diem*- seize the hour!"

Now Pete jumped to his feet and climbed onto the table.

"O Captain! My Captain!"

He collapsed off the table, obliterated about twenty Cobra bottles and narrowly escaped braining himself on an ornate statue of the Hindu god Ganesha. His fall was broken by a plush, red chaise longue underneath the statue, which creaked ominously under his weight.

"Hey, be careful, man," said Carl. "The elephant god never forgets."

He sat back down, and turned to me.

"Soooo- do you think the tattoo idea went over well, man?"

"Hmm, I'm not sure. You're kind of flaunting your naked lack of ambition with a tattoo, aren't you? Generally employees with any sort of prospects will like to preserve the notional threat that they might move on, if their employer doesn't meet their professional aspirations. But the corporate tattoo is more an expression of unconditional loyalty, isn't it?"

"Oh, I don't know, man," said Carl. "It wouldn't take that much alteration from 'Ofcable' to 'Ofcom' or 'Ofgem' or, er, 'Ofwat', would it? The whole world of regulatory quangos is still your oyster. From a body art perspective, I mean."

"Yeah, 'cause if you had 'Ofcable Twat' tattooed onto your neck, you'd only need to have 'cable T' removed if you ended up at Ofwat, right?" said Pete, peeling an obliterated After Eight mint off his knee, and sitting down next to me gingerly. "Job done. And no new needlework required."

"That's pretty punchy talk from you, Evel Knievel!" I said.

"What? 'Cause I slipped on a slimy piece of lime pickle?" said Pete, indignantly.

"Yeah, just the slip off the top of the table- could have happened to anyone."

"Or Ofmedia, man," said Carl. "I mean, the more I hear about what we do, the more it sounds like Ofmedia's remit anyway! What's the point of Ofcable, you know? No one's actually done anything since I've been there. And why is Torquemada really here anyway?"

"You might think that, mate," said Pete, "in the bitter watches of the night- but you must never, ever say it. Not within earshot of Colin, anyway…"

"OK, thanks, man. I'll repress those doubts."

"But if you were ponderin' the Ofmedia fall-back, I reckon the best tattoo option would be 'Ofcable media twat'," said Pete. "More letters to be removed, but it gives you the option of Ofmedia *or* Ofwat. Doors are openin', mate!"

"Hey man, what do Ofwat actually do though?"

"It's like Ofmedia," said Pete. "But they regulate water as well as sewage…"

"You seem to have been giving Ofmedia some thought then, Pete?" I suggested. "Ever been tempted to cross over to the dark side?"

"Never- those Ofmedia bastards!" barked Pete. "They're only in it for the porn!"

"Aren't we all?" said a new- female- voice. That was actually quite a shock in the painfully male preserve of 'Standards'. A fifty-something bluestocking had appeared at the table. She pulled up a chair next to Pete.

"Just busting your balls, Pete. Though for goodness' sake don't get started on Ofmedia again. Change the record, old son." She looked curiously at Carl and I. "Sorry I'm late, all- Colin suspects that *TV Buddies* may be harbouring a ring of lesbian Nazi fetishists. He wanted a female operative to try and infiltrate it. Go deep undercover."

"Your words?" I asked. She chuckled, and adjusted the sombre navy Alice band on her head.

"His, of course. No doubt some nonsense he's picked up from those ridiculous Sylvester Stallone films of his. He spends a fortune on that memorabilia, you know."

Pete had perked up noticeably on hearing about this secret mission.

"Do they really have lesbian Nazis on *TV Buddies*?" he slavered.

She laughed.

"Of course not, Pete, don't be so bloody silly! But would it really matter if they did? Whatever Colin may think, it's not the *Boys from Brazil* out there on the cable network. And this isn't the Bankside branch of the Simon Wiesenthal Centre, so far as I'm aware."

She started shaking the dead Cobra bottles.

"Any brewskis going? You chaps have done a pretty thorough job! This must be you new boys, because young Peter here is considerably more mouth than trousers when it comes to drinking!"

"There were a lot of speeches," I said. "Thirsty work."

"Carp *diem* and all that, eh?"

"Yeah, the Carp bobbed up again, the queen of rivers. That was the friggin' least of it!" said Pete. "But I'm forgettin' my manners- V, have you met Matthew? Matt- Veronica. A fellow posh person for you to talk to, if you find the peasants too revoltin'. And, er- vice versa. You two should get on like a house on fire. The one reading *thelondonpaper* is Carl. I don't know why he's doin' that. But hang on a sec, V, an' I'll go and see if I can get you a drink. A complimentary port on the house may be in order, we've been eatin' Cobras here, I can tell you…"

Pete staggered off. Veronica held out her hand for me to shake.

"Ah- one of the new lawyer chappies. How are you finding it, then?"

"The Bear Gardens Tandoori?"

"No, no- I can easily follow your thought processes regarding that. After the initial disappointment that Bear Gardens is not a nudist colony, as its name so clearly suggests, the realisation that the BGT is the best and only curry house in Bankside slowly starts to sink in. What I really meant was, how are you finding this motley crew?"

I looked around the table.

"Yeah, I think it's quite a good fit for me, to be honest…"

"God help you then!" chuckled Veronica. She looked at the splattered lime pickle, mango chutney and mint yoghurt on the table. "What happened to the assorted condiments?"

"Pete did a stage-dive after the speeches. It was like a Sex Pistols gig in here."

"Well, never minding the bollocks is certainly an important prerequisite to listening to any speech by Colin. Speaking of which, at least Pete still seems fully clothed. That's always something. It's not pleasant watching a naked man try to catch a Frisbee, let me tell you. Even Colin only suggests seizing the day."

"That's what happened on the Summer Ramble?"

"Ah- you are well-informed. One of the things that happened. The 'rambling' element of it really came more from Colin's interminable pep-talks than the event itself- which was just in that little park area outside the Tate Modern."

"What, so about a hundred metres from the office?"

"That's right! The rather Tolstoyan grove of silver birches that they have there. It does seem to be true that just getting out of the office is enough to release people's inhibitions. As we can see this evening."

She looked quizzically at Carl, still reading his *thelondonpaper* at the table. It had a muddy footprint on the front page, I would estimate a UK size 10 or 11, which gave him a pronounced resemblance to a lunatic on a bus. But in a benign phase, as he was in a world of his own, chuckling away to himself.

"What on earth can he be reading with such relish in that pitiful rag?" she asked. "The wretched 'Cityboy'?"

"I don't think it can be- one of the few blessings of this financial crisis is that it seems to have effaced Cityboy from the free press forever. Carl was distraught to see him go, though- he was convinced that he was really an ingenious socialist *agent provocateur*, just posing as a broker. Determined to fatally discredit the rotten capitalist system from within."

"An interesting theory. I always assumed that he was just a deeply annoying twat."

"I think that was the more generally-held view, yeah."

"Old Carl doesn't look much like a lawyer himself. More like the defendant, I'd say. Perhaps he's just posing too."

"There's certainly more to him that meets the eye. Part legal *apparatchik*, part revolutionary- part anarchist, part watchdog. He's a riddle wrapped in a mystery, inside an enigma."

"Really? That's nice. Colin and Pete I should describe as insultingly easy to read. Of course it's far too early to tell about you. You may yet prove to have hidden depths."

"Why hidden? I wouldn't say hidden, exactly. More latent… But what about Thomas? Have you had a chance to consider how he fits in?"

Veronica twisted her pearl necklace between her fingers pensively.

"Thomas- well, I suppose he's a fairly enigmatic character too. Not in a very pleasant way though, I suspect."

"I've actually heard that he's the resident Samaritan."

"Maybe so. But then there must have been some reason why no one liked the Samaritans in the first place- otherwise they wouldn't have been so surprised by the good one, would they?"

"Did someone mention my name?" asked Thomas unpleasantly, appearing behind us. He was clutching a garish green drink.

"We were talking about you actually, Tommy," I said. "Trying to figure out what makes you tick. I'm guessing that in your case it isn't Cobra?"

"And what on earth are you drinking? Green chartreuse, eh? Good man, good man," said Veronica approvingly.

"Hardly, Mrs Andrews," said Thomas coldly. "I never touch alcohol when on duty. This is a *diabolo menthe*. French mint syrup and lemonade. Highly recommended by the *Tricolore* French textbook series."

"Of course, of course," said V soothingly. "But are you really on duty now?"

"Naturally I am," said Thomas. "Do you think I would be participating in a gathering of this nature for my own enjoyment?"

"You certainly know how to sweet-talk a girl, I must say! But listen, chaps, we've simply got to get out of here. There's absolutely no beer left after Seaman Staines' little hornpipe routine on the table, and my feet are already sticking to this disgusting carpet. And it is a little depressing to be at a party where someone is reading a newspaper that doesn't even have any narrative content..."

"What do you have in mind?" I asked.

"As it happens I do know a late bar just over Southwark Bridge- not more than ordinarily horrendous. From a distance it looks like it's full of complete and utter scumbags and low-lives, but on closer inspection they nearly all turn out to be off-duty accountants."

"OK, sold- let me just grab Pete," I said.

"How about you, Thomas?" asked V. "I can't guarantee that they have *diabolos* there, but I certainly wouldn't rule out *crème de cassis*, if you can be tempted by a walk on the wild side?"

"Please excuse me, Mrs Andrews," said Thomas, inclining his head slightly. "I have a very busy day tomorrow, with a full programme of philanthropic activities. To answer your earlier question as to what 'makes me tick'- my real passion is for philanthropy. With a particular focus on helping orphans."

"Wow, that's great," I said. "I actually did see 'engaged in philanthropic activities' on your out-of-office email, but I obviously assumed you were just taking the piss."

"Thank you," said Thomas. "I'm much obliged to you for your approval. Particularly as my way of life clearly differs so markedly from your own in that respect."

"Well, if you do have to dash, don't let us hold you up," I said. "Have a good one tomorrow. Don't let the bastards grind you down, alright?"

Thomas drained his *diabolo menthe* grimly, and slunk off into the night.

"You two really seem to be hitting off!" said V. "Colin will be pleased!"

"Ah, it's only because we're just so damn close that we can kid around like this, you know? I'll get Pete."

"What about the others?"

"What about them? Look at the state of them!"

Colin was stretched out on the chaise longue underneath the Ganesha statue, snoring loudly. If he was the sacrificial offering to appease the god after Pete's sacrilegious capering, it looked like Ofcable was in for some serious divine punishment. Pete was in deep and, on his part, apparently vehement negotiations with the management to obtain a free glass of port. Meanwhile Carl was busily tearing a series of stories out of *thelondonpaper* and folding them neatly into his breast pocket, for his future delectation.

"Social convention requires that we do at least extend the invitation to them, Matthew. The 'Carp' is not a solitary fish."

"OK then, you're in charge of herding carps," I said. "I'm already sticking my neck out enough here by accepting any degree of responsibility for Pete..."

Veronica nodded, and addressed herself to Colin and Carl.

"Come on, you fellows- are you coming for a night-cap or not?"

Neither of them seemed in any condition to continue festivities, so I joined Pete at the counter. He was still engaged in good-natured, but clearly futile, haggling with the waiters.

"You need to reward the good customers. The good *guys*. I mean, we could've trashed the friggin' place or anythin'! What if we was West Ham fans, on a booze-fuelled rampage after the Millwall match? Or strikin' Tube-drivers, goaded into anarchic frenzy by Bob Crow?"

"Well, sir, you did get up onto the table and knock everything off it," said the head waiter affably. "Bottles and everything. Some of the other customers were very far from pleased! They wanted us to throw you out and beat you up, you know. We told them you were a valued customer, coming here all the time. Basically docile."

"Listen, Pete, Veronica doesn't want a port anyway," I said. "She wants to make a move. To some after-hours place over the bridge."

"The Casbah? The City's premier Islamic-themed squalid drinkin'-den… V's like friggin' Joe Strummer with this Casbah fixation of hers. But whaddaya' mean she don't want a port?"

"Is that really so outlandish to you? She's a woman, mate, she's not an Oxford don. And who drinks port in a curry house anyway?"

"She's posh, ain't she? An' who has puddin' in a curry house? Your mate over there couldn't get enough of his Mango Surprise!"

There were a number of strands to this debate, but fortunately Veronica arrived to take charge before we could get too bogged down in it.

"OK, chaps, Carl is going to take Colin back home. At least, I think that's what he was saying. So come on, I could murder a brandy and amaretto!"

"You mean a port and lemonade?" said Pete.

"Not a port thanks, Pete! How old do you think I am, eighty-five? Though it was awfully sweet of you to persist so very long with the notion."

Pete and I followed Veronica up the stairs and back out onto Bear Gardens. The return to street level seemed to highlight the reduced condition that we were in- at least if I looked anything like Pete did. Veronica looked at him disapprovingly.

"Pete, can you please either do your tie up properly, or take it off completely? You look like a Hollywood drunkard with it at half-mast like that."

Pete started struggling ineffectually with his tie.

"I know what you mean, V- because I am pissed, there's no denyin' it- but in no way am I like any Hollywood depiction of drunkenness... That's more like takin' friggin' laughin' gas. Do you see me gigglin'? Or hiccupin' comedically? What about the seedy reality of drinkin'- the demons? No one wants to see that on the big screen, it would seem."

"The demons are inside you already, Pete," I said. "I'm pretty happy when I'm pissed."

"Well that's jolly lucky, old bean, or you wouldn't have had many moments of happiness outside working hours recently!"

"I've been under a lot of pressure lately," I said, as we climbed an endless set of stone stairs up onto Southwark Bridge. "Personal and professional."

"Mopin' round like a lovesick teenager ain't personal pressure, mate," said Pete. "An' I really can't imagine how any job could be less professionally stressful than workin' at Ofcable!"

Pete was a great believer in speaking *in vino veritas*. But fortunately he also had a very short attention span.

"This is like friggin' Kilimanjaro!" he wheezed. "I'd like to see some of these extreme marathon-triathlon-mountaineer guys do that after a curry and a few beers- then we'd see what they're really made of!"

"Oh yes, anyone can rock-climb sober, can't they?" said Veronica.

"It's not a bad idea though," I said, pausing to suck some air into my burning lungs. "It's all about new frontiers. Now you've got guys running ten marathons through the Sahara in a week, rowing the Atlantic..."

"... Consumin' sixty-six hot dogs and buns in twelve minutes," interrupted Pete. "Fact! That was Joey 'Jaws' Chestnut of Vallejo, California in 2007. Un-friggin'-believable!"

"Exactly- what are they going to do next? When all the mountains have been climbed? Doing that shit under the influence of booze or drugs is the only way to keep on pushing the barriers. It could even bring the excitement back into Formula One. Although you obviously don't want people literally hitting the wall."

"Blootered Ice Road Truckers!" said Pete. "Now that's a show I'm definitely gonna' make- as soon as we move into cable production!"

"Oh, do come on, you pissed twats!" said Veronica, from the top of the steps.

"No, no- that's Matt's new thing. Production!"

"That's Carl, Pete!" I said. "Let's preserve some boundaries of identity here, shall we?"

Spurred on by Veronica's patrician taunts, we both made a dash for the summit. By the time I reached it, I was definitely seeing little purple stars dancing in front of my eyes. I looked at Pete, bent double with his hands on his thighs.

"Hey, it actually is like Kilimanjaro!" I said. "The altitude sickness is coming on, the bridge is spinning. The lights- argh, the lights…"

There was a flash flood of headlights over the bridge in both directions, as the taxis bounded together through the darkness like racing cockroaches. Suddenly the traffic lights changed, and a black cab stopped right next to us. For some reason the occupants had turned on the light in the back, so that they looked like performers in a fifties television programme, illuminated against the gloom of the river at night. The realisation that we, as viewers, could not hear their dialogue changed the tableau again, so that it seemed more like a silent movie from an earlier age. That impression was intensified by the fact that both characters were wearing formal evening dress, rather than more obviously contemporary attire. The realisation that it was Emily and Xavier made my stomach lurch. It was a horribly voyeuristic moment, but somehow I couldn't look away. Not until Emily saw me. She stopped laughing and then opened her mouth again, as if to defy the impossibility of making herself heard. Then the lights changed again, and the cab moved off.

I felt as though it had hit me, breaking every hope in my body. I could have cried out in agony, but then somehow I couldn't say where it hurt. By now Veronica and Pete were staring at me too. I could read in their faces that I wasn't looking too good. In fact I could feel the shock and pain paralysing my face. I kind of wanted to start crying, but then I couldn't seem to dislodge my facial features from that grimace. Maybe that was a good thing, because I'm not sure what else was holding me together. Pete shaped to say something, but I knew that I couldn't take it at that moment, whatever it was. Any speech, any consolation, any human contact or emotion would be completely inadequate, because just then the only antidote was reconciliation with Emily- or total oblivion. Veronica seemed to sense that, because she took him by the arm.

"Just shut up, Pete, OK? Shut up for a moment."

She led him away. For some reason I stood there, watching the two of them walk over Southwark Bridge towards the City. It took me a while to realise that in my mind they were just proxies for Xavier and Emily, headed in the other direction, already far out of sight. Somehow I knew I had to keep her in view as long as I could that night, painful though it might be, because when she was gone this time, she really would be gone forever. The river below would have stopped flowing before we could get back to where we'd been- what was it, five minutes ago? But pretty soon Pete and V had disappeared too. I wondered idly how it would feel to tumble through that gusting Thames breeze, down to the onrushing black wall of rank river water below. I felt it once, in a dream- falling free, almost joyfully, a headlong rush of liberation, until right at the last moment, when you suddenly realise that you've never been less willing to let go of life. Then you cram every possible regret and hope for salvation into a desperately fleeting moment. Only in the dream, of course, you never hit the blackness, or whatever horrors hide beneath that inscrutable sheet of water. So I lit a cigarette instead. Then more practical considerations took over, in the form of a pressing need to throw up as soon as possible.

Chapter 6

Bankside, London, 7 November 2008

You wouldn't ordinarily mistake the workspace at Content Standards for the MIT Media Lab or the Large Hadron Collider, but there was certainly a thoughtful, contemplative mood there the next morning. With the alcoholic guilt seeping out of my pores, I could definitely get on board with that type of self-hating introspection. I had to keep reminding myself that it was only the depressive effect of the alcohol that was taking me down so far, but even then I wasn't quite sure that I believed it. It didn't help that I was effectively in solitary confinement, having failed to wake Pete from his patented persistent vegetative state before leaving the flat. 'The Fear' loves company, and even his would have been an improvement on subterranean sick blues, alone in the office.

Even Pete had some standards though. When the clock struck eleven, he walked shakily into the office and silently handed me a brimming mug. He sat down sombrely and drank deeply from his own. I took a sip, then spat it straight back into the mug. It brought back sickly sweet, tangerine memories of Southwark Bridge the night before.

"What is this shit?"

"Tea, of course, mate."

"With a Mango Surprise depth-charge?"

"I put some Berocca in- for the hangover."

"In the tea, you moron? With milk? Why didn't you just piss in it?"

Pete shook his head at this rank ingratitude.

"I was too dehydrated."

I tilted up the mug, to show him the disgusting mass of cottage cheese that had formed inside it.

"Look, you idiot- the milk has curdled from the citric acid. This is like having a Cement Mixer for breakfast."

Pete just grunted and continued to drink his own. I was too physically and morally debilitated to go and get anything better, so we sipped manky tea and Berocca together in companionable silence. It was actually OK if you avoided the biggest lumps of congealed milk. Kind of a low-stakes game of Russian roulette. Every now and again Pete would lose, grunt again and spit a bit out into his waste-paper basket. I followed suit, and I would definitely recommend that strategy if you ever find yourself in the same situation. In any event, it held me engrossed for a while, until I gradually became aware of scratching noises coming from behind Pete's desk. I looked at Pete, who raised an eyebrow.

"Ratty?" I asked.

"I prefer to think of 'em as semi-aquatic mammals, old chap. But it would certainly not be unprecedented!"

With a manful effort, he stood up to investigate. In his reduced state, he gave the impression of an extraordinarily ineffective mime artist attempting to convey the act of search for a lost object. Perhaps it would ultimately turn out to be his mind. This hapless performance finally ended when Pete jumped back in alarm, and Carl calmly got up from behind the desk. Carl straightened his tie, took Pete's mug of tea out of his hand and drained the dregs, with apparent satisfaction.

"Do you wanna' biscuit with that?" said Pete.

"No thanks, man. It seems to contain solids already. And if you'll be guided by me, you won't take disco biscuits at this time of the morning yourself, either."

"Jesus Christ! I meant a friggin' Rich Tea. But don't change the subject, Swampy- what were you doing down there, anyway- blockin' the third runway?"

"I had to improvise, man. It was too late to get home."

"Why- where do you actually live, Carl?" I said. "You've never mentioned a, er, home before…"

"Wiltshire, man. I have to be near the Stones, know what I mean?"

"The Rolling Stones? Is that where they live?" I asked. "I always assumed that they lived on the King's Road. Or in L.A. Not all together though, I guess."

"No, man. Not those Stones. The Standing Stones. Stonehenge. It's like one massive battery-recharger, man, focussing cosmic energy from all over the, er, cosmos. Harnessing the, er, ancient wisdom of every druid who ever walked the earth. It's the source of all my strength and calm, you know?"

Carl picked up one of Pete's Chas n' Dave CDs, angling the shiny side towards himself to check that his tie was straight. He nodded at his reflection, obviously satisfied with what he saw.

"Lookin' good, baby!" said Pete.

"Thanks, man. But if you'll excuse me, esteemed colleagues, there are others whose need for me is even greater than yours," he said. "I have an important meeting with Colino. Strategy, man. He likes the way I think. *Outside* the box."

He nodded at us, but so ponderously that he actually seemed to forget that he had already bidden us farewell.

"Colin thinks I have a big future here," he said complacently. "Oh, speaking of which, Pete, the new, er, *Cable Enforcement Bulletin* is just out."

"No shit!" said Pete, suddenly energised. "Did I get anythin' in it?"

"No, man," said Carl. "That's what I mean. Time for a new way of thinking. Later, 'gator…"

This time he did manage to shuffle off down the corridor. Pete looked at me in astonishment.

"Big?" he said.

"Future?"

"Do you think Carl has a big future?"

"Yeah, big like the Hindenburg Disaster was big for the Zeppelin business. Listen, the guy eats temazepam fritters for breakfast, Pete, he is hard-wired for fiasco. However promising things may look, however copper-bottomed a sinecure Carl may appear to have carved out for himself, sooner or later he will screw it up irreparably. Colin might think he's very clever taking a docile, empty mind and moulding it for his own devious, cable supervision purposes. But the dangerous thing about Carl is that he does occasionally have his own ideas. It's like the Fifty Year Storm- it's just a matter of time before it happens again. And when it does, Colin will be lucky if he, any of us- or even Ofcable- has a future."

Pete grunted, pushed away the waste-paper basket, and put his head in his hands.

"What was that about temazepam? I need some shit like that, opiates, King Kong pills. Normal pain-killers just aren't workin' for me any more."

He writhed in his chair.

"You'd need to speak to Dr Carl about that. From me it's more spiritual solace."

"Argh, I'm in a whole spirit-world of pain too," he moaned. "There is one thing that you can do for me before I die actually, mate... call Chatterbabe for me? They're on the friggin' Ofcable 'Ten Most Wanted List' this week. That means daily spot-checks..."

"But why?"

"Who can say? But will you give 'em a bell for me?"

Pete looked at me with what he clearly imagined to be beseeching, puppy-dog eyes.

"What's the point? It's like fucking *Mary Poppins* over there. They're adding to the public morality. They should be checking up on us. If they could take the horrible truth when they saw it..."

"Whatever, mate, I think I'm gonna' be sick again..."

He left the room hurriedly. I waited a few minutes for him to return, but there was no sign of him. The walls of the broom cupboard were starting to close in on me, so I decided to call Chatterbabe TV after all. Pretty close to replicating the authentic caller experience, I should think. I flicked the TV on. The same skimpily-dressed blonde was pouting at the camera.

"Party time's over, sugar-plum," I muttered, and picked up the phone. There was a familiar voice at the other end.

"Welcome to Chatterbabe TV! You're talking to Jane- what's your name?"

I stuck with a losing formula.

"Art- Art Vanderlay."

"Art! How are you?"

"Hello, Jane- why is it always you when I call?"

"It must be fate. Or maybe the fact I only get screen-time during Ofcable office hours."

"Is that a bad thing?"

"Not so bad, but you know- every girl has her vanity. We don't want the producers to love us only for our minds. The highest call volumes are at the weekends- and public holidays, of course."

"Well, I think you look lovely. Maybe we could get up some kind of petition? Phone-line Tarzan seeks Jane?"

"That would be sweet. Probably management are more interested in what the real callers think, though. But then I guess that Ofcable calls make up a pretty big part of our income these days. That and former Tottenham Hotspur players, of course. Those guys are obviously finding retirement very tough. They're always phoning up."

"I can imagine. It can't be easy sinking into obscurity when you've been used to the glory and adulation of playing for North London's second-biggest football team."

"It's great that Ofcable takes them on as Standards Supervisors then! Sort of care in the community?"

"Yeah, exactly. Working here- that's what I really meant by obscurity…"

"You sound a bit more cynical than usual, Art. Is everything OK?"

"Things could be better. You know my girlfriend?"

"The one who brutally dumped you?"

"Er- yes. Well, now she's involved with my worst enemy."

"You have a worst enemy- I'm impressed! You must be very important."

"Not really. Just strong on the negative emotions."

"So what are you going to do now- fight him?"

"The first step in my plan was just to get extremely drunk."

"Oh. Did that work?"

"I managed to get drunk OK, but it turns out that's just left me stranded in a parallel world of guilt and self-loathing."

"It sounds like my home-town in Poland."

"Which is?"

"Swinousjcie."

"It sounds awesome. More towns should build 'swine' into their names."

"They've certainly built them into the population. Is that what you call onomatopoeia? Because it's not what you'd call an upbeat town."

"You sound pretty cheerful yourself."

She laughed.

"That is quite important for the job! Besides, things could be worse. I'm not actually in Swinousjcie. And, unlike my friend Katinka, I'm not about to be deported to the Ukraine."

"Exile to the endless steppes... That would not be good. What did she do?"

"Nothing! Unless you count the heinous crime of not being born in the EU. We need to find a lawyer for her, or she's history."

"Definitely not good."

"Do you know anyone who might be able to help out? It would have to be for free- to start with. She just doesn't have any more money to spend, and you can't get legal aid for Asylum and Immigration Tribunal hearings. I've been working as her 'McKenzie friend', taking notes, you know, and sorting out the paperwork for her- but I don't have any legal training at all. I hate to ask, but you do sound- educated."

"Yeah, but that really isn't my type of law..."

"So you're a lawyer!"

"Well- I was... But a, er, corporate lawyer."

"You are! You can help Katinka! Any solicitor can appear in the Tribunal."

"But I never did any immigration law- or criminal law, or anything like that. Litigation. I've never even been to a court."

"So what type of law do you do if you're a corporate lawyer?"

"Well, none, really. It isn't a very legal type of a job, to be honest. It's more about getting everyone organised. Sending them conference call dial-in details. Preparing all the documents, and checking them for typos. Then you give them pens to sign the agreements with at the end."

"The last bit sounds easy enough!"

"Oh, you'd be surprised, Jane…"

"But is that really true? Why would they pay you a lot of money for that?"

"It's pretty hard work. And you have to stay up very late at night for, I don't know, a few months at a time."

I think Jane had stopped listening a few beats before.

"Art, you're what we've been waiting for- to try and save our friend! You must help her! And you know, you sound so dispirited on the phone. To lack any real pride in what you do, isn't that right? This could be what you need too. To give you that pride back."

"I don't know, Jane. They say that pride comes *before* a fall. This would really be turning that old saying on its head."

Jane tutted in frustration.

"Don't be so stupid, Art! What does that really mean? You need to stop just saying silly things that you don't really believe, and actually *do* something. Stop just- just watching life!"

"We are watchdogs…"

"Oh, I know- but just think- this could really help someone! A real person! Doesn't that mean anything to you?"

"Of course it does- I just… With all this chaos in the City, I don't know if I'm coming or going. What I'm going to do with myself. I'm still adjusting to where I've ended up now…"

"Yes, but you're still in London, aren't you? You still have a job, you know there'll be food on the table, you know where you're going to be- what country you'll be living in. Whatever else happens, and I know it isn't easy, at least you'll always have that to hold onto! Which is more than Katinka can say right now. That's real loss of control over your destiny- just think how powerless she must feel!"

Her tone softened.

"Listen, we're meeting in a pub round the corner from the studio at seven o'clock. To discuss what to do, I mean. It would be really great if you could come along. We don't know anything about English law, and we just can't afford another lawyer. Please, Art?"

"What? Seven o'clock tonight?"

"Yes, tonight! What were you planning- a Fireworks Night? We don't have any time to waste- she only has ten days to lodge her appeal! If she's even going to make one this time…"

"You know, it's a highly specialised area. It might do her more harm than good to have input from someone without any practical experience of immigration law. Couldn't she go to a Citizens' Advice Bureau or something? Or just type it into Wikipedia? That's what I would do myself. We definitely don't need any more fireworks round where I'm staying, though- kids are letting them off at head-height down the pavement as it is…"

I let my voice tail off, as Pete stalked back into the office. He looked a lot better already. The guy really did have the powers of recovery of the monster in a horror movie. And in fact a fairly pasty complexion with it that day. When I came to think about it, there were lots of shared characteristics between Pete and the Evil Dead. He also had some pretty strong psychotic tendencies- at least as viewed from your bed, whilst he was erratically launching darts into a board a foot above your head. Unfortunately he seemed to have overheard the previous phase of my conversation with Jane.

"Oh, Christ- posh chat!" he muttered.

Hopefully that was as deep as his analysis had got. But I couldn't risk another entrapment lecture from Pete- not in his present state of mind. I had to kill this call.

"Listen, she's Ukrainian!" said Jane. "She was born under a Communist dictatorship. A simple, ordered world. She really doesn't have the educational tools to deal with the intricacies of the English legal system. Look, I understand that you might not know all the rules off the top of your head, Art. But surely you must at least know how to research them- where to go to find out what they are? And be able to understand what they say- interpret them- once you have found them? I honestly don't think you understand what this country is like for a foreigner. How hard it can be just to get people to take you seriously. Even to want to understand what you're saying! That's where you come in. People here will listen to you. You're part of the establishment, a professional. Someone to be respected by the immigration officers- by the system."

I laughed. Wrong response.

"Do you know how much I- or any of us- would give to be that person now? Just to have that respect. To be someone they couldn't simply brush aside. Like an irritating little- swine from Swinousjcie! To help our friend. And you just take it for granted. You're laughing about it! Do you have any idea how that makes me feel? Do you?"

"Do people actually pay their own money for these conversations? I felt better before I called."

"Listen, Art, forget what I said. Just come along at seven. We really need you. I'll see you at seven, OK? Tonight. At the studio. You must have seen me on the channel. I'll wait for you outside. Take care!"

She hung up.

It was too little, too late so far as Pete was concerned, because now he swivelled his chair into prime lecture position.

"I'm gonna' tell you a little story now, my friend. About a Chinese bloke."

"What was he called?"

"I don't know! How should I know? Just a Chinese bloke, alright? Anyway, this Chinese bloke- whose name is not at all germane to the friggin' story- went and spent all his money on a seventeen-year-old girl he'd met in an internet chat-room. He sent her presents, he sent her flowers, he sent her friggin' homeopathic medicines- God knows what else. Eventually he travelled all the way across China to meet her, real trans-Siberian shit, and when he got there… Oh ho ho, did he not like that!"

"Well? What happened?"

"She turned out to be a middle-aged geezer, mate! I thought you would have read about that. One of the top stories on the BBC website, that was. Proper cautionary tale. Credit to her- him, I mean- for turnin' up in person, though. Some people would've bottled the moment of truth, I reckon. Bound to be awkward, really."

"Your point being? You think that Jane is a man?"

"She could easily be a friggin' bloke. Or even worse- arguably worse- she could be a minger, she could be a nutter, she could work at Ofmedia. You wouldn't even know until it was too late!"

"And by then I would have spent all my money?'

"Well basically, because you would've been sacked, wouldn't you?"

This didn't seem the ideal moment to bring him fully into the loop on the big meeting at Chatterbabe TV. In any case, there was absolutely no way I was getting involved myself. With an eviscerating hangover. On a Friday night. And God and Colin alone knowing what the Ofcable Code of Conduct implications would be. Besides, judging by his encyclopaedic knowledge of Gerard Depardieu's 1990 marriage of convenience classic *Green Card*, even Colin probably knew a hundred times more than I did about immigration law. I couldn't even remember whether or not the big guy got to stay in the US at the end of the movie. He certainly didn't feature in many Hollywood pictures after that. All in all, the only person who could possibly be of less practical use than me would be Carl.

Right on cue, Carl slouched into the broom cupboard. His actual physical movement was as sluggish as ever, but there was something new about him- a freshness, an innocence, a child-like enthusiasm.

"Has Colin secretly had you lobotomised?" I said. "Just twitch convulsively for 'yes'. Oh my God, he has- that sick bastard! But perhaps in the end this was the best thing- for everyone."

"Hey, I wasn't twitching- just, er, shaking my head. Anyway, your attention please, 'cause this is business not pleasure, man. Team meeting, to be precise. Colin wants to build on the progress we made last night. He thinks we're really getting some traction with the team building now. Two words for you: 'Mo' mentum'."

Pete groaned, then slumped wordlessly back down onto his desk.

"I just hope there's no tattooist on the premises, Carl," I said. "You better not have smuggled some disgusting biker body-artist masquerading as a motorcycle courier in through the tradesman's entrance. Anyway, I'm invoking my statutory right to ten shots of tequila before the needle goes in. I'm not getting taken down sober."

Carl twitched again.

"Oh, uh, that was just brainstorming, man. You don't find the prince of ideas without kissing a few frogs along the way. You'd, uh, do pretty well to remember that yourself- if you hope to find a place for yourself in Colin's New Model Army, that is. There's a new broom in town, and it's sweep, sweep, sweeping the old order away..."

"Oh, come on," said Pete, prising himself up out of his chair again. "We might as well go and see what that silly sod has cooked up this time. Whatever it is, there'll be no friggin' peace for any of us till he's got it off his chest. Carp *diem*! Seize the koi! O Carptain! My Carptain!"

He barged unceremoniously past Carl, and we followed him down the corridor to the 'Conference Room'. This was none other than the dingy interview room where my Ofcable career had first begun. What a long way I'd come since then. It was now equipped with such extraordinarily bulky and antiquated audiovisual equipment that Colin could hardly be seen, standing impatiently behind the flimsy table he was using as a makeshift podium. Veronica was sitting on a lime-green chair at the front, looking anxiously at a precariously affixed overhanging projector above her head.

"Don't worry, V," said Pete reassuringly. "If that bugger comes down, no one'll be safe- it'll take the whole friggin' buildin' out, no questions asked. Rats an' all..."

"Hey, I found them, Colin!" said Carl, now interposing himself in front of us.

"Ah, Messrs, er, 'Tango and Cash'- glad you could make it!" said Colin. "Only Thomas to come... Oh, there you are Thomas. Didn't see you come in."

Somehow Torquemada had infiltrated the room and occupied a lime-green chair next to Veronica.

"Good morninggg, Team Cobra!" said Colin. "Now you might very well be wondering why I've summoned you to my side this morning... Even Stone Cold Pete Staines looks a bit curious, amn't I right, Peter?"

"It's jus' trapped wind, Col," said Pete.

"Right, well, to answer your question, I suppose you could say it's all about reflecting on what we've learned about each other. By spending some time together outside the constraints of the office last night, I mean."

"Yeah- now we know why we need those constraints…" said Pete.

"But what else?" probed Colin. "What else have we learned, do you think?"

I noticed for the first time that there was a large BHS plastic bag on top of the carousel slide-projector on the table. Colin rested his hand on it.

"Now, some of you might recall that we discussed the possibility of new Team Cobra T-shirts last night?"

"That was the friggin' least of it," said Pete. "Some tool wanted his face tattooed, as I recall!"

"Yes, indeed- and of course in the cold light of day, that all seems a little far-fetched," continued Colin. "You can't really wear a T-shirt to work- not in compliance with the official Ofcable dress guidelines, that is! And we won't all be together at the weekends- that often."

He pulled open the BHS bag in front of him triumphantly.

"What you can, however, wear in the office, both with comfort and with decorum, is a jumper!"

He pulled a handful of jumpers out of the plastic bag. They were in various colours, but all shared the same telltale dull gleam of 100% acrylic fibre.

"More importantly, we can also recognise the unique contribution that each and every one of us makes to the team. For example, I- like Captain Kirk himself- will sport a chartreuse jumper."

He held a yellow jumper up against himself.

"Are you sure that's chartreuse?" asked Pete.

"Well, it's the closest they had, alright? Work with me on this, Peter!" He rummaged in the bag again. "And what's this? Another one? There's another one here, er, Lady and Gentlemen... It's for you, Carl!"

Carl stepped forward to receive it.

"Chartreuse- command personnel. That means more to me than I can say, man."

"It's your destiny, Carl. Embrace it. Veronica, meanwhile, who is the proud holder of a PhD, will wear a blue jumper- like Dr Spock!"

He handed a blue jumper to Veronica. She also held it up against her. It was evidently the same size as Colin's own.

"Room to live long and prosper in, man," said Carl.

"Next up is Matt," said Colin. "Matt will wear a red shirt, like Lieutenant Sulu..."

"Because he too is quite extraordinarily camp..." said Pete.

"... And here's a red jumper for you too, Peter," said Colin.

"You'll probably get whacked on a trip to some far-flung planet, man," said Carl. "Both of you. You red-shirts don't last two minutes when the, er, photon torpedoes start flying. Alien bait, man. Heh heh."

"Thomas- please step forward," said Colin. "Although, technically speaking, you are of course an Ofmedia secondee- a different galactic species from us- like the noble Klingon, Worf, son of Mogh, you have won our trust here at Starfleet!" He pulled another red jumper out of his bag. Torquemada looked at it in disgust.

"Beamed down, then blown away, man," said Carl with relish. "You too, Tom. Heh heh."

"Wouldn't a blue one be rather more appropriate for me?" said Torquemada. "If only in light of the higher academic entry standards required by the exclusive Ofmedia Graduate Recruitment Programme?"

"Two words for you, Thomas- 'earn your stripes'. I mean, er, 'earn it'."

Thomas looked around in disgust.

"But Carl?" he said, helplessly. "What has Carl done to earn his?"

"I see something in Carl," said Colin. "Something I haven't seen for a long time."

"Respect for you?" suggested Pete.

"Yes, well, the presentation ceremony is now complete," said Colin. "It only remains to share our new mission statement with you…"

"Carp *diem*!"

"New, Peter! New! Are you ready, team? Then 'let's boldly go-where no team has gone before'! Oh, Matthew- maybe you could write all this up in the next issue of *Being Ofcable*? Perhaps in the style of Jim Kirk's Captain's Log?"

"Being what?"

"*Being Ofcable-* our, er, inflight magazine! We in 'Standards' have our very own page in it. And you did English Literature at uni, didn't you?"

"Er- yeah."

"Well, then! This initiative is all about harnessing the, er, unique talents that each of us bring with us on the mission. Editing our page of *Being Ofcable* is your chance to show us all just what you can do, Matthew! OK?"

He lifted his hand, in what may have been some sort of Vulcan farewell, and Carl started ushering us all back towards the door.

"Well, Colin's quite obviously still pissed!" said Veronica. "What on earth were you fellows drinking before I got there last night, White Lightning?"

"Speaking of lightning, what on earth do we do with these jumpers?" I asked. They crackled lightly with static as we walked.

"Oh, just bin that, for God's sake!" said Veronica. "He'll have moved onto something else in a week or two. Even the team Frisbee sessions only lasted a couple of weeks. And that was the symbol of the whole blessed Carp *diem* movement!"

Pete grunted agreement.

"What Colin really needs is to boldly go where no Trekkie has ever gone before- on a date with a real human female!" he said. "You must have a mate that you can set him up with, V?"

Veronica laughed.

"Maybe one of the girls from the channels- although I rather suspect that they would eat someone like Colin for breakfast!"

"It's funny you should say that, V..." said Pete. "Because this numpty here has a crush on one of the *Chatterbabe* girls!"

"Really, Matthew?" said Veronica. "How very *Romeo and Juliet*! I do hope you won't prove 'star-cross'd lovers'- as Colin so memorably described Ofcable and Ofmedia on last year's Globe visit..."

"Two households, both alike in dignity? I don't think so. But don't you start- this is all in Pete's mind!"

"I'm glad to hear it!" She waved and disappeared into a slightly more capacious, Laura Ashley-inspired version of the broom cupboard. Pete and I trudged wearily back to our desks.

"There's only one thing for it now, mate," said Pete as we collapsed back into our chairs. "The final solution..."

"McDonald's?"

"Yip. Toss a coin for who goes?"

"Well, I'm not going, coin or no coin. It's miles away. On the other side of the river, I mean. Let's go to Pizza Express next door."

"I don't have a friggin' yuppie hangover though, mate- it's the real thing. Anyway, we've been through all this before. There's one at Guy's Hospital. No river crossin' required."

"That's actually further away though, Pete. I've checked the numbers."

"It's all psychological though, ain't it?"

"Whatever. I'm not going anyway- just get me a Quarterpounder with Cheese meal. Diet Coke. Not Super-sized."

"Really? This is how it's gonna' be?"

"You've got no negotiating position here, Pete- because I *know* you're going to McDonald's, come hell or high water."

That was when the phone rang. Afterwards it struck me that the strangest thing about that call was that it took me a moment to realise that it was Emily. At the time I felt that the strangest- and the stupidest- thing about the call was that, in trying to give Emily the impression that I wasn't sitting in the Darts Room pining for her night after night, I indicated that I was going out that very Friday night. But then maybe it was actually stranger and stupider that, simply by saying that within Pete's earshot, I somehow got into a position where I really did have to go out, just to avoid being caught in a demeaning lie to Emily. Objectively speaking, by far the dumbest thing of all was that by genuinely not having anywhere else to go, I ended up going to the Chatterbabe studio for seven o'clock after all. OK, so that course of action would probably also involve having to give an as-yet-unknown Ukrainian girl vital, life-changing immigration law advice. But when I looked at it in the round, that was probably the easiest thing to fix without serious loss of face. And maybe Katinka wasn't the only one who needed her life to change, anyway. She definitely wasn't my type, but there was something about speaking to Jane that almost made me see life as, I don't know- something to consider engaging with again. Or at least worth another try. I reached out to the computer and typed 'UK immigration law' into Google.

Chapter 7

Gray's Inn Road, Camden, London, 7 November 2008

It didn't take me too long to find the Chatterbabe studio- after all, the address was at the top of all the Standards Supervision Reports I had filed on them in the past few weeks. Unfortunately that was about the only known quantity in the whole expedition, and getting there was always likely to be the easy bit. They were at the Chancery Lane end of the Gray's Inn Road, so I took a leaf out of Xavier's book and took the Tube. As always happens when you're early- and jumpy- the public transport ran like clockwork, and I arrived at Chancery Lane well in advance of seven. I felt as though I could have used some time stuck in a tunnel that evening- it may be better to travel hopefully than to arrive, but sometimes even travelling hopelessly can be an improvement. Nothing plays tricks on you like time does though, because as I walked past the medieval rabbit warren of barristers' chambers in Gray's Inn, it transported me back even further. Not to when Gray- or whoever it was- built the thing in the first place, obviously. No, to about seven or eight years before, to an unfeasibly sunny morning, when a girl and I were walking down that same part of the Gray's Inn Road. We weren't holding hands or anything, just chatting- but then again there was something, there was something more to it than that. You could tell, because the jokes sounded funnier, the pre-Starbucks, polystyrene-tainted coffee tasted richer, the visible surface area of my re-worn shirt looked crisper, than should really have been possible that morning. That's the whole point, isn't it, that's what everyone's looking for- the alchemy that can turn one morning's commute into a moment that you remember for the rest of your life. It wasn't as though we were watching the sun set on the Ngorongoro Crater together- we were going to the firm's old offices, in fact, to play at being lawyers on the summer vacation scheme. Absolute beginners. As it happens, I was probably pretty hung-over then too, I think we both were- but in a different way. Like students, fearless and unrepentant, basically invincible. And a hell of a lot younger, of course. For whatever reason, I hadn't been back to that spot since, but it was still infused with the romance, the sheer freedom of that moment. It unsettled me, because you couldn't say that things had worked out precisely as I had hoped back then. Being hit by that memory was like running into the last person in the world that you would have expected- or wanted- to see, at the worst possible moment, without being able to run away. Because for once there was no avoiding the realisation that she always had been that beautiful and special- she always would be. And of course there was also the fact that the girl was Emily.

That's the Inns of Court for you, I suppose- the land that time forgot. Back in 2008, and looking at the neat rows of leather-bound law reports through the windows, I was suddenly uncomfortably conscious that almost any one of the chambers' inhabitants could have made an infinitely better job of this Katinka business than me. But then maybe they weren't Chatterbabe callers. It struck me that most barristers I knew were sufficiently talkative characters to make a chat-line an unnecessary, maybe even prohibitively expensive, hobby for them. By then I had crossed the Clerkenwell Road though, and I was facing the Chatterbabe studio- and the music.

'Studio' was actually rather a grandiose term for the dismal premises from which Chatterbabe TV sought to engage and inspire Britain. It wasn't exactly the Warner Brothers lot in beautiful, downtown Burbank. On reception there was an amiable but off-hand guy of Mediterranean appearance, who only intermittently favoured visitors with his attention, being more occupied in animated, moustache-tugging conversation with a group of unshaven cronies. As well as thick stubble, the cronies were sporting PVC-look leather jackets, garish football strips and slip-on shoes (socks optional), and sitting sprawled around the small bank of leather-effect sofas in the reception area. They were all speaking loudly and authoritatively at the same time, in a language that I couldn't immediately place. This left no space in reception for any visitor to sit down, or even to stand in without being uncomfortably positioned right in the middle of a highly expressive, but completely incomprehensible, conversation. This might partially have explained why there were a number of other blokes hanging around on the pavement outside. That and the fact that they were all chain-smoking, of course. Any brand so long as it was contraband. It was also possible that the main reason these characters preferred to remain *al fresco* was that they were subject to restraining orders, of varying degrees of legal formality, against making their presence felt in the studio. Although this was in no way a homogeneous group, the 'outsiders' did share one striking characteristic: an uncanny resemblance to former Bulgaria striker Hristo *'El Pistolero'* Stoichkov. As I stepped out onto the pavement to join them, I quickly realised that there was one other unarticulated bond between them- an inherent suspicion and dislike of me as an interloper. So on the whole I was fairly pleased when the time gradually crept round to seven o'clock, the aluminium-framed glass doors of Chatterbabe swung open, and the bottle blonde from the TV show emerged. She looked quickly around the *Pistoleros*, many of whom she seemed to recognise. Those were the ones she tried to avoid making eye contact with. She gave me a dazzling smile, which didn't seem to endear me much to my new friends.

"Hi-yah!" she said.

"Hi! Hello. How are you?"

"So- you're famous lawyerrr?"

Her accent was a lot heavier in person than over the telephone. Maybe they had to put on the old Queen's English when they were on air, like in the early days of the BBC. I could understand her alright, though- I just wasn't sure how to respond to this description. On the one hand, it wasn't entirely borne out by recent events, and I was instinctively unwilling to accept such undeserved plaudits. On the other hand, I didn't want to pour too much cold water on my legal credentials at this stage. No one wants their lawyer constantly telling everyone how incompetent he is.

"Well, sort of…"

"You're verrry modest!" she said, with a loud peal of laughter.

I smiled back, but I wasn't relishing the attention that this brought to our conversation from the *Pistoleros*. Another girl, a pretty brunette clutching a huge ring-binder, had come out of the studio now. She was also looking around the crowd at the stage door, but the *Pistoleros* weren't showing much interest in her. They seemed drawn to Jane like moths to a flame.

"So how do you want to do this?" I asked. "Did you bring your friend along?"

"You wanted me to bring frrriend?" she said, giggling.

"You know, the Ukrainian girl. Katinka?"

"No frrriend," she said. "Especially not Ukrainian! *Ukrajinci!*"

She scowled, spat on the pavement emphatically, and then looked at me coquettishly.

"Most peoples verrry happy with me. Alone."

I laughed nervously. The conversation was taking a slightly different turn than I had expected from her business-like tone on the telephone. The grumbling from the *Pistoleros* was also making me feel increasingly uncomfortable. Where they came from, committing a violent crime of passion was like jumping a red light. It's a primal, passionate land, the Seven Sisters Road. Even the brunette was staring at me now. She looked puzzled, and somewhat less than impressed. The evening was going about as well as I had expected, in my most pessimistic assessments of it.

"Where is camerrra?" asked Jane.

"Camera? What do you want to do? Before and after extradition shots?"

She stared back at me.

"How do you do it, if no camerrra?"

"Well, you know, words. Writing. Tell her whole story- how she's been treated, how she feels about it all... What should have been done differently?"

She giggled.

"I've never worked with storrries before. But you still need pictures for storrries, no? Next to picturrres?"

"Some pictures can't hurt, I guess. Help them get an idea of what type of person they're dealing with. A decent, hard-working type. Salt of the earth."

She giggled again.

"Harrrd-worrrking! You're verrry funny!"

I smiled uncertainly again. One of the *Pistoleros* had approached now, and was standing right next to us. He was wearing a smart business suit, although the respectability of that look was slightly tempered by the sinister leather overcoat that he was wearing on top of it. He put his hand on her arm.

"What's goin' on here? Who's this guy? Who are you, my friend?" he asked brusquely.

"Who are *you*, darlink?" Jane said flirtatiously, not in the slightest intimidated by this peremptory approach.

"Kostas. Kostas Alexandrou, 'course," he said. "I've got the kit in the Beamer, so let's get a wriggle on, shall we, love? You're on an hourly rate, an' you're not getting paid for your social networkin' skills!"

The blonde stared at each of us in turn, in blank incomprehension.

"Kit? Camerrra? You'rrre both here for photo-shoot?"

For some reason she accompanied this question with another irritating peal of laughter. It didn't help me get my head around the situation. Fortunately at that moment the brunette also approached the group. She looked shorter up close, and prettier, with her dark bobbed hair and strikingly pale blue eyes.

"Are you the Ofcable guy?" she asked. "The lawyer? I'm Jane. Or, actually, since we're off duty now, Monika. We should be on real name terms if we're going to work together, I suppose!"

"Hi. Matt," I said, holding my hand out. "Very, er- relieved- to meet you. Although you're not who I was expecting!"

"You seem to be having fun- making new friends."

"Yeah, I love it here. It's like sniffing petrol in a match factory."

Kostas' scowl had lifted slightly, which was a relief, because the guy had some beetling brows when he put his mind to it.

"You a lawyer, mate? Matt, I mean! Me too. Criminal, ecclesiastical, genocide trials- you name it! What's your game, my friend?"

"Erm, I'm not quite so versatile, unfortunately. Just corporate and, er, immigration law for me."

"Well, where you from? You English-qualified?"

"Yes…"

"Then don't sweat it, mate! You can turn your hand to anythin' in this caper, once you're a few years qualified, believe you me. Anyway, I'm not here on business! Or not the day job, anyhow," he said, winking at the blonde. "This is just for the creative hit," he confided to me. "Erotic photography. Art. I mean, don't get me wrong, I like the scenery too! But it's not really about that- it's about comin' up with the perfect shot…"

"The money shot?" I asked.

Kostas guffawed and slapped me on the back.

"If you want to call it that! Capturin' the moment, my friend. You picture it in your mind- then it's all about makin' it reality. Every shot tells a diff'rent story. A thousand and one nights, you know what I mean?"

"Yeah, you're the Scheherazade of soft porn, mate."

Kostas stared at me for a moment, before winking again.

"You're a cheeky *bastarde*, you know? But I like you! You've got a bit of the Greek about you, know what I mean?"

"I'm tragic?"

Right on cue, the blonde girl pointed at me.

"This guy wanted me to bring frrriend!"

Kostas looked at me again.

"You're a dark horse, fella!"

"Yes- well- that was just a misunderstanding…" But it did give me an idea. "Kostas, you might actually be the very man to speak to about this! Do you have any form in immigration law? I bet you do!"

Kostas laughed.

"Is the Ecumenical Patriarch of Constantinople an Orthodox Christian, my friend? 'Course I do! The worst thing that ever happened to me was Greece becomin' part of the European Communion. Without that..." He rubbed his fingers together expressively. "As it is, I gotta' office full of Turks- you should see my house, it's full of Turkish Delight, they keep sendin' it to me every time I get 'em a new purple passport! I don't touch that shit myself, who wants a sweet with more talcum powder on it than a baby's behind? But my Mum likes it, what can I say? She tells my granddad they're York Fruits though- he really hates those Turks, I don't know why!"

"Well, I understand there has been a bit of historical animosity between the Turks and Greeks," I said.

"Yeah, that's right!" said Kostas. "That's exactly it. That's what his beef is, no doubt about it. Historical. Anyway, that don't mean shit to a professional, you know what I mean? A Turk is- well, almost as good as a Greek to me. Anyway, immigrants is not all- not by a long shot. I've got my resident domestic workers; my Gangmasters Licensin' Authority cases- cocklepickers, fruit-pickers, winklepickers, you name it an' they can pick it; my Seasonal Agricultural Workers- that's basically your gangmasters for Bulgarians and Romanians. I'm gangbusters for gangmasters, I tell you, my friend!"

"A boom area, for sure. But listen, Kostas, if you're an immigration expert- and it certainly seems that way to me- maybe you could help out Jane's..."

"Monika's..." said Jane.

"Monika's friend. She's a Ukrainian..."

"*Ukrajinci!*" said the blonde. She spat on the ground again.

Kostas looked at her in disgust.

"Oi, watch out for the Hush Puppies, love! Different ways from us, my friend! We're all Orthodox though, right?" He crossed himself devoutly. "Listen, Matt- I like you, I do. And there's a certain professional curtsey to think of too. But time awaits no man, an' I need to take Frank Rijkaard here back to my studio for the photo-shoot. So, look, here's my card."

He handed me a business card, black with silver writing on it, then stood back to watch my reaction. It read: "Kostas Alexandrou: GCSEs, A-Levels, BA, CPE, LPC, Duke of Edinburgh's Award (Bronze)- Lawyer of Discretion. Photographer of Discrimination. Person of Distinction."

"Wow," I said. "This really is a calling-card."

"You like it?" Kostas smiled. "Not too shabby, eh? One of my clients who's in PR- well, he writes the classifieds for a used-car dealer- he came up with it. I wanted somethin' that said a bit more about me than just my technical legal skills, my friend. A mission statement, if you know what I mean? An escalator pitch, they call it."

"Yeah, we tried something like this at my old firm," I said. "It didn't come across as well as this, though. This captures the man, as well as the mission. I like it."

Kostas nodded enthusiastically, and looked around to the girls.

"You see? He likes it! 'Lawyer of Discretion', baby!"

"So what do you say, Kostas?" I asked him. "Are you in?"

"Like I said, mate, I'm in a rush just at the minute. But you've got my card- if you have a problem, if no one else can help, an' if you can find me, just give me a call, OK? If I can keep all these Turks in the country, a nice Ukrainian girl should be a piece of piss, know what I mean?"

The blonde girl started to go through the motions of spitting again, but Kostas took her by the hand and led her off, giving Monika and I a jaunty wave with his massive car-key fob as he went.

"Oh, and Matt, my friend!" Kostas shouted back to me, leaning out of the window of his car. "If all else fails- Three Stage Plan, right?" He held up a finger. "Stage One, get her to marry some

English bloke. Any punter will do, it don't matter so long as he's got the old purple passport himself." He held up another finger. "Stage Two- when the Home Office interview comes round, get her to talk about his favourite football team. I mean every-dam'-thing about them, she's gotta' be Alan Hansen in drag by the time she gets in there!"

"Great, thanks! What's Stage Three?" I shouted.

After what seemed like an eternity, the third finger went up into the North London sky.

"Stage Three- the team. Very important. Gotta' be Spurs! You can't go wrong with Spurs, 'cos even the Home Office know that no one outside Britain has ever heard of 'em. Start talkin' about Chelsea in there, and she'll be back in the USSR with the rest of the fan-base before you can say '*Dasvidaniya,* Pet'! Get too cute and start talkin' about Barnet FC, and they'll smell the rat a mile off. Even girls who like football don't like the minnows. They like a bit of glamour, know what I mean?" He looked at my suit. "OK, so maybe you don't... But take it from me, my friend. Spurs!"

"Got you- Spurs it is! Cheers, Kostas!"

He waved, and the BMW roared off towards King's Cross.

"I can certainly help with *that* back-story," said Monika. "You wouldn't believe the number of Spurs players- past and present- we've had calling Chatterbabe TV!"

"You don't say? That's perfect- she'll be able to give the Home Office the low-down on the most intimate peccadilloes of the Spurs Legends. What could be more British than an unhealthy pre-occupation with the love lives of footballers?"

"Will she really have to get married though, Matthew? I don't know how she'll feel about that."

"Don't worry, we'll find another way. Kostas is probably used to handling these cases on a fixed fee arrangement. If he can't come up with a decent case before he hits his fee-cap, they get marched off down the aisle, I guess."

"And you want him to work with us?"

"We need to consider every option. Then we'll exclude the illegal ones."

"OK. I just don't think that Katinka is ready to get married. It's a big step, you know."

"Definitely. I'd think hard on it myself."

She tutted.

"You sound just like you do on the phone, you know?"

"So do you- now that it actually is you. I was wondering what had happened to your language skills when that blonde girl turned up. Suddenly it was all 'r's. You…"

"She!"

"She… Seemed to be purposely seeking them out, just to roll them into oblivion."

"Galina! Aargh- how could you mistake her for me- she's so- so bloody Russian! Galina, of all people! I told you quite clearly that I was Polish! Didn't I tell you that I was Polish?"

"Yeah, sorry about that."

"What were you thinking! Me- a Rrrussian!"

"You're not going to spit on the floor, are you? It's an ugly thing, xenophobia. And remember that it was a pure case of mistaken identity. She was just the one who always came up on the TV screen while you were talking."

"You never saw me? Not even once! So she was why you came here! You thought you were speaking to Galina the whole time!"

"Well, you can see how it happened. A completely innocent misunderstanding. She was always on the screen when we were talking. Then she shows up at the stage-door, at the exact time we were supposed to meet. A real comedy of errors, eh? All very embarrassing."

"Really? Sometimes we see what we want to see, I think. But come on, we have to go and meet Katinka."

I followed her down the street.

"This is it," she said, pointing out a nondescript, old man's pub on the corner. She held the door open for me.

"This is your local? The Sheep's Head?"

"You don't like it?"

"It doesn't seem the most, er, scintillating place."

She shrugged.

"Katinka works here in the evenings. She says it's soothing."

"It's her party, I suppose."

We walked up to a table that was already groaning under the weight of half a dozen huge ring-binders, otherwise solely occupied by a sturdy girl with a huge mop of blonde ringlets and chunky black glasses.

"Christ, what's this? The National Archive?" I asked.

Monika blushed.

"This is just a dossier that I helped Katinka put together on her case. The 'Sheep' let us keep it here. It has all of her correspondence with the Home Office- it seems to take them about twenty letters just to confirm that they're considering your application! And I put together all of the legislation on the Points-Based System, the Immigration Rules, the Immigration Directorate Instructions and Entry Clearance Guidance, the Nationality, Immigration and Asylum Act 2002, all relevant decisions of the Immigration and Asylum Tribunal and the Court of Appeal case-law, to save you some time. Is that right? Did I miss anything?"

"No, er, that should definitely be enough to get started with. I'll let you know if we need to, er, dig deeper. Once I've got all of the facts from Katinka."

I shook hands solemnly with Katinka and sat down at the table.

"Would you like a drink?" asked Monika. "Nothing alcoholic for you whilst you're working, I guess, Matt?"

"No, I never touch the stuff when I'm on duty," I said, reluctantly. "Total focus."

"Maybe just a beer, then? A Stella Artois?"

Thank God for the Poles- I'd forgotten that they regard beer as a light thirst-quencher.

"So you were going for the Tier 1 route to enter the UK under the Points-Based System- 'Post-Study Work'?" I asked Katinka. "You had leave to remain as a student?"

"Yes, yes, no problem with that- I was studying Sleep Therapy at Ruislip University. That was a Masters Degree course, so it was only the 'maintenance funds' requirement that was a little bit of a problem for me... Just after I graduated, you know?"

"But you had a job already, right?"

Katinka nodded.

"Yes, working. No problem."

"She was already working as a sleep therapist, but freelance," Monika explained. "Self-employed. So she didn't have a fixed salary or anything like that. The thing is that they seem to change the maintenance funds rules the whole time, there are old rules, new rules and transitional rules, and no one knows whether they're coming or going! I mean, even the Home Office officials and judges! When Katinka put in her application- that was back in September, September the twenty-ninth- all applicants had to have £800 of cash held in a savings or current account. Afterwards they changed the rules, so that anyone applying after 31 October 2008 had to show that they'd had the £800 for the whole three months before putting their application in."

"And Katinka had the £800?"

"She did when she applied. And she'd had £800 for some of the month before she put her application in. But she hadn't had it for the whole of August- which was the month before she put her application in- and she definitely hadn't had it for the whole three months before that. It was only when she started to get her first few cash clients that she managed to pull it together, you see."

"It's not easy to build up a sleep therapy practice," said Katinka. "Sufferers from sleep deprivation can be very lethargic. It's not easy for them to get out and seek help."

"Right... So what exactly did you submit to the Home Office, Katinka?" I asked.

Monika flicked through one of her immaculate ring-binders.

"Here it is... Like I said, Katinka thought she had to show that she had a 'closing balance' of £800 or more in the month immediately preceding her application. But National Colonial Bank wouldn't give her a statement covering the exact period of the calendar month of August. It was out of synch with their statement calendar, they said. So Katinka's 'August bank statement' actually ran from 4 August to 25 August 2008. You can see that it shows that Katinka had more than £800 at all times after 18 August. I mean, she's no idiot. She always knew that she had to hit that level for her Tier 1 application."

"I hardly ate! Nothing except home-made pickled cucumbers, for a whole month!" said Katinka. "I had a real hydration problem, to be honest. I was drinking gallons of water. Then I swelled up like a balloon…"

"She got to the magic £800 though," said Monika. "But then the Home Office refused her application anyway. They said she had to have £800 for the whole month before her application, not just some of it. And even if she had, her bank statement was for the wrong period. She should have had one dated no later than 29

August. But that was the only one she could get for her NCB current account. What else could she do? You think that the National Colonial Bank cares a damn whether Katinka gets to stay in the country or not? That they are going to tell the millionaires to wait, while they prepare some special, bespoke bank statement for Katinka?"

"They probably couldn't even if they wanted to," I said. "And I imagine they had a few other things on their mind at that point, given that the whole bank was hours from oblivion... So you made an appeal?"

Katinka nodded.

"To the Immigration Judge. No problem. It was Monika here who made it happen. She was brilliant, really fantastic. She managed to get National Colonial to issue a new bank statement for me. This one covered 29 August to 29 September 2008. Perfect! And by then I had saved more money, so it showed a closing balance of over £800 the whole time during the period of that statement. Monika had thought of everything. We were ready for the appeal. We submitted the statement to the judge before the hearing. We had it all covered."

Here Monika broke in again.

"Except that there was a problem, obviously. The judge said that the PBS Guidance was very clear- Katinka had to submit a bank statement covering the one month period immediately before her application, with no exceptions. He would have looked at the new statement from National Colonial *if* we'd sent it in together with her original application to the Home Office on 29 September, but we hadn't. He wasn't interested in looking at it at the appeal. He just ignored it! And without that, Katinka's original statement was only up to the twenty-fifth of August, and that wasn't good enough. He agreed with the Home Office that she should have had the £800 every day, and then he said that by the time he heard the appeal, on Monday- the third of November that is- the rules had changed anyway. We didn't just have to have the money every day for one whole month. Now we had to have it every day for three months. Every day! And not even some of the days in the month- because you know how bank accounts go up and down. That's normal, right?"

"Yes, it is..." I said.

"But none of these rules had even changed from one month to three months at the time Katinka made her application in the first place. It's so unfair! It's not about actually having the money, you see- you need to be able to show that you had the money at that precise date, and they won't put two and two together from the fact that you had it a few days before and realise that you're not trying to go on benefits. Why would she need benefits- she's a brilliant sleep therapist! Things are really taking off for her now. It's just so frustrating!"

"What do you do?" I asked Katinka.

"I tell them to count sheep," she said.

"So what do you think?" said Monika.

"I'd recommend whisky myself- counting just stresses me out."

"About the case, idiot!" she said.

"What did your lawyer tell you at the time?" I asked.

"He didn't know what he was doing, I think," said Monika sadly. "He said that if we wanted a lawyer to make legal history, we had to find the money to pay for that. He was only there to do his best with a tricky case. But he did get paid! He just took the money and let Katinka lose her appeal. When she had done everything that she needed to do!"

"OK, OK. What does the Policy Guidance say?" I asked.

Monika flicked through another file.

"This is it... 'Transitional arrangements for maintenance (funds)'. Let's see... 'You must only show you have the required funds at the time you apply'. But what does that actually mean? 'Time you apply'? How long exactly do you have to have the £800 for?"

"What does it say about the documents that you need to send in as evidence of that?"

"It says 'The types of documentary evidence you need to send to support your application are as described in this document. However, until 31 October 2008, they do not need to cover the three-month period, but they must be dated no more than a month before your application'."

"So they don't actually talk about having that cash every day during the month at all?"

"Not that I can see. Have a look."

"Hey, I think we're onto something here, Monika. 'No more than a month'- that just sets a maximum age on the information. How could they extrapolate from those words that you need to have the money for a whole month? I don't think a court would. That's the point of substance. I think the problem for us is the evidential point: the fact that the second bank statement wasn't available until after the initial application to the Home Office. So we're tripping over the 'no more than a month' rule. We've got to get the Tribunal to accept that the Immigration Judge should have considered the fresh evidence submitted to him, that wasn't available to the Secretary of State on the original application- even if the rules had changed by then."

"Do you think we can?" asked Monika.

She was excited now, and that did make me nervous. I just couldn't get their hopes up about something that I still knew so little about. Whatever I may have intended, I was going to have to stick with this until I could give them a real answer. The one they deserved to get when they paid a lawyer to do this work in the first place.

"Listen, Monika- and Katinka- I need to look at this some more. There are a few points I need to check up on. I could maybe call in some favours from barristers that I've worked with in the past, just in terms of how the laws of evidence would work here. But there's definitely something in this- don't pack your bags yet, Katinka!"

"You really think so?" asked Monika. Her enthusiasm for Katinka's cause was contagious- I mean, it had to be virulent if it was even affecting me. And the longer I spent with her, the more I felt a need to- well, to make her like me. Maybe that was why I also felt the need to level with her.

"Yeah, I do. Like I told you, this isn't really my area of the law. But let me do some more research on it- this weekend- because we need to know that it's going to work, if we're going to lodge an appeal next week."

"You said 'we'! That's great, Matt!" said Monika, smiling.

"What will all this cost?" asked Katinka. "I still don't have much money, you know."

"Let me look at it, OK?" I said. "Can I take the dossier with me?"

"If you can carry it!" said Monika. "Come on, I'll give you a hand carrying it to the Tube station. Katinka has to stay here."

"I'm working," said Katinka by way of apology.

"After this?" I asked.

"No, now, actually," said Katinka. "This is kind of a drop-in surgery for me. Here at the Sheep's Head. They know me in the neighbourhood now. People will come and talk to me about their sleep problems. I can advise them, and then they go home and sleep. I mean, some of them actually drop off at the tables here. But they sleep."

"And the pub encourages that kind of custom?"

"They say there's no such thing as bad publicity."

"This must really be pushing the boundaries of that saying... But the punters- I mean, the, er, patients- pay you for this advice?"

"Oh yes. I mean, they generally buy me drinks or, er, pork scratchings, rather than cash as such. But they do pay me."

"No wonder it took so long to get the £800 together..." I said. "If only the court accepted pints as 'Maintenance (Funds)', you would probably have been one of the most solvent people in Britain when you made the application."

"But it's not about the money for me, you see," said Katinka. "It's about reaching out to the people who need me most, when they need me most. The pubs of London are full of sleep-deprived people who just want to drink themselves asleep- they need my help. Just as much as neurotic people in offices who can afford to have an hour of therapy during surgery hours. This is where my real work is done. Out here on the front-line of insomnia."

"Listen, I'm sorry if I was kidding with you a little," I said. "I can see it's important work. And we'll do- I'll do- everything I can to help you carry it on. Well, good night, sweet dreams."

"Ha, ha," said Monika. She grabbed a bundle of files, and helped me to lug them out towards the Tube.

"Thanks- you don't have to do that," I said.

"No, I want to," she said. "And you don't have to do this either- any of this."

"I know. But I think it's something that I can do. Something I can really help with."

She looked at me curiously.

"You sound surprised!"

"I suppose that I never really thought about my work- my, er, qualifications- in terms of helping people in that way. It didn't seem so personal. Now it seems important."

Monika laughed.

"You see- maybe you needed Chatterbabe TV too!" She put her files on top of the ones that I was carrying, so that they completely blocked my vision.

"So- shall we meet again on Sunday then?" she asked.

"Sunday- as in the day after tomorrow?"

"Well, you did say you were going to look at the case this weekend, didn't you? And it's not as though you have a girlfriend to distract you any more, is it?"

"Ouch. You know, I had actually not thought about that fact for two hours and, er, thirty-four minutes. Maybe I did need Chatterbabe. But now it's right back in there. Front of mind."

"Sorry... But this- this is someone's life, you know!"

"A life? It's some time since I've had first-hand experience of such a thing. But OK, Sunday. Six p.m. here. That will give me a chance to get into the law library and try to get my head around this first."

"Brilliant! See you then. I look forward to it. No, I mean it. Good night, Matt!"

Her head darted around the files, and she kissed me on the cheek, then disappeared again before I could respond- physically or mentally. I paused for a moment, then struggled down the escalator and back underground.

Chapter 8

Bloomsbury, London, 29 November 2008

It took me a moment, letting the undulating shelves of Immigration Appeal Reports and Immigration and Nationality Law Reports stretch my gaze up to the high ceiling of the UCL Library, to make the connection. I had been walking back home to the flat one night- pissed, probably- when I saw one of those low-tech, rotating advertising hoardings on the Balls Pond Road. The reel of adverts had been taken off it to be replaced, so that all you could see behind the screen was a series of horizontal electric strip-lights like a giant, glowing Jacob's ladder, steepling right up into the sullen Dalston night. It surged upwards, rippling and blinking in its limitless energy and possibility. That had kept me standing there too, looking at a billboard without a bill, feeling an irresistible wave of hope rise in me. I hadn't expected to recapture that feeling spending my Saturday mornings in a law reading room in Bloomsbury, but if life's a game of snakes and ladders, you have to enjoy the ladders where you find them. And I had to admit that it was the meetings with Monika- with Monika and Katinka, I mean- at least twice a week, sharing their elation at any progress we could make, that I really looked forward to. I bundled up my photocopying and hurried to Warren Street on foot, to catch the Tube to the office.

I met Monika and Katinka at Southwark Station, and we walked up to Ofcable together.

"Why couldn't we just meet in the Sheep's Head?" grumbled Katinka.

"Well, Katinka," I said. "Firstly because it's ten o'clock in the morning, and as one of its most loyal clients for the past month, I can tell you that the 'Sheep' doesn't open until midday; and secondly, because it doesn't contain any word processing equipment, and the purpose of this meeting is to finalise the written grounds for your appeal."

"It's got a new video juke-box," she said.

"Right- similar to a PC, but with some important functional differences. Come on, Katinka, lift, lift! This is what we've been working towards for all this time, we've really got to nail it today!"

"This is where you work?" said Monika admiringly, as we swept through the glamorous reception of Ofcable. It looked especially impressive on a Saturday, because you had the impression that it must be frequented by suave media executives all week. Come Monday, the harsh reality of shiny suits and M&S for Men cardigans would quickly dispel that illusion. But I still enjoyed the moment, because I knew that it couldn't last for long.

"Maybe you should reserve judgment until we get to my actual office…" I said.

Katinka followed, completely impassive. She obviously didn't think much of a working environment without any bar towels or fruit machines in it. She must have been wondering how we actually got paid- given the almost insurmountable logistical difficulties of transporting pints of lager from The Tempest Inn all the way down to 'Standards' without spilling them. Even Monika's enthusiasm for Ofcable was dwindling slightly by the time we got there ourselves.

"You should ask them for an office upstairs- somewhere where there's some natural light!" she said. "It can't be healthy working in artificial light all the time…"

"Does it disturb your sleep?" asked Katinka, with interest.

"It used to, but I've been sleeping like a baby since I've been spending so much time in the Sheep's Head," I said. "Very therapeutic."

"Have you asked them to move you higher up in the building?" asked Monika.

"You'll make someone a great wife one day," I said. "The problem is that they tend to reserve that kind of floor-space for the senior executives."

"And what makes someone a senior executive?" Monika asked. "You have a degree. Even a professional qualification. What more do they want?"

"Hmm, I'm not sure what the precise definition is, but I reckon that your day job has to involve spending no more than fifty per cent. of your time cold-calling cable TV channels…"

Katinka was sitting at Pete's desk now, admiring the 'Diamond Lights' record-sleeve.

"Who are these guys- 'Glenn and Chris'?" she asked. "Big stars in this country?"

"Perhaps in their own field of expertise…" I said. "But listen, shall we get started? I'm not sure when they turn the lights off. No one seems to do much work at the weekends around here."

Katinka nodded, but she seemed much more interested in Pete's Spurs memorabilia. Perhaps she thought there were some useful sleep therapy props in there.

"Did you find what you were looking for at the library?" Monika asked.

"Yeah, I think so! The key thing is the point we talked about on Thursday," I said. "We all agreed that Rule 245AA didn't impose any requirement for the production of documents at a particular time, right? What we were worried about was Rule 34C- which says that failure to produce the specified documents would make Katinka's application invalid, so that it didn't even have to be considered by the Home Office. But the point I keep coming back to is that the Secretary of State actually *did* make a decision on Katinka's application, under Rule 245Z. She decided that the bank statement showed that Katinka didn't have the requisite maintenance funds for the correct period. OK, it was the wrong decision- it was a decision that we've spent weeks challenging- but it was still a decision!"

"So?" said Katinka.

"So the Home Office could simply have said that the application wasn't properly prepared, and thrown it straight into the waste-paper basket," said Monika. "No legal decision, so no mistake of law to challenge. But they didn't! They've given us a shot!"

"Exactly!" I said. "Rule 34C is out of the game. And section 85(4) of the Nationality, Immigration and Asylum Act 2002 says that 'the Tribunal may consider evidence about any matter which it thinks relevant to the substance of the decision, including evidence which concerns a matter arising after the date of the decision'. I checked the case-law this morning, and it's crystal-clear that nothing in the Immigration Rules dealing with the PBS can exclude section 85(4)- as an express provision of an Act of Parliament. Parliamentary sovereignty and all that. So we're going to be saying that precisely because section 85(4) gave him the ability to look at

Katinka's new bank statement, the Immigration Judge should have done so."

"Because by that time, it was available, and had to be considered to evaluate the merits of the application?" said Monika.

"Right!" I said. "I think we've got them!"

Monika squeaked with delight, and jumped up to hug me. Which was great on one level, but which also gave Pete the opportunity to display unsuspected powers of dramatic timing in making his presence known for the first time.

"An' what do we have here?" he said, stepping into the doorway.

"What- what are you doing here, Pete?" I asked.

"What am I doin' here? What am *I* doin' here? I work here! Just like you soon won't. I'm not, let's say, one of the employees of a friggin' supervised cable channel! In fact, if I'm not very much mistaken, one of the actual telephone operators we're supposed to be regulatin'!"

"Pleased to meet you," said Monika. "I'm Monika. But you might know me better as Jane from Chatterbabe TV…"

"Oh, I recognise your voice, luv!" said Pete darkly. "I never forget a voice…"

"Yeah, but Pete," I said. "Have you ever actually been here at the weekend before? In all the time you've worked here? You must admit that this a bit of a coincidence."

"That's not the point, mate," said Pete. "'Course I'm only here 'cause I followed you! What legitimate activities actually need to be carried out here? But I was startin' to worry you was Jack the friggin' Ripper! All these inexplicable early mornin's at the weekend… 'Doin' legal research'- hardly a credible cover-story, was it? So it's not *my* professional conduct we're dissectin' here now, is it? Or are you seriously tryin' to tell me this is official business? What is this, Ofcable's first bust since the good old days of Telewest?"

"He was just helping Katinka with her immigration appeal," said Monika. "To continue her work in the country she loves- her home!"

"OK- sounds like bollocks so far. So why are *you* here, Chatterbabe?"

"She's the brains of the operation, Pete," I explained. "The question is more whether it's strictly necessary for Katinka herself to be present…"

"She likes to keep track of what's going on," said Monika. "But Clive- I mean, Pete- none of this had anything to do with Ofcable! Or, you know, Chatterbabe TV. That was just the way that I met Matthew- and asked him to help us. It was all my idea."

"We'll see about that," said Pete impressively. "Can we have a word alone, please, Matthew? In my, er, friend's office, if you please."

There was nothing for it but to follow him into Veronica's office. He slammed the sliding-door shut behind me.

"You really have screwed up royally this time, mate! Are you out of your friggin' mind, bringin' her and her woolly friend here? What do you think Colin would say if he found out about this? He would go absolutely ape-shit, that's what! And he would not be wrong, either! You would be out of here before you could say 'industrial espionage'. Besides, he's basically been waitin' for his whole career to uncover an inside job like this!"

"An inside job like what, Peter?" asked Colin, sliding the door open with a flourish.

"We're all ears," said Torquemada, gliding into the office after him.

I have to admit that that was a serious blow.

"Like, like our, er, preparations for the 'Standards' tenth anniversary party?" said Pete.

Colin shook his head slowly.

"You disappoint me, Peter. Not just because 'Standards' has already had a tenth anniversary party, so you can't possibly be telling me the truth. But because you were actually at that party yourself! I think it's about time someone told me exactly what has been going on here, don't you? And today of all days!"

I looked at Pete, searching for inspiration. That was when Monika and Katinka came wandering in too.

"Is everything OK?" asked Monika. "We were worried."

"Right- Colin, can I introduce you to Monika and Katinka?" I said.

Monika smiled, and Katinka gave Colin what seemed to be a rudimentary curtsey.

"Katinka is a Ukrainian national who I've been helping with some immigration law troubles that she's been having. On a *pro bono* basis, you know. Monika, Katinka- this is Colin. Our boss, and the head of the Content Standards Supervision Team here at Ofcable."

"Trouble with the law!" said Colin.

"They want to throw me out of the country!" said Katinka, unhelpfully.

"So is she actually- a fugitive?" asked Colin.

"She's not on the run, Colin, she's in a legitimate appeal process with the immigration authorities," I said. "She just needed some legal advice, and she couldn't afford a lawyer."

Colin nodded.

"Innocent until proven guilty, right?" I said. "This is all going through the proper legal channels."

"So I have nothing to worry about, Matthew? There has been no breach of Ofcable protocol?"

Torquemada sniggered.

"Right..." I said.

"So this is not, in fact, Ms Monika Antoniak from Chatterbabe TV then?" said Colin.

"Oh, bloody hell!" said Pete.

"Do you think I don't know the key operatives of these channels as well as I know my own team?" said Colin. "That I don't have a file on each and every one of them? That I don't know exactly what they look like- how they operate- how likely they are to cross the line? The, the arrogance of it! You have absolutely no idea of the dedication that this job takes. No idea at all, based on your conduct today! Can't you see the manifest security risks- the breach of confidence- involved in this behaviour? It's like the Profumo Affair writ large! The Dreyfus Affair!"

"Well, it's not really like the Dreyfus Affair," I said. "That was an anti-semitic miscarriage of military justice in pre-War France..."

Colin ignored me.

"And can you imagine what would happen if the press were ever to get hold of a scoop like this: 'Ofcable Mandarin Caught in Honey-trap'? 'Police Quiz Ofcable Mole?'"

"Chatterbabe Charmer Cons Channel-supervision Chump?" suggested Pete. "Pole Potty?"

"Shut up, Pete..." I said. "Listen, Colin, I'm sorry- I know it looks bad. But there's really nothing underhand about it. I heard about Katinka's situation from Monika- from speaking to her on monitoring calls. Of course I should have told you that I'd made contact with her outside work. I do regret that. But to start with I didn't know that anything was going to come of meeting Katinka- so it would have seemed a bit crazy to be bringing it to you anyway. And now- well, now you know."

"But do I, Matthew? Do I really know? What is there between you?"

"Me and Katinka? Absolutely nothing. Well, kind of a solicitor-client relationship."

Katinka nodded.

"No, I mean between you and Chatterbabe Operative 211... Between you and Monika?" said Colin.

I felt myself blushing.

"Nothing at all, Colin- we're just working together on Katinka's case."

Monika looked at me, then laughed and turned back to Colin.

"He actually seems quite keen on one of my colleagues, if that helps!"

"Not really..." I said.

"He only came to meet me in the first place because he thought I was her."

"Well, that's not strictly true," I said. "Although that isn't really the point here..."

"It's perfectly understandable, you know," said Monika. "She is very blonde and pretty..."

"His ex is blonde as well," said Pete. "Cruella."

"Oh, really?" said Monika. "Maybe that's why he was watching my, er, colleague on Chatterbabe then!"

"You refer to Ms Galina Artemyev, I presume?" said Colin.

Monika gasped.

"It's really fairly elementary..." said Colin modestly. "You see, I have personally witnessed Matthew closely scrutinising Ms Artemyev's broadcasts on more than one occasion!"

"Oh, for Christ's sake..." I said.

"It was probably the time-delay when they're on air that fooled you there, Matthew!" said Colin. "It's easy to see you're still a bit green, my boy! That's the oldest one in the book, that is. Some, er, greenhorns don't even realise that most callers aren't even speaking to the girl on the screen- there's a whole room of operators behind the scenes in the studio, you know!" He cleared his throat. "But, that's not, that is not the point either. Sometimes, Matthew, it is not good enough for Ofcable just to be impartial. It must look impartial too. That is the principle that seems to have been allowed to fall by the wayside here."

"One of many…" said Torquemada. Colin glared at him.

"We'll talk about this further on Monday, Matthew," Colin said. "But I'm afraid that until then, you must consider yourself suspended on full pay and benefits, pending further disciplinary action."

"I'm, er- I'm actually on holiday next week, Colin," I said. "For Katinka's immigration appeal…"

"That's what you're doin' with your *holiday*?" said Pete disgustedly.

"What? It's not as though he has a girlfriend to spend it with," said Monika.

"Yeah, thanks for mentioning that, Monika…" I said. "Again."

"You can jolly well stew on it next week then, Matthew," said Colin. "I'll deal with you when you get back."

"What!" said Monika. "That's so unfair! He hasn't done anything wrong!"

Colin didn't reply, but set his jaw defiantly. There didn't seem to be much point in trying to change his mind for the moment. Pete had obviously reached the same conclusion, because he started to usher us out.

"C'mon," said Pete, "Let's all sleep on this. We can talk about it again next week. Sorry about all this hassle at the weekend, Colin, mate."

"See you on Monday, Peter," said Colin, sinking down into Veronica's chair and gesturing to us to leave. "I hope…"

"You got it, boss!" said Pete, as we stepped out into the corridor.

"So this is the way the world ends," I heard Colin say. "Not with a bang but a, erm, whimper!"

"What did he say?" Peter whispered to me.

"Something from T.S. Eliot? He really seems to be taking this hard..."

"Yeah- something don't make sense here..." said Pete. "Just one thing, Col," he said, popping his head back into Veronica's office. "What are you and Tommy doin' here on a Saturday, anyway?"

Colin glanced at Torquemada, then pulled himself upright in his chair.

"Oh, I suppose there's no point not telling you now!" he said. "The cat is all but out of the bag anyway..."

"Colin..." said Torquemada.

"They'll find out for themselves soon enough! And they- they deserve to hear it from me. Peter, Matthew- I'm sorry to have to tell you that Thomas here has just informed me that we're being merged into, er, another regulatory quango."

"Not Ofmedia..." said Pete. "Anyone but Ofmedia!"

Colin hung his head.

"Oh, Christ, it is Ofmedia, isn't it?" said Pete. "You are havin' a friggin' bubble bath!"

"It's all part of the 'Bonfire of the Quangos', Peter."

"It's been coming for years!" said Torquemada. "Surely you must all have expected this- sooner or later."

"Well, of course everyone knew that there was no real need for two separate organisations regulating cable," said Colin. "But no one could have foreseen this: Us- merged into them. Them taking us over! Or how it would be done! And now it emerges that this, this little snake in the grass, Thomas, knew about it all along! Oh yes, we welcomed him here with open arms, but it turns out that he's only been here to spy on us! Now he's reporting back to his Ofmedia superiors on who should keep their jobs in the reshuffle!"

"If anyone…" said Thomas.

"Today I found out exactly what he's been saying about us. Not enough busts…"

"Check!" said Pete.

"Too much focus on team-building initiatives…"

"Check!" said Pete.

"Too many 'gimmicks'…"

"If the *Star Trek* jumper fits, wear it…" said Pete.

"Pete!" I hissed at him. "Whose side are you on here?"

"There's going to be a bloodbath at Ofcable!" continued Colin. "No one is safe- not you chaps, not Veronica and Carl, not even me. Not anyone!"

"Especially after Matthew's little stunt today," said Torquemada unpleasantly. "Not to mention your own childish tantrum just now, Colin. I'm disappointed in you. I thought you might have some- transitional- part to play in my integration planning. Now I'm really not so sure I can recommend that…"

"I'm sorry, Colin…" I said. "How- how do you feel?"

"How do I feel? How do I feel? This has been my life's work. How do you think Noah would have felt- if they suddenly told him to, er, pack three of each animal instead of two, just as the floodgates of the heavens were opened onto Canaan? And maybe not make the trip himself, after all? That's sort of how I feel, to be perfectly honest. Now, chaps- leave me alone with Thomas… We have a lot to discuss. We'll speak about that disciplinary matter when you get back, Matthew."

"OK- see you then, Col," said Pete, sliding V's door closed behind us.

"So what do we do now?" I asked him, as we left the 'Standards' floor.

"I think we probably oughta' go for a pint, don't you?" said Pete.

"Yeah, definitely. Monika? Katinka?"

"Yes, let's go. I'm so sorry about all this, Matthew," said Monika. "This is all my fault!"

"Damn right!" I said. "I was actually doing quite well here... Now we're all buggered!"

She hit me on the arm.

"You're supposed to say it was always going to happen anyway! You heard what Colin said about Ofmedia! Are you at least friendly with that Thomas guy?"

Pete laughed grimly.

"Let's just say that Matthew here is gonna' be first one up against the wall when that particular revolution comes! But c'mon, I could murder a Cobra."

Outside the office, down at river level, Pete led us through a nondescript Bankside alleyway. Despite its unpromising appearance, it was punctuated at various points with huge heritage placards.

"Wait, wait! I have to read this!" said Monika. "It's just amazing to think that this is where some of Shakespeare's greatest works were born! It doesn't look like much- but it gave the whole world unforgettable art. You asked me, Matt- what I'd like Chatterbabe TV to be like. Well, like this- turning something shabby into something- inspiring!"

"I think you need a bit more than some fake tan an' a few friggin' oil bubbles to make unforgettable art, darlin'," said Pete. "No offence, obviously!"

Monika shook her head.

"Oh, of course, of course we would have to change a lot of things around there. It's the participation aspect of it that we need to capture- letting people create their own art, giving them a forum to express themselves, however they choose. That's something to build on, isn't it?"

"So how would you shake it all up then?" asked Pete. "Put it on after the watershed? Get licensed for adult material?"

"Of course you would think that!" said Monika. "You Ofcable guys seem to be obsessed with sex! But that's not it at all. For a start, I would get rid of the whole scantily-clad bimbo thing. I would focus it back on the performance art. Like I said to Matt, kind of a YouTube television channel. Focus on the interaction between the channel and the public. Bring people's own ideas to life on our channel, and help them reach an audience they would never have dreamed of! We could have weekly or monthly themes for some of our time-slots, to give viewers the chance to work within a bit more of a structure: to find their feet in creating content. Almost like a living film and drama school, you know? And then definitely slots for videos and short films, of course, for those who'd already started to blossom as artists. We could even give Katinka a late-night slot to help people with insomnia- she could talk it through with them, give them the benefit of her sleep therapy experience. Help them drop off."

"Sounds like BBC2..." said Pete.

Monika ignored him.

"Initially people would still be paying for their calls, but over time the advertising revenue would allow us to reduce that- hopefully to nothing. The *auteur* slots would attract more free-thinking brands as advertisers- people who prefer the *avant-garde* to the obvious."

"It sounds amazing! Like subverting the whole trashy ethos of cable TV today, and turning it into something incredible- Art for the People! But do you think you could really pull it off?" I asked.

Monika nodded.

"Absolutely we could- the channel is in some financial difficulties, you could buy it for a song, I think! I mean, Dimitrios is completely open about it- he would sell it for whatever he could get, if he could only find a buyer. But he's a kind man at heart- he would help us to get it up and running. And the girls would love to get involved in something a bit more- positive- than Chatterbabe TV. Maybe not that Galina, but the rest of them. And as for Katinka, well, you know she lives for her sleep therapy!"

"And it definitely wouldn't hurt her to have a sponsoring employer for her immigration appeal, either," I said.

Monika nodded again.

"That's right," she said. "It might sound silly to you, but I'm just starting to feel- to feel as though it's time to do something about it, you know? That this is the right moment to do something really special?"

"Did Dimitrios tell you how much cash he wanted for Chatterbabe?" I asked her.

"He said about three hundred thousand pounds," said Monika. "But I think he would take two hundred and fifty. After all, everyone keeps telling us that the world is coming to an end, don't they? And I know that Dimitrios would love to sell the business to his employees, if we could raise the cash. He's a very emotional man..."

"How much do you have at the moment?"

"Well- counting all of our savings- about five thousand..." admitted Monika.

"OK- so that is a bit of a funding gap," I said. "Does that include Katinka's access to a lifetime supply of free beer? That's got to have some financial value."

"Don't be so stupid!" said Monika. "Don't you know anyone who could help? Any of the people you worked with in the City?"

"The thing is that all those guys are getting fired by the dozen right now… And people who do have cash don't necessarily want to spend it on slightly, uh- speculative- ventures like this. I mean, you could probably buy an investment bank for three hundred grand right now."

"There you go- a bank!" said Pete. "Wouldn't a bank just lend them the money? A small business loan or somethin'? What about a NINJA loan- they seem to be all the rage!"

"That's kind of the problem… The banks aren't even lending to each other at the moment- and I'm guessing that Chatterbabe TV is not exactly a Triple A-rated credit."

"There must be some way we can do it," said Monika. "Can't you at least think about it? You really are clever, Matt- even I can see that, from all the work you've done on Katinka's case. If you could just find a way to express that positively. So this is it- this is your chance to turn it into something good!"

"My chance?"

"Well, why not? We're not going to do it without you, are we? And I don't think we're in much of a position to pick and choose. You too, Pete. This could be something that you can be really proud of."

"Whoah, cool the beans there, darlin'- I'm a valued employee of Ofcable! I'm not gettin' sacked next Monday! So don't lump me in with this twat…"

"It doesn't sound as though there's going to be much left of Ofcable by the time Monday comes round though, is there, Pete?"

said Monika gently. "And you two are a great team- that's obvious. At least think about it, OK?"

"Christ- first the City, now Ofcable. If you're not safe working in a regulator- what then?" I said.

"That's exactly it, isn't it?" said Monika. "We all need to adapt- every one of us. Our jobs are on the line too, along with Katinka's future in the UK. But we have an idea that could create something spectacular for all of us- so now let's get on with it!"

We sat down at a table in the dingy, deserted front bar at The Tempest. It may have been close to the office, but it was certainly no enchanted isle. Pete proudly lined up four pints of Cobra Lager.

"You see?" he said to me.

"Wow, this really is a brave new world…"

"*Na zdrowie!*" said Monika, clinking glasses with Katinka.

"I think- I still think- the Chatterbabe buy-out is an amazing idea, Monika," I said. "But I've just got quite a lot on my mind today. I seem to be getting through the careers pretty quickly this year. And this time there are also Colin, Pete and V's careers to think of."

"And Carl's…" said Pete.

"Well, Carl I don't really count," I said to Pete. "Not after the Mont Blanc Incident."

"Speakin' of Carl, there is one thing you can do to make it up to me…" said Pete.

"What's that, mate? Just say the word!"

"What was the famous 'Ketamine Incident'? The one you two chumps speak about with bated breath in the office?"

"Ah, the Ketamine Incident… That must never be discussed."

"I don't understand the point of ketamine," said Katinka suddenly. "Why bother with it? If you want to be tranquillised- or you know, to get some sleep- there are proper techniques. Or just have a few beers."

"It's not always as simple as that, Katinka- although your professional curiosity does you credit," I said. "Sometimes there can be cultural sensitivities surrounding alcohol that might make other alternatives- superficially- more appealing."

"For Christ's sake, you've got to tell us now!" said Pete. "What happened?"

"Was it for a rave or something?" asked Monika.

"Perhaps the closest analogy to that- in the culture in question," I said. "We had a client- a young client, a very nice bloke- at the firm, who happened to be a Methodist."

"So he couldn't drink?" said Pete.

"Exactly. I mean, I believe he may have had the odd pint or two when he was at university- and no elders were watching. But on this occasion they were very much watching, because he'd rashly promised his mum he'd go to one of these special 'Methodist Speed Dating Evenings' at John Wesley's House on the City Road. Not far from where Carl and I used to work in the City, in fact. He was a very eligible bachelor, because apart from anything else, he was an M&A investment banker, and he was starting to make some real money. And this event was chaperoned to the nines."

"What is 'speed dating'?" asked Katinka.

"Well, they get together a big group of single people. And then, instead of going on a proper date for drinks and dinner, *amuse-bouche* and getting dumped, one person at a time, you have five-minute dates with loads of people in turn. As many as you can see in the time available, basically."

"You have sex with several people in turn?"

"No, no, no- just a chat! To see if you might be compatible. The furthest it goes is ticking the box next to their name, to indicate that you might be interested in seeing them again. If you both tick the box, they put you in touch with each other. Then the sex is up to you, I guess. Probably the Methodists actually hold off a bit longer than others might, as a matter of form."

"It's all the rage!" said Monika. "The London Polish Society even organised a speed-dating night. I did hear that they're planning not to provide any vodka at the next one, though. Only the girls could still sit upright by nine o'clock..."

"But what did all this have to do with you and Carl?" said Pete. "You're not friggin' Methodists, are you?"

"I'm coming on to that, Pete," I said. "The point was that we happened to be working with Arminius on a deal at the time."

"Wait a second- Arminius was the guy's name?"

"Yeah. It must be a Methodist thing. We were running a data room for them. I was the associate on the deal, and Carl was filling in as a kind of 'para-paralegal'. Which, of course, he was allowed to do before the Ketamine Incident. Arminius would call Carl when he had bidders who wanted data room access, and Carl would open up it up for them, then sit in there with them. Just to make sure no one took anything away with them. Or copied anything without submitting a formal photocopy request form. There were all kinds of data room rules to abide by. Although we didn't think to include substance abuse..."

"That's all he had to do?" said Katinka. "That sounds like a great job!"

"It really was an Arcadian existence for Carl. Ever since then, he's been trying to recapture that paradise lost... Anyway, we were speaking to Arminius all the time, and it soon became clear that, although he was a pretty confident bloke in other ways, he was absolutely bricking it about this Methodist speed dating business. He was worried he wouldn't have anything to say to these girls- or their mothers. The event was getting closer and closer, and he was losing his mojo in a big way. But he couldn't get out of it, because he'd promised his own Mum that he would be there, and she in turn had promised the rest of the gang. The noose was tightening around his neck."

"So what did he do?" asked Monika.

"For some reason- I still don't know why- he consulted Carl and me."

"No shit!" said Pete. "He must've been friggin' desperate! What did you tell him?"

"I obviously suggested that it was a case for a spot of Dutch courage," I said.

"Only that was the last thing he could do- with the eyes of the whole community on him?" said Monika.

"Right. So that was really the end of it from my point of view. It's not as if I'm in any position to provide tips to others on the art of romantic repartee…"

"You seemed to be chatting away very happily with Galina when you came to Chatterbabe TV!" said Monika.

"So… Like I said, that was the end of it in terms of my involvement. But Carl must have spoken to Arminius again afterwards. At any rate, between them they somehow agreed that Carl would give him a pill he had legally acquired, that was guaranteed to calm anxiety. It wouldn't get him high, or have him dancing on the speakers or anything- it would just relax him enough to do his thing, talk to everyone freely and breezily, and then call time on his speed-dating career while he was ahead."

"Ketamine?" said Pete.

"Right. It nearly called time on his Methodist career. It turned out that Carl had got this particular dose from some clinical trials he was doing in his spare time. No sooner had Arminius washed it down with a glass of mineral water, than it launched him on an intense out-of-body experience. Which you can imagine had both pros and cons from a speed-dating point of view. On the 'pro' side, apparently he did prove quite a success with the more spiritual, mystical girls present."

"Oh my God!" said Monika. "And on the 'con' side?"

"Even now he still receives at least one Methodist tract a day, urging him to mend his ways. He used to, er, send them onto us- to show us the grief we'd caused him... Carl and I actually know quite a lot of John Wesley's teachings now, as a result: 'Ye see the wine when it sparkles in the cup, and are going to drink of it. I tell ye there is poison in it! And, therefore, beg ye to throw it away!'"

"I notice that you haven't followed them particular teachin's just yet..." said Pete.

"I'm still reflecting on them- absorbing them... But to be fair to Arminius, he was in a bit of a cleft stick at this point. The thing is that it isn't just alcohol that's frowned on for Methodists- it's all intoxicants. So he couldn't just tell them that, far from having a few sharpeners and disgracing his religion, he'd actually just popped a Class C drug at a religious event. And, let's face it, it can't have been easy to weigh all of that up- not whilst suffering from the double-vision and hallucinations. That may have been why he called Carl, and asked him to come down to the venue. For moral support, I suppose. Of course the problem was that Carl actually did head along there- to the, er, spiritual home of Methodism. It was just around the corner from the office, you see. With the benefit of hindsight, that caused more problems than it solved for Arminius. Because Carl adopted a Methodist persona- at least until his position there became, ah, completely untenable..."

"Shit! A Crystal Methodist! So what did this Arminius guy say to you afterwards?" asked Pete.

"Initially he was cool. But of course he had to come down eventually, and when he did, he was very cross about the whole thing. Obviously he blamed Carl, but then he also felt that the firm shouldn't have anyone so completely out of control on the pay-roll at all- someone who might inadvertently get innocent people wrecked like that. I had to promise that Carl would never be assigned to any matters that Arminius' bank was involved with again- otherwise they'd be looking elsewhere for legal advice in the future. And it was a big account for us."

"What did Carl say about it?" said Monika.

"He took it hard. Of course he offered to consume ten times that amount there and then, in order to demonstrate scientifically that Arminius should have been able to take it with no ill effects. But ultimately he had to concede that from a pharmacological perspective, it was unlikely that Arminius would have quite the same tolerance to the stuff as he did. He saw it more as a case for a rap on the knuckles than a permanent ban on client contact, though. He's never quite forgiven me for that. Especially after his engagement fizzled out…"

"Carl was engaged? You're friggin' jokin'!" said Pete. "Who to?"

"Afterwards it transpired that he had plighted his troth at the Methodist speed dating. Under completely false pretences, of course- he was pretending to be a direct descendant of Charles Wesley. 'Trevor Wesley', I think he called himself. I still don't know how he had found out enough about Methodism to develop that persona. I didn't even know there were two Wesleys. But anyway, that was when things really started to get out of hand. We had serious words."

Pete laughed.

"You're pretty matey really though, aren't you?"

"Circumstances do seem to have thrown us together a bit. And I'm the first to accept that Carl has a difficult path to walk, along that fine line between idiot and idiot savant... Wait a minute, though- that could be it!"

"What could be what?" said Monika.

"Speed dating!"

"What do you mean?"

"First of all, let's figure out if we can get this money from the bank! Then I'll explain 'Plan B'..."

Katinka swallowed her final mouthful of beer.

"Well, I'm definitely not taking any ketamine," she said.

Chapter 9

City of London, 4 December 2008

"So, let me just get this straight, one more time," said Veronica, twiddling her pearl necklace through her fingers and taking a deep draught of triple espresso. "Why am I the one leading the meeting with the bank manager again?"

"There are really two reasons for that, V," I said. "Only one of which you will actually be communicating to the bank manager himself."

"The real reason is that you're the only one both old enough, and posh enough, to carry it off…" said Pete.

"And the reason you tell them- is that you're the Chairman of our acquisition vehicle," I said.

"Chairperson," Monika corrected me.

Veronica nodded.

"And talk me through what we actually want from them again, Matthew? Sorry for being so clueless."

"No problem, V. Non-executive directors are always a bit vague on these details. What we want- what we ideally want- is a three hundred and fifty grand loan. That way we can buy the channel, plus have fifty to a hundred grand of working capital to get us through the first year of operation, put on the first programming schedule, and generally get ourselves up and running. After that the station should be throwing off revenue itself, so we can use that to fund our operations going forward. We might even try and pay ourselves some salary then."

"What are you going to do until then?"

"We'll largely be eating home-made pickled cucumbers until then," I said. "It worked for Katinka."

Veronica was making careful notes on a Waitrose shopping-list pad.

"OK- got you," she said. "So we're meeting Nigel Thorne- Small Corporates Manager?"

"Yep. He sounds like a nice enough guy on the phone- but you need to watch out for his nervous laughter. He always seems to laugh just when he's about to give you some bad news."

"How reassuring… And who are you guys, again?"

"We are Matthew Verreaux: Chief Executive; Monika Antoniak: Head of Programming; and Peter Staines: Interim Finance Director," I said.

"And Katinka Kovalenko: Executive Producer of all Sleep Therapy Programming," said Monika.

"Why is Pete only the Interim Finance Director?"

"Because he doesn't actually know anything about accounting yet- we'll have to hire a real FD once we've raised some cash. But Pete can do the book-keeping to start with. Then we'll move him into an area more suited to his, er- unique skill set."

"I actually worked in the bookies' in Romford for a while," said Pete. "Little known fact. School of hard knocks that, let me tell ya'!"

"Really? OK, great- don't mention that, V," I said. "Now- are we ready to rumble?"

Veronica looked anxiously at the bar of the coffee shop.

"Perhaps I should just have one more coffee before we go?"

"Hmm, I don't think that's a good idea, V. You just need a bit of chairperson-like calm and gravitas now."

Even without the extra caffeine hit, she was shaking visibly as we left the coffee shop and headed across King Street to the bank on Cheapside.

"Right, I'm out of here," said Pete. "I'll cover for you in the office, V. Give 'em hell guys! Break a friggin' leg!"

"Ready, V?" I asked.

She nodded and took a deep breath, and we went into bat. Actually that might be overstating the urgency and immediacy of the whole banking experience a little, because it certainly wasn't like walking into the board room for the Project Behemoth closing meeting. That had only been a few blocks away from Cheapside, but it felt like a world apart. This time we had to queue up at the cashiers' desk in the branch for ten minutes, before we were able to make it clear that we were there for a meeting with the Small Corporates Manager about a business loan. Finally however, we were ushered into a characterless meeting room with a ceiling almost as low as the 'Standards' section, and overhead projectors suspended virtually at shoulder-height. I wondered where they kept the signing pens. Maybe there was a troupe of attendants waiting to bring them in ceremonially, if we somehow managed to get the green light for the deal.

That was when Veronica swung into action, and grabbed the situation by the scruff of its neck. She strode into the meeting room, brushing past the proffered hands of the bank manager and his henchperson, and sat down at the head of the table. This was evidently already occupied by their notebooks and pens, so she scattered these with a deft back-handed swipe and spread out her own papers. Nigel approached, slightly disconcerted, and moved his stationery to a discreet distance away from her. I looked at

Monika next to me. She looked a lot more worried than Veronica. In fact, she looked exactly how I felt.

"What's going on?" she whispered. "What's got into her? Did you tell her to do this?"

"Of course not!" I hissed back.

"Would you, er, like some coffee, Veronica?" asked Nigel.

"Mrs Andrews. And yes. Yes, I would. Black as night and sweet as sin."

He poured out some coffee with a shaking hand and ladled in some sugar, and she drained it, reached out for the pot herself and poured herself another cup. With the utmost deliberation, she poured in sugar and stirred it, whilst fixing him with her gaze. Then she leaned forward towards him, and gestured him forward. He tried to ignore the gesture, but she was clearly not going to break the deadlock until he moved closer to her. In fact I was starting to get worried that she was actually going to grab his tie and pull him closer. Finally he gave in to the inevitable, and edged closer with the utmost reluctance. Then she repeated the exercise with his colleague. The seconds were passing like hours. Once they were both sitting there, totally focussed on her, with no alternative but to hang on every word, she finally started speaking- slowly and intensely.

"Now don't fuck with me, fellas, this ain't my first time at the rodeo."

"I can assure you, Mrs Andrews, we have absolutely no intention of…"

Veronica slapped him on the back jovially.

"Say no more about it, Nigel, I just wanted to set the tone. Put down some ground rules. Boundaries. We want to do business with you. But we also want to do it our *own* way. That's very important to us." She leaned forward again. "Very important."

Nigel exchanged a glance with his colleague.

"Can we just have one minute to confer, Nigel?" I asked him. "There are a couple of figures on our business plan that I just need to run by Veronica before we get into the, er, nitty-gritty."

"No problem at all!" he said eagerly. "Just let Sandra know when you're ready for us to come back in."

They scarpered in double-time. As soon as they were gone, I leaned across to Veronica.

"Now, V, please don't take this as criticism- or at least not as destructive criticism- but I think we need to change tack a little. I know this isn't a familiar environment for you, but the whole dominatrix thing is sending out completely the wrong messages. Non-lending messages. Kind of panic signals to the brain. It's like dealing with a schizophrenic in here. These guys must feel like they've wandered onto the set of *The Shining*!"

"And the swearing- it may be best to cut down the swearing. I don't think he liked the swearing," said Monika nervously.

"To be fair, I think there was only one actual incidence of swearing- but it really stayed with us," I said.

"Oh, I'm so sorry!" said Veronica. "All I wanted was to seem, you know, business-like!"

"I know, I know. And you're doing brilliantly, V. I just wanted to get the meeting back on track, OK? Absolutely no harm done."

Veronica nodded.

"So shall we get them back in?"

"Absolutely. And I will be as nice as pie, Matthew- just wait and see."

Monika squeezed Veronica's hand, as I tried to rouse Sandra the receptionist sufficiently to call the bank manager back in. Eventually she deigned to put through a call, and he approached the meeting room cautiously.

"I'm, er, I'm sorry about before, Nigel," said Veronica. "I just feel so very passionately about this business plan!"

"No problem at all, Mrs Andrews," he said, as he sat back down at the table. "But before we get started again, I must just ask you how your first time at the rodeo went? Did anyone, er, fuck with you on that occasion?"

V blushed demurely.

"They tried, Nigel, believe me, they tried! And that's one of the reasons that I've put together this all-star management team for this project. To protect me- and all of our other investors. So without further ado, I'd like to ask Matthew, our Chief Executive, to take us through the detail on the financing proposition."

"Thanks, Veronica! So, guys, I'd like you to think of this as 'YouTube on TV'..."

"Can I- can I take you back a step please, Matthew?" said the bank manager. "Now what exactly is 'You Tube'? It sounds rather rude!"

"Right- OK- that's OK- that was just the elevator pitch. We've got more detail on exactly what we do in the business plan. But YouTube, you know, it's a video-sharing web-site owned by Google. Users can post their own video clips- home videos, cute pets, infomercials, independent movies- any self-created content."

"Ah yes- I know all about Google, of course, of course! That's what people use to find things on the internet when 'Ask Jeeves' is busy, isn't it?"

"Really? I don't think many people do that... But yes, that's definitely the concept. Anyway, you can see that we've set out here in the business plan what our key revenue streams will be..."

We walked through them. It was increasingly clear that Nigel had no clue whatsoever about social media, why we wanted to do this or how it could possibly make any money. But even so, he knew more than enough to expose some pretty gaping holes in our strategy.

"There is one thing I would like to understand a bit better- just on the management side, Matthew," said Nigel. "And that's the amount of, ha ha, independent cable TV experience in the management team? As I understand it, Mrs Andrews, you will be a non-executive director, and so not involved in the day-to-day running of the channel?"

"Oh, good God no! I mean, no, I will be leaving that side of things to the management team," said V.

"Right- and Ms Antoniak, you have a lot of experience in television production, but for a major TV station in Poland. Whilst Matthew here has only recently gone through a, er, career change- from working at a law firm. And Mr Staines has some experience, at a relatively junior level, in the Content Standards team at Ofcable. So doesn't that leave you a little, how can I put it, light, on actual UK cable TV experience? Especially in a small channel, where cash flow will clearly be tight to say the least... Won't the equity investors be expecting to see a little more grey hair- a few war stories, you know- on the cable side of things?"

"What kind of, er, what kind of equity investment would you be expecting to see going into the business, Nigel?" I asked.

"Of course we'll get back to you with the details on that, if we are able to put together a term sheet for you to take this loan proposal forward. But in the current climate, the, ha ha, 'Credit Crunch', you understand, you can imagine that our internal credit committee is being very exacting as to the terms of the loans that we can advance!"

"Oh, of course, I'm sure they're just being jolly careful with all our hard-earned tax-payers' money!" said V sweetly.

"Absolutely, absolutely... Well, as you can imagine, if there aren't sufficient assets to be provided as security for the loan, with something to spare in case they lose value- and the business plan obviously suggests that there won't be- then that gap will need to be filled with equity capital from the, ha ha, from the backers of the project."

"So to put it another way- real money?" I asked.

"Yes- definitely real money. First risk money, of course. We'll certainly want to make sure that someone else has plenty of, ha ha, skin in the game..."

"Of course, of course, we always understood that. And we're exploring a number of promising avenues to raise that equity as we speak- virtually as we speak," I said, as Monika kicked me under the table.

"So the equity won't be coming from management's personal resources then?" said Nigel.

"Er- no. External finance."

"Who exactly do you have lined up as equity backers, out of interest? We deal with almost of all of the leading venture capital houses here. If you let me know who you're speaking to about the VC, we can obviously keep them in the loop on the debt side. No problem at all."

"Oh, great, great... As it happens this is actually more likely to be private investors- high net worth individuals from our network in the City. Family offices. Business Angels. You know the drill!"

"Of course, of course!" said Nigel. "It all sounds very exciting. I'm sure it's all, ah, coming together very nicely indeed."

"You bet. So you think we need to look again at our, er, 'bench strength' on the cable side?"

Nigel cleared his throat.

"I think it's essential, to be honest, Matthew. I'm just not sure the team is, ha ha, remotely credible as currently constituted. I'm not an expert in the, er, media world, but I would have thought that you do need someone who knows what they're talking about in the cable market."

"OK, thanks, it's helpful to understand that- because we have been kicking around one other idea. We haven't come to a complete landing on this yet, as a team, but our boss in 'Standards'- Colin Stebbins- is a real expert in the field. He has years of experience in cable, right, Veronica?"

"Colin? He has, er, he certainly has worked in cable TV for a long time, if that's what you mean…"

"Sounds perfect!" said Nigel. "So can we add him to the business plan? I think that would make the credit committee look rather more favourably on the application! Especially as we would need formal confirmation from Ofcable and Ofmedia- as your dual regulators- that the channel is in good regulatory standing. As a condition precedent to advancing the funds, you understand. A mere formality, I'm sure."

"That should be fine… We'll tie up the, er, final loose ends with Colin."

This time I ignored Monika's kicks- and Veronica's startled glance.

"Well, thank you so much for coming in and working through this, er, fascinating proposal with us, Mrs Andrews! We'll be in touch just as soon as we can discuss it with our credit committee. Though I must warn you that in this, ha ha, 'Credit Crunch-ed' world, the credit committee… Well, you know…"

We all stood up and shook hands cordially.

"Please do feel free to contact me if you have any more questions!" I said.

"About what?" said Nigel.

"You know, about this project we hope to work with you on."

"Oh, that, of course, of course! Yes, we'll be in touch just as soon as we can! Sandra will show you out…"

———

Chapter 10

Holborn, London, 5 December 2008

I've always been fascinated by that scene in *Bleak House* where the monstrous Krook, collector of a suffocating morass of legal documents spewed out by the Court of Chancery, is burnt alive in a spontaneous human combustion- consumed from within by the legal system's putrid moral corruption. That was on Cursitor Street, just round the corner from our court- or, to be more precise, the Upper Tribunal (Immigration and Asylum Chamber)- so hopefully Katinka had skipped that chapter. Maybe she would have wondered what all the fuss was about anyway when, half a mile away, the whole City of London was still going up in flames. I was guessing that fire would take a lot longer to burn out than Mr Krook's brimstone-infused, booze-kindled carcass. In any event, Monika and Katinka were already waiting nervously outside the Tribunal at Bream's Buildings when I got there.

Field House is actually a modern building, indistinguishable from the glass and steel fortresses of the innumerable law firms clustered together throughout the legal district, but the whole area is so imbued with the fearful majesty, battlements and quadrangles of the Royal Courts of Justice and Inns of Court that it might as well be medieval. To me it felt like- well, like justice- but then they say that the British are always soothed by tradition. After her recent experiences in the English legal system, I wasn't sure that Katinka would feel quite the same way.

"Alright? How did you sleep?" I asked Katinka.

Whatever she said was drowned out by the roar of a slightly dated BMW screeching down the narrow street and pulling up, with the merest suspicion of gangster parking, outside Field House.

"Matthew! Monika! How are you, my friends?" boomed Kostas, leaning out of the driver's window and carelessly tossing the end of his cigarette onto the pristine steps of the Tribunal.

"And you must be the client," he said, stepping out onto the pavement and holding his hand out to Katinka. "*Enchanté, mademoiselle!*"

"Hey, thanks for coming along, Kostas," I said. "But I really don't think you can just leave your car outside here, can you?"

"Relax, Matty-boy, relax! Didn't I tell you that I'm, what can I say, acquainted with one of the court clerks here? No parking tickets for Kostas on this street, my friends! This is a bona fide emergency…"

He gave us an extravagant wink and led us through the automatic doors into Field House. "Lorraine!" he exclaimed, as we walked into reception. "Lorraine! Lovely Lady Lorraine! How are you this sunny mornin', my darlin'? I've been searchin' for you everywhere under the sun, let me tell you!"

The receptionist blushed and flapped at him with a piece of paper.

"Oh, hello, Kostas- we all know who you're really here to see…"

"You know that's not true, Lovely Lorraine," said Kostas with a winning smile, "I'm just usin' her to get to you... But don't tell her, she must never, ever know!"

"I can't believe this works!" I muttered to Monika.

"I don't think it would work very well for you..."

"I'll tell her you're here, Kostas," said the receptionist, "that'll bring her right down, I'm sure!"

"Tell her to leave it a few minutes- jus' so's you and I can have some quality time together first!" said Kostas, sliding his arm across the reception counter. He drew it back quickly though, as almost instantly an elaborately made-up woman in her late twenties or early thirties appeared, with a tight pony-tail, slightly over-sized glasses and clutching a pink 'Hello Kitty' clip-board. She obviously knew Kostas too well to leave him languishing in reception for long.

"Cathy! I jus' had to come and see you, darlin'," said Kostas, stepping forward to take her hand, and artfully giving her a peck on the cheek as he did so.

"Not in front of the appellants, Kostas, not in front of the appellants!" said Cathy indulgently. She consulted her clip-board, and turned to Monika and Katinka.

"Ms Kovalenko? One of you two, I suppose!"

Katinka stared back at her blankly.

"That's her," explained Monika. "I'm her McKenzie friend."

"Lovely, lovely. Well, good morning, Ms Kovalenko and her McKenzie friend!" She consulted her clip-board again. "So Kostas- Mr Alexandrou here- isn't representing you today, then?"

"No," said Katinka.

"Oh- that *is* a pity..." said Cathy.

"I'm just the co-pilot today, Cathy, darlin'," said Kostas. "Any excuse to see your beautiful face again! My good friend and colleague Mr Verreaux here will be doing the honours on the legals. Very clever man, believe you me."

"Well, tickety-boo from a clerical perspective," said Cathy, "because that's the name I've got on my list. But I don't think we've ever seen you here before, have we, Mr Verreaux? I never forget a face! Do much Tribunal work, do you?"

"Er, no," I admitted.

"Whereas Kostas is a very familiar face here, aren't you Kostas? One of our favourite solicitors, we all like to say. Well, anyway, we do have two lovely judges sitting for us today, Senior Immigration Judge Gittins and Senior Immigration Judge Holland, so I'm sure that everything will work out just fine. And your Home Office Presenting Officer today will be Mr Makepiece."

"Gittins!" said Kostas, under his breath. "*Bastarde!*"

"Is that a problem?" asked Monika.

"No problem, no problem," said Kostas, with an unusually unconvincing smile. "Nothing to worry about. Matty-boy here will have him eating out of his hands, you'll see!" He leaned forward to whisper to Cathy, "Maybe I'll sit at the back today, darlin'..."

"Righty-ho, shall we go through to the waiting room then, peeps?" said Cathy. "You can find complimentary water and, er, water- in there. Kostas, 'course you can just ask Lorraine if you'd like a cuppa'... There's a fire exit at the rear of the room. In the event of power failure, emergency lighting will come on to show you the way to it. But really you can just following the lawyers stampeding for the exit- that's what people tend to do whenever we have a drill! And I'll be right back for you, just as soon as the judges are ready for you."

"How long do you think that will be?" asked Monika.

"Well, I'm not exactly sure this morning," said Cathy. "There are some really rather miffed Gurkhas in today, I'm afraid. That

Joanna Lumley has been whipping them up into a right frenzy. It's a very good cause, I must say, and she's a very charismatic lady by all accounts. The judges just don't know what to make of it though, because the law's the law, really, isn't it? Anyway, I'll be back as soon as I can!"

Kostas gave her a languishing look as she went out.

"So- are we going to be up against it in there?" I asked Kostas.

He held his hand out and tilted it to and fro.

"Oh my God, that Gittins… He's a real bastard, my friend- an intellectual, the worst kind, what can I tell you?"

"Yeah, I guessed that from your '*bastarde*' comment…"

"Ah, you speak Greek? Anyway, right, that's not so good for us, 'course. But Holland, him I know fairly well, I can do business with him. He heard one of my greatest ever Gangmasters cases!"

"And you won it?"

"Like I said, it was a Gangmasters case, my friend! And not to blow my own trumpets, I don't lose on the Gangmasters. Johnnie Cochran for murder trials, Kostas for Gangmasters. If OJ Simpson had been up for runnin' a gang of winklepickers on the Ribble Estuary beat, I'm the one he would have called, you know what I mean?"

"Yes, but what does all this *Ghostbusters* stuff mean for my case?" asked Katinka.

"Yeah, Kostas, what does it mean?" I said. "Are we in with a fighting chance with Holland, or what?"

"You've always got a chance in a two-horse race, my friend. And Makepiece is no ball-breaker. He'll always settle for a draw, if you know what I mean?"

I didn't get the chance to find out, because just then Cathy bustled back in.

"Right, you're on! Those Gurkhas are out already."

"Of court? Or the country?" I asked.

"Well, both, I suppose. Sad, really- that brave gentleman risked his life for this country. But, rather unfortunately, one of his sponsors did wave a dirty great knife at Mr Makepiece right in the middle of his submissions. And after he'd worked so hard on them, with all the press being in today! He's still having palpitations now, he's a very excitable man, Mr Makepiece is. Says he's had all the stuffing knocked out of him by it. So I told him he was just lucky not to have been carved first! That Joanna Lumley has got a lot to answer for, I must say. But come on, shake a leg, now, chop chop! Judge Gittins is in a fearful bait already, I'm afraid. Says he'll have Joanna up for contempt, but I'm really not sure that would be the ticket at all. Still, it'd be lovely to see her in here, I did enjoy *Ab Fab*, didn't you? P'raps Jennifer Saunders could be her sponsor. I don't think our judges would take Jane Horrocks seriously, to be quite honest. That Bubble, she did make me laugh though!"

"I don't think Joanna Lumley would need a sponsor," I said. "She is English, you know."

"Oh, I thought I'd read somewhere that her father was an officer in the Gurkhas! Where are you from yourself, Mr Verreaux? New Zealand?"

"I'm from this country too!"

"Oh, are you really? Never mind that now, though, come along, come along..."

She ushered us into one of the Tribunal's hearing rooms. There were a handful of spectators, presumably Nepalis, sitting at the back of the public gallery, two of them holding up a small banner with an extremely badly photocopied picture of Joanna Lumley on it. It must have been from an old *Radio Times* or something, because you could just about make out that she was clutching a bottle of

Bollinger and a very long cigarette. Katinka held her fist up to them, in the international gesture of solidarity.

"Are they really supposed to be here?" I asked Cathy.

"Well, the Tribunal is open to the general public, so as long as they don't have any more of them carving knives with them, it should be absolutely fine, I would have thought. Lord knows why they're interested in Ms Kovalenko's tribunal though, they certainly don't look Ukrainian to me. Perhaps they got here a bit late, and they don't realise that Mr Gurung has already been and gone. Still, best not to rile them up any more than we need to, I suppose. We should probably just keep *schtum* about that, and I'm sure they won't bother you or your client, Mr Verreaux. True Britons, I call them…"

We sat down.

"I'll be off now," whispered Cathy, "But have a lovely hearing, and I'll be back for you once you're all done, and the judges have beetled off to make their cups of tea! Oh, and reach their decision too, of course."

"Well, Mr Verreaux," said one of the judges, "We have had the opportunity to review the appellant's painfully detailed- if rudimentary- written grounds for reconsideration of the Immigration Judge's decision at the First Tier Tribunal. Is there anything that you would like to add or amplify before this- Upper Tribunal- hearing?"

I looked at Katinka. She was staring blankly at the judge. He was a small, pugnacious-looking man with white hair and alarmingly bushy black eye-brows. Katinka gave the impression that she didn't understand a word he was saying. Still, she already had her points for acceptable English language ability under the Points-Based System, and no one could take those away from her now.

I looked back at Kostas. He mouthed "Gittins! Intellectual *bastarde!*"

"Thank you, Sir- Sirs. Is that the plural?"

"Sir will suffice, Mr Verreaux," said Gittins.

"OK, thanks. The first thing to say is that, in the circumstances, it's really not surprising that the Immigration Judge got it wrong, and we're certainly not criticising him for that."

"That's a very gracious concession, Mr Verreaux," said Gittins dryly. "Please feel free to elaborate."

"Well, Sir, it was a bit unlucky for everyone that there was a change in the legal requirements for maintenance funds, slap bang in the middle of Katinka's appeal process. Some sort of misapplication of the transitional provisions was just an accident waiting to happen. Like when they introduced the automatic yellow card for taking your shirt off when celebrating scoring a goal. They made the change, it was publicised, but it still took a while for people to get to grips with it, and in the meantime quite a few players picked up needless bookings."

"You are referring to the 'Laws of the Game' of association football, Mr Verreaux? Is that really on all fours with the present case? Though I am no authority on those particular, hem hem, 'Laws', as I understand it, the change that you advert to was more in the nature of a permanent change to what jurisprudentially might be better described as 'rules' of the game, without a transitional regime in the strict legal sense of the term? And, as such, transgressions of that new rule by the players would perhaps be more accurately characterised as a demonstration of engrained behavioural patterns on their own part- or even ignorance of the then-prevailing rules, not directly referable to any deficiency in their publication by the sport's legislative body- rather than misapplication of a transitional regime by the officiating referees?"

This was starting to look like a tough gig.

"I take your point, Your Honour- Sir. Let that football analogy be struck from the record. But the point is, that the Immigration Judge mixed up the rules that were actually in force at the time of Katinka's application to the Home Office, with the rules that were subsequently in force by the time that she managed to submit the right bank statement to the First Tier Tribunal. Then he got confused about the evidence that he had to take into account in working out whether those requirements had been satisfied. Section 85(4) of the 2002 Act couldn't be clearer in saying that- hang on a second, Sir, I'll just read it out to you: 'On an appeal under sections 82(1), 83(2) or 83A(2) against a decision'- so that includes Katinka's appeal to the IJ, obviously- 'the Tribunal may consider evidence about any matter which it thinks relevant to the substance of the decision, including evidence which concerns a matter arising after the date of the decision'. So clearly the IJ should have taken account of the bank statement that was submitted after Katinka's Home Office application, but before her First Tier Tribunal hearing."

"But the IJ did take full account of the provisions of Section 85(4)- with which I am, it would appear, considerably more conversant than yourself- at the hearing though, didn't he, Mr Verreaux? Let me read the transcript from his decision back to you: 'I am only permitted by the Act to consider the relevant circumstances at the time of this hearing'."

"Yeah, he definitely said that, and that must be right, but how could that have led him to the conclusion he actually reached? The new bank statement had already been provided by the time of the appeal hearing, so he should have taken it into account- what could have been more relevant? But that's precisely what he then proceeded not to do! The words 'this hearing' clearly refers to the appeal to the IJ, not to the initial Home Office decision. And there's nothing in Section 85 that would freeze the evidence at the application stage, if we're talking about the same Act?"

"That, at least, is not in doubt, Mr Verreaux," said Gittins.

"Great! So with respect, and all of that, to the IJ, his statement at the hearing about Section 85(4) was not especially helpful- or even, you know, correct."

"But, Mr Verreaux, your submissions also depend on the requirement for evidence of the requisite funds under the transitional provisions in force at the date of the appellant's original application having been satisfied by the 'new bank statement', as you choose to characterise it (without, perhaps, great service to your client's case)- that is to say, the bank statement that was only submitted by the appellant prior to the First Tier Tribunal hearing?"

"That's right, Your Honour- but I don't think that's a problem for Katinka's case. Let me just read you the transitional wording in the Policy Guidance, because it isn't especially clear: 'Up to 31 October 2008, you do not have to show you have had the funds for at least three months before your application. You must only show you have the required funds at the time you apply. The types of documentary evidence you need to send to support your application are as described in this document. However, until 31 October 2008, they do not need to cover the three-month period, but they must be dated no more than a month before your application. For example, if you apply under Tier 1 (Post-Study Work) on 12 July, a single bank statement with a closing balance of £800 dated between 12 June and 12 July 2008 will meet the maintenance requirements. A bank statement dated before 12 June 2008 will not be acceptable.' Did you follow that?"

"Tolerably so, Mr Verreaux, you are perhaps confusing your own grasp of the facts with my own- relatively stronger- one."

"OK, so my reading of that is that all Katinka needed to do was prove that she had £800 on any one day during the month directly preceding her application. If that's right, then we have no problem, because she had £976.20 on 29 August 2008. But even if that's not right, and she actually had to have £800 or above for the entire period of one month directly preceding her application- and I really can't see how that's required…"

"But the IJ- as an immigration law professional- could see how it was required, could he not, Mr Verreaux? Because he said 'the clear policy behind the Rules is that applicants must prove to the satisfaction of the Secretary of State that they are adequately financially self-sufficient. This self-sufficiency would hardly be satisfied by evidence that, on any one given day only, a sum of £800 was held by the applicant, if thereafter that sum was no longer maintained by the applicant'."

"With respect, Sir, it wasn't the IJ's job to decide what the Rules should have been, only what they were. But, like I say, even if he was right, and Katinka had to have over £800 for the whole month- which he wasn't, and she didn't have to- then we can still get there using the bank statement that was submitted prior to the First Tier Tribunal hearing. It covered 29 August to 29 September 2008, and it showed a closing balance of over £800 the whole time during the period of the statement. Four-square within the Policy Guidance. We've already discussed why Section 85(4) required the IJ to take account of that statement, but to be honest it would only have been basic fairness, natural justice, for the IJ to do so anyway, even in the absence of Section 85(4)."

"How so, Mr Verreaux? Do you imagine yourself to be in a court room of the United States of America- a jurisdiction, or to be more precise, assortment of jurisdictions not even falling within Her Majesty's Commonwealth of Nations- constructing emotive, rabble-rousing appeals to abstract principles of justice, for the benefit of a susceptible and hand-picked jury?"

"No, Sir. But you and I both know, Sir, how banks work. Initially Katinka could only get her bank to issue a statement from 4 August to 25 August 2008, despite repeated requests for the single, up-to-date statement that would save her from expulsion and keep her in the country. The bank were unmoved by phone-calls, emails and even branch visits. On each occasion they indicated that the means of communication that she was not then deploying to obtain the required information was in fact the only way to secure such a statement."

"What you might call a 'Catch-22' situation, Mr Verreaux? To coin a colloquialism conceived by the late Mr Joseph Heller in the eponymous novel. Hmm, well it is true that even customers of, dare I say, considerably greater substance than your client appears to have had, cannot invariably count on the timeous co-operation of the clearing banks," said Gittins.

"Very true, Sir. Who knows what bizarre internal procedures led them to choose the dates of Katinka's original bank statement? It cannot be right that the National Colonial Bank's own fetishes and foibles should be allowed to determine whether bona fide Tier 1 applicants get leave to remain in the country or not. Otherwise the bank, not Parliament or the elected government, is in effect determining the practical course of immigration policy in this country. To put such power in the unaccountable hands of a private sector corporation…"

"Albeit one now largely owned by the British taxpayer, Mr Verreaux?" said Gittins.

"Indeed, Sir- but hardly a democratic institution. Well, Sir, to vest such power in a bank would be to create a Kafka-esque nightmare in which…"

"Alright, alright, Mr Verreaux, you've made your point. Although in any event I utterly fail to see the relevance of Herr Kafka's writing to the case at hand. He, as you may or may not be aware, was writing of the condition of the rule of law in a land far less happy than our own- to wit, the Bohemian province of the former, and largely unlamented, Austro-Hungarian Empire."

"Indeed, Sir, though I believe that there are more universal messages that should be taken from his work. It's also worth bearing in mind what František Palacký observed on the subject, Sir: 'If there were no Austria, we would have to create it.'"

"We're obliged to you for your submissions, Mr Verreaux- both legal and Austro-Slavic. Mr Makepiece, have you any submissions to make on behalf of the Secretary of State for the Home Department as respondent hereto?"

Makepiece dragged himself to his feet. A tall, anxious-looking man with a pronounced thousand-yard stare, he looked visibly shaken by the Gurkha incident.

"Judge Gittins, Judge Holland, the Home Office notes Mr Verreaux's submissions. Accordingly, the IJ's alleged misunderstanding of Section 85(4) is not disputed by the respondent, and the Home Office can accept that if the relevant date to determine satisfaction by the appellant of the maintenance funds requirement was indeed the date of the First Tier Tribunal hearing, then the appellant should have been given points under Appendix C."

"You accept that, Mr Makepiece?" said Gittins. "Are you satisfied that you have recovered fully from your brush with the Nepalese *kukri* earlier this morning?"

"*Kukri*! *Ayo Gorkhali*! *Ayo Gorkhali*!" shouted the Nepalis from the back of the room, suddenly animated by their ancient war cry.

Makepiece uttered a silent shriek, and slumped back down into his chair, clutching at his heart.

"Silence in Tribunal! Silence there, sir!" barked Gittins. "This is not a Rudyard Kipling novel, sir! Mr Makepiece, pray resume your submissions- you are quite safe in my Tribunal hearing room."

"Yes, Sir. Thank you, Sir," said Makepiece. He looked nervously back at the Nepalis, but rose gingerly to his feet again. "However, my, er, my submission for the respondent is that paragraphs 245Z and 245AA of the Immigration Rules do make it perfectly clear that the relevant date for deciding whether an applicant met the maintenance funds requirement or not was in fact the date of application, not the date of decision or date of hearing. If you will indulge me, Sir, paragraph 245Z(e) provides that 'to qualify for leave to remain as a Tier 1 (Post-Study Work) Migrant, an applicant must meet the requirements listed below', which includes a requirement under sub-paragraph (e) that the applicant has a minimum of 10 points under paragraphs 1 to 2 of Appendix C (dealing with maintenance), and goes on to provide that if the applicant does not meet these requirements, the application will be refused. Paragraph 245AA, Sir, specifically states that 'if the specified documents are not provided, the applicant will not meet the requirement for which the specified documents are required as evidence'. Or to put it another way, Sir, if the application fails at that stage, there is simply no discretion under the Rules to allow evidence to be produced post-application, whether before the First Tier Tribunal hearing or otherwise. If an applicant fails to get their application right, that's the end of that application, and it cannot be remedied on appeal. There is no valid application for the points to attach to. To use Mr Verreaux's own analogy, a, er, 'red card', Sir."

"Very well, Mr Makepiece," said Gittins. "You explain yourself with admirable clarity and, if I may be permitted the observation, a more seemly diction and address than we have thusfar been vouchsafed this morning by the other legal representative in attendance.

But in light of that analysis, and to follow it to its natural conclusion, when would Section 85(4) ever apply to make later evidence in favour of the appellant available to the Tribunal?"

"Never, Sir," said Makepiece. "The respondent's submission is that the purpose of Section 85(4) is to allow the Tribunal to take into account the fact that someone might have the requisite savings at the date of application, but not by the time of the hearing. Public policy requires that an applicant who subsequently becomes indigent not be given leave to remain under the points-based system."

"Do you have anything to add to this most pertinent line of reasoning, Mr Verreaux?" asked Gittins with relish.

"Sure... Well, Sir, I would like to know where Mr Makepiece is finding these words, because I certainly can't find them in the statute book. When I look at Section 85(4), it looks pretty wide- 'the Tribunal may consider evidence about any matter which it thinks relevant to the substance of the decision, including evidence which concerns a matter arising after the date of the decision'. These Immigration Rules- Rules 245Z and 245AA- are just to tell people what paperwork they have to put together. There's nothing in them precluding the application of the Tribunal's discretion to consider evidence that is submitted later. And if they really were found to limit the Section 85(4) discretion, well, Sir, that would irretrievably shift the balance of the constitutional system of the United Kingdom, in a way that might change life here for ever."

"Really, Mr Verreaux? That is a typically hyperbolic suggestion on your part, is it not?"

"The fact is, Sir, that the Nationality, Immigration and Asylum Act 2002 is an Act of Parliament. It reflects the sovereign will of the supreme legal authority in the United Kingdom, which can create or end any law..."

"I'm obliged to you for this most enlightening lecture in constitutional law, Mr Verreaux, but are you at least approaching a point?"

"Yes, Sir- as I say, the 2002 Act is primary legislation, in contrast to the Immigration Rules which, as Lord Hoffman so perspicaciously observed in *Odeola v Secretary of State for the Home Department*, are not even a form of subordinate legislation- just administrative regulations. They have the force of law, but they can never override primary legislation. That means that nothing in the Immigration Rules could have qualified the IJ's Section 85(4) discretion to look at Katinka's new bank statement.

And if the Tribunal has that discretion, and valid evidence has been submitted after the Home Office decision, then the most basic natural justice requires that it exercise that discretion. The point is, Sir, that the Secretary of State didn't reject Katinka's application because it didn't meet all the requirements of the Immigration Rules. The decision clearly states that it was made under para 245Z(e) of the Immigration Rules- so the application was made, it was considered, but it was wrongly decided because Katinka wasn't awarded any points under Appendix C. If the Home Office wanted to complain about the paperwork, then that was clearly the time for the Secretary of State to say so. I don't know why she didn't- perhaps she regrets it now. It's Jacqui Smith, isn't it? But, Sir, we're dealing here with a question of substance- did Katinka have the funds required by law, or not? And when you look at it that way, it's really pretty simple: she did, she's proved it, and neither the Secretary of State, the IJ nor- with respect- you, Sir, should close your eyes to that proof."

"We are much obliged to you for your advice, Mr Verreaux..."

"What Mr Makepiece, nice though he otherwise seems, is saying is that unfavourable evidence can always be considered by the Tribunal, but that favourable evidence can never be. I submit, Sir, that it's perfectly obvious to all of us that that just isn't fair! I was taught at university that 'Equity is Equality', Sir. And that should apply whether the parties are Government ministries, or hard-working sleep therapists from the Ukraine. Mr Makepiece is right that the IJ could have looked at evidence that Katinka had lost all her money- well then, he should have looked at evidence that she had made it too, as part of an ongoing application for leave to remain in this country. Thank you, Sir."

"Thank you, thank you, Mr Verreaux, that's really quite sufficient for now. We are particularly obliged to you for your repeated musings on the philosophy of justice. As a Tribunal, we are accustomed to spend so much of our working hours concerned with the dry application of what happens to be the law of the land. However, if neither of you have any further submissions to make- and here I would ask Mr Verreaux to restrain his no doubt overwhelming impulse to make a tear-jerking closing summation- my colleague and I will adjourn to consider our decision. The court clerk will summon you all back in, once we have reached that."

We all filed out.

"Well done, Matthew!" said Monika. "That was really wonderful!"

Katinka looked as impassive as ever, but Kostas clapped me on the back.

"Yes, yes, nice one, my son! If I hadn't known better, I would honestly have thought you knew what you were talking about in there, believe me!"

"Thanks! How do you think it went?"

"There's no such thing as a dead cert in this game, my friend," said Kostas. "It's not like Gangmasters, with Kostas in your corner. But now she's got a real fighting chance, I can tell you that! You're still alive, Katinka, baby, you're still alive!"

Cathy came to collect us and take us back into the waiting room.

"Now, how was Judge Gittins?" she asked anxiously. "Because I've just been looking at his Judicial Feedback Forms from this morning, and they do not make for pretty reading! I mean- just look at this one!"

She held out a green A4 form, with five white text boxes for feedback to be inserted into. The reviewer had simply scrawled 'Die Judge Git!' in each section.

"That's not too bad, is it? He must have had that his whole life."

"But from Harold Jackman QC- arguably the leading immigration lawyer in the United Kingdom? And what about this one then?"

"Lumley Posse gonna' dick your hoes," I read. "Listen, Cathy, it's just an idea, but maybe you should just throw the crazy ones away? I can't believe this is the kind of feedback the Courts & Tribunals Services is really looking for?"

"Ooh, do you think so? Because the last thing we want is for Judge Gittins to see these- put him right off his deliberation, they would! I do hope he didn't see any of them on his way out."

"He did seem a little tetchy…" I said.

"Oh, that's just his way," said Cathy. "What you want to watch out for is more the, er, outbursts…"

We had barely settled down in the waiting room when my mobile phone started vibrating furiously. I ran outside to take it.

"Mr Verreaux? This is Nigel Thorne from HGF Bank. I wondered if we could have a word about the, er, Chatterbabe TV acquisition financing?"

"Sure. Hi, Nigel. Thanks for getting back to me. How did it go at credit committee?"

"There are a certain number of, ah, issues to discuss… Not all of them strictly speaking credit issues, in actual fact."

"Go on."

"What you have to understand is that HGF is- in principle- very keen to support you. Between us, this does tick a few boxes for us. It seems that we need to make some loans to small businesses, rather as a matter of urgency- the political pressure on the top brass is becoming overwhelming. And the bank is also trying to position itself as the, er, 'tech bank' of choice in the City. Which you can imagine is a bit of a leap for some of us older chaps…"

"I don't know, Nigel- you know all about Ask Jeeves…"

"Yes, that's exactly what I said! But back to Chatterbabe. There are three main conditions, so, in no particular order: The first thing- and this is nothing personal- is that you need to find a credible chairman. Chairperson. Admirable though she is, Mrs Andrews…"

"You didn't like the Joan Crawford thing?"

"Er- no. No, we didn't."

"OK. I think this will actually be a massive relief to her. I should never have put her in that position. She obviously wasn't comfortable with it. What's next?"

"Secondly, Chatterbabe is *not* a strong credit. We're going to need a big buffer of equity before we can get comfortable with your business plan."

"Which means?"

"Which means that we'll lend you two hundred and fifty grand, if you can raise one hundred of equity. Skin in the game, I like to call it!"

"A hundred grand! Is there any chance of tweaking that debt-to-equity ratio a little- to increase the debt part, I mean?"

"Absolutely none, Matthew. To be perfectly honest, lending money to a start-up cable TV channel is, ha ha, the last thing I want to be doing at this stage of my career. So I'm not going to be going out on any kind of limb for this business- if you understand me?"

"I think so."

"So how exactly is your fund-raising going? Are you going to be able to raise that kind of equity?"

"Well, the ink isn't dry just yet... But we do have something up our sleeves."

"You've got, ha ha, two weeks to pull the rabbit out of the hat, Mr Verreaux."

"Two weeks?"

"Call it fifteen days then. You assured me that you had realistic funding options. Time to pursue them."

"OK, OK. What's number 3 then?"

"Ah- our legal team happened to, er, put in a preliminary call to Ofcable this morning. Just as a matter of form. As I think I mentioned, they wanted to check that there were no regulatory issues."

"Should you really have done that, Nigel? We never gave you permission!"

"Legal got the, er, wrong end of the stick on that, timing-wise, I'm afraid! And anyway, Mr Stebbins is part of the management team, isn't he? So we can speak to him whenever we please. And it, ha ha, pleased us to call him today."

"OK- so did they speak to Colin then?"

"As it happens- no. We did try to get hold of Mr Stebbins, but as it turned out the call was actually taken by someone else. You know how these things are..."

"Go on."

"One Mr Thomas Taylor. And this Mr Taylor unfortunately informed my legal colleague that there is indeed a, ha ha, an ongoing investigation into Chatterbabe TV, that will oblige him to qualify significantly any assurances that he can give us concerning its relationship with Ofcable. Which in any case is soon to be subsumed into Ofmedia and cease to exist as an independent entity at all, as I understand his remarks. By all accounts Ofmedia has no reason to look kindly on this particular channel or, ha ha, any of you. Quite the contrary, if he was to be believed."

"Torquemada! What else did he say?"

"In fact he indicated that you and certain other members of the proposed Chatterbabe management team might potentially be, ha ha, involved in the investigation yourselves. As, well, as the subject of the investigation, rather than as the investigators, if you see what I mean? According to Mr Taylor, even Mr Stebbins is unlikely to be in a position of influence within Ofcable for very much longer."

"What! OK. Listen, there's been a serious mix-up here, Nigel. I'm not sure that Mr Taylor is really in a position to be making allegations of that nature. But let me straighten all this out at the Ofcable end. I'll be back in the office on Monday…"

"Not for long, from what I understand…"

"We'll see about that! But the one thing I would ask is that you keep the dialogue open with us on this? We will get there, and we're very keen to do the deal with HGF, believe me."

"I do believe you, Mr Verreaux, because I very much doubt that anyone else would lend you this money! I would just, ha ha, remind you that the offer period for your loan facility is only- I think we said fifteen days. And we still haven't seen any detailed plan for how you propose to put the equity in place. I certainly can't authorise any expenditure by the bank on legal fees or further due diligence until we have a satisfactory understanding of how that's going to work, built into a credible financial model. And I'm sure you appreciate that this issue with Ofcable, Ofmedia or whoever it might be is, ha ha, an absolute deal-breaker from the bank's perspective. We simply can't take the reputational risk of getting involved with a project that doesn't have the absolute backing of all applicable regulators."

"No, of course not. Totally understood. But we're on the case. I'll get back to you as soon as possible."

"Goodbye for now then, Mr Verreaux."

I staggered back into the waiting room.

"What happened? Was it the bank?" asked Monika.

"Er- yeah…"

"Quickly, quickly, everyone!" said Cathy. "We do not want to keep Judge Gittins waiting now, believe me! Oh, ah, Mr Verreaux, any idea where Kostas has got to?"

"No, sorry, Cathy- Monika?"

"He had, er, he had to go for an, uh, urgent client consultation, I think. A very important client- Miss Galina," she said meaningfully.

"Oh yes- that one's on a very tight deadline, Cathy," I said. "And very hush hush… A strictly need-to-know basis."

"Will it be an Upper Tribunal case, do you think?" Cathy asked excitedly. "That would be lovely!"

"Er, quite possibly. He couldn't go into much detail- client confidentiality issues- legal privilege… You know the form, Cathy!"

"Ooh, yes," she said. "Sounds awfully exciting! And lucky her getting Kostas! She's, er, she's not awfully pretty, is she?" she asked anxiously.

"Some people seem to think so…" said Monika darkly.

"Oh!" said Cathy. "Well, anyway, the judges are ready for you now."

"Do they seem in a lenient frame of mind?"

"Ooh, I really couldn't say, Mr Verreaux. Sometimes Judge Gittins does enjoy an expulsion after a day like this. Good luck to you though, darling!" she said to Katinka.

We filed back into the hearing room. For the first time, Judge Holland, who I had kind of forgotten about, made his presence felt.

"Hem hem. We will send a reasons statement to each of Ms Kovalenko and the Secretary of State within three working days of this hearing, in the form of a written statement stating the reasons for the following decision. In the meantime, our decision is as follows: For the reasons to be stated in full in that reasons statement, we find that as a result of Ms Kovalenko having applied for further leave to remain under the Tier 1 (Post-Study Work) scheme before 31 October 2008, her application clearly fell under the express transitional provisions set out in the version of the Policy Guidance applicable to that period. She therefore only had to produce one single bank statement dated at some date between 29 August 2008 and the date of her application on 29 September 2008, showing a closing balance of at least £800 for one or more days during that period, in order to be awarded 10 points under Appendix C."

"Yes!" shouted Monika.

"*Jai Mahakali! Ayo Gorkhali!*" shouted the Nepalis.

"Hem hem. It therefore falls to us to consider whether Ms Kovalenko had in fact complied with that requirement, as the bank statement she initially submitted only covered 4 August to 25 August, and it is not disputed that this was before the earliest possible date allowed, namely 29 August 2008. It is similarly not in dispute that, subsequent to her application and immediately prior to her hearing before the IJ on 3 November 2008, she had submitted a further bank statement covering the period from 29 August 2008 to 29 September 2008. Happily for Ms Kovalenko, this 'second statement' shows a closing balance of over £800 within the latter period. It is our finding that as a matter of natural justice Ms Kovalenko was entitled to expect the IJ to have acted under section 85(4) of the Nationality, Immigration and Asylum Act 2002, and to have taken this further evidence into account. Accordingly, the IJ's error of law, in concluding that Ms Kovalenko had to demonstrate that she held at least £800 for the entire period of one month preceding her actual application, was undeniably material. Since Ms Kovalenko had therefore demonstrably satisfied the transitional requirements for Maintenance (Funds) in full, the decision we must substitute for that of the IJ is to allow her appeal. Thank you."

The judges got up and walked out of the hearing room. Monika threw her arms around my neck.

"We did it! We did it!" she shouted. "I can't believe we did it! You're staying, Katinka! You're staying! Oh, thank you, thank you, Matthew!"

She kissed me, and this time I found myself kissing her back. It felt amazing, a rush of affection for her that finally seemed to be releasing me from the emotional paralysis of that night on Southwark Bridge.

"What are you two doing?" said Katinka.

"We did it, Katinka!" said Monika, letting go of me and hugging Katinka. "Let's go out and celebrate!"

"OK," said Katinka, putting her coat on.

"What did the bank manager say?" Monika asked me.

"First let's toast Katinka!" I said. "The bank manager conversation is hangover news, and the White Swan is just around the corner from here..."

Because that night was about Katinka. And there was something else I wanted to hold onto- something I wasn't even ready to discuss with Monika yet. For the first time the law had really meant something to me- something more than a job, or proud parents, or a trip to L.A., free jelly-beans and a mortgage.

"We did it!" I said. "We really did it!"

Chapter 11

Bankside, London, 8 December 2008

Colin was engrossed in sorting a huge pile of Stabilo Boss fluorescent markers into different colour groups, then testing them and sub-dividing them according to remaining ink reservoir. I knocked on the sliding-door, but he made me wait a while, before speaking without looking up.

"I do find that it's generally more efficient to manage highlighters centrally," he said. "A, er, command supply chain system, if you will. Not an easy job, but someone's got to do it. Takes a little dedication to do this- before anyone else has even arrived in the office on a Monday morning- takes a certain willingness to play for the team, if you follow me?"

"Definitely. But thanks- mine were all dried out."

"Indeed! Well, you will get your pro rata share of the depleted ones back too. That's only fair, you know. Should you return to the team at all, that is."

"Right. Listen, Colin, there's something I need to ask you, if this is a convenient moment?"

"No, Matthew, no it is not. Now it's my turn to speak to you. Oh, yes."

Now he was drumming his knuckles on his desk. Not very hard- he was too fundamentally cautious for that. But definitely firmly enough to indicate extreme irritation. Finally he spoke.

"When I brought you on board, Matthew," he said, "when I gave you important responsibilities in this team- it was because I trusted you implicitly. I believed that you shared my vision, my values. Our values, here in 'Standards'."

I bowed my head.

"Not all of them, perhaps," he continued. "I knew, of course, that we didn't see completely eye-to-eye on everything. The jumpers, for example- although I still genuinely believe that the colour-coding initiative is worth persisting with. But I was happy to put differences like that behind me, if you were. To pull together for the greater good. To play for the team."

He tossed a document towards me. A termination letter? A compromise agreement? It missed my side of the desk completely, so Colin hopped up and bustled around behind me to pick it up. He placed it carefully in front of me.

"Well then, just imagine how I felt when I saw this!" said Colin.

I lifted it up. It was the latest edition of the *Being Ofcable* newsletter. I peered at it.

"When I asked you to run with our page of *BO*, it was because I wanted you to have the chance to express yourself- the opportunity that you had always craved in the City. With you studying English and all that. And this? This is how you repay me?"

"Isn't this the one with your profile in it, Colin?"

"Correct. Turn to page 6."

"OK, Colin, but all I did was jot down the responses to the standard *BO* profile questions that you dictated to me! And I think you even came up with the questions yourself, didn't you?"

"That I dictated to you!" spat Colin. "You think I dictated this- this filth? Look at this- just look at it: 'Who is your all-time hero?'"

"Oh yeah- nice one, intriguing choice there, Colin. I actually thought you were going to go for Arnie or something. You really surprised me, I must say."

"Jean Nicolas Arthur Rimbaud!" spluttered Colin. "A French…"

"Legend?" I suggested.

"Nancy boy, Matthew!" he said, shaking with emotion. "You think a French nancy boy is my hero? Because now, that's precisely what all of Ofcable does think!"

"That certainly isn't how I'd describe him, Colin," I said. "But yeah, that's what you told me. Jean Rimbaud."

"I told you John Rambo, Matthew! First Blood! 'To survive war, you have to become war'!"

"Hey, I'm really sorry, Colin," I said. "I'm sorry for any professional embarrassment I may inadvertently have caused you by including a famous poet and novelist as your hero, rather than a fictional drifter and disillusioned war veteran…"

Colin held out his hand.

"Apology accepted, Matthew." We shook hands solemnly. "We'll say no more about it. But there is one piece of unfinished business. The Chatterbabe TV affair. You and your, er, little friend coming in here at the weekend…"

"Look, Colin, I'm, er, I'm really sorry about that too. I realise that it was a serious misjudgement. And that it hasn't helped things with the whole Ofmedia merger business either. It's just that, you know, I knew that I wasn't doing anything wrong, so I didn't think about how it would look. But I understand exactly what you mean- why you were so annoyed about it."

"As I always say, Matthew, it isn't good enough for Ofcable just to *be* impartial. It must *look* impartial too."

"Absolutely- I understand that now."

"Well then- for what it's worth with this, this Ofmedia Sword of Damocles hanging over our heads- welcome back on board, Matthew!"

"Thanks, Colin- it means a lot to me."

"Now what did you want to ask me about?" asked Colin.

"Ah- yes. How can I put this… Why did you opt for Rambo and not Cobra anyway, Colin? As your hero in that *BO* article we put together, I mean."

"Hmm… That is an interesting question. Are you putting together copy for the next edition of *BO*? I suppose I'd have to say that it's just a phase I'm going through at the moment…"

"Kind of anti-establishment? Edgy- rebellious?"

"You could say that. I'm not a, er, believer in rules for their own sake, you know- oh, no, no, no! I know when to cut loose. Take a few, er, chances."

"Well in that case, I've got a proposal for your consideration…"

"Not an indecent one, I hope!"

"Er- no. Colin, you're interested in cable TV, right?"

"You could say that, Matthew. I've devoted my adult life to it." He held up the fingers on both hands, and then quickly raised one hand again. "Fifteen years in cable regulation! Oh yes, you could say that."

"Well, what if I told you that we had an opportunity to buy our own cable channel- to turn it around and make a decent channel out of it? With you as the Head of Content?"

"But what about my work in 'Standards'? I've been a watchdog for longer than I care to recall, Matthew. I've, er, paid the cost to be the boss. It's asking a heck of a lot for an old gamekeeper to turn poacher now, you know!"

"Yeah, but that's sort of the point, Colin. The game's up for Ofcable. Torquemada and his mates at Ofmedia are stitching us up as we speak, but the truth is that- with or without them- our world would have changed forever, and quickly. We need to find a new place in it, while we have the chance. Because soon it simply won't be Ofcable any more- not as we know it."

"Oh, I know that we're all up for review, Matthew- but that's fine, we can reapply for our jobs, we've been through all this before- and we're still standing!"

"Not this time, Colin. This time it's an existential threat- Torquemada is plotting to get us all out. You know as well I do that it's them against us here. And he's been telling anyone who'll listen at Ofmedia that none of us are going to make the cut."

Colin stared at me in horror. "Not even…"

"No, Colin. Not even you. And that's the really unfair part about it, to be honest. Most of the rest of us are… Well, I probably deserve to be fired anyway, don't I? So, listen. The choice is to wait until, sooner or later, we're all on the scrap heap- or to go down fighting, trying to build a new TV channel that we can all believe in."

"Which, er- which channel did you have in mind, Matthew?" he asked.

There was no easy way to say this.

"As it happens, it's actually, ah, it's actually Chatterbabe TV," I said.

Colin stared at me, aghast. Then he started laughing.

"Matthew! You really had me going for a moment there! Chatterbabe, indeed! They're one of the worst of the lot…"

"They're not really though, are they, Colin? They never put a foot wrong. I think that's part of the problem here. Now all of these channels have got their own compliance sorted out, no one really needs 'Standards' any more. And there aren't actually all that many channels in this space any more, anyway. It's all done in Internet chat-rooms. They've moved on with the times, and we need to do the same."

"Move into Broadband Roll-Out, you mean?" said Colin. "BRO?"

"I'm not sure about that- BRO makes the NHS look under-staffed," I said. "Any more people there, and they'll have more employees than there are UK broadband users."

"Then what?" said Colin plaintively.

"Like I say, we stay in cable. And you would even be staying in the standards business, in your new role as Head of Content. What better position to monitor standards from? It's like a new generation of regulation. Proactive. Pervasive. Perfect."

"PPP," murmured Colin to himself. "But why me? Why do you need me?"

"Quite simply, Colin, it's those fifteen years in the cable business that you were just talking about. We need to tap into that. And the bank also, er, need to see someone with a bit of experience in the industry on board."

"Why?" Colin asked. "Who else do you have on board? Lord Grade? Alan Yentob? Melvyn Bragg?"

"Same energy, more youth," I said. "Tomorrow's media moguls. Me. Pete…"

"From 'Standards'?"

"Yep- Team Cobra!" I said. "Plus Monika from Chatterbabe TV. And Katinka- she's the free-lance sleep therapist who was getting chucked out of the country."

"The one who looks like a sheep?"

"Er- yes."

"Anyone else?"

"Yep, at the bank's suggestion I'm also currently interviewing for a new chairman of the board. And I think I've lined up the perfect man for the job. A real City heavyweight. Laden with gravitas."

Colin sucked his teeth.

"I'm just not sure about all this... It seems a bit too much of a conflict of interest. Sometimes you have to apply the smell-test. And I'm really not sure about this one..."

"Oh, come on, Colin," I said. "There's no conflict of interest. We were regulating them. Then we step down from that- which may or may not involved being made redundant first. We buy them. Someone else regulates them." Colin stiffened at that, but he had to hear this. "There's no conflict. Everyone's happy. And just imagine it, Colin- we'll have moved from regulation into production: really living the dream! Picture the scene: Tomás de Torquemada, gloating over having taken over Ofcable, desperate to get a really big cable bust to prove himself, and only too conscious that he's got some mighty big boots to fill. He'll be eating, drinking and sleeping standards enforcement, scanning the cable horizon like an implacable hawk, but he'll have to watch our channel, day after day, putting out such impeccably high-standard content that he won't get so much as a sniff of a story in the *Cable Enforcement Bulletin*! Your content. Think about it, Colin- he'll be counting on Chatterbabe as a soft target to get the elusive first bust- but with you at the tiller, he just won't get a look in!"

Colin's eyes blazed. There was life in the old dog yet.

"Even if someone did have a lapse in judgment- and you can never rule out human error, especially with Pete on board- with you as 'the Cleaner', there wouldn't be a trace of smut by the time it hit the airwaves! That's why we need you. For the ultimate game of high stakes, cable cat-and-mouse- all wrapped into an epic battle between good and evil!"

"It's true!" he said, punching the air. "The perfect- unspoken- revenge. Just let him try to find a content breach in my, er, content!"

"That's the spirit!" I said. "Now there is just one thing…"

"What's that, Matthew?"

"Your first mission. As part of the team." I picked up one of the highlighters. "And we all know what a team-player you are, Colin! It's how we're going to raise the money to buy this new channel of ours. It's an, er, unorthodox plan, but it might just work. So let me explain exactly how you fit in…"

Chapter 12

Shoreditch, London, 10 December 2008

"Is that friggin' barbed wire?" said Pete. "Quite the Hitler's bunker theme they've got goin' on in here, innit? Shoulda' known from all them BNP posters on the community notice board!"

"I think you'll find it's actually tinsel, Peter," said Colin, sipping morosely at his pint of Stella. "A coarse strand tinsel, I grant you, but festive Christmas tinsel nonetheless. And- physically intimidated though I frankly am to be in a place like this- I have to tell you that the funereal décor is the least of my worries. Oh, the very least!"

"Hey, I know what you mean, man," said Carl. "I don't know if 'Wife Beater' is really the right beer to whet our, er, whistles for tonight's programme, Pedro? Kind of the wrong mind-set for when you're a-wooing going, isn't it? I'm going to need every detail in my preparation to be just right if I'm going to bring the, er, heat tonight, man."

"Well, I double-dare ya' to ask Lenny McLean behin' the bar there for a half of oh-so-light and refreshin' German *weissbier*, mate!" said Pete defensively. "You heard what he said when I asked him if he had Cobra Lager on tap. He'll have the rest of Combat

18 round here, beatin' *you* into a persistent vegetative state, before you have time to ask for a wafer-thin slice of lemon on top! Or even to think the word 'wooing'- which I definitely wouldn't recommend in here, by the way….."

"Not the beer, gentlemen," said Colin imploringly. "Oh, I'm not talking about the beer! Think of the bigger picture! Are we really- uh, is this *really* a good idea? I mean, there must be another way to raise the money, mustn't there? There's no shame in coming up with a different plan, is there? Plan 'C', if not Plan 'D' or indeed 'E'? No shame in that at all, I'd say! And did HGF Bank really unequivocally- irrevocably- say they weren't prepared to lend us the whole amount anyway? Would this not be a sensible time to appeal to their sense of decency- to throw ourselves on their mercy?"

Pete reached out to pat him on the shoulder empathetically, whilst simultaneously sliding another pint of Stella over the table towards him. Slightly too hard, so that Colin could only parry it awkwardly from going straight off the end of the table, and a mini-tsunami of lager sloshed out of the glass and cascaded over the untouchable acrylic of his cardigan onto his trousers.

"The thing is that there is shame in it though, Colin, mate! In throwin' the towel in. I don't- really- like this any more'n you do. But if we give up on it now, we'll always wonder what could've been. And let's face it- aintcha' seen Bobby Peston talkin' about banks on the Beeb lately? The boy is a friggin' broken record on the subject. HGF probably ain't good for all the wedge itself right now! Now, c'mon, Colin, you're a smooth operator, you could sell ice to the Inuit, right?"

Colin nodded slowly. I thought I could see burgeoning resignation in his eyes. Unfortunately that was the moment that Carl decided to give him a pep talk.

"No way, man, you're more the regulator type than a salesman- I'll bet you couldn't sell coke in the Priory!" he said encouragingly. "But don't worry, at this stage all you can really do is relax, get into character and put your faith in the, er, 'Method', man. A'ight?" Colin stared desperately back at him, ashen-faced. "Hey, what character have you developed for this gig anyway?" continued Carl.

"What? We need a character? I was going as myself, of course! Why, who are you going to be?"

Carl chuckled complacently.

"This is beautiful, man!" He slapped his leg. "Heh heh heh. You'll love this. A completely new persona…"

"C'mon then, mate, spit it out," said Pete.

"Ahem. Only Britain's greatest playwright."

"Andrew Lloyd Webber? He does love the laydeez…"

"No, man. Shakespeare!"

"Shakespeare? But he had a beard!" said Colin.

"An', of course, has been dead for approximately two thousand years…" added Pete.

"All of which occurred to me, man. Ergo- not William Shakespeare: 'Darren Shakespeare'. A direct descendant of the great man. In whom the name and, er, unquenchable spirit of the 'Swan of Avon' live on. Nickname…"

"… 'the Bard'?" I suggested.

Carl smirked.

"Forsooth and anon, man. Women love poets: Lord Byron, Oscar Wilde, Andrew Motion. The sonnets. The soliloquies. The 'exit, pursued by bear'. They just can't get enough of that shit. They'll be entranced. High on *my* supply- of Class A, er, chat."

I could tell that, in spite of himself, Pete was deeply impressed.

"Course you'd also be proper minted," he reflected. "Some of those shows've been runnin' for years. West End, Broadway,

Queen's Theatre Romford. They make *The Mousetrap* look like *Aspects of* friggin' *Love*. Would you be a direct relation, then? Collectin' royalties every Burns Night?"

Carl shrugged.

"I believe those works are mainly by the late, er, 'Rabbie' Burns, man. But as for my family tree- that won't be articulated. Ever-present, but unspoken. Part of the mystique, if you will. I definitely don't want to get lost in the detail. It could open me up to, er, inconvenient questions."

"Yeah, like: Were Shakespeare's plays actually written by Francis Bacon?" I said.

Carl blinked.

"Who?"

"OK, so it probably is best not to go into too much detail…"

"Right, I'm going into character now anyway, man," said Carl, holding his hand up with an air of finality. "Which way to the noisome privy, varlets?"

I got up too, but to get the next round of beers in. This was definitely no time for half measures. Colin's mojo had clearly left the building some time ago. He was still bogged down in the role-playing issue when I got back to the table with the pints.

"So do the rest of you chaps have characters too, then?" he asked. "Spurs legend Clive Allen as usual for you, Peter, I suppose? Hmm, a *nom de guerre*, eh…" He looked at me, eyes illuminated with sudden inspiration, then shook his head ruefully. "I'm not, ah, I'm not sure how appropriate Lieutenant Marion 'Cobra' Cobretti would be for me in this- in this, ah, particular format, Matthew?"

"No, that would probably work better if we were in the L.A. underworld of the early eighties," I said. "But listen, Colin, we're trying to get hold of some cash for the channel here, remember? You don't see door-to-door salesmen notching up the sales in false names, do you? The whole point is that we need to be able to pick up the cheques at the end. Could be tricky if they don't know what we're really called."

Colin shifted uncomfortably in his chair.

"What about Carl, then, Matthew- this new Darren Shakespeare persona of his?"

"Well, that's a little different. I think it probably is a good idea for Carl to have an assumed name. That should make it harder to trace him back to the rest of us."

"But what about the money he raises?"

I laughed.

"I hadn't really considered that- fucking remote- contingency. But to quote his great-Grandpa Willy, anyone who agrees to give that boy cash will clearly have eaten the insane root that takes the reason prisoner. To the extent that it probably doesn't matter what we tell them. We may as well claim that he actually is William Shakespeare."

Colin nodded earnestly.

"Sent from the past, to rewrite the future. Got you! So- for the avoidance of doubt- using my own name then?"

"Right..."

Carl returned from the toilet. He didn't look much different from before, except that he was now wearing a single hoop earring and a T-shirt with a huge hypodermic syringe emblazed on the front of it.

"'My Kingdom for Some Horse'," read Pete. "Nice one, mate. Elizabethan for real! But where's the cod-piece?"

"That's under my breeches, man," said Carl. "Where it always is."

"For now, mate, for now... Who's ready for another sharpener, then? My round, fellas. Same again, Col? Or are we ready to ratchet it up a level, eh?"

Colin groaned, and continued performing his own toilette with ever more demented intensity. This consisted of elaborate rearrangement of his thinning hair with an enormous tortoise-shell effect comb. Carl watched in fascination.

"Wow, parting really is such sweet sorrow tonight, man! Heh heh heh."

"What do you mean?" said Colin suspiciously.

"Nothing, Colin, he's just getting into character. Limbering up with a spot of the old *Romeo and Juliet*, you know?" I said. "Don't mess with his confidence!" I hissed at Carl. "Tonight- for one night only- he has to believe that he's irresistible to women."

Carl looked at me archly.

"Cupid is a knavish lad; thus to make poor females mad…"

"Oh, don't start with all that shit again, Bard."

Pete reappeared with a sticky-looking tray, every inch of available surface area covered in squat shot glasses.

"Vodka- completely odourless… The ladies won't even know what's hit 'em! Not until it's too late anyway, eh, Col? Right- down in one, fellas! Bottoms up!"

Mine went down alright, but it didn't do much for the butterflies in my stomach. They were just fluttering more erratically now. I took Pete to one side.

"Are we really going to do this, then?"

"What, mate? It's just a coupla' shots. Get with the programme, willya'?"

"Not that- tonight, I mean."

"Not you too? It was your idea, woznit?"

"Kind of…"

"Well then… C'mon, you're, what- thirty-six years old?"

"Twenty-seven!"

"Really? Twenty-seven?"

"Yes, Pete. Colin is thirty-six. And look at the state of him!"

"Well then, er, twenty-seven and never been kissed, young, free, single. The perfect candidate to speak to a few chatty, charmin'- minted- young ladies then, aintcha'?" He passed me another shot, gesturing at me to drink it. "Course we're gonna' do it. Biiig time we're gonna' do it. Why ever not, old chap?"

"Because it can't possibly work? Because we'll look like complete tools? Because..."

Pete laughed.

"Now I'm gonna' have to stop you there, mate... That's just an inherent risk for us in all male-female contact- don't be makin' *that* into some kinda' special quirk of financially-motivated speed-datin'. The way I look at it, we're actually de-riskin' the datin' part of this. It's like a built-in emotional hedge against sexual rejection, innit? Yes, our chivalric spirit may be questioned, yes, we might get knocked back once or twice, and yes, we might ultimately get slung out on our cabooses. But then we're not actually here to hit on the girls at all, are we? Just to raise some moolah for the business, remember? An' to follow your own analogy: does the superstar salesman top himself, just because he gets the door slammed in his face a few times?"

"Actually I think there is quite a high incidence of suicide amongst travelling salesmen."

"Yeah, man," interrupted Carl. "Didn't you see *Death of a Salesman*? I believe my, er, fellow man of the theatre, Mr Arthur Miller, would answer your question in the affirmative."

"An' no doubt so too would many of your fellow astronauts. But back in non-freak world, the answer to my question is 'Hell, no!' He dusts himself down, saddles up the executive edition Mondeo and then rides straight on to the next sale. Just exactly what we're gonna' do. Right, peeps?"

"Shakespeare, man, not Pepys," sniffed Carl reproachfully, and turned back to Colin. Pete put his hand on my shoulder.

"Listen, it's not really us gettin' KB-ed in there, see? Just think of your speed-datin' persona as a kinda' money-makin' avatar of yourself, if that helps?"

"Oh yes, very helpful. Except now it sounds like you really are going there to hit on the girls."

"Well aren't we all, mate, deep down? Just a little bit? I certainly hope I for one would never be so depraved as to put base lucre before lurve. If the right opportunity to combine the latter with our operational objectives were to present itself, of course."

"But in that case this brilliant 'emotional hedging' of yours isn't going to work too well, is it? It's actually more like two rejections for the price of one. Haven't you in fact buggered up the fund-raising and reaffirmed your lack of attractiveness to the opposite sex, in one fell swoop?"

Pete shook his head at this naivety.

"Swoop- is that the same thing as 'lunge'? The point is, mate, that none of the above applies if you just remember the golden rule at all times…"

He paused for effect.

"Oh, go on then…" I said.

"Jus' don't ever, ever admit that you're interested in romancin' the ladies!"

"Not even to yourself?"

"Partic'ly not to yourself." He slapped his forehead. "Obviously!"

"OK, thanks, Pete- I'm really glad we had a chance to talk this through. I feel so much better about the whole thing now."

"Great stuff! Now come on, sunshine, let's get this freak-show on the road! Before Colin loses it completely. Talk about big match nerves! That's the third time he's gone off to the khazi in the last half hour…"

"Do you think he's adding much value here anyway? The guy's a basket-case tonight."

"Oh, some girls like that, mate. 'Straitjacket chic', they call it. He's bringin' a bit of breadth to our offering. 'Cos it's gonna' be horses for courses in there, believe you me. There's no tellin' what might tickle their fancy. What dark corners of the female libido Colin may be called on to explore…"

I took a deep swig of my pint.

"Blimey!"

"Even the 'Bard of Avon Ladies' might have his own small part to play, before the long night is through…"

We watched Carl as he approached the bar and engaged the landlord in earnest conversation. After a while he held his pint-glass out towards him, apparently commenting on the contents. I just hoped it was complimentary. There was the etiquette of the situation to think of- and also the fact that this guy had three tear-drops crudely tattooed onto his face. Suddenly there was a roar from the bar.

"You're fackin' barred, son!"

"The Bard, man!" said Carl, with his best thespian enunciation. But I noticed that he didn't let this retort interrupt his swift retreat.

"Oh, no, no ya' don't… Don't you come this way!" hissed Pete. "What didya' say to him?" he asked Carl, as he loped up to us.

"Masters, spread yourselves!" said Carl, not breaking stride.

Some of the pub's most heavily-tattooed locals were getting up from their bar-stools now, and approaching us menacingly. In fact some of them seemed to be bringing the bar-stools with them. "OK, forget it- let's nash," said Pete. "Now, people, now, now, now!"

We bundled Carl out through the double doors, just as the first pint glass hit the wall beside them. It splintered against a tinsel-fringed photo of the Millwall Supporters' Club, group portrait, circa 1980. It looked like it had already taken a fair bit of punishment, but given that some of them seemed to be sporting surgical masks for the photo, maybe that was just the state of the Millwall supporters themselves. Sepia lager-soaked and lightly studded with broken glass.

"Oi- come back here, you fackin' wankers!" yelled the landlord. "You an' your so-called fackin' firm!"

"A pox on *your* house, man!" Carl shouted back, as the doors swung shut behind us and another pint glass crashed into them. "Bald-pated, sheep-biting rascal!" A cascade of broken glass tinkled down onto the pavement outside. "Exit, pursued by beer!"

"Just- stop- talkin'- willya'?" panted Pete. We were pegging it back down Shoreditch High Street towards Bishopsgate now, putting some clear water between us and the Third Reich. "No one's- safe- till we're in the City. No nutters- south of Commercial Street!"

"What?" I gasped.

"Them's- the rules! It's like- the Geneva Convention- innit? D-M-Zee, mate. I know that- they know that- an' you damn well- oughta'- know it too!"

"So- why- were we- north of it, then?"

"Jus' shut up- and run- we're nearly there!"

Even so, we didn't stop running until we got to the police station on Bishopsgate. Better safe than sorry- after all, Commercial Street is hardly the 38th Parallel. To my amazement Carl got there first, then doubled over, hands on spindly thighs, panting hard.

"Hey, er, cool your boots, man! I think we've lost them!"

Pete scanned the pavement behind us.

"Yeah, it can't be too easy to run in them 20-hole Doc Martens…"

"Especially when you're swinging a crowbar like that, man- that had to be some powerful, er, centrifugal force that thing was exerting. Doowwwn-force, man."

"Speaking of boots, Carl, what happened to your own, uh- eccentric footwear?" I asked.

There was something impressive in Carl's philosophical acceptance of the fact that he was standing in a grimy puddle in Central London, with nothing except slightly perforated, skin-coloured pop-socks on his feet. But then there was also something a little disturbing in it.

"Well I, er, I had to slip my sandals off back there, man. They were impeding my running style, if you know what I mean?"

"Who are you- Zola friggin' Budd?" said Pete.

"Did her shoes also turn out to be a couple of sizes too big when the cookie, er, crumbled, man? But I actually did hear that she got spiked once too. Like me at the staff Christmas party, Matt, you remember that?"

"Yeah, I do… I could be wrong, but I think in her case it was with running spikes- not pharmaceutical strychnine."

"Hey, I wasn't running too fast after that either, man, let me tell you!"

"No, you wouldn't have been- not when you were experiencing near-fatal muscle spasms. But like I told you at the time, Carl, there's no point crying over spilt milk, is there?"

I turned to Pete.

"And as for you, douche-bag- what's with taking us to the National Front Disco back there, anyway?"

"Just a bit of local colour, mate! The Kray twins used to drink in there, did I mention that?"

"A few times, yeah. Their unquenchable spirit lives on too, clearly."

"Plus, Colin does my nut in with his penchant for the Pitcha' and friggin' Piana'. Pitcha' me in a chain pub, know what I mean, mate?"

"Colin!" I said. "Where is Colin? Did we leave him in that dump? Christ, we're the worst blokes in the world! We've got to go back for him!"

"Hey, do you think he's still in the Gents, man?"

"If so, he ain't gonna' thank us too kindly when he finally does emerge, izzee? Not when he finds out that the Egon Ronay of strong continental lagers has kicked the place off, and then done a swift Dexys Midnight Runner!"

"Listen, Pete, focus. Focus. This is serious. We can't just leave him. It's fucking *Fists of Fury* back there! Those boys were going absolutely mental."

"Yeah, what about our creed? 'Leave no man behind', er, man?"

We pondered this for a moment.

"So, Colin, he's a pretty handy bloke, isn't he?" said Carl hopefully. "Tooled up, was he? Liable to go a bit *loco-* when the, er, when the shit goes down?"

"Yeah, he's insane in the main vein. What the fuck do you think?" said Pete.

"Er- no. So what do we do then, man? Call the cops?"

"That's actually not as stupid as it sounds, you know," I said. "Pete, mate, do you want to just duck into the police station there? Bring them up to speed on the situation? Put all your cards on the table? *Mano a*, er, *mano?*"

"Oh yeah? And say what?"

"Ask them to come back to the pub with us, obviously. Those psychos can't do anything to us with the Five-Oh there, can they?

Even north of Commercial Street. Outside the Demilitarised Zone, I mean."

"Not with their faces full of CS Gas, man!" said Carl with relish. "Let's see how they fancy the ring of that truncheon thing!"

"Yeah, but why me?" said Pete. "You're the friggin' lawyer, aintcha'?"

"Exactly- I really can't be associated with public affray. Even if we were, er, eventually exonerated ourselves…"

With hindsight, I can understand why Pete wasn't that keen either. But we wasted a couple of precious minutes arguing about it anyway, before Carl interrupted, grabbing Pete's shoulder and pointing down the road towards Shoreditch.

"They comin' after us? Let's get into the cop-shop pronto…"

"No, man. The bus, the bus! Look at the top deck of that, er, omnibus!"

A number 63 was passing us, headed south down Bishopsgate towards London Bridge.

"It's getting away, man!"

"Keep your hair on, mate, it's only goin' about 15 miles an hour! What about it anyway?"

"It's Col! Colino! You know, Colin!" said Carl.

"You what? It only bloody is him, you know!" yelled Pete. "C'mon, Shoeless Joe!"

The buses stop every 50 yards on Bishopsgate, so even knackered after the Escape from Colditz, it didn't take us that long to catch it up.

"Hey man, do we still have to pay if we're, er, just visiting?" Carl asked the driver.

"Yes, mate," said the driver. "What the fuck do you think?"

"Why does everyone keep saying that to me, man?" said Carl.

"It's a bleedin' bus, not a visitin' library!" said the bus-driver, warming to his theme. "Who d'ya think I am- Cliff Richard in *Summer Holiday*? Who d'ya think you are- Una bleedin' Stubbs in a mini-dress? Where d'ya think I'm goin'- Athens via the former republics of Yugo-bleedin'-slavia? What model bus d'ya think this is- a pre-Routemaster 1960s AEC Regent..."

"Alright, alright, Cliff..." I said.

We paid, then followed Pete up the stairs.

Colin was kneeling awkwardly on the row of seats at the back of the bus, peering anxiously back down Bishopsgate out of the rear window.

"So, we meet again, Meester Bond!" said Pete.

Colin swivelled back round and gaped at us.

"How- how on earth did you find me, chaps?"

"Never min' that," said Pete. "How did you get away? An' are you alright, mate?"

"Well, I- I climbed out of the toilet window," said Colin. "But I did get a bit of that blue urinal cake on the bottom of my trousers when I was scrambling up that, that porcelain Matterhorn, since you ask! It won't stain, will it? It's really not that easy to work out what chemicals could possibly give it that- that uniquely livid hue- is it? Copper sulphate? But otherwise, yes, generally unscathed, thank you kindly! Neither shaken nor stirred, to follow your Meester Bond theme, young Peter!"

"Pretty resourceful, Col!" said Pete admiringly. "I never knew you had it in you!"

"You're not- you're not annoyed then, chaps?" said Colin anxiously.

"Course not- we thought you'd be pissed off with us!"

Colin shook his head and patted Pete on the arm magnanimously.

"I never liked the idea very much, you know that, Peter. But if you don't hold it against me that I, er, expressed that via direct action, well then, there are certainly no grudges on my part! All's well that endeth well, eh, Bard?"

"Hang on a minute!" I said. "Did you just do a runner back there then, Colin? Even before the fight started?"

"Fight?" said Colin unguardedly.

"The static, man," explained Carl.

"I don't Adam an' Eve it!" said Pete. "Here we are- riskin' our necks to go back to Dodge an' bail you out- an' you had just bottled the datin' night, climbed over the pisser like Sherpa Tenzin', an' then caught an oh-so-convenient bus back home!"

"Pretty cold, man," said Carl. "We were risking everything for you. Everything."

"Well, in theory," I said. "We hadn't actually done anything yet."

"Whaddaya' mean, we was about to head back for him with the Sweeney!"

"With the police constabulary? But, what on earth happened in the pub then, chaps?" asked Colin.

"Yeah, good question- what did you say to the Missin' Link back there?" Pete said to Carl. "None of your *Pride and Sensibility* shit, I hope?"

Carl shrugged his shoulders.

"Hmm, Ms Austen- not really my era, man. And besides, I was just relaying some much-needed objective feedback on the, er, overall drinking experience there. I suggested that in the long run it might be better for business if he encouraged people to express themselves more freely in what they ordered. Be a facilitator, not a, er, dictator. Live *La Vida Loca*. Like I told him, I would have been much happier with a lager top or, er, shandy all along. But then when I asked him to top up the rest of my Stella with cider and blackcurrant cordial as a goodwill gesture, he became actually quite abusive."

"Snakebite Black? Nice one!" said Pete.

"Right, but as I observed to him: how sharper than a serpent's tooth it is to have a graceless landlord, man, heh heh heh… His reaction was not cool. Then when he asked me- something to the effect of where we had come from- and I told him I knew Matt from being in the same firm, well, things did start to get regrettably personal."

"You told that psychopath you were lawyers! Are you out of your friggin' mind?"

"Er, no, man. Or at least, that was not the meaning he derived from my remarks, anyway. It seems that 'firm' can also refer to some sort of grouping of fans of, er, association football clubs. Sire Bald-Pate back there affected to believe that we were from the 'Inter City Firm'. When I explained that the firm in question did indeed have a strong cross-border focus, well, you could see for yourselves what happened. Shit got a little, er, crazy, man."

"I specifically told you *not* to bugger about in there!" said Pete. "Did you really think that stylin' yourself as a shandy-sippin', Shakespeare-spoutin', poncified West Ham hooligan in a Millwall pub was completely consistent with those instructions?"

"The guy didn't look so tough to me, man," said Carl. "You saw that, er, 'Cry-baby' tattoo that he had, didn't you? Right down his face!"

"Yeah, what a wuss- only done time for triple murder!"

"Hey, is that what it means? Heh heh heh- I thought it was a reference to some kind of, er, relic of childhood innocence. I hope he didn't mind me calling him 'Tiny Tears' then, man. Just rattling his, er, cage, heh heh heh…"

"Er- I really don't mean to interrupt this fascinating study of prison anthropology, but shouldn't you gents be getting off the bus right about, erm… Now?" said Colin, pointing out of the window. "Isn't the place you're going to in fact situated on Bishopsgate? By my calculations, we're already on Gracechurch Street. And any minute now we'll be at London Bridge. Completely the wrong side of Old Father Thames for your present purposes, I think you'll find!"

I looked out of the back window, to see the venue disappearing behind us. I didn't know it then, but within a few hours, I would be wishing I'd stayed on that bus. Well, I didn't actually know it, but I suppose I did have my suspicions.

"Yeah, right you are," said Pete. "But let's get one thing absolutely straight, sunshine- jail-break over! You're comin' with us. No one's gonna' mess with you now, anyway…" He gestured towards Carl and me. "Not now you're runnin' with the notorious, nefarious 'Legal Business Crew'!"

Colin was too dispirited even to resist. He must have thought he was out on the open prairie and home free when he got away on that bus. I felt for him, I really did, but at the same time we had unfinished business to take care of. We scrambled down the narrow staircase of the bus and back out onto Bishopsgate.

"That's right, bugger off, you tossers!" shouted the bus-driver after us. "D'ya think *I've* got no more bleedin' worries for a week or two?"

Five minutes later we were standing outside the bar. It seemed chic and imposing, garrisoned by a crack team of glammed-up PR girls, an unrepentant yuppie sanctum in which we had no place.

"Can I just take your names, guys?" one of them purred.

Carl stepped forward.

"Shakespeare," he said. "Darren Shakespeare."

"Like the novelist?" asked the PR girl.

"Forsooth. And, er, anon!"

"Is Mr Alexandrou with you?" asked the PR girl.

"That's a good point- where is Kostas?" said Pete.

"I don't know," I said. "He did say something about a concept photo-shoot he had in mind. Involving Galina and a terrapin…"

"What?"

"I really don't want to go into it now… As the terrapin probably said."

"It's time to go in now, gentlemen…"

"OK, OK, come on, guys. Kostas will just have to catch us up later."

The rest of us gave our real names. We were each given a starting table number and a pink sheet of paper to mark our preferences on. Something told me that we'd have to be thicker-skinned than Senior Immigration Judge Gittins when it came to reading our feedback at the end.

"But these table numbers are all different!" said Colin in despair.

"We're not gonna' be on the same table, are we, Colin?" said Pete. "Do you think it's a friggin' dinner-party? Do you wanna' do a speed-date with the Bard? If so, let me save you some time- he's called Darren, he likes *piña colada* an' gettin' caught in the rain without any shoes on. Next! Now, come on- time for a quick sharpener. Justa' get into the zone, and after that it's every man for himself. An' Colin…"

"Yes, Peter?"

"Man the fuck up, willya'? This is not a drill, soldier. This is a live project, and you are a go!"

The high priestess of the PR girls, sunglasses perched on her head in defiance of the wintry conditions outside, tapped daintily on her white-wine spritzer glass with a spoon.

"Ladies and gentlemen- speeders- welcome to the Christmas edition of the City Beehive Accelerated Courtship Evening- where we know all about the birds and the bees!"

"I'll get the drinks in, lads..." Pete whispered.

"Now then, I am Belinda- your 'Queen B' tonight!" she continued. "All you lovely ladies have numbahs for the evening, and the gents have the numbah of the first hive they will be visiting. Now, you handsome fellows will be the worker bees tonight. You will have four minutes at each fragrant flower, and then we'll tinkle the bell a teensy, weensy bit like this..."

One of the PR girls sounded a huge shipping-klaxon, leaving everyone within a twenty-foot radius momentarily dazed.

"...To tell you when to buzz off to the next table. And so now, without further ado- time to find your very own honey!"

Somehow Pete materialised almost instantly with another copious clutch of shot-glasses. The guy had the bar presence of Oliver Reed.

"Right- we're doubling up again, *compadres*! It's last orders for the last man standin' in the Last Chance Saloon here, right?"

I swallowed one of the shots. Suddenly an intense burning sensation enveloped my throat and neck. My vision flickered, then blurred over completely.

"Bugger me! What is this?"

"Absinthe!" said Pete. "Wicked stuff, mate. French philosopher shit, know what I mean?"

It certainly hit the spot. It left me reeling. Meanwhile Colin was staggering around in a ragged, myopic circle, like a BSE-afflicted cow doing dance therapy on a theme of *Bohemian Rhapsody*.

"Next!" barked Pete, passing around the rest of the glasses.

Colin opened his mouth. He seemed to be about to protest, but if so it was a self-defeating strategy. Pete just forcibly tipped his head back and poured the absinthe straight down his throat.

"C'mon, Rimbaud- chase the friggin' fairy!"

Colin was still convulsing from the impact when Queen B came right up behind us and sounded the shipping-klaxon in his ear. It was a total sensory assault. He writhed in agony.

"Chop chop!" She shaped to make another blast of the horn, leaving Colin shuddering in anticipation, then lowered her hands. "Now hurry along, boys, don't be bumbling bees- honey and nectar wait for no drone!"

I had been planning some motivational words- maybe even a team hug or a recitation of *Invictus*- before we went over the top, but with the combined effect of the absinthe and the foghorn, it was all I could do to avoid blacking out myself. I stumbled uncertainly towards my first table.

I can't remember much about the girl at Hive 8, largely because I was still partially blind for the first couple of minutes of the date. By the time I had got my head together, events at Hive 9 had sort of taken centre stage anyway. For a moment I thought I was still hallucinating when Carl stood up from his chair, apparently to make some kind of theatrical declamation. That done, he crouched down awkwardly on one knee. I could only stare at him in silent horror. Number 8 followed my gaze, then blinked in astonishment.

"Do you *know* that guy?" she asked.

"Er- yeah. A valued colleague."

"What is he *doing*?"

"I'm still trying to piece that together in my own mind. But I don't want to ruin the surprise for you- you'll find out for yourself in about an hour and a half."

"Uh, intriguing. And what about his *shoes*?"

"Lost- running away from skinheads. After a fracas in a pub."

"Oh my *God*!"

"It's really not as bad as it sounds…"

"Well that's good- because it sounds *really* bad!"

She pondered for a moment.

"Do you happen to know if it's compulsory to do, er, *every* date?"

"Hmm, I certainly hope so, or this could be a pretty short evening for us boys…"

I could see Queen B at the front, welling up to give the klaxon a blare. I had to go in for the kill.

"So, what do you do again?"

"Oh *sorry*, I thought I mentioned that. I'm an employment lawyer."

"Any contacts in the fund management industry? Alternative asset management?"

"Um, not really, no."

The klaxon rent the air. There was a seismic domino effect on the neighbouring tables, as the sonic boom flattened everything in its wake.

"Well, OK then, nice to meet you! Enjoy meeting the Bard."

"The *what*?"

"Wait and see!"

I moved onto Hive 9. This girl was definitely pretty, but she was also pretty shell-shocked.

"So, is this you engaged now? Because I saw the last guy go down on one knee. Just tell me if you're already out of the dating game. I don't want to tread on any toes here."

She laughed- but nervously.

"He was reciting lines from, er, *Romeo and Juliet*, I think. Quite a lot of them, actually. I think it was intended to be romantic.

Although he did major a bit on the death scenes, which was kind of weird."

"Romantic? He didn't ask you about your work?"

"Why would he?"

"Er, no reason. So, he just spouted lines from Shakespeare? Absolutely no shop talk?"

"I don't think shop talk is even allowed. It's not actually a business networking event, you know. But then this evening is certainly not going to be a great success if all the dates are just a post mortem of the previous one! Especially that particular one…"

"Yeah, sorry. I can see that could make it a bit of a Groundhog Day experience."

"Do you often indulge in this type of speed-dating voyeurism?"

Suddenly she pointed over my shoulder to Hive 7.

"Speaking of which…"

All we could see from our vantage point at Hive 9 was the broad back of a girl, apparently necking enthusiastically with someone.

"… Some bees seem to be quicker workers than others!" she said.

I tried to keep an open mind, but in my heart of hearts, I think I always knew that it was one of my boys. It became a bit clearer which one it was when I saw Pete convulsed in laughter, pointing helplessly over to the table. That meant it had to be…

"Colino! ¡*Olé, olé*! ¡*Andale, andale*! ¡*Arriba, arriba*!" yelled Pete.

"Oh, what," I said. "I don't believe this…"

"You were holding out hopes for Hive 7?"

"Well, not for the girl."

"Oh, really?"

"Nothing like that… I was just hoping that my boss- Colin- wouldn't make a complete fool of himself."

"How are those hopes working out for you?"

"Dashed."

"And if that's your boss- how do you behave?"

"I aspire to his self-control."

The klaxon went.

"So do you think Darren Shakespeare went the whole hog, and actually proposed to Number 10, then?" she said.

"I'll find out soon, I guess! Sorry for being a crap date."

"Oh, it's all relative, you know."

She was right, of course- everything is. I mean, I had thought I was utterly hammered, but it turned out that was relative too, because at that moment Pete appeared with another tray of shots and immediately forced me to down one.

"So this must be another of your colleagues, then?" asked Number 9, without much gusto. That must have been how it struck Pete too.

"Who pissed on your chips, luv?" he said. "You look like a bulldog chewin' a wasp. But not to worry- I'm workin' my way over here. Be with you shortly!"

"Right- bye for now, then!" I said to Number 9, with a jaunty wave. Probably best to leave her alone with that thought.

"How are you getting on then, Julio?" I asked Pete, en route to Hive 10.

"Better'n you, for a start. But not quite as well as 'Don Colin' over there…"

He nodded over towards Hive 7, where Queen B had now resorted to armed intervention in an attempt to separate Colin and Number 7. They were still locked together in a clinch, as she tried desperately to lever them apart with her clipboard.

"C'mon, put your back into it, luv!" shouted Pete. "Inadequate hardware, 'course…"

"She should've come for a quick half in Shoreditch- they're literally throwing crowbars at your head up there. I would've picked it up myself if I'd known crowd control was going to be an issue. But what's Colin playing at? Not exactly hunting as a pack, are we?"

"Well, you know what they say, mate- love will tear us apart…"

"Hmm. The thing about you, Pete- and I know you won't mind me saying this- is that it can be hard to tell whether you're inside the tent, pissing out, or outside the tent pissing in, if you know what I mean?"

"It's a bit of both with me, to be honest, mate! I jus' hope young Number 7 over there has committed a lot of dough to the cause, that's all I can say…" He paused to knock back another shot of absinthe complacently, like Verlaine during Happy Hour at the Café François 1er. "'Cos Mr C's out of the friggin' game now, M.I.A.! I'm not sayin' there's no way he can pull a millionairess now, but… well, you really wouldn't wanna' start from here, wouldya'?"

"No, I would not- in fact I'm just trying to work out how we got here in the first place. I wasn't really expecting this from Colin, I must admit…"

"He may not have much form with absinthe… But it's like I told you, mate- horses for courses! And that stallion has found his paddock…"

I groaned, and sat down at Hive 10. Not great body language, I admit, but then hers wasn't much better. By that stage I was getting quite familiar with the facial expression of a girl who had just spent four minutes with Carl. It was a complex blend of sheer disbelief, overwhelming relief that it was over and utter disillusionment with the speed-dating process- possibly the entire male sex.

"Hi- I'm, er, Matt."

"Emma…"

"So- how's your night going, Emma?" I asked.

"Slightly weird," said Number 10. "I haven't done this before. I was kind of expecting more small-talk."

"Right... What have you actually had?"

"Oh, so the last guy told me I was 'the very antidote to desire'."

"Well, that's not true. Definitely not the antidote. I mean, you're pretty- pretty."

And that was true. She had honey-streaked brown hair and quick, bright eyes that seemed to wait shyly under long lashes before darting right through you. I hadn't noticed how beautiful she was until I sat down, but now it struck me more every time I looked at her.

"So what did you do to provoke that type of feedback?" I asked. "Could this be an inner beauty issue, do you think?"

"Shut up! I radiate with inner beauty."

"Yeah, I'm feeling that, definitely. So what happened then?"

"He started off by suggesting that we forget about the whole speed-dating thing and get out of here. He wanted to go down to the Globe Theatre and picture London at night- in Shakespeare's time. When gruff bear-baiters, bohemian actors and exotic courtesans all rubbed shoulders- and, er, loins- in 'Merrie Southwark', he said."

"You passed on Merrie Southwark then?"

"I told him he should watch *Shakespeare in Love* on cable, and save himself the Tube fare. He said that the movie was a sacrilege. I cited the universal critical acclaim and multiple Academy Awards it received."

"And that was when he came out with the 'antidote to desire' line?"

"Correct."

"Strange choice of quote!"

"I thought it strange. He said it was Shakespeare."

"Shakespeare! Bard my arse. Congreve, I'd say."

"Oh, do you like literature, then? *Reading*, I mean?" Her dealings with Carl had obviously left her with a poor impression of the mental capabilities of the adult male. But there was nothing I could do about that, I didn't have the time or emotional energy to undo the trauma of four minutes with Darren Shakespeare. Not all at once, anyway. I had to re-map our strategy, and quickly. There was still no sign of Kostas. Colin and Carl were both irretrievably off-piste. Pete had made it totally clear that he was being led by his libido, not by the business-plan. And all of us were wasted.

"Me? Reading? No, no, I wouldn't say so."

"Really? What on earth do you put down as a hobby on your CV then- if you can't use 'Reading'? Most civilised human beings include it after 'Travelling' and 'Going to the theatre with friends'."

"If you would put down reading and travelling, you might as well just put down 'making toast', or 'walking to the Tube station'. I mean, going inter-railing hardly makes you Marco Polo these days, does it? So, if I was going to include hobbies on my CV- which I wouldn't - I would probably go long on the daily rituals. That would at least imply hidden depths. A weird- but strangely alluring- talent for finding fascination and wonder, even in the mundane…"

"Hmm, the *American Beauty* approach… Do you find that works well for you? In getting jobs, I mean?"

"I was just about getting away with it- until the 'Bonfire of the Quangos', anyway."

"Your one got burnt then?"

"Like a wicker effigy of a hedge fund manager. So it turns out that we don't need two separate regulators for cable TV after all. Who knew, right? Or that Ofmedia was the bloody asbestos quango, of course."

"Ah… Well, look on the bright side. You got the job in the first place. Wow. How on earth did you pull that off?"

"Circumstances kind of swept me along, to be honest. Ofcable really saved me when the financial crisis hit. Now I just need something to save me from the public sector funding crisis. But enough about my stellar career- what do you do?"

"I'm a, er, hedge fund manager."

The klaxon went.

"Wow, really?"

"I know, I know- not very PC right now!"

"No, no, I think that's great- I was just kidding with the, er, burning effigy thing. I'd love to find out more, actually…"

"Hem hem. Drone Numbah 21!"

"Ah, bugger…"

The Queen Bee had bustled over to the table. She thrust her clipboard towards me assertively.

"Am I right, Drone Numbah 21, in thinking that you are in some way affiliated to Drone Numbah 19?"

"Who?"

"Drone Numbah 19!" She impatiently consulted the clipboard. "Or, to put it another way, Mr Colin Stebbins?"

"In some way… Why- what is he up to now?"

She looked meaningfully at Number 10.

"What?" I asked.

"Step away from the table, Drone Numbah 21," she said.

I looked around for Colin. No sign.

"Step away from the table!" repeated Queen B firmly.

Actually, there was a sign of Colin. As my vision fully returned, I could dimly make out a figure rolling around on the floor of the bar area, apparently in imminent danger of being crushed or asphyxiated by Number 7, whose bra-strap was now dangling alarmingly out of her sleeve. Unless she really was having a night to remember, I was starting to see what the problem might be. Queen B spoke in a low hiss.

"Are we going to have a problem here? Come quietly, Drone Numbah 21- don't force me to implicate you in this, this disgraceful scene, this sickening display, in front of a sweet girl like Numbah 10. Is that really what you want? Right now there's still a hard way and a- a slightly less hard way. But those options are closing down in front of your, your freaky little compound bee eyes." She tapped her watch. "Oh, that's right- it's coming right up for Taser O'Clock, Drone Numbah 21. We're going to shoot you down like Chico Mendes…"

"Wasn't he a conservationist?"

"Whatevah. Tick, tock…"

I sighed and stepped away from the table.

Queen B pointed her pen over to Colin, then rapped it sharply on the clipboard.

"Need I, in fact, say more, Drone Numbah 21?"

"Well, yeah, you do actually- what do you want me to do about it? It takes two to tango, you know. And doesn't this go down as a success for the event? Actual coupling? Ring up the sale, I'd say, Your Highness!"

"It only takes one person to decide that you have to leave my Apiary, Mr Verraxe, and that person is *me*. And my definition of success most certainly does *not* include watching a pair of distinctly over-grown teenagers making out like it's Prom Night at the local special needs school. So, either you get your little friend to stop acting like a sailor on shore leave, or he- and the rest of you complete and utter prats- will have to buzz off. For good! *Comprendes*, Mendes?"

I couldn't, in all conscience, look around me and say that the plan was definitely going to work. But on the other hand, it definitely wasn't going to work if we got chucked out at this point. I stared around the room desperately for inspiration. There was one notable demographic trend.

"Listen, er, Queenie, we may be complete cretins, but we're also all blokes. So if you do decide to go nuclear and give us our marching orders, there's going to be a lot of disappointed girls in here…"

Queen B arched her eyebrow.

"… Well, maybe not so much disappointed then, as lonely. Stranded. Solitary bees. Exceeding the number of drones available for speed-dates at any given time. Unlikely, therefore, to return to the hive for highly lucrative future City Beehive events. Wondering, in fact, what the refund policy for this one might be?"

She pursed her lips.

"I'm going to do something for you, Mr Verraxe, that I've nevah done for anyone in the entire history of this illustrious Apiary. I'm going to turn a blind eye to Mr Stebbins'- antics. For now. But don't let me see you, or any of the rest of these- these immature idiots you've brought with you- taking a leaf out of his filthy book. Or you'll be out of here quicker that you can say…"

"Botox?"

She flounced off.

"Merry Christmas!" I called after her.

I had missed Number 11 completely but, in my state of mind at that moment, I think it's fair to say that the loss was all mine. I was just shaping to move towards Hive 12 when I noticed that no one had come to sit with Number 10. Emma the hedge fund manager. Which figured, because Colin was clearly hard at it with Number 7. And Number 10 was a hedge fund manager. I sat down at her table again.

"Hello again, Emma- only me. Do you want me to go and notify the Queen Bee that you don't have a new drone of your own?"

"You're pretty close, are you?"

"God yeah, she's my sister from another mister."

"I see that, are you?"

"I see that, I could feel the love. I do like what she's done with the whole 'Queen B' thing though!"

"Yeah, it's short for 'Bitch', apparently."

"Oh, come on then, sit down. Better the devil you know tonight, I think. If you, uh, forgive the expression! Do you realise that the bloke who's actually supposed to be here is your friend Number 19? The one she was just talking about- another total freak, in other words! No offence, obviously."

"Another total freak?"

"As well as Shakespeare's Sister, I mean. Come on, this guy is actually snogging another girl- during the date!"

"Ouch, that must be tough to take. Especially coming hard on the heels of another crushing blow to your confidence."

"What do you mean?"

"You know, the whole 'antidote to desire' thing…"

"Shut up! My confidence is just fine!"

"I do feel kind of responsible for this, er- probably quite temporary- blip in your self-esteem, I must admit…"

"You? Why?"

"Well, because I actually am responsible. It was me who brought the, er, principal offenders here."

"All of them? Why on earth would you do that? How do you even know people like that?"

"The last bit- well, that really is a long story. But I brought them here because we had to give it one last shot to raise some money. For our business. Or maybe it would be truer to say 'our dream', you know?"

"So you thought you'd pitch it to people here- whilst they were trying to find their one true love?"

"Well- yeah."

"Unbelievable! And what is this business? I suppose you have a pitch book with you, do you?"

"Yes! I mean, uh- no. Carl- Darren- had them. In this big Shakespeare folio thing he was carrying. He must have left them in the pub, when we did the runner. Thank God there was no one who could read back there... It's basically a video-sharing cable TV channel- 'YouTube on TV', we call it."

She shook her head, then laughed.

"Wow, I really wasn't expecting to hear any social media pitches tonight! But surely you weren't actually expecting this to work, were you?"

The klaxon blared.

"It certainly has been- interesting- talking with you, Matthew! And keep the faith- maybe there's a pot of gold at the next table!"

"Maybe!" I said, but then I already knew I wasn't going to make it there to find out.

"And if all else fails- there's always *Dragon's Den*. You guys are absolutely made for TV! It'd be priceless, wouldn't it? I'd stay off the sauce ahead of that one, mind you. No one can hear you scream in prime-time. And God knows what Sir Alan would make of you lot..."

"You know, now I kind of wish I was here dating," I said. "It would've been good only to crash and burn in my capacity as a suitor."

"As opposed to?"

"My, er, money-making avatar?"

She shook her head again- this time in dismissal. I stood up wearily and looked around the room. It was carnage out there: everywhere you looked, my men were down- or out. Kostas hadn't even reported for duty. Pete was absent, presumed deserted. Incredibly, despite the somewhat unpromising start to their relationship he seemed to have won Number 9 round and gone off somewhere with her. Colin had copped a huge, livid love-bite on his neck, and was being dragged to the exit by Number 7. Meanwhile Carl had mounted the stage area and was delivering a rambling soliloquy to two bemused-looking security guards, whilst the Queen Bee tugged doggedly at his T-shirt. When she caught sight of me, she mimed an excruciating convulsion of neuromuscular agony under the effect of a Taser gun, and barked some orders to the security guards. They started threading their way through the tables towards me.

"You're going down, Mendes!" she screamed. "We'll give you a bleak midwintah, scumbag! Come back here and sing *Away in a Taser* with us!"

Clearly another hasty retreat was called for. On my way out, I turned to look back at Emma's table. She was already in apparently animated conversation with a new drone. There was a strange sense of hollowness inside- of missed opportunity- in walking away from her. What I wasn't completely clear on was how much that had to do with her personally, and how much it had to do with the fairly obvious regrets surrounding the night as a whole. I was starting to notice that once you get into a real cycle of failure, it can be hard to break the whole spectrum of debacle out into all its constituent shades. That takes a little brooding after the event. And there was no time for that then, because out of the corner of my eye, I could see Carl finally felled by a prolonged blast of the shipping-klaxon, accompanied by a vicious chop to the shins with Queen B's tungsten steel-edged clipboard. As if in slow motion, he sank to his knees, hands held up in a gesture of placation to the unforgiving heavens.

The Bard had it right about one thing: 'We make guilty of our disasters the sun, the moon, and the stars: as if we were villains by necessity; fools by heavenly compulsion'. But sometimes we just get desperate, and make bad decisions. I shrugged off the green haze of absinthe, and staggered back out onto Bishopsgate.

Chapter 13

Bankside, London, 12 December 2008

Sometimes- in a dream- I find myself confronted by an unbearably vivid situation, demanding immediate and decisive action, but at the critical moment my body is paralysed, unable to respond at all to the crisis. The more clearly I see the problems facing me, the less able I find myself to deal with them- even to move a muscle. It's a nightmare, but at least morning generally comes to the rescue. Two days after my speed-dating debut, I was still trying to wake up.

"Cheer up, man," said Carl, sloping into our office. "Worse I may be yet: the worst is not; So long as we can say 'This is the worst'.'"

"What are you on about now, Bard?" said Pete. "Is it the friggin' worst now, or isn't it?"

"I think it may in fact be the worst now, man. 'Cause Tomás de Torquemada wants everyone in 'Standards' to come to the Conference Room. Urgent meeting."

"Thomas?" Pete said. "How come that scrote gets to summon us to meetings?"

"He's the, er, *eminence grise* around here these days, man," said Carl. "C'mon, hurry up, guys! My burgeoning reputation as the Ofcable 'Mr Fix-It' is jeopardised every time you drag your heels like this… Don't be so freaking selfish, you know?"

"Comin', comin'…" grumbled Pete. "All hail to our new friggin' Ofmedia overlords…"

Torquemada had prepared a complex organigram on the whiteboard in the Conference Room to demonstrate exactly how Ofmedia would subsume 'Standards', apparently designed to cause the maximum humiliation possible to Colin.

"So this diagram should largely speak for itself, I think?" said Thomas. "But does anyone have any questions- before we get into some of the detail around integration?"

Carl put his hand up.

"Yes?"

"Hey, man, why does it say 'Fuck Ofmedia' up there? I mean, I get the 'Fuck Ofcable' bit, obviously, 'cause that's what's going down here…"

"It was already written on the whiteboard, you moron! In permanent marker! I've even heard you ask that exact question- in this very room- before!" said Thomas. "This is absolutely, utterly typical of how things have been allowed to run around here! Certifiable cretins like this roam free, obstructing valuable work- and quite possibly vandalising valuable quango property in the first place. It's no surprise that Darwinian evolution has selected Ofmedia to continue at the expense of Ofcable! Now if there are no other idiotic blitherings, can we please move on to the merger synergies piece now?"

Colin put his hand up.

"What on earth is it now, Colin?"

"There's a big, wrinkly grey elephant in this room with us, Thomas, and it seems to me to be a little bit pointless to be talking about merger benefits until we've addressed it!"

"Well? What is it?"

"This elephant- let's call her 'Nelly'- happened to tell me that no one from the Ofcable Standards Team would be coming across to Ofmedia on a permanent basis. That going forward, all cable matters will be dealt with by the existing terrestrial and satellite TV teams at Ofmedia. Ignoring, of course, the considerable expertise that we have built up here in the specialised field of cable! Can you please confirm or deny what, ah, 'Nelly' told me, Thomas? Because until you have, I really don't think anyone wants to listen to much of your- your pompous rambling! Today, tomorrow or ever!"

"Hear! Hear!" said Veronica.

"O Captain. My Captain!" shouted Pete.

"That really hasn't been finalised yet," blustered Thomas. "I can assure you that you will all be informed of the status of your, er, positions, in the fullness of time, and at the appropriate time. And to keep spirits up and boost morale, I think you'll find that you have been awarded what, in the circumstances, is an extremely generous budget for the, er, last Ofcable Christmas party!"

"Just answer the question, you insufferable little twirp!" said V. "You've been bragging for days now that this is all in your gift. What's it to be: do you know, or were you just lying all the time- to inflate your feeble little ego in some pathetic way, when you're just as much out of the loop as we are?"

"I can, er, I can confirm that not *everyone* currently working in the Ofcable Standards Team will be losing their jobs…" said Thomas. "Beyond that, the communication of the precise, ah, employment law outcome for each member of the team is in the- more than capable- hands of the Ofmedia HR department. As is quite right, proper and appropriate."

"Hey man, what he means is that *he's* staying on," said Carl. "Neat play on words, man. You would have fooled me with that. If I hadn't happened to see your email to the Ofmedia Chief Exec, that is!" Now Carl stood up and addressed us from the front of the room, next to Thomas. "Because what that email said is that we're all gonna' be laid off, even Colin! And that junior Ofmedia staff on lower salaries are gonna' be promoted into our positions, with Torquemada in charge! Which sounds like a pretty bad deal for us, man!"

"What!" said Veronica. "You mean we're not actually redundant at all! Those bastards!"

"Sit down this instant!" said Thomas.

"I will not, sir!" said Carl.

"And how on earth did you get hold of that email? This is absolutely outrageous! I, I demand to know- this instant- how you, of all people, got access to a, a Category Three Ofmedia confidential missive? I demand it! This is, well it's an unheard-of security breach!"

"I'm certainly calling my solicitor!" said Veronica. "With the damages we'll get for this, perhaps I will buy that new Merc after all…"

"How could you possibly have seen it?" persisted Thomas. "I don't print that type of email off- not in this office! And I certainly wouldn't have left it lying around on top of the printer!"

"No, man, I hacked into your computer," said Carl. "I wanted to find out what was going on, and no one would tell me."

He addressed the rest of us again. "Officially, these Ofmedia dudes are saying that it's all in the hands of Ofmedia HR now- but that's only because the decision's already been made and, according to Tom here, they really don't want to pay us any damages over and above statutory redundancy pay! But you can't just, er, sack people who aren't even redundant without going through the proper procedures! And like Miss Veronica says, we can't be redundant if they plan to replace us with other Ofmedia dudes! That's the law of the land, man. We've got rights!"

"But you can't just hack into my computer and read confidential Ofmedia correspondence!" said Thomas. "You- you just can't! This is a very serious matter. And now you're telling me about it! Have you completely lost your mind?"

"What are you going to do about it, man?" said Carl. "Sack me? Deduct it from my, er, golden shower, or whatever you call it?"

"Good work, Carl- but why didn't you tell us sooner?" said Pete.

"Hey, man, there were confidentiality issues," Carl said. "Plus, I was hoping that Colino and I might still get a reprieve. Can you believe they didn't even want us two?"

"It must be hard to take- after all your days of service, Carl!" Veronica said. "Some of us have actually been here since the beginning. But it seems to me that you may have over-played your hand a bit here, young Thomas. Thanks to your machinations, we all have extremely lucrative claims for unfair dismissal against Ofcable- and I suppose once the merger has gone through, against Ofmedia too. Ker-ching!"

"It's pretty much an open and shut case, with all that email evidence ripe for document discovery," I said. "You really do need to make sure that isn't mysteriously deleted at this stage, Tommy-boy…"

"Or rather, you could delete it, if you fancy picking up the soap for Bubba in the prison showers!" said Carl. "Because that's where you're headed, man, if you perjure yourself in court. Just ask Jeffrey Archer. That's some more law. Besides, I printed off your whole inbox to be on the safe side, man."

"You what!"

"Yeah, man. Orphan shit and all. I have it stored in a super-secret, maximum security data warehouse. At my Mum's house."

Now Torquemada was deathly pale.

"I do wonder what the famous Ofmedia Chief Exec we keep hearing about will say- when he sees a black hole in his annual budget, because of all the extra compensation being paid out to us!" said Colin. "I should think he'll be more than a little bit concerned already about financial matters, given the economic outlook. Hard to imagine that public spending on quangos is going to go up any time soon, what with the 'Bonfire of the Quangos' in full swing out there! But they can't cancel the merger now either, because the Minister's already boasted about it in public. And now he's got the Ofcable mandate to think of too… More costs, and less money to play with. He might start to think that the person who made such a dog's dinner of all this would be quite a natural candidate for a, er, cost-saving trim of the Ofmedia staff…"

"Let's cut to the chase here, Torquemada," I said. "You're screwed, and you know it."

"But you, you only know about the email because that moron Carl hacked into my computer to get it! That's illegal! He would be in trouble too!"

"Well, I for one could not give a damn about that!" said Veronica. "He's made it perfectly clear that he was only interested in trying to save his own skin anyway."

"Damn right!" said Pete. "I'm suing Ofmedia. Carl can look after himself!"

"The truth will come out- if there's a tribunal hearing," I said. "But of course there is one way- to make all this go away…"

Thomas stared wildly at me.

"What is it?" he asked.

"I say one way- but it has two parts." I turned to the team. "Firstly, do any of you guys actually want to stay here, instead of coming across to Chatterbabe with us?"

"Whoah- are we all invited, man?" asked Carl.

"Of course, Carl, we're all in it together now! And you're the one who's got us back into the game here. Pete- don't you agree?"

"100 per cent., mate. You may be a bit of a tosser at times, Carl, but I'd rather have you inside our tent tossing out, than outside our tent…" "Alright, alright, Pete, we get the message," I said.

"OK, well I'm on board then, thanks, man! My Mum always said I'd end up on TV!"

"You'd make a wicked Shaggy in *Scooby Doo*, mate…" said Pete.

"Leave it out, Scrappy," I said. "So does anyone want to stay here?"

"Matt, I think I'm going to stay put," said Veronica. "The experience with HGF the other day really showed me that- well, that you can't teach an old dog new tricks! And there's the pension to think of too at my age, you know. All the very best of British, though!"

"No problem, V, completely understood. But we're counting on you to do a show for us, one of these days! Well then, Thomas, part one of your side of the bargain will be telling Ofmedia that V is indispensable to the current cable supervision regime, OK?"

"Fine," he said sulkily. "She's more competent than the rest of you idiots put together, anyway."

"That's definitely true… With the, er, honourable exception of Colin, I mean. As for part two- you're going to phone Nigel Thorne at HGF Bank, and tell him that you were inexplicably mistaken in your belief that Pete, Colin and I were in hot water with Ofcable. Then you're going to tell him that, for so long as Chatterbabe has a Head of Content like Colin, it's highly unlikely that we'll ever have any regulatory problems with Ofmedia either. And of course then you'll make sure that we don't..."

"How can I say that?" hissed Torquemada. "What if you go off the rails?"

"Firstly, you know as well as I do that that's inconceivable with Colin at the wheel. And secondly, you simply don't have any choice, you'll just have to take a chance on us, won't you? And Torquemada, if you think it would be difficult for me to find a job in this environment, as a qualified lawyer, how easy do you think it would be for you to find a job- outside the comfortable confines of Ofmedia?"

He looked at the wall.

"I didn't think so! So we have a deal?"

He nodded sullenly.

"Right then, there's no time like the present for you to phone Nigel- some of us have got a business plan to write!"

Before Torquemada could slip out of the room, I took him to one side.

"Listen, Thomas, I know this hasn't played out exactly as you might have planned it, but you've still got what you wanted- Ofcable is wiped off the face of the earth, and we're all out. So we can still make this right, and part friends. We're not going to make any more trouble for you, OK? We just want our shot at buying this business!"

He nodded again.

"Alright, Matthew. I'll let you know when I've spoken to Mr Thorne."

"Cheers, Thomas." My phone started vibrating. "I'll speak to you later..."

"Hello, Matt? It's Emma. Emma from the City Beehive."

"The what?"

"Speed dating. Number 10 here."

"Number 10! Is it really you? One of the few people who had as bad a night as I did! How are you? Do you want to form a survivors' group? We've got a lot of issues to work through…"

"Really? Because actually I want to talk to you about that business plan of yours. It can't be easy raising cash right now- in the middle of a financial crisis, I mean?"

"Not exactly- and I reckon the speed-dating option has got to be pretty close to the bottom of the barrel… But it's a weird thing, too- because of course I know that the economy has gone to hell in a handcart, we all read it on the BBC website every day, ten times a day- but it's taken this for me to understand what that actually means in practice. I guess my idea of a financial crisis was all premised on a series of black and white photos from the US of the '20s and '30s. I couldn't take an economic melt-down seriously without at least some sepia-toning."

"Ah, I think I know the ones you mean! I think that's the case for everyone who did GCSE History in the late nineties. You mean the ones in the 'Primary Sources' section at the back of the textbook?"

"Yeah, exactly!"

"First you had American teenagers dancing a boisterous Charleston, above a caption that said 'The Roaring Twenties'. So that would be your epitome of the allure of economic boom, then?"

"Yeah, I guess so, although saying that I don't know how much I would really have enjoyed the Charleston when it actually came down to it. But don't get me wrong, I do occasionally enjoy a bit of a bop when extremely inebriated."

"Quite complicated steps, I understand. I'm not sure that conventional modern 'bloke dancing' would cut it. Not to imply that you're no Fred Astaire on the dance floor, of course... But listen, much though I'm enjoying this trip down sixteen-year-old memory lane with you, I did want to talk a bit of shop too. How much were you looking to raise?"

"We need a hundred grand of equity- to raise two hundred and fifty grand of debt."

"And the debt's lined up?"

"We've got an agreed term sheet with HGF. Subject to equity and, er, regulatory conditions."

"How much equity is committed?"

"Just about enough to cover the legal fees. If I do the drafting..."

"Right. Listen, Matt, the fact is that we're looking to get some traction in social media right now. People are saying it's going to be the next big thing and, whether you believe that or not, it's our job to make sure that we can give our investors some kind of exposure to it. If we can get to that cost-effectively, of course! Well, I happened to mention your idea in the office, and there was a lot more interest than I expected. There's an obvious cross-over to a website, once you get the TV asset up and running. And at the level of funding you're talking about, frankly people see this as a bit of a shot to nothing. So if you have a business plan that you could ping over to me, I can try and put together an investment case to chuck you the £100K on a convertible loan?"

"No way! That would be amazing. What kind of coupon? How much of the equity would that give you?"

"Let's talk about that some more once we have the detailed business plan. Look, I'm not promising anything, Matt. But £100K is chump change for the fund, and I'd like to find a way to back you on this. If it works, we all look like fucking heroes, don't we?"

"Er- yes. That sounds good. I don't think I've ever been an actual hero. So listen, Emma, we're just in the process of putting together something for HGF," I lied. "Something all-singing, all-dancing. We'll get that through to you too, as soon we can."

"That would be perfect. I'll send you my contact details."

"Brilliant, thanks. Er, out of interest- where did you get mine?"

"From Queen Bee, of course!"

"Really? I thought she was still, er, holding me responsible for the date night fiasco…"

"How ridiculous!"

"I know, but you can kind of see her point. Quite a lot of the girls missed out on three or four of the dates that they were supposed to have, because my boys kept copping off with people and going AWOL."

"I know, I was one of them! So how are the rest of your little band of *desperados*?"

"Loved up with their lady-friends from the other night, of course. Settling down. The pitter patter of, er…"

"Shut up!"

"It's strange actually- no one has ever really discussed what happened that night. It's kind of a 'don't ask, don't tell' thing in the office, you know?"

"Like homosexuality in the US Armed Forces?"

"Just exactly like that, yeah. Although Pete was making 'royal jelly' gags fairly persistently for the first twenty-four hours after the Beehive expedition. So perhaps further details will gradually emerge over time."

"So you all work together?"

"Oh yes. And I've actually been staying with Pete, too. I'm only moving back into my old flat later today…"

"How did that happen?"

"Well, I was, er, thrown out by my ex-girlfriend..."

"So you are at least single? Even if seeking to exploit that status to raise cash?"

"Yes... Anyway, I had to wait to get my tenants out of my place in Dalston."

"Kind of a chain of eviction?"

"That's right, although I like to think that I took my medicine better than the ex-tenants did- they cut up a bit rough."

"So will Pete miss you desperately then?"

"He seems to be taking it quite well, to be honest..."

"With hindsight, I'm actually quite sorry I never got to have that speed-date with him- it sounds like it would have been quite an experience!"

"It was all his loss..."

"You're very gallant. But then you did come back for seconds, as I recall. And then what happened?"

"I, er, made a tactical withdrawal. I'd experienced the best hive, twice in a row, and I wanted to make sure I went out on a high. And then there was also the fact that, for the second time that night, I was chased off the premises by crazed people, threatening me with extreme physical violence. It was getting to be a bit of a habit."

"Oh yes... I did hear Queen B inviting you to sing, er, 'O Little Town of Electroshock', with her..."

"Quite. Christmas in her house must be pretty twisted. Singing 'Good King Waterboard' around the tree. Anyway, I explained all that background to her the other day, but she took a more mercenary view of the whole thing. She said some of the, er, sweet honey bees had been in touch with her trying to negotiate pro rata repayments of their entry fees. That's the problem with having City lawyers as clients. She even argued that we had breached the implied contract to attend all of our dates. Fortunately I could remember all of the speed-dating law I had learnt at university, so I was able to talk her down from the breach of contract suit."

"She did sound a little surprised that an actual girl was trying to get in touch with you! So you were a lawyer, were you? That was the job you got canned from- before you became a cable guy?"

"That's right- and my next job will probably be actually installing cable TV."

"Not if we make Chatterbabe fly. Although that's a good point- my first stipulation as an investor will be to change the name. 'Chatterbabe' is lame, to be perfectly frank. It sounds like a Victorian children's weekly…"

"I see what you mean- the whole *Water-Babies* vibe… Not cool. So what would you suggest? Anything you like, just say the word. 'Emma TV'… Or how about 'Em TV', that has a ring to it, no?"

"MTV? Really? I think that's already been done to death, hasn't it, Matt? But how about 'Phoenix TV'?"

"Reborn from the ashes of Chatterbabe? I like it!"

"Well, sleep on it. I have to dash. But make sure you send me that business plan, pronto. Who knows how long social media will be hot for, it could be the next big bust. The old-timers still talk about some of the dotcom turkeys they backed!"

"Perfect, will do. And thanks a lot, Emma. This could be really exciting."

"I think so too! Speak soon."

Just like that, we were back in business. And I wasn't worrying quite so much about the Emily situation either, for some reason. Emma was like a less intense, more down-to-earth version of Emily- almost how Emily used to seem to me, before the City had got to her.

"Carl? Carl!"

"What's up, man? What's going on?"

"Tell me some more about these unsuspected I.T. skills of yours…"

Chapter 14

Dalston, London, 14 December 2008

"Here is Dalston, giddy Dalston. Is it home of the free- or what?"

The music kept running through my head. I think Morrissey was actually talking about London generically in his song, but this made a lot more sense to me. For the first time in years, I felt like I was doing what really mattered to me at that moment.

"Oh, here is Dalston: 'Home of the brash, outrageous and free'."

"Do we really all need to be here for this?" said Pete. "I haven't missed the Sunday night of the George an' Vulture Darts Double-header since 2002…"

"Listen Pete, I don't care how long it takes, no one's going anywhere until we've nailed this business plan, alright? Last time we put too much pressure on V, and it all fell to pieces. We're all in it together this time. Team Cobra, right?"

"Oh, yes indeed!" said Colin, rolling up the sleeves of his chartreuse jumper. "That's the spirit, Matthew!"

"Is this the part where we have the team hug then?" asked Pete. "Or can we at least wait till the luvverly Emma is here?"

"Who's Emma?" asked Monika.

"She's the one who's trying to get us the equity we need," I said. "If we can just make the debt work with HGF. She's not coming along this evening though- Pete's just buggering about."

"The 'equity' is not all she's tryin' to get…" said Pete.

"What do you mean?" Monika asked.

"Well, don't you think it's a little strange that this- otherwise financially savvy- girl seems to be movin' heaven and earth, just to invest a chunk of change in a flaky business idea that no one else will touch with a barge-pole? All I'm sayin' is that she does seem to have taken a little bit of a shine to the gaffer here, that's all! And what's wrong with that?"

"So she's the girl you met at the speed-dating?" Monika asked me.

"That's right- that was the whole point of it, remember? Though admittedly some of the boys did go a little off-piste. So I really don't know why you, Pete, 'Mr Lover-Lover', are stirring up reminiscences of that particular episode!"

"I still don't understand how that all worked," said Monika. "Don't any of you actually have girlfriends?"

"What are you trying to do- mock us with our sexual ineptitude again? No, we don't. I got brutally dumped, Colin's married to his work, Pete's married to his darts, Kostas doesn't believe in monogamy and Carl- well, you know Carl, don't you? Do you have a boyfriend?"

"You know I don't, Matthew."

"Well, there you go then. Sometimes people just end up being single for a while. And obviously that does include everyone connected with Phoenix TV."

The doorbell rang.

"Ah- the final piece in our jigsaw…" I said.

"Pizza, man?" said Carl. He opened the door. "Holy Shit! It's, er, it's Father Christmas! Yo ho ho, man!"

"It's not Father Christmas, Carl," I said. "And anyway that would be 'Ho, ho, ho'. 'Yo ho ho' is more Captain Blackbeard. It's Bob!"

"What are you, er, wearing then, man?" said Carl.

"These are my, ah, Yuletide ceremonial robes, of course. I've been at the Sexennial Stilton Soirée in the Hall. And very festive it was too!"

"Bob!" I said, getting up to shake his hand. "Thanks so much for coming. It's great to have you on board. Come on in, and I'll introduce you to the rest of the team. Guys, I want to introduce you to our new Chairman- Mr Bob Walker. Bob has a huge amount of experience in the City, and he knows everyone worth knowing…"

"The other thing that may be worth mentioning at this stage, Matthew, is that I currently occupy the post of Second Warden of the Worshipful Company of Cheesemongers," Bob announced. "Hence the, ah, formal Yule attire this evening."

"Christ, Bob, you're a braver man than me, walkin' around here dressed like that!" said Pete. "How, er, how do you two know each other? Or rather, in which particular posh City circles did your paths first cross? The club?"

"Funnily enough, no- though as Matthew has probably told you, I am certainly no stranger to 'posh City circles'! But in actual fact, young Matthew here used to step out with my daughter Emily- she's an investment banker in the City herself, in fact. Some people may have been kind enough to refer to us as part of the 'City Aristocracy', but I think that's a little, 'OTT', don't you, Matthew! Oh yes, the two of them may have had some little spat, but he's like a son to Doreen and I, and we're quietly confident that they'll patch it all up in due course."

This last part was definitely news to me- we'd only talked about Bob coming on board as chairman, to satisfy HGF's craving for some City white hair- not so much the wider dynastic agenda. I didn't know anyone else of the right age and background who would be prepared to do it simply for the kudos, before we had any money for non-executive director's fees.

"Not to air the dirty laundry in public," I said, "but I was actually always under the impression that you considered me to be- well, not really ambitious enough to keep up with a shooting star like Emily. And obviously you were, er, proved pretty spectacularly right on that score!"

"Not at all, not at all," said Bob. "It's not about the past, it's about the here and the now- and here you are, coming to me for advice, bringing me in to your new company as Mr Chairman. Getting me back into 'the Game'. I couldn't be prouder to help out, Matthew!"

He put his hand on my shoulder paternally.

"But what about Xavier?" I asked.

"Xavier," said Bob, with some displeasure. "Xavier may have a lot of money, but other than that he seems to have absolutely no redeeming features at all! Not only is he a completely inappropriate age for Emily, but Doreen agrees with me that he is quite the graceless fellow. Just to give you an example, selected purely at random: I recently invited him to the annual guest dinner of the Worshipful Company of Cheesemongers, explaining that it was something of a City institution- which I can confidently say that no one in the Guildhall or its environs would gainsay- and you won't believe how he responded!"

"How, man?" asked Carl with interest.

"He said that he'd been coming to the City for thirty years now without ever encountering the Company, and he saw 'no, you know, pressing need to remedy that situation now'!"

"So what did you say, man?"

"Of course I explained the history and origins of the Company. In some detail. It was clearly essential to put it all in the correct historical context for him. But before I had even finished describing an important particular of the grant of the Cheesemongers' charter by Lord Mayor Bartholomew Robards, he had cast doubt on the role of the livery companies in the 'modern City'! Does he think the Ceremonial Cheese-cutter burnishes itself? Or that Boris-bloody-Johnson organises the Lord Mayor's Show? Ridiculous!"

"That's cold, man," said Carl sympathetically. "Dissing the 'Mongers like that!"

"Monika, I was wondering if you could just give Bob a bit more detail on what Chatterbabe does today- and about our vision for taking Phoenix forward?" I asked.

"Perhaps you should- after all, you're virtually his son-in-law!" she said.

"OK, OK. Look, Bob, this is what we took to HGF," I said, passing him version 1.0 of the Phoenix business plan. "Obviously we still need to jazz it up a bit. But this is the fundamental business proposition- how the key revenue streams will kick in. Believe it or not, it actually makes some money today, so break-even in the new format should only be a couple of months out."

Bob put his reading-glasses on to peruse it.

"You know what you need?" said Bob. "What they call a 'Powerpoint Presentation'. You can put all kinds of snazzy graphics into it. Emily and her lot work wonders with them. Have you ever seen one, Matthew?"

"Yeah, I have actually, Bob," I said. "And that- in case anyone was wondering- is where Carl here comes in. Carl, I think it's time for you to start working your magic!"

"Just leave it with me, man," said Carl. "If I can hack into the Iranian nuclear program and prime their centrifuges to auto-destruct, then I think I can manage a PPT. But there are a few things I need, to make it sing."

"What?"

Carl ticked them off on his fingers.

"One packet of Rizlas (large); one Clipper lighter; one large selection pack of Nik Naks (must include at least three packets of Nice 'N' Spicy); at least two litres of SunnyD; and one large tin of condensed milk. Also a small enclosed area- that too is crucial, man."

"Will the spare room be alright?"

"Hey, that's perfect, man."

"OK- Pete, will you go to the Costcutter on the corner and buy all that crap for Carl then?"

"Why me?"

"What else are you doing? Everyone else is useful. And I need to call Em."

"Ooh- Em, is it now? OK then, OK, I'm goin', I'm goin'. Anyone else want anythin'? Box of Black Magic for your hedge fund coochy-coochy?"

"Just get some beers, will you, mate? This could be a very long night."

I went into the kitchen to call Emma.

"Hi! Matthew from Em TV here."

"Phoenix TV! I was just thinking about you actually, Matt. Because I turned on the TV to find something to watch- and what I really wanted was to see a programme some of my friends had made themselves. Really get involved, you know? If only there was a TV experience like that out there…"

"There could be soon! We're putting the finishing touches to the business plan tonight, and you should have it in the morning."

"Brilliant. Is it going to be a late one?"

"It definitely has all-nighter potential…"

"You must be used to that at least, from being a City lawyer!"

"Yeah, although historically I've had quite mixed results with all-nighters…"

"Oh… Well, good luck! And how about the debt?"

"I'm off to HGF with our new chairman first thing tomorrow. Big meeting."

"OK, great, but do try not to tell them to fuck off too early in proceedings this time. I don't want to put you under any more pressure, but we *really* need that loan to make this whole deal work."

"Oh, no, no, Emma, you're making it sound much worse than it really was. She only told him not to fuck *with* us."

"I stand corrected. I hope it wasn't some subliminal, anti-banker sentiment driving this negotiating strategy though? Now you're entering our domain. And you certainly haven't had the easiest Credit Crunch so far!"

"Well, yes and no, Emma. I can't deny that there's been a bit of fun in it too. I mean, at the peak of the banking crisis, the numbers in the press were just so mind-blowing that I completely lost all sense of proportion when all those banks kept falling over. There was a kind of excitement- almost titillation- about what was going to happen next. The business section of the paper was like the sports pages, with new heavyweight boxers getting knocked out every day."

"I know what you mean! I think we all started to lose our perspective on it, to be honest. By the time I'd seen Lehman Brothers, Merrill Lynch, Bear Stearns and AIG hit the skids, I was frankly a bit bored to hear about dull old Washington Mutual or Wachovia going under."

"Exactly! Anyway, I'm not really what you'd call a class warrior here. We were knee-deep in the financial services sector at the firm."

"So it's not a question of the powers of good at Phoenix against the evil forces of the City, then?"

"Not at all- that's my world too. And I definitely don't think you're evil. Not in a bad way, anyway."

"That's good- because apart from your appalling speed-dating etiquette, I actually think you're very nice. And I was rather hoping that we could catch up for a drink- once this is all tied up?"

"Definitely, I'm well up for that."

"Go get the debt then, baby!"

"Er- OK!"

I felt a rush of exhilaration, an excitement I hadn't felt since the first moments when I realised that Emily and I had made a connection. In fact, the only thing that worried me was how similar that had felt.

That was when I noticed Monika standing next to me in the kitchen.

"Matt, I don't want to interrupt," she whispered. "But there's smoke coming out from under the door of your spare room!"

"Carl! Shit! Em- got to go. I'll call you tomorrow, OK?" I hung up.

I followed Monika to the spare room. She pushed the door open intrepidly and ventured in.

"Oh my God!" she said. I burst in after her.

"That's amazing!" said Monika. "I didn't even realise that was possible!"

She stood in a dense cloud of cannabis smoke, watching the computer screen morph and evolve into extraordinary geometrical shapes and shifting hologrammic images, behind the slouched form of Carl himself.

"Wow- what on earth is that?" I asked Carl. "It's mind-blowing!"

"This is our Powerpoint presentation, man. Although I did have to, er, borrow, some graphics from the NASA Astrophysics Data System. I guess that will all be open source some day… But come on, close the door, man," said Carl. "I can only create in the right atmosphere. It's like the, er, Guild space navigators in *Dune*, man."

"Which Guild is that?" asked Bob with interest, closing the door behind him. "I'm not sure I've come across them in the City?" He seemed impervious to the thick cloud of dope smoke all around him.

"They, er, can only work immersed in clouds of spice gas."

"Ah- we don't have anything like that at the Cheesemongers'. Unless you include the, ah, Great Gorgonzola Day, perhaps…"

"They end up weirdly mutated by the process, man," he said. "But it's a small price to pay for folding space. You 'Mongers should consider that."

Monika was still watching the presentation in amazement.

"It's as though you're folding space and time with this!" she said. "It's more like a Tamagotchi- like an avatar- than just a presentation!"

"It's at the very intersection of, er, science and art, man. When I'm working, I try to visualise what Picasso would have done with Powerpoint text boxes at the height of his cubist phase- and then project beyond that, to another technical level of possibilities, you know? Powerpoint is actually a, er, highly sympathetic medium for the, er, simplification of natural forms into conventional geometric images."

Suddenly the screen went blank.

"Oh my God! What's that then, Pablo- *Guernica?*" I asked him.

"It's crashed, man- I was worried that this machine wouldn't have the power to deal with what we're creating here…"

"Christ! Can you rebuild it? Because, Carl- it was absolutely amazing. This could change everything!"

"I think so, man. But now I need solitude. Otherwise this will just be left- a, er, fragment of the complete work. Like *Kubla Khan*, man…"

I gave him the additional slides that we had roughed out on paper to go into the presentation, and the rest of us went back into the living room.

"What happened to Kubla Khan?" asked Monika.

"Seemingly Coleridge was in an opium-induced haze of some type when he had a vision of what later became the poem *Kubla Khan*. 'A damsel with a dulcimer' and all that… When he woke up, he started scribbling it down as quickly as he could, but he was still in the middle of it when he had an unexpected visit by a man from, er…"

"St Ives?" suggested Pete.

"No, I think that was the dude with seven wives. Anyway, after this visit, Coleridge couldn't recall any more of the vision. The rest of it was lost forever. So let's leave Carl to it, shall we?"

"But when is it goin' to be ready?" asked Pete. "I'm friggin' knackered! And aren't you due at the bank at eight a.m.?"

"I've got no idea. Carl moves in mysterious ways. But you guys can leave now, if you want. I think we've got everyone's input on the document. Great team effort!"

"Who's, er, who's actually going to the bank tomorrow, Matthew?" asked Colin. "I hear from Veronica that's it's, well, it's quite a test of fire! Though we are, of course, no strangers to *that* after our, er, speed-dating experiences…"

"We thought it would just be Bob and I this time, Colin, if you don't mind?" I said. "We don't want to look too mob-handed. And, through no fault of her own, V made a rather, er, eccentric impression on them last time…"

"Sounds like an excellent plan to me!" said Colin.

"How did you get in touch with Bob again, Matthew?" Monika asked me.

"Via Emily, of course. He's her dad. We've never had a direct line of communication before. Absence seems to have made the heart grow fonder- on Bob's part anyway."

"I think I'm going to go home now," she said. "It is getting really late! Good night everyone. Good luck at the bank! And with everything!"

I lay back on the sofa, closed my eyes for a moment and passed out for six hours. I woke up with a start in the living room, alone, fully-dressed and covered in Nik Nak crumbs. I scrabbled for my mobile phone.

"Christ! Seven o' clock! The bank!"

I ran through to the spare room. Carl was slumped in front of the computer.

"Carl! Wake up! Wake up! I need it now!"

After an eternity, Carl looked slowly round at me.

"Cool your boots, man. I'm just applying the very final touches to a, er, minor masterpiece of its kind. Cinderella *will* go the ball…"

He gave the keyboard a final caress, and a spectacular *aurora borealis* rippled and cascaded across the screen. There was something about the image that reminded me irresistibly of that bare advertising billboard, just around the corner on the Balls Pond Road, now trapped underneath a new endless loop of slogans and cellulose smiles.

"My work is done now, man," he said, flipping the laptop closed. "And I emailed it to Emma, like you asked. Now it's all over to you, man."

"Carl- thank you! I never thought I'd say these words... But you're a bloody genius!"

By the time I was shaved, suited and leaving the flat fifteen minutes later, Carl was sprawled out on the spare bed, snoring loudly.

"*Vaya con dios*, man," I called quietly to him, as I closed the front door behind me and ran for the bus.

Chapter 15

City of London, 15 December 2008

The Worshipful Warden pulled his costly velvet cloak tightly around him against the cold, before striding out onto the cobbled street outside. He stepped carefully, to avoid the filth and detritus of Olde London beneath his feet. Insolent rain-drops splashed off the enormous, bulbous jewels that encrusted the golden chain of office resting heavily on his shoulders, like tear-drops on the rheumy eyes of some ancient sea-monster arisen from the unspeakable depths of uncharted northern oceans.

"Er, Bob- do you really think the full regalia is a good idea for a business meeting?" I asked cautiously. "Is that what people do these days?"

He looked at me, amused at my naivety.

"This is the City, Matthew- this is exactly what you need to show these guys that you're part of the club! A calling card, you might call it. Because in the City, if you're not inside, you're outside! You must have heard that…"

"I have heard it- but I thought it meant something a little different from this…"

"Trust me on this, my boy…" He rubbed his hands together. "You're in my world now!"

We walked along Cheapside to the bank. We got a few funny looks on the way, but not as many as you'd expect for a group which included someone in a violet, velvet three-cornered hat, at eight o'clock on a Monday morning. People must have an unusually high pomp and circumstance threshold in that part of the City.

"So what did Emma say about the old Powerpoint presentation? Pretty snazzy, eh?" said Bob.

"She absolutely loved it! She texted me on my way here- she wants to hire Carl to do their own presentations. Although I assume that's subject to interview and satisfactory references. They're pretty informal in hedge funds, but I don't know how Carl's working practices would fit in there..."

"So is she going to make the investment, do you think?"

"Yeah, I think she wants to, but now this whole thing is completely inter-conditional. To get the debt we need the equity, to get the equity we need the debt."

"How can that possibly work, then? Isn't it a bit of a chicken and egg situation?"

"There's an element of the chicken and the egg, there always is, but if you can just get all the plates spinning at the same time, somehow- somehow- everything generally seems to fall into place. Or at least it used to before this September, anyway... So if we can swing it in this meeting- the deal is on!"

"Come on, then- break a leg, old chap!"

"Let's do this, Bob!"

We were shown straight through to the meeting room this time. Bob winked at me and pointed to his three-cornered hat.

"So tell me, Nigel, are you in the 'Great Twelve' yourself?" said Bob, as we sat down at the board table.

"I'm not, er, exactly sure what you're referring to, Mr Walker?" Bob chuckled.

"The 'Great Twelve' livery companies, of course, Nigel! As you're no doubt well aware, in this strategically crucial position near the Guildhall, we of the Cheesemongers are often said to be the missing tribe of the 'Great Twelve'!"

He leaned forward confidentially, his chain of office swinging alarmingly close to Nigel's nose.

"As a matter of fact, Nigel- and don't tell anyone from the so-called 'Worshipful Company of Forkwrights' this- this might just be the year we finally squeeze them out of the 'Great Twelve', and take our rightful seat at the top table!"

He tapped his own nose meaningfully and winked.

"Let's just say that the Worshipful Lord Mayor happens to be a very good friend of mine, if you know what I mean?"

"So, like you suggested, Nigel, we wanted to bring in a new chairman," I said. "Someone like Bob, who could use their contacts in the City to help us get the business off the ground."

"And the fact is, Nigel," Bob said, "it's really my responsibility now to give something back to the City, which has given me so much, isn't it?"

"Yeah, thanks, Bob," I said. "So, Nigel, shall we run through the revised business plan? Things have changed a bit since we last spoke on the equity side, because now we have backers with some serious dry powder. Yes, they were single-handedly responsible for bringing down at least two multinational banking groups. But on the bright side, they are prepared to put some of the profits into Phoenix TV. I've actually got it set up on my lap-top here, which is probably the best way to look at it."

In a perfect world, the best way to look at it would actually have been to hook it up to the big screen that they had mounted on the wall there, but I'd been to far too many botched presentations to go down that road. You spend the first half hour of the meeting just trying to work out how to use the system. To begin with, you all have a bit of a chuckle at its vagaries and some good one-liners are bandied about. Fifteen minutes in, the joke is starting to wear a little thin, and you realise that there's nothing for it but to give up and desperately ask the home team how to use it- however bad that looks. They are eventually forced to reveal that they don't know how to use it either, feel humiliated by their own inept blunderings, and secretly blame and hate you for it. Finally they summon their own IT expert, who spends another half an hour testing various implausible theories, turns out to be in total denial as to the fallibilities of his own system and charmlessly pronounces your memory-stick, software and business practices to be hopelessly antiquated and unfit for modern purposes. By that time, the allotted period for the meeting is over, you and the home team both hate each other and possibly irreparable damage has been done to your technical, professional and ethical credibility.

"I've also got some hard-copies of the slide-deck here for you, Nigel. You can hold onto them, in case you can't read anything off the screen."

"Great, thanks," said Nigel. "Normally I'd suggest pulling the presentation up on the big screen, but since you're happy not to use it, I have to tell you that we have had a few glitches with it! In fact there is a theory in the bank that it's part of the reason we haven't closed any small business loans since 2007…"

"I really don't think that's going to be a problem today, Nigel," I said. "You see, this isn't so much a presentation- as living artificial intelligence."

I smiled, flipped the lap-top open and let Carl and Powerpoint weave their alchemical tendrils around the room.

"It's- it's just so beautiful…" gasped Nigel.

Chapter 16

Holloway, London, 22 December 2008

"More *baklava*, anyone?" asked Kostas, passing around a sticky white cardboard box.

"What's that, mate?" asked Pete, straining to hear him over the roar of traffic noise pouring in from the Holloway Road outside.

"Just asked if you wanted more *baklava*, my friend," Kostas said, yanking away the traffic cone that was holding the window open. "I thought it would be a nice touch for the closing meetin'. The famous Greek hospitality, know what I mean?"

We all winced involuntarily as the window slammed shut, and the pane trembled in its rickety frame.

"I thought *baklava* was Turkish, Kostas?" said Pete.

"Greek, Turkish, whatever, right? I don't fear Turks bearin' gifts, know what I mean? Don't tell my granddad I said so though! He hates those Turks with a passion, believe me…"

We waited in silence for another ten minutes.

"More coffee, anyone?" Kostas said. "I think there's another jar of Nescafé somewhere… Or Rita can go and get one from the Nag's Head Shopping Centre. Spare no expense- that's the way Dimitrios rolls, believe me, my friend- especially round Christmas time!"

"Yeah, but where exactly is Dimitrios, Kostas?" I said. "He was supposed to be here half an hour ago. We were supposed to close this deal on Friday! The sale documents are all agreed- you drafted them yourself. But we need Dimitrios' signature to take to our investors before they'll release the cash to us. It's as simple as that. This is the worst closing meeting I've ever been to. Well, one of the worst... It's almost as though we're being deliberately slowed down here."

"I know, my friend, I know, you're preachin' to the incense-burner here!" said Kostas. "What can I tell you, I've called Dimitrios ten times, I'm movin' heaven and earth here!"

"And there's one other thing that's bothering me, Kostas..."

"What's that, my friend?"

"Where were you on the night of the speed-dating?"

"Oh my God, come on, come on, don't start with this again, now! What are you, my wife? I told you, I had a photo-shoot with Galina, I was already committed, money had changed hands, I couldn't make it. I wanted to work on that high-concept idea I had with her and the terrapin- you know, the idea I had after I saw some of the wrinkly little *bastardes* in the pond at Clissold Park- where it'd look as though its head was emergin' from between her breasts, instead of out of his shell, know what I mean? Artistic. I mean it was tricky, technically speakin', to set the shot up, because she'd heard somethin' about Florida Snappin' Turtles, an' she kept worryin' it was gonna' bite her..."

"What on earth are you talking about, Kostas? Just answer the question, will you?"

"How long are you gonna' hold this against me, my friend? I'm sorry I missed this speed-datin' of yours, but it all worked out, you played a blinder, you got lovely Emma on board, life goes on, everyone's happy, right?"

"The thing is that I happened to check the rota at Chatterbabe for that night. When we were doing our due diligence on the company last week. And Galina was working at Chatterbabe that night."

"Oh, Sweet Jesus! You checkin' up on me? I'm disappointed, disappointed, my friend! I wouldn't expect this from you... You couldn't have seen her yourself, you were out at the speed-dating, right? So what can I tell you, she nipped out for a while..."

"You can say what you like, Kostas, but I *know* you wouldn't have missed that City Beehive. Not unless you were doing something a hell of a lot more important than a photo-shoot with Galina. Christ, you were the only one of us who had any real chance- barring a miracle- of actually making it work!"

Kostas opened the window, lit a cigarette, dragged furiously at it and still managed to toss the burning cigarette butt out of the window and onto the heads of the passing Christmas shoppers below, before it dropped shut again with a slam.

"Matt, my friend, it's killin' me not to be completely open with you about this, but as a fellow lawyer, you really gotta' understand that there are client confidentiality issues here!"

"But Dimitrios is your client- and he's selling us Chatterbabe! Isn't he?"

Kostas paced the room restlessly.

"Look, I jus' can't tell you the whole story," he said. "It's not my story to tell you. But what I can say, is that at this time of day, Dimitrios would normally go to the Greek-Cypriot Social Club on the Hornsey Road. So if you really wanna' see him, then let's go down there, alright, my friends?"

"Of course we want to see him!" I said. "You know we do. We want him to sign these bloody documents! We agreed to meet him here- now you're making it sound as though we're hassling him on some whim!"

"Well, what can I tell you my friend? I look around, an' I see that he's not here. An' I know he won't be at home, because that's where his wife and mother-in-law are. So, Hornsey Road is the next best bet, believe me!"

"I thought you kept telling me that your client- that Dimitrios- was a man of his word?"

"Yes, an' he comes from a long line of proud Greek men of their word: Odysseus, Daedalus, Agamemnon…"

"Really? Because from what I remember from school, those were some pretty perfidious *bastardes* too. Daedalus designed the bloody Labyrinth!"

"He's a man of his word, believe me, my friend. Jus' not of his calendar! But, listen to me, you're overreactin', he's late, he's somewhere else, we'll go and find him and we'll get him to sign the documents. So what have you lost? An hour? You sleep for eight hours every night, my friend! So get up a little bit earlier tomorrow, an' you have the time back already, am I right?"

"Can't we try callin' him- before we go out drivin' round London?" said Pete.

"He's not goin' to speak on the telephone! Dimitrios doesn't believe in telephones…"

"He doesn't believe in telephones?" I said. "I'm not being funny, but aren't we buying a cable chatline channel from him?"

"Mary, Mother of God, will you just relax, my friend? He acknowledges the technology of telephony. If you wanna' know the time, call the speakin' clock, that's fine with Dimitrios. He just don't believe in doin' business that way! No, if you want to talk business with Dimitrios, you got to go an' see him, man to man. Sit down together. I told you where."

"Yeah- you told us here!"

"An' now I'm tellin' you Hornsey Road! Sweet Jesus, I'm a reasonable man, but you're really pushin' me here, my friend!"

"OK, OK, let's go to Hornsey Road then."

We headed downstairs and out onto the Holloway Road.

"Where's Monika, mate?" Pete asked me, as we picked our way carefully down the stairs. "I was expectin' to see her here."

"Shit, I don't know- I tried to call her earlier, but she wasn't picking up. I haven't heard anything from her."

"I'll try her now. Let's sort this friggin' deal out, and then we'll track her down."

The Holloway Road is not the thoroughfare that you'd choose if you want to get somewhere in a hurry, but the advantage of travelling with Kostas was that he tended to use the bus lane and pavements more than the road itself. In three minutes flat, the BMW screamed to a halt outside a dingy shop-front, festooned with over-elaborate lace curtains infused with years of grime.

"This it?" said Pete. "I thought Dimitrios was a friggin' leadin' Greek-Cypriot entrepreneur?"

"An' what does that say?" said Kostas, pointing at a scrap of paper taped to the window.

"I dunno', mate," said Pete. "It appears to be written in Greek! Or possibly Cypriot."

"Greek-Cypriot Social Club! So follow me, OK, my friends?"

Kostas was parked at his customary forty-five degree angle, so Pete and I in the back of the car found ourselves considerably further from the kerb than Kostas in the front. Nonetheless, we all piled into the club. The walls were decorated with dusty lace doilies and yellowing pictures of moustachioed Greek football teams of some unspecified vintage, together with various Liverpool teams from the nineteen-eighties. The front room was filled with small tables, mostly occupied by late middle-aged men drinking tea and playing what I assumed to be backgammon. Many of them greeted Kostas warmly as we walked through, leading to animated bursts of Greek on both sides. No one paid the slightest attention to me or Pete.

"Er, Kostas," I asked him in one gap between bursts. "Is Dimitrios actually here then?"

"Yes, my friend, he's in the back room. He takes his backgammon very seriously- he doesn't like to be watched. Says it would be like being watched in the bed-room, if you know what I mean!"

"Kind of… But can we maybe go and speak to him then? It's getting pretty urgent. Tomorrow is the last day the bank can fund this deal before Christmas. And they are men of their calendars."

"OK, OK, I'm hurryin', can't you see, my friend? I had to blank several old friends of the family back there! God only knows what will come of that! But come on."

Ten minutes later, we were knocking on the door of the back room. A loud rant in Greek ensued.

"He's not happy bein' interrupted," conjectured Kostas.

"Well, I'm not happy being dicked around here! This sale process is a joke, Kostas!"

Kostas tilted his head to and fro.

"Maybe so, maybe not. But who owns the TV channel? And who wants to buy it? That's what you got to ask yourself, my friend."

He knocked on the door again. There was another burst of Greek, but this time Kostas walked in, ushering us through after him. Dimitrios looked extremely sulky, but he kissed Kostas on each cheek nonetheless.

"Dimitrios, we're very sorry to disturb your backgammon like this," I said, "But we really need to get your signature on these documents today. The banks and our equity provider are waiting for them. If we can't get your signature back to them today, the whole deal could be in jeopardy."

Dimitrios looked at us impassively, then started a new sally in Greek. When he finished speaking though, Kostas nodded and turned back to us.

"Let's go back to the office. I'll explain to you there."

"No, no, wait just a second. Is Dimitrios coming, or not? I'd like an explanation right here and right now. What's going on here? We need the signatures now. Do we have a deal, or don't we? I'm getting a little tired of being fobbed off here!"

Dimitrios launched into Greek again.

"Listen, Dimitrios, I know for a fact that you speak perfect English- so would you please pay us the courtesy of telling us what's going on?"

"Matt, take it easy, mate, alright?"

"No, Pete, we've got to have it out with him here. C'mon, it's time to open your kimono, Dimitrios!"

Now Dimitrios was raging at me, and Kostas stepped in between us.

"He's sellin' Chatterbabe to someone else, my friend," said Kostas quietly. "He got a better offer, and he's signed up an exclusivity agreement with them. The deal's off. Now come on, let's go, let's go, before you make matters a whole lot worse, my friend. Dimitrios really din't like the kimono thing. An' if he found out you were referrin' to a traditional Japanese robe favoured by women, then that would definitely would definitely be feudin' talk…"

He ushered us back into the front room of the club.

"Kostas, I'm going to ask you again- where were you on the night of the speed-dating?"

"Matt…"

"Just tell me now!"

"I was reviewin' the exclusivity agreement for Dimitrios, my friend. He needed me!"

"Jesus Christ, Kostas, you've really shafted us here!"

"What could I do, my friend? You know we have to do what the client tells us! Solicitors' Practice Rule Number One, mate: 'I promise to do my best.' Or somethin' like that, innit?"

"I think that's actually the 'Cub Scout Promise', Kostas…"

"Same idea, innit? Anyway, this is jus' the kind of person Dimitrios is, to be honest, my friend. He makes this big thing of bein' a man of his word, an' so the wrong kind of people can exploit him in that, by gettin' him to sign up documents that he probably shouldn't. You know, the whole demonstration of good faith thing. He's a sucker for it. All you have to do is doubt his word, and there's a grand Dimitrios gesture on the way, regular as clockwork, signed, sealed and delivered. It's not the first time this has happened, if I'm honest, an' it probably won't be the last…"

"So who is he selling to?"

"It's called, er, it's called 'Luxembourg Capital Partners'…"

"Luxembourg Capital Partners! Bugger me! That's Xavier Tempel's fund! This is just getting better and better! But how on earth did Xavier know about this deal? This is fucking insane!"

"You know this man, my friend? The other bidder?"

"Yes, I know him! And I am not losing this deal to him! So what can we do to make Dimitrios change his mind back now?"

"Listen, my friend, no one could be sorrier than me about what's happened here. Really, it's a horrible thing, my heart goes out to all of you, it breaks for you, an' if there was anything I could do, anything at all, I'd do it in a heart-beat. But this Xavier guy, he offered more money, you know what I'm sayin'? Dimitrios has his family to think of, and he always puts his family first. Call it a Greek thing."

"You think we don't put our families first here too? What do we do, prefer complete strangers? But hang on a minute…You are related to him though, aren't you?"

"Course I am! He's like a father to me. Although if you wanna' be a stickler about it, he's even more like a father to my cousin, if you know what I mean ?"

"Yeah, I think so- he's your uncle. So what if you were to get involved in the Phoenix TV project yourself, Kostas? We've still got funding lined up from Emma's fund and HGF, if we can get the deal done with Dimitrios by tomorrow. You're a businessman, and an artist- with your, er, photography. And you know everything there is to know about cars. We'd all love to have you on board. Pete and Monika think the world of you. Your integrity. Except when it comes to terrapin rights, obviously…"

"Listen, Matt, my friend, I appreciate the offer, an' I like the business, and the team, a lot. I think the world of you all, you're like family to me. You're forgettin' one thing though, and I'm surprised at you as a lawyer, my friend. What about the exclusivity agreement? Even if we can get Dimitrios to ditch this Xavier guy, it's out of his hands, innit? We can work all the magic we like in Tribunals, but that's a binding contract, mate. Nothing to be done."

"Can you get me a copy?"

Kostas hesitated.

"OK. OK, my friend. I've got it in the Beamer. You take a look at it, an' if there's any wriggle-room, then we'll speak to Dimitrios and have a go. You can't say fairer than that, right?"

"No. Thanks, Kostas."

"Matt, mate," said Pete. "Just had a message from Bob. Says he can't speak now- but he's got some important news. On the deal. Some terrible mistake he's made. And some guy called Xavier?"

"Xavier! Did Bob say where he was?"

"He said he's in a procession to the friggin' Guildhall, if that means anythin' to you?"

"Right, Kostas, can you take me to the City?"

"Now, my friend?"

"Yes, now! We need to speak to Bob. I'll read the exclusivity agreement on the way- if I don't black out from the g-force on Highbury Corner. And Pete- can you try and get hold of Katinka? I'm worried about Monika. We can't do this without her! I'll text you her mobile number."

"Katinka? Friggin' hell, this is gonna' be fun…"

"Thanks, mate. Kostas, just head for Moorgate will you? I'll direct you from there. I can't believe those guys venture too far, in their condition. They carry all kinds of crap with them in these processions. We'll just have to drive around the area until we find them."

"Drop me at Highbury Corner, willya'?" said Pete. "Katinka ain't answerin' either. But I'll find them! Christ, Kostas- is that strictly in accordance with the Highway Code? You do know that we drive on the friggin' left hand side of the road here, don't you?"

"Highway Code? Pete, my friend- Kostas' Code is 'Who wants it the most, *bastarde*?'"

"C'mon, let's channel that into gettin' this deal done! Hang in there, mate!" said Pete, slapping me on the shoulder. He slipped out of the car and Kostas gunned it down Canonbury Road, headed for the City.

"Do you think this could be them, my friend?" said Kostas ten minutes later, sounding his horn as we sat behind a procession of robed marchers moving solemnly down Basinghall Avenue.

"Hmm, judging by the extremely large cheese those two guys with the silver platter are carrying, I'd say it might well be," I said. "Do you think you could stop beeping the horn for a minute though, Kostas? It's really riling up those dudes with the bowler hats and aprons over there… I'm actually going to get out and look for Bob on foot, OK? Thanks for the lift- and for the exclusivity agreement."

"No problem, Matty-boy- and, listen, I'm sorry about how things have turned out, alright?"

"Sure. I'll speak to you later."

I got out, and Kostas threw the car into an abrupt U-turn, scattering the Cheesemongers' rear-guard, and causing the left cheese-bearer to lose control of the platter momentarily. The cheese's huge weight caused it to slide alarmingly leftwards on the silver platter, and the right cheese-bearer over-corrected and tipped it too far back towards his side. The 'Mongers in the vicinity looked on in horror as the super-sized cheese toppled down onto the road. It thudded down onto the tarmac, then split agonisingly in two.

"Out of the way, you benders!" shouted Kostas out of his car window at the scurrying Cheesemongers. He reversed back over the dissected cheese, obliterating one half completely and leaving a deep tyre-mark through the other. "Later, Matt! Call me, mate!" He accelerated away, churning the cheese into Dairylea as he went.

"Sorry… sorry…" I muttered at the forlorn Cheesemongers around me, who were desperately trying to scrape the remnants of the cheese back onto the platter. "You might want to try Cheestrings when you're out and about in future- more durable…"

I picked my way through the procession to the front, where Bob was leading the way, holding a fearsome-looking pike before him.

"This is it, Matt- the Ceremonial Cheese-cutter!" he said, brandishing it belligerently when I finally attracted his attention. "Unworthy churl though I be, I've been, ah, entrusted with the signal honour of cutting the ancestral Cheddar!"

"Ancestral, eh? You might actually be better off with an ice-cream scoop for that today…"

"What do you mean?"

"Er, nothing, nothing... But what did you want to tell me about Project Phoenix, Bob? There's a serious problem on the deal. And I'm really hoping that you're going to tell me that you're not part of it?"

"Sorry I couldn't get away, Matthew," he said. "But for the Second Warden to miss the annual Cheesemongers' procession to the Guildhall. Well..."

"Yeah, yeah, it would be the end of civilisation as we know it, I know. But Bob, you did mention that you had something important to tell me?"

He transferred the Ceremonial Cheese-cutter from one shoulder to the other uncomfortably.

"The thing is, Matthew... Well, the thing is that I'm afraid I might have been guilty of a teensy-weensy bit of an indiscretion on the Phoenix side..."

"What do you mean?"

"Well, I was just so pleased to be getting back into 'the Game', you know- to be giving something back to this dear old City of ours..."

"Spit it out, Bob, we'll be at the bloody Guildhall in a minute!"

Several Cheesemongers behind us were glaring at me now.

"Ssshhh... ssshhhhh..." hissed Bob urgently. "Solemnity is of the essence. Otherwise it's just- well, a walk through the City with a big cheese, isn't it? Right then, well, to be quite honest with you, Matthew, I told Emily about it. That I was getting involved with the Chatterbabe buy-out, that is. Chairman of the Board! I just wanted her to see that her old man still has what it takes to be involved in a real deal, you see. Raise some finance. Perhaps you wouldn't understand- you're young, you've got it all front of you. But I don't want her to see her Dad as an old man, not yet. I didn't mean any harm by it..."

"And she told Xavier! I don't believe this! Pete was right- she *is* a grade 'A' bitch!"

Now all the Cheesemongers were staring at me. I didn't want to be there when these guys saw the state of the ancestral Cheddar.

"Sorry, guys," I said. "I was just talking about the Second Warden's daughter. No offence, no offence. But why does Xavier even want Chatterbabe? Surely he's not doing it just to spite me? He's already won, hasn't he? What more does he want? My blood?"

"The thing is, Matthew… Xavier was actually there too- when I told Emily. She had brought him round to the house to meet Doreen and I. I suppose in some way I, er- I wanted to show him that the Cheesemongers and I still do have a place in the, er, 'modern City'. Whatever he and his jumped-up private equity cronies might think! But it gave him an idea, apparently- he's been planning to set up a gambling channel on cable TV for some time, he said. So when he heard about this- about a licensed cable channel available on the cheap, with a motivated seller- he got Emily to call Dimitrios, to make a deal…"

"That utter, utter shit!"

"He doesn't seem to like you very much either, I must admit… But, Matthew- I'm so terribly sorry. Let me help to make this right…"

"No, Bob, you've done more than enough for one day. You stay here and, er, cut the cheese…"

I turned to the nearby Cheesemongers, who were now loudly tutting at me.

"And as for you twats, I prefer aerosol cheese anyway!"

Chapter 17

City of London, 22 December 2008

"Where are the jelly beans?" I asked Ken. "That's what I miss most about this place. Well, actually it's the only thing. But we definitely don't have anything like that at Ofcable."

"Oh, you know how it is, Matthew… In the present, er, climate, it's really no longer considered appropriate to have, er, luxury confectionery in all the meeting rooms. Certainly not for the small deals."

"There aren't even any mint imperials any more, man," said Carl. "Although they were actually quite minging, anyway. They had an aftertaste like amyl nitrate, man… That's poppers to you, Ken."

"Ah, yes, well, shall we push on with the agenda, now we're- finally- all here?" said Ken. "And of course, we're delighted to host you, to wrap this up once and for all!"

"I don't know about agendas," said Dimitrios. "I just wanna' explain why I asked for this meetin'," he said. "As all of you knows, I'm a plain man, a man of my words."

"And so am I, you know," said Xavier.

"A man of my words," continued Dimitrios. "So when all of you starts getting upset, telling me I have to sell to one person, then another person, my head is spinning with it, and I says to Kostas- he's like a son to me, this boy- I says, 'let's get everyone into the same room, and let's talk it through, we puts the cards on the tables and we decides between all of us what to do. OK? Like businessmen!"

"I'm a man of my words too, you know," said Xavier. "So when my lawyer tells me that I have a, uh, watertight, bombproof, copper-bottomed, binding exclusivity agreement to buy something, and I want to buy it, I find it a little bit difficult to understand why I have to, uh, why I have to talk about it anymore, you know? This may be the Greek way of doing business, you know, but it's not the way we do deals in New York, London, Luxembourg, uh…"

"Solihull…" said Darren.

"Those are my cities, you know. I don't know how it's done in, uh, Istanbul…"

"That's in Turkey! Istanbul is in Turkey!" hissed Dimitrios. "We're all Greek here, *bastarde*!"

"The thing is," I said, "the exclusivity agreement actually works a little bit differently from the way that you described it to Dimitrios, Xavier. I'm pretty familiar with the wording, because it's based on this firm's standard form, right, Ken?"

"Of course it is. Why wouldn't it be?" said Ken. "They all are! Do you want them drafted from scratch on every deal? Who do you think's going to pay for that, eh?"

"Right, except that when you read it, there's one important difference from the signed exclusivity agreement that Xavier's fund had on Project Behemoth," I said. "On that deal there was a 'hard' exclusivity obligation- so the seller couldn't do a deal with anyone except for Xavier's fund, at any price."

"The same as this one, you know!" said Xavier. "That's what a bloody exclusivity agreement is, you know. And Ken used the same document for this one, I, uh, asked him to."

"Not quite, Xavier- for this one he must have used the version of the standard form with a 'soft' exclusivity obligation. This one says that Dimitrios can't do a deal with anyone to sell Chatterbabe to them for 'total consideration lower than' Xavier's offer price. And Xavier's offer price is defined as £300,000, not as whatever offer Xavier might make from time to time- if he decided to increase it. So provided that we offer £300,001- which we do- then all bets are off under that exclusivity agreement. We're back on a level playing-field."

"Nonsense!" said Ken, but he was frantically flicking through the agreement, "I told the trainee just to use the exclusivity agreement from Project Behemoth... He told me he'd found it on the system. So it, er, it must be the same!"

"Surely you guys remember that the Behemoth deal changed quite significantly in the course of negotiations though? The first draft was intended to reflect the 'low-ball' offer Xavier made at the start- no offence, Xavier- so the seller got the hump, and refused to give him full exclusivity. He was still hoping to find someone else to sell it to for a better price. It was only when Xavier eventually increased the offer to a level more acceptable to the seller- a more reasonable offer, to be honest- that we prepared the final draft of the exclusivity agreement, granting full exclusivity this time."

"So you're saying that Ken, you know, prepared the wrong agreement?" said Xavier. "Is that true, Ken? Is it, you know?"

"Well, I- that bloody trainee- I was on the partners' retreat in the States at the time, I didn't have time to check everything myself... Wait, doesn't that say that, er... Oh."

"Are you saying, you know, that, he's right?" thundered Xavier. "Are you, Ken?"

"Of course, I'm sure that no one would try to argue now that we didn't intend to have full exclusivity- whatever the, ah, actual piece of paper might say!" said Ken. "So I think the parties would all accept that it should just be read in that way anyway... If it was just a mistake by some very junior lawyer- who I might say has let me and Xavier down very badly indeed- using a cookie-cutter precedent..."

"Nice try, Ken," I said. "You don't have a leg to stand on, and you know it."

"You! You have a, uh, conflict of interest!" said Xavier. "You were acting for *me* on this deal! Project Behemoth! You can't say this, you know! You're in breach of duty! Breach of trust!"

"I'm not acting for anyone, Xavier. I'm the competing bidder. I can say what I like, because what I know about Behemoth doesn't make any difference whatsoever. The issue is what's written in this agreement. And that's just a question of fact. It's there in black and white for all of us to see."

"Is that right, you know?" Xavier spat at Ken.

"Well, er, we could, we could try reporting it to the Law Society, and see what they say... But I don't know what they could really do about it."

"About what?" said Kostas. "The fact that you drafted a different agreement from the one your client wanted? Maybe they'll ask you a few questions about how that happened, my friend! I've seen a fair few cowboy solicitors go out that way in my time, believe me! You would definitely not be the first!"

"Of course I assumed that Xavier would have read it before he signed it!" said Ken desperately. "Didn't you look at it, Xav, and tell the trainee that you were happy with it before you signed it? You would hardly just have signed anything we put in front of you, would you?"

"That's what I pay you for, you know!" screamed Xavier. "Maybe I should train as a bloody lawyer, and draft all the agreements too, you think?"

"But now, Uncle Dimitrios," said Kostas, "The real question is who you're gonna' sell your Chatterbabe too? To Matthew, Monika and me- or to this *bastarde*!"

"I'll give you £350,000 for it!" said Xavier. "But that's my final offer, you know. I'm not haggling like a, uh, grubby market trader, you know!"

"I started my careers working in a market!" Dimitrios shouted. "*Bastarde!*"

"I can see that, you know!" said Xavier, looking round the room. "This is the most, uh, amateurish transaction that I've ever been involved in, you know. First, we have these, uh, unspeakable Greeks…" He turned to Ken. "And then your bloody firm, you know! How much did you say you wanted to get paid for this? £150,000? That's, uh, nearly fifty per cent. of the consideration for the whole deal, you know, and you couldn't even get a simple exclusivity agreement right! You'll never work for this fund again, you know, never!"

"A hundred and fifty grand!" said Kostas whistling. "That's a bit steep innit, Ken? I'm doin' this for ten large, no questions asked…"

"How would you know what super-premium legal services cost? You? A crummy high street lawyer!" shouted Ken. "You haven't the first idea what goes on in the City. Do you have any idea how few deals there've been since the Credit Crunch started?

Xavier, we need your business! None of the banks will touch us after all the deals we've done for you!"

"Shut up! Shut up!" Dimitrios shouted. "I told you before what we gonna' do, we gonna' talk it through, and then we decides who to sell Chatterbabe to! The talkin's not goin' too well, so I'll tell you how it's going to be. You each have 24 hours to come up with your bid, then you writes it down and puts it in envelope. I'll open the envelope, and whoever's made the highest bid, I sell Chatterbabe to. OK?"

"But how do we know you won't just change your mind again, you know?" Xavier said.

"I'm a man of my words!" screamed Dimitrios.

"I hear that, but I don't see it, you know! Anyway, I don't have any more time to waste on this, I have to fly to Monte tonight, you know. Ken, will you set up a video conference call for tomorrow so that we can, uh, put this to bed? Get all these, uh, people on the line. Do you think you can manage that, you know? I'll speak to Emily later about the bid."

Xavier got up to leave, but pointedly did not shake hands with anyone.

"I'll speak to you later too, you know," he said to the wretched Ken. "You better pray to your, uh, lucky star that we win the auction, you know! Although something tells me that we might, uh, we might just be able to raise just a little bit more money than a failed lawyer and a bunch of civil servants, you know!"

"Come on, Uncle, let's go too," said Kostas. "I'll give you a lift, Matt."

As we walked out of the firm onto Coleman Street, Kostas shook his head.

"Why did you have to say that about the sealed bids, Uncle? That *bastarde* has money to burn. How we gonna' come up with a bid to match him now?"

"This is business, my son!" said Dimitrios, shrugging. "And besides, what I could do? I gave him my words we would do some business together…"

"I know, I know… But now this Xavier guy is goin' to get his hands on Chatterbabe, Uncle! You think me and Matt here can raise enough money to outbid some private equity hot-shot overnight? We're stretchin' it to the max just to pay the price we agreed, believe me!"

He put his hand on my shoulder.

"Listen, Matty-boy- you gave it your best shot, buddy, but it just hasn't worked out for you this time. So what? 'Cos I gotta' new idea- why don't you come and be my partner at Alexandrou & Associates LLP, OK? You've already had your first big immigration win, I'll show you the ropes on the Gangmasters, before you know it we'll be bigger than that *bastarde* Ken, no problem! What do you say, my friend? Matt?"

"I've got Pete on my mobile, Kostas! Give me one sec, will you?"

"You got it. I'll get the car, my friend."

"So what did Katinka say, Pete? Has Monika been in touch with her? She hasn't been taking any of my calls."

"She was a bit arsey with me, to be honest, mate. Well, to the extent that she could be, within the limits of her slightly dozy personality, if you know what I mean? To start with, she was askin' me why she should do anythin' to help you, after what you'd done to Monika. So that's when I reminded her that you had risked your job, and spent hours workin' for nothin', to help her remain in the UK. That did have some effect on her, I must admit."

"What I'd done to Monika? What's happened to Monika?"

"Right, well, you're not goin' to like this part much. It turns out that Monika's buggered off back to Warsaw. Left this afternoon apparently. Decided there's nothing left for her here."

"What! What can we do- do you think we should go to the airport? To persuade her to come back?"

"She's not Jennifer Aniston, mate. She's Monika. Like Monica from *Friends*, see what I mean? Seriously though, people don't just go chasin' each other to airports in real life. You need some kind of mature, adult response. You're just gonna' have to speak to her, I think. That's if you actually want to get her back."

"What do you mean? Of course I do- we're so close to doing this deal now! And she's such an important part of the business!"

"That's just the point though, isn't it, mate? She doesn't just want to be part of the business. She thought that you were goin' to build this together. Now she doesn't know what to think. You've got your new best mate Bob tryin' to set you up with Emily again, and Emma the minted- and fit- hedge fund manager ridin' into town with her investment, savin' the day and generally bein' loved and, er, fancied by all. Neither of which were exactly part of how Monika imagined it all turnin' out. Remember that this whole City world that you and Emily and Emma- Em n' Em, ha- come from, well, it's just all a bit confusin' to her, isn't it? Intimidatin', even. But look on the bright side, who would have thought you would have turned out to be such a Casanova? Not me, for starters. I mean, I'm friggin' astonished, if that's any consolation!"

"I need to speak to her, Pete."

"Fine, fine. I'm not promisin' anything, but I'll see what I can do. But first you need to work out what you want to speak to her about. I'm not sure that you even know that yourself right now, do you, mate?"

"OK- thanks, Pete."

"An' there is one other thing- Bob W asked me to pass a message on to you. He says you're not takin' his calls. Which seems a bit friggin' ironic, seein' as no one else is takin' yours! Anyway, he told me to tell you: 'Message from Emily- Luxembourg Margin Call'. Bit cryptic, innit?"

"Pete- you're absolutely sure those were her words- 'margin call'?"

"Absolutely sure, mate. I repeat: 'Luxembourg Margin Call'. Over and Out."

Chapter 18

City of London, 23 December 2008

Xavier, Darren, Emily and Emma were all hunched up next to each other in their little square boxes, like battery hens in some sick financial services factory farm.

"Hey, you guys look like the world's worst advent calendar up there!" said Carl.

"I don't know, my friend, some of them look pretty good to me, am I wrong?" said Kostas.

"Right then, if everyone on the video conference lines can hear me alright, shall we get this show on the road?" said Ken, unconvincingly installed at the head of the table. "In case anyone doesn't have a good picture, we've got me, Matthew, Dimitrios, Kostas, Mr, er, Staines and Carl here in our offices, and Xav, Darren, Emily and, er, Emma on the videocon. It looks lovely in Monte Carlo, Xavier- are you absolutely positive you don't need some on-the-ground legal support out there?"

"Not from you, you know!" said Xavier's box. "Maybe if you could recommend someone, uh, half-way competent?"

"Right, yes, well, I have Xavier's sealed bid here. Matthew, do you have your, er, consortium's bid there? If so, shall we pass them down to Dimitrios and, er, Kostas?"

"Why is this Kostas guy at the end of the table, you know?" said Xavier. "He's one of the parties, just like Verreaux!"

"He's like a son to me, this boy!" shouted Dimitrios. "He's the only one of you that I trust!"

"It's alright, Xavier," said Ken. "I'm sure that Dimitrios will not object to allowing me to, er, verify the quantum of the bids on your behalf."

"What's he talkin' about?" Dimitrios asked Kostas.

"Don' worry, Uncle…" said Kostas. "Come on, let's get on with it, people- Christmas is comin'!"

Ken and I passed the sealed envelopes down to Dimitrios, who impatiently ripped them open, then fumbled for his glasses.

"OK, OK, let me see. Luxembourg Capital Partners offer- £375,000! Very good, eh, Kostas, very good start! Mr Matthew offers- £300,001. Not so good… That's no more than you offered yesterday! I'm not sure you understand how an auction works so well, my friend! Looks like Chatterbabe goes to Luxembourg …"

"That's £300,001 in cash, Dimitrios," I said.

"In cash?" he said, bemused. "In cash, yes, of course in cash, what else would it be in, *dolmades*?"

Kostas was studying the bid letters carefully.

"Uncle, Xavier's fund has offered £375,000 in deferred loan notes- payable in 2011!"

"Loan whats?" said Dimitrios.

"Loan notes- so basically, if you sell him Chatterbabe now, then three years from now he gives you the cash- if he's got the money by then, know what I mean? This is just a fuckin' I.O.U.! 'Scuse my French, ladies…"

"What!" screamed Dimitrios. He unleashed a withering sally of Greek. I was pretty sure I recognised some of the words from our trip to the Greek-Cypriot Club. "What is this bullshits! You want to take my company for a piece of paper! Give me the cash! Or no deal!"

"You're selling it to me, you know!" screamed Xavier. "You promised!"

"Over my dead body!" hissed Dimitrios.

"Listen, Xav- if you're such a friggin' big-shot, why don't you just pay my uncle in cash?" asked Kostas.

"You probably wouldn't understand this, you know, because it's more of a, uh, high finance thing," said Xavier. "Not the kind of thing you would have any experience of, you know! But our hedge fund has a slight, uh, very slight liquidity issue. Like most hedge funds, we do have a credit facility- ours is with the Benelux Banking Corporation, a very, uh, prestigious financial institution- that we've been using to buy significant holdings of financial stocks in the markets…"

"A bank loan," Kostas explained to Dimitrios. "An' I've had plenty of experience of people who can't pay, believe you me, Unk- the used car business is full of 'em!"

"So with the current temporary, uh, blip in asset values, you know, and just as a precaution, Benelux are asking for, uh, a bit more cash from the fund. Just to cover the facility."

"What is he talkin' about?" Dimitrios asked Kostas.

"Matt, can you explain, my friend?" said Kostas.

"Xavier, are you trying to tell us that you've had a margin call from Benelux?" I asked innocently.

"That's a, uh, bit of a ridiculous, uh, hysterical way to describe it, you know- it's more like a, er, routine margin adjustment, you know."

"Routine!" yelped Ken. "And now you don't have the cash for Chatterbabe! Jesus Christ, Xavier, why didn't you tell me about this! This has been sinking funds all over the world... And I was going to give a solicitor's undertaking for the completion funds to Kostas yesterday- this firm would have been on the hook for the whole consideration! I could have had personal liability, for God's sake!"

"This fund is too big to fail, you know, everyone knows that!" said Xavier.

"But unfortunately Benelux Banking Corporation seem to be under the impression that it's too stupid to save..." said Ken bitterly.

"Can someone please tell me what's goin' on?" asked Pete.

"It seems as though Xavier borrowed some money to buy bank shares on the cheap, after Lehman Brothers collapsed," I said. "He must have thought share prices couldn't possibly stay so low. But unfortunately, with the benefit of hindsight, that turned out to be something of a high point for them... The loan was only secured on the bank shares themselves, so when their value really started falling off a cliff, the bank asked him to increase the amount of cash he had deposited with them against the loan. Or they would sell the shares out from under him and sue him for the rest of the money."

"So that means..."

"That means that Xavier is absolutely buggered!" said Ken in despair. "Who would take your loan notes for any price, with a margin call against you! Benelux aren't about to just let you off, Xavier- they desperately need that cash themselves!"

"Nonsense, you don't know what you're talking about, you know!" said Xavier. "This won't finish me! I'll do a deal with Benelux. Everyone in the City knows that I have a charmed life in the markets!"

"Despair thy charm, douche-bag!" said Carl.

"Well said, Bard," I said. "Now, since we seem to have agreed the big picture deal here, I'd just like to get Dimitrios' signature on the sale agreement… We've got a financing to complete with HGF today!"

"Here you go, uncle," said Kostas, putting the SPA in front of him and opening it at the signature page.

"Stop! You can't do this, you know!" said Xavier. "I offered the most money! Me! These guys are nobodies, you know!"

Dimitrios signed the agreement with a flourish and handed it back to Kostas.

"Cheers! Now, Matt, if you could just sign this for and on behalf of Phoenix Acquisitions Limited…"

"Wait- use this, man…" said Carl, leaning forward with both hands to present me with a chubby black fountain-pen, basking in a luxurious case.

"Carl- is this…"

"The missing Mont Blanc, man!"

"But where has it been all this time? Was it really you…"

"No, man- I got it from Darren yesterday. It twisted my melon too, but he'd had it all along! Seems Xavier always makes sure they're one short, just to keep the other dudes on the deal in their place. He asked Darren to take one out of the box they sent us for the closing meeting- pen roulette, man. Only on our deal it was him who didn't get one… He never thought we would make him take one for the team! When I told Darren the trouble it'd caused us, he most civilly gave it to me as a, er, keepsake. And now I want you to have it, man. Closure, you know?"

"Wait- that's my pen! You can't do this- tell him, Ken! Tell them they can't do this!"

"Oh, come off it, Xavier," said Ken wearily. "The game's up, wouldn't you say? Let's just leave them to it. Unless you have anything more to say to Xavier, Matthew?"

"Well, I do actually, Xavier: fuck you!"

Xavier's box on the screen flickered, and then disappeared into blackness.

Suddenly another box opened up on the screen.

"Mary, Mother of God, where do all these beautiful ladies keep coming from, Matty-boy?" said Kostas. "If I'd known about this, I would have been on board from the start, believe me, my friend!"

"Who, er, who just joined the video conference?" said Ken.

"It's me- Monika Antoniak."

"Where are you, Ms Antoniak?"

"I'm actually in your, er, your firm's Warsaw office right now…" said Monika.

"I thought you wouldn't mind in the circumstances, Ken," said Pete. "There wasn't any other way to get her on the call. An' believe me I tried everythin'!"

"That's er, that's absolutely fine," said Ken. "But I think the formal business of the meeting is completed now, isn't it, Matthew?"

"Not quite, Ken," I said. "Monika, I really need to talk to you. You haven't been answering any of my calls."

"Don't do this, Matt…"

"Do what? Talk? I'm not giving up without a fight. I need you!"

"For the business?"

"No- I need you."

"Why didn't you say anything- before? You never gave any sign of that when I was still in London!"

"You should have chased her to the airport, man," said Carl.

"I know!" I said, glaring at Pete. "I know I fluffed my lines again. But the truth is that it's taken me all this time to figure out what I needed to do- who I needed to be with- to be myself. Because, let's face it, I was way wide of the mark in how I spent my time and lived my life in every other respect too. So did I know immediately that you were the right one for me? Maybe not. I think I thought I could find something exactly the same as Emily and I had, only somehow make it work out better this time- but it turns out that just isn't me, after all. They always tell you that you learn from your mistakes, but I keep finding new ways to screw up. But there is one mistake that I'm not going to make: Letting you leave this video conference without telling you now that I love you. So I do. I love you. I'm just a boy- standing in front of a screen- with a whole bunch of other people watching…"

Xavier's box suddenly flickered back on, next to Monika on the big screen.

"Oh, piss off, Xavier!" I said.

Xavier disappeared again.

"…And asking you to love me!"

"I do!" said Monika.

"I hope someone's recordin' this for Phoenix TV!" said Pete. "It's friggin' reality TV gold dust! I'm seein' *Little Lord Fauntleroy* meets *The Bachelor*… I'm seein' *Little Lord Fauntleroy* meets *The Bachelor*…"

"So you'll come back?" I asked Monika.

"I'm on my way!"

"Tell reception there to charge the taxi to the airport to my personal account!" said Ken, wiping a manly tear from his cheek.

Monika's box disappeared from the screen.

"Wait- wait, Matt," said Emily. "This isn't exactly the way I'd pictured this- because this was supposed to be the part when I ask you if there's any chance of us getting back together. But I think I've just seen the answer to that question, haven't I?"

"You know, I don't want you to think I'm enjoying this, Emily. I mean, I would have enjoyed it, really enjoyed it: Two months ago- six weeks ago- yesterday. But now, I'm just sorry there's no happy ending for us. And anyway, it's perfectly obvious that you deserve to meet someone infinitely better-looking, richer and cooler than me, who owns a vineyard in Champagne, and end up blissfully happy."

Emily laughed.

"Oh, you're so full of it! That's one thing that hasn't changed, however much you have! But I did the right thing, didn't I? I redeemed myself, right?"

"Damn right!"

This time it was Emily's box that blanked out.

"Anyone else got anythin' to say?" said Pete to the video camera. "Does anyone know of any cause or just impediment why these two persons should not be, er, joined together? The luvverly Emma?"

"I'll hold my peace, thanks Pete!" said Emma.

"The 'antidote to desire', man…" whispered Carl.

"I heard that!" said Emma. "Just remember: you work for me now, boy!"

"In that case I, er, declare this video conference over!" said Ken. "Congratulations, Matthew! And, er, no hard feelings?"

I shook his hand.

"You brought us all together, Ken!"

Dimitrios delved into his coat pocket, brought out a bottle of clear spirit, wrenched the top off it and started sloshing it into our water glasses.

"Now the deal is done- time to taste the true spirit of Greece! Courtesy of the Hornsey Road Greek-Cypriot Club!"

"Ah- ouzo, nice one, Unk!" said Kostas. He clapped me on the shoulder, as we downed the spirit together. "*Yamas*! *Yamas*! Keeps the goddam' cold out, eh? *Yamas*!"

"This boy, he's a fuckin' madman- but I like him!" said Dimitrios, pouring me some more ouzo. "Where you from, my friend? You speak funny, if you don' min' me sayin' so?"

"From London- but I lived in Glasgow as a kid," I said.

"Glasgow? Scotland? Like King Kenny?" said Dimitrios.

"Kenny Dalglish- yeah, exactly. I am a Celtic fan actually…"

"Why din't you say so before, my friend! I love King Kenny- a great, great man… We can sort somethin' out with this money, I think! Maybe to you I give a loan…" He sloshed more ouzo into my glass. "But don' ever refer to me and woman's clothing in the same sentence again! I don' care if it's Japanese silks, French lace or fuckin' Eskimo furs, my friend!"

"*Yamas*, *amigos*!" said Carl, joining us, knocking back several fingers of neat ouzo and holding his glass out for a refill. "I have absolutely no idea how, but we seem to have done it, man!"

"You really pulled it out of the bag with that Powerpoint presentation, Carl," I said. "You can be my Planchet any time!"

"No, man- you can be mine."

"Where's Colin, by the way?"

"He had some unfinished business at Ofcable, man. It turns out that Miss Veronica got the top job in 'Standards'…"

"What! What happened to Torquemada?"

"Considered to have blotted his copybook during the merger. Not a team-player, man."

"In fact, V is forcin' him to apologise to Colin this very afternoon…" said Pete. "Part of his rehabilitation. Twelve steps to not bein' such a friggin' numpty!"

"Wow, this is a bloody great day!"

"*Yamas*, man, *yamas*!" said Carl. "So when are you heading out to the airport?"

"You think I should go and pick Monika up?"

"I know it, man. Those who forget the mistakes of the past are, er, doomed to repeat them."

I nodded and passed him my glass of ouzo.

"Hold the fort, boys- see you tomorrow for Day One of filming!"

Later that night, I walked back down the Balls Pond Road with Monika, past the rotating advertising hoarding. We stood watching it for a moment, and then strolled hand-in-hand home down Dalston Lane.

―

Chapter 19

PHOENIX TV- DAY 1- TRANSCRIPT OF THE TOP 10 MOST-WATCHED CLIPS

#1 Carl's Socialist Interpretation of All Popular Culture
Title track: sequence of Carl painting a hammer and sickle onto a large picture of Captain America.
INT. STUDIO
Carl and Sir Fred Goodwin sit next to each other on a spartan bench, watching *Teenage Mutant Ninja Turtles* together on a very large TV screen.
CARL
(clasping his hands together)
So, er, Fred, one of the first things that arrests the viewer's attention in this episode is that the evil villain of the show- the leader of the thinly-disguised military–industrial-congressional complex 'the Foot'- is known as 'the Shredder'. An uncanny resemblance to your own nickname, 'the Shred'. So my, er, question for you, 'Sir' Fred is: how do you like them apples, man?
(long shot of Sir Fred looking uncomfortably into the camera)

#2 Veronica's All-Time Ragga Classics
INT. STUDIO
VERONICA
... And in at Number 7, SL2's legendary 1992 smash, *On a Ragga Tip*. Massive props to Slipmatt and DJ Lime, because this is one sick track!
(the song starts)
VERONICA
(singing along)
'Ay- ba day, ba wa-da-da-di-day, Ay- ba day, ba wa-da-da-di-day, Ay...'

#3 Emily's No Pain Champagne
Title track: sequence of Emily trying a supermarket own-brand champagne in the kitchen of a luxurious flat. She spits out the champagne and pours the rest of the bottle down the sink, before tossing the empty bottle out of the window. It tumbles down, nearly braining a pair of working-class pensioners on the street below.
INT. STUDIO
EMILY
When selecting champagne, I always try to bear in mind Polonius' immortal advice to his son Laertes: 'This above all; to thine own self be true'. It's all too easy to be influenced by herd mentality or, even worse, by the craven counsel of lesser palettes, you know?
KEN
(woodenly holding out a glass of champagne towards Emily)
A drop of jolly old Moët Non-Vintage, Emily? It's Britain's best selling brand, dontcha' know!
(Emily takes the proffered glass and takes a sip from it, then grimaces and tosses it contemptuously over her shoulder, hitting Ken and drenching him in

champagne. A good-looking waiter appears with a huge bottle of Krug, pours it into an incredibly long-stemmed champagne flute and hands it to Emily)
That's *much* more like it, Antoine darling!
(taking a sip)
Hmmm, biscuity…

#4 Bob's Livery Company Pageant

Title track: sequence of Bob in long gown, three-cornered hat and chain of office, wielding the Ceremonial Cheese-cutter Darth Maul-style, like a martial arts weapon.
INT. STUDIO
BOB
People often ask me the secret of my success in the City… Well, it's not what you know- it's what you know about the Lord Mayor!
(Bob laughs heartily)
But seriously, I'm delighted to be joined on the show today by His Worship The Lord Mayor of London himself- Barrrryyyy Jeeeenkinssss!
(Enter Barry Jenkins, thumbs hooked around his gold chain of office)
BOB
And who better than Barry to give viewers some top tips on how to, er, 'hustle and grind', in the modern City?
BARRY
Thank'ee kindly, Bob, thank'ee, delighted to be here. But first I'd like to say a few words of thanks to you, Bob, personally, for your superhuman efforts in raising the profile of the 'Great Twelve' via this fine program. This is the biggest shot in the arm for the movement since my, er, illustrious predecessor Dick Whittington arrived in London! And as a token of gratitude, it gives me great pleasure to announce that, from this day forward, the Worshipful Company of

Cheesemongers will be ranked as one of the 'Great Twelve' livery companies of the City of London!

BOB

What a moment, what a moment…

(dabs his face with a silk hankie)

BARRY

I know that this will come us a shock to many of our esteemed friends and colleagues in the Worshipful Company of Forkwrights, who will graciously make way for the Cheesemongers. But I'm sure that I'm not alone in wishing them all the best in their future endeavours outside the 'Great Twelve'!

(Camera-man's hand appears in front of the lens, drawing his finger across his throat to indicate that the program is out of time)

BOB

I'm afraid I'm going to have to stop you there, Barry- but a thousand thanks to you for coming onto the show tonight!

(Barry nods smugly)

Good night- and Guild bless!

(voiceover off camera)

BOB

Seriously, though, Baz, I just can't thank you enough- the 'Great Twelve' means everything to me! I mean, finally in the Lord Mayor's show as of right, rather than merely by invitation!

BARRY

Say no more, Bob old boy! Between you and me, I never liked those twats from the Forkwrights anyway. Worshipful Company of Fuckwits, more like! This isn't live on air is it, Bob? You can edit that bit out, can't you, Bob? Bob?

#5 *Cupid's Darts*

Title track: Pete walks into a night-club wearing a fur coat and shades, with each arm around a glamorous dolly-bird. He carelessly disengages one arm to throw a volley of darts at a dartboard on the wall. The darts appear to go nowhere near the board.

(Anguished shouts from off-screen)

INT. STUDIO

PETE

Good evenin', and welcome to Cupid's Darts- television's second-best pro-am darts-based datin' programme! No other programme in television history has led to so many couples gettin' married and openin' pubs in the county of Essex. In fact some experts believe the pub landlord species would be facin' extinction were it not for our efforts on this show! But, without further ado, let's meet this week's beautiful contestant: the luvverly Emma from Chelsea!

(Enter Emma)

PETE

Helloooo, Emma! And are you ready to meet your dashin' partner this evenin'...

EMMA

He better be dashing this time, Pete...

PETE

... Carl from Wiltshire!

(Enter Carl)

EMMA

Oh, you really cannot be serious...

#6 *Colin's Film 1989*

Title track: Colin wearing a *Miami Vice*-style suit, medallion slung around neck, sitting in a director's chair with 'COLIN' stencilled onto it. The first four letters are too large for the whole name to fit in one line, so the 'N' has been added below as an after-thought.

INT. STUDIO

COLIN

This week, we'll be considering one of the great unsolved mysteries of early '90s cinema- why there was never a sequel to 1992 crime-comedy-caper *Kuffs*!

(cuts to the film poster)

Now, this film has it all- a young Christian Slater at his cheeky best; *Resident Evil* zombie-slayer in training, Milla Jovovich; Ashley Judd's first movie outing; beautiful San Francisco itself, and an original music score by *Axel F*-penning synth-pop genius Harold Faltermeyer. Sure, Slater was still not at the peak of his considerable powers as an actor- but as the movie's tag line reminds us, 'When you have attitude who needs experience'?

Next week- another San Francisco classic, in before-its-time artificial intelligence fairytale *Electric Dreams*, and why I don't agree with the revisionist boo-boys who say that the only memorable thing about it was Phil Oakey and Giorgio Moroder's timeless soundtrack collaboration, *Together In Electric Dreams*…

(Colin singing off-screen)

'We'll always be together/ However far it seems/ Together In Electric Dreams!'

#7 *Katinka's Sleep Clinic*

Title track: sequence of long file of sheep jumping over a fence, ended by Katinka in a very thick, white woolly jumper. She looks vacantly into the camera.

INT. STUDIO
(Extended shot of Katinka in another thick white woolly jumper, staring blankly at the camera. Suddenly we lose the picture as the cameraman slumps into sleep himself, before he comes round and sits up with a start)
KATINKA
(singing)
'When I'm worried, and I can't sleep/ I count my blessings instead of sheep…'
(Camera-man slumps back into sleep)
(Fades out)

#8 Queen B's Secret History of Paramilitary Activity

Title track: sequence of Queen B inspecting a crack team of bouncers on parade before a speed-dating event. Noticing that one of them isn't wearing a tie, she deals him a vicious blow across the head with her clipboard. He crumples to the ground, where she continues to rain in blows.
INT. STUDIO
CAMERA-MAN (*off-screen*)
I'm not making this bonkers, right-wing crap!
PETE (*off-screen*)
Oh, c'mon, you big girl! It's no worse than *Ross Kemp on Gangs*- and that got a friggin' BAFTA Award!
QUEEN B (*on-screen*)
(*miming sparking up a Taser*)
Do we have a problem here?
CAMERA-MAN (*off-screen*)
So that's 'Paramilitary Activity': Take 1!
QUEEN B

Next week- the Nicaraguan Contras: how they waged a just war against the Sandinista menace, won the admiration of the late, very great President Ronald Reagan- and found true love on the way!

#9 Darren's Cribs of the Rich and Famous

Title track: Darren wearing golf clothes, with a Ralph Lauren sweater draped over his shoulders, peering at a gated mock-Tudor mansion through a pair of binoculars.

EXT. GATED MOCK-TUDOR MANSION NEAR BIRMINGHAM
DARREN

Lots of people fink there's nao celebritoys in Burminum…

(*lifts binoculars and peers through the gates*)

Well, moi message to them is: Yow couldn't be more wrrronggg! Todayyy we're at the crrrib of former Aston Villa boss, 'El' Ron Atkinson, in beautiful Barnt Green, an' it is absoluuutely bostin'!

Next week- we visit the crrrib of another huge Broomeye nime, former UB40 front man Alie Campbell, in, erm, pictuuuresque Barnt Green…

CAMERA-MAN (*off-screen*)

It's next door, isn't it, Darren? Shall we just go and film it now?

DARREN

Yerrokay, our kid…

#10 Kostas' SuperKars of the '80s

Title track: sequence of Kostas driving a souped-up Ford Capri at high speed past a file of Sinclair C5s, spraying them with mud and water, then winking roguishly at the camera.

EXT. NONDESCRIPT INDUSTRIAL ESTATE
KOSTAS

(*driving a dubious '80s Jag*)

The 1982 Jaguar V12 XJ-S- this car screams 'class' louder than the world's scariest headmaster, innit? I'd rather be in this car, than in Kerry Katona's knickers!

(Kostas pulls up next to a white Austin Maestro campervan conversion at the traffic lights and waves two fingers together in salute. Matthew is driving the Maestro, with Monika in the passenger seat next to him. Matthew responds by revving up the engine. There is a tinny sound)

Whereas Matthew's vehicle- well, my friends, it's the choice of a man without the flair and dress-sense to carry off a Vauxhall Astra. Britain's offical ninth most-scrapped car of the last 30 years, the Maestro is to turbo-diesels what the Trojans were to ancient warfare…

(drumming his fingers on the roof of the XJ-S)

… Greek chariot-fodder! Ready my friend?

(Matthew revs up the Maestro. Kostas hits the accelerator, and the two cars take off, the Maestro chugging audibly as the XJ-S pulls effortlessly away from it. Monika giggles uncontrollably)